THE HIGHLANDER'S WELSH BRIDE

The Hardy Heroines series (book #5)

By Cathy & DD MacRae

PRINT EDITION

PUBLISHED BY
Short Dog Press

www.cathymacraeauthor.com

ISBN-978-0-9966485-7-8

License Notes

The Highlander's Welsh Bride

It was over. Prince Llywelyn was dead, his soldiers fleeing before King Edward's army. Carys, a distant cousin to the prince, herself a princess of Wales, had picked up arms alongside her husband more than a year ago. Now homeless, her husband buried beneath the good Welsh soil, she seeks shelter in the north, far from the reach of Longshanks's men. Carys and Wales would never be the same again.

Birk MacLean has been ordered to take a bride and produce an heir. He grows weary of the lasses paraded before him, women of delicate nature and selfish motives. He desires a wife strong enough to help lead one of the most powerful clans in Western Scotland.

One like the Welsh woman sitting in his dungeon, arrested for poaching MacLean deer.

Can Birk convince Carys marriage to him is preferable to a hangman's noose? And will the heard-headed Scot be worthy of a Princess of Wales?

From the towering Welsh mountains to the storm-swept Scottish coast comes a tale of betrayal and loss, deceit and passion. An epic tale of honor and the redeeming power of love.

WORDS OF INTEREST

Welsh:

Mi gerddaf gyda thi dros lwybrau maith. – I'll walk beside you over many paths.
Cer i grafu - go to hell
Dim gwerth rhech dafad - not worth a sheep's fart
Rydych chi'n ferch ddewr – you are a brave girl
Fy merch(ed) – my daughter(s)
Bychan – little one
Nain - grandmother
Cymru = Wales
Cymry = Welsh people
Cymraeg = Welsh language

Gaelic:

mo chridhe – my heart (a term of affection)
mo luran – my baby
a leannan – sweetheart (baby, daughter, other young person)
a nighean- my daughter
mo charaid – my friend

Norse:

eldhúsfífl (EHLD-hoos-feef-uhl) — "hearthfire idiot", an idiot who sits by the fire all day; a good-for-nothing
elskan mín – my love *(gender non-specific)*
sonr mín – my son
móðir – mother
faðir - father
kerling – old hag
amma – grandmother
bikkju-sonr – son of a b*tch

Prologue

MacLean Castle
Morvern, Lochaline, Scotland
1279

Birk MacLean stood at the window overlooking the Sound of Mull, rain misting the air, whorling in glistening patterns across the thick, leaded glass pane. He stared at the missive in his hands as emotions too powerful to identify seeped into his soul.

All hands aboard the Mara Cu' lost in a storm crossing the North Minch.

"My laird, be there anything else?" the messenger asked, a wobble in his voice.

Birk glared at the source of interruption and crushed the parchment. The slight man paled.

"What?" Birk growled and stepped toward the man.

"I asked if there be anything else, my laird." His clansman backed toward the door of the laird's solar.

"Nothing," Birk bit off.

The sound of his hasty retreat tempted Birk to feel guilty for frightening him, but his anger swept aside the notion as easily as a feather on the wind. He finally had proof the wench was unfaithful. Now she and her lover lay at the bottom of the sea, robbing him of the right to revenge. No one would wish to speak ill of the dead, leaving pity to be her legacy rather than the scorn and banishment she deserved.

"What is it, son?" his father called from the next room, his voice soft and infirm.

Birk strode to the open doorway leading to his father's chambers, halting at the cloying stench of sickness hanging in the air. The lung fever which had claimed many older clansmen this past winter left the laird in a diminished condition. Birk had taken on his father's responsibilities since and was the MacLean in all but name.

"'Tis news of Rose," Birk answered with a calm he did not feel.

"What of the MacDonald bitch?" Alex MacLean asked bitterly.

"She and Lyal MacLeod died during their passage to Stornoway. A storm sank their ship crossing the Minch. No survivors."

"Thank God for His good judgement," his da pronounced, his eyes glittering above the blanket clutched to his chin. He sputtered then heaved a wet, wracking cough.

Birk grabbed the cup of mulled wine on the table next to the bed and helped his da sit up to drink. He tried not to think about how his once robust sire—even at his advanced age—had been reduced to the skeletal form before him in a matter of weeks. Unable to rise on his own, Laird MacLean had become bedridden less than a month ago.

"I should have never asked ye to marry that jezebel. Had I known her true colors, I'd have told MacDonald to go to hell. His offering of peace brought more bad blood, no doubt his intention. The only good to come of your debacle of a marriage are my wee granddaughters. At least the Almighty wrought two miracles from my misjudgment."

"'Tis over, now, Da. Ye need yer rest," Birk replied.

"Bah. I have lived long and buried three children and my first wife, though yer ma will always have my heart and will outlive me by years, God willing. I'll be resting in my grave soon enough. The mantle falls to ye now."

6

Birk was tempted to offer reassurances, but knew they would ring as insults, hollow words more befitting the weak-spirited, not a man who had lived a braw life leading one of the strongest clans in the Highlands. They both understood his time drew nigh and naught could be done to change their circumstances.

"I'll ask the elder council to schedule the ceremony. No need to wait until this frail auld man becomes a corpse to do what needs doing."

"As ye wish, Da." Birk wanted to say more, but could think of nothing that didn't sound like the sentimental talk of a woman.

"Ye know what this means?" Alex asked.

Birk tilted his head in invitation.

"With no male heir, ye'll have to take another bride."

Birk's lips thinned and his jaw clenched. As much as he hated the idea, sooner or later, he'd be forced to wed again. Heaven help the woman who agreed to be his wife.

Chapter One

Battle of Orewin Bridge, Wales
December 1282
Three years later

Three English soldiers emerged from the woods, footsteps crackling on frozen branches and snow. Carys caught her brother's arm in warning, but the alarm arrived too late. They'd been spotted.

"Stop!" one of the soldiers shouted, drawing his sword. He burst across the small glen, the other two men at his heels.

Hywel snatched his bow from his shoulder. "Take the one on the left." In a swift move born of too much practice killing the English, he nocked and released an arrow, dropping the lead soldier in his tracks.

Carys flung her javelin. The leaf-shaped blade struck her target in the chest, piercing his leather armor and knocking him to the ground. The instant her hands were free, she drew her bow, aiming for the third Englishman whom Hywel had already staggered with an arrow. She added a feathered shaft of her own to ensure he fell and stayed down. Drawing her short sword, she stalked the bodies.

"Carys, we must fly!" Hywel called softly. "The prince has fallen. More of Longshanks's men will be upon us anon."

The scream of steel on steel and of men dying rose on the air behind them, adding urgency to his plea. Carys nodded, pausing to stuff the few coins the dead English soldiers had in their possession, along with their daggers, into the small pack she carried. She spotted a silver necklace and yanked it from the neck of its owner. A fine silver ring with beautiful filigree work set with an amber stone hung from the chain. She hastily stashed it into a pocket.

8

Unbuckling the belt from the man with two arrows in his chest, she sheathed his short sword in its scabbard and tossed it to Hywel. The man in leather had been an archer, so she blended his quiver with hers, slung her bow over a shoulder, and reclaimed her javelin. Carys then trotted after her brother into the forest. The fresh, clean scent of snow and evergreens replaced the stench of death as they loped silently through the wood, away from the battle. They moved like ghosts in the long shadows of the afternoon. Their footsteps crunched softly on the frozen ground, leaving little evidence of their passage. Sunlight filtered weakly through the heavy canopy, leaving the dense underbrush deeply shadowed.

The sounds of battle faded, and the eerie quiet unnerved Carys. It seemed the forest along with all of Cymru grieved the loss of her prince.

"Where are we headed, Hywel?" she asked, her voice pitched on a whisper. Though most English soldiers wore chain armor and lumbered about like oxen—easily heard in the silent forest—she didn't wish to draw attention in case scouts roamed this direction. Sound carried easily on the crisp winter air. Wearing dark green woolen leggings, leather jerkins, boots, and leather cowls covering their heads and shoulders, Carys and her brother blended in with the evergreen foliage and shadows.

"Our cousin, the prince, is dead," Hywel reminded her. "That means Cymru has fallen to the English. We've naught left of family and nowhere to turn. I say we travel to the coast and find our way beyond Edward's reach."

The reminder of her husband Terwyn's death in battle only a few weeks past tore a fresh wound in Carys's aching heart. They'd been married only a few months, and her dreams of hearth, home, and children died along with him.

She considered her brother's words. She didn't know much of the world but knew Longshanks's reach stretched far. Was there such a place where his presence wasn't a blight upon the land?

Somehow, the English had crossed the Irfon River downstream today and attacked the Cymru army from behind. Carys and her brother had been part of a small band of archers charged with holding the Orewin Bridge, keeping the English on the south side of the river. Once the Marcher Lords attacked the Cymru flank, the English cavalry crossed the bridge unopposed. Equipped with better armor and weapons, the English had soon turned the battle into a slaughter. Carys and her brother were among the few who had survived. Their next steps would lead to their safety—or death.

The coast lay a good two or three days' march south on foot. They had traveled farther before, though typically not in the dead of winter, or with an English army at their backs.

More at home in the forest than in any dwelling, Carys settled into her stride, keeping her eyes and ears open for the enemy. By nightfall, she and Hywel had put many miles between them and the battle. Hywel placed a finger to his lips as they approached a cluster of cottages in a small valley ringed by hills. The rock walls and thatched roofs appeared in good repair.

"Ho, the house," Hywel called, keeping a respectable distance between himself and the cottages. Carys hid behind a tree, an arrow nocked and ready. With as much treachery as they'd witnessed today, she'd guard her brother's life with her own.

A large man opened the door to the nearest cottage. "Aye? What the devil do ye want this late of an eve?"

"My companion and I seek a hot meal and mayhap a place in yer barn for the night. We have news of the battle and of Prince Llywelyn." Hywel held up a brace of hares they'd shot along the way.

The big man motioned for them to enter. "Come in, come in. 'Tis cold and I'm lettin' out the heat."

Carys stowed her arrow and caught Hywel at the doorway. They stepped into the warm cottage. Her nose twitched and her mouth watered as the aroma of freshly baked bread and simmering pottage struck her. It had been days since they'd had a home-cooked meal, and she prayed for the goodwife's hospitality.

"All Cymry are welcome in me home if they come in peace. Seat yerselves. Alis makes the best *cawl lafwr* in all of Cymru, and we were about to sit to supper."

Hywel and Carys leaned their bows, javelins and packs against the door frame and eased onto the bench their host indicated.

"I'm Mal, and this is me wife, Alis. Our oldest son, Derwyn, daughter, Begwn and youngest boy, Derfel."

"I'm Hywel ap Pedr, and this is my sister, Carys. Many thanks for your hospitality."

Alis set two mugs full of cider and bowls of lamb stew in front of them. "Here, this will take the chill off. Ye needn't have to pay for yer meal with game."

"*Mewn pob daioni y mae gwobr,*" Hywel replied.

Alis planted both hands on her hips. "A reward in every goodness, aye? I can see yer mam taught ye well."

Carys glanced downward while Hywel offered a sad smile.

"How'd they go?" Mal gently asked.

"When Longshanks' men took Ynys Mon, they were counted among the dead that day."

"We'll pray for their souls this eve," Alis said.

Hywel nodded as Carys heaved a sigh.

"Ye said ye had news." Mal motioned for them to fill their bowls, and Hywel obliged with his tale.

"We fought the English at the battle of Moel y Don and drove them into the sea nigh on a month ago. We then followed the prince to Orewin Bridge. Our numbers were in the thousands, and we would have won the day, but someone showed the English where to cross the Irfon beyond the bridge. They attacked from both sides. We did what we could but ran once we saw Prince Llywelyn fall."

Mal shook his head, a heavy frown on his face. "Our dear prince has died? Aye, 'tis dire news, and no mistake. There's no shame in living to fight another day. Our strength is in our knowledge of these forests, mountains and hills, and in the ambush. We're no match for the English on an open field."

Carys drank the cider and soaked in the heat from the fire. Seeing this herder with his family enlarged the hole Terwyn's death left in her heart. In another year, she would have been picking up their first child. Instead she picked up arms against the cursed invaders. Her ancestors had done the same against the Vikings, Saxons and Romans before them. She longed for the violence to end.

Mal sent his two youngest to bed shortly after supper. Hywel regaled their hosts and eldest with tales of their recent battles. He had the soul of a bard and entertained everyone with his stories. He and Mal speculated how long until Longshanks would send his Marcher Lords and their men deeper into Cymru to crush any further rebellion.

Carys watched her brother. Hywel's black wavy hair mirrored her own. They both were tall and slender and shared the same brown eyes, an inheritance from their parents. Carys spotted their da's humor when her brother smiled, though he did so less these days.

Their da had taught them both woodcraft and how to hunt at an early age, something all Cymry learned, even nobility. She speculated they'd spent more time in the woods than on their small holding while growing up. Cymru's mountainous terrain was unfit for farming, though they grew enough crops and livestock in their small vale to allow them and their tenants to prosper. Like Mal and his family, they'd kept sheep, pigs, chickens and a few goats.

Hywel tapped her on the shoulder. "Sister mine, 'tis time to find our rest and allow these fine people to sleep."

Carys nodded and sat upright, blinking against the red glow of the banked fire. She must have dozed. "My thanks for yer generosity," she murmured.

"Ye are welcome to sleep before the fire. 'Tis too cold in the barn this time of year," Mal said.

Carys smiled. "We've slept on the ground the past several nights. Yer barn will be a welcome comfort. Besides, we'll be off afore light and do not wish to disturb ye."

"Here, at least take some laverbread for yer journey," Alis said as she handed Hywel a linen-wrapped bundle.

He accepted the gift. "*Dduw bendithia eich teulu,*"

Mal smiled. "May God bless your family as well."

Carys and Hywel settled deep into a straw-filled stall and tucked their cloaks and blankets around them. Carys nestled into her seal fur-lined cloak, a wedding day gift from Terwyn. He'd taken her wool cloak without her knowledge and his mother and sister had sewn the hide of a seal he'd killed into the wrap. Too flustered by the details of her wedding day, she never realized the cloak was missing until he'd offered the sumptuous gift. Tears brimmed her eyes as Carys recalled the joy of receiving something so thoughtful and practical. More than a warm garment, it was a sign of a caring husband and of acceptance by the women in his family.

From her pocket, Carys fished out the ring she'd claimed earlier in the day from the dead man. She took her own ring, the thin gold band Terwyn had given her at their wedding, and placed it on the chain with the other. She then drew them around her neck, the cold metal soothing against her skin. The delicate filigree circlet was obviously a woman's ring and she wondered who it had belonged to. Had the soldier purchased it as a gift for his wife? If so, there was an Englishwoman soon to be grieving the loss of her husband. Her mother told her once, men went to war while women bore the burden of it. Carys hadn't understood what she meant at the time. She did now.

Rising before the sun, she nudged her brother awake. "Time to be on our way, Hywel."

Hywel stretched and walked to the back of the barn to relieve himself. Gathering their weapons, they resumed their journey. Breaking their fast with a piece of laverbread as they walked, Carys recalled when her mother taught her how to make the staple. Boil seaweed for hours until soft, then chop it fine and roll in oats before baking or frying. Alis had baked this batch, making it harder, ensuring it traveled well. Carys carefully tucked the memory of her mam away and sent a silent blessing to Alis for her thoughtfulness.

Though unlikely the English were nearby, Hywel set a brisk pace to devour the miles between them and the coast.

"Where exactly are we headed?" Carys asked, eager to learn of his plan.

"Aberystwyth is the nearest port of any size. We should reach the Rheidol River today. It will lead us to Aberystwyth and to the sea. From there we can find a ship to take us to either Éire or Scotland."

"Which has better forests?" Carys wondered, anxious to return to a familiar life.

"Scotland, I think. 'Tis the larger of the two. Vikings and their decedents still hold parts of the northern end. We can either buy passage when we sell the sword and the daggers ye took, or we can hire on as crew for a merchant vessel. Either way, 'tis time to find another home, though it pains me to say."

Carys frowned as she considered their future. "We'd die within the year battling the English if we remained. I do not fear dying but would rather not throw my life away fighting for a hopeless cause."

Hywel dipped his head. Treachery among their kinsmen had cost them dearly.

As predicted, they met the Rheidol by noon and followed it toward the sea. They exchanged two grouse and a pheasant for another hot meal, more laverbread, dried meat, and a night in a barn. The third morning they encountered the coast.

Carys and her brother stood on a hill overlooking the seaside hamlet of Aberystwyth. The sun lay just behind the mountains to the east, sending orange and pink streaks to announce the day's arrival. The briny smell of the ocean filled her nose. A crying seagull wheeled in the brisk wintry air. She saw no sign of English soldiers, nor were any naval vessels moored nearby. The small fishing village appeared to be awakening to a new day as if unaffected by recent events.

"Come, sister mine. We will need to find a ship quickly as they will want to sail with the tide."

They trotted toward the docks where fishermen—their nets at the ready—launched, and merchant vessels—both large and small—loaded goods.

"Wait for me here," Hywel said, handing her his bow and javelin.

Her brother's easy style gained the attention of the old men gathered around the pier closest to them. Hywel said something to make the men laugh then shook his hand in greeting. One old man pointed toward another dock. Her brother patted him on the shoulder and strode back to her. Carys grinned.

"What?" Hywel asked as he approached, his smile mirroring hers.

"Ye could charm the Almighty Himself if given half the chance."

"Mayhap, but I have found us a boat. The captain sails around Scotland, trading as he goes."

She nodded approval and stepped in behind him, the hood of her cowl pulled low. They passed taverns and inns, the aroma of cooking food in the air.

"Wait, here, Princess," Hywel teased, "and I will sell the steel we took from the English to yon blacksmith."

Carys punched his arm. "You know I hate it when you call me that."

His eyes softened "Aye, I do, but ye are a true princess of Cymru."

"As ye are a true prince, Brother."

Hywel offered a sad smile and removed the signet ring given him by their father, a symbol of his place in the royal house. The heavy gold ring was embossed with the Dragon of Cymru, Llywelyn's symbol.

"Keep it safe with yer others," he bade, then strode toward a building, smoke rising from its stone chimney.

Carys surreptitiously placed the ring on her chain and watched Hywel enter the smith's shop, her nose twitching at the scent of baked goods. She spotted a vender selling fresh meat pies and bought four bundled in a cloth.

A gnarled hand grasped Carys's arm. "Ye've the stench of death on ye, lass."

Carys wheeled, meeting the gaze of a half-blind old woman, her milky eyes staring from a deeply wrinkled face.

"Aye, *nain,*" Carys replied kindly. "I've just come from battle where our beloved prince was struck dead by the English."

The old woman clucked her tongue. "Dreadful news that is, indeed. What I sense is not simply the death behind ye, though there be plenty, but the death afore ye."

A pit gaped in Carys's stomach at the thought of more loss. "What shall I do?" she asked, her voice a choked whisper.

The old crone patted her arm. "It matters not, *fy merchd.* Stay or go. Death follows ye like a hound. Though if ye leave this day, 'twill send yer own death into the distant future."

Stunned by the prediction, she absently handed the old woman one of her meat pies and settled a brief kiss on the wrinkled brow. "God be with ye, *nain,*" she whispered.

"And with you, daughter." The woman accepted Carys's gift and blended into the crowd.

Carys strode toward Hywel as he left the smithy and handed him his pies.

He gave her a pleased grin. "The English may be a curse upon the land, but their steel isn't. The blades fetched a good price. Hmm, this is good," he mumbled around a mouthful of lamb and root vegetables as he took a bite.

"If we are to be at sea, there's no saying when we'll have an opportunity to eat anything other than fish for a while," Carys replied distractedly, still stunned by the prophecy she'd received.

Finishing their pies, they hurried to the pier as one vessel prepared to sail and two others finished loading.

Hywel approached a sturdy man whose shock of red hair gleamed in the morning light. "Captain Ferguson?"

"Aye, I'm Murdoc Ferguson," the ruddy man replied. A sandy-colored Cymru Shepherd marked with a black saddle and white belly bounded next to Ferguson, its front paws on the rail. The man placed a hand on the dog's head. "Easy, Dewr."

Carys pulled her cowl low over her face to hide her features and smiled at the dog's name—*brave* in her native tongue. Dewr was much like the dogs their father's sheep herder kept.

"I was told ye are in need of hands," Hywel said.

"Do either of ye know yer way around a boat?"

"Aye. Our uncle was a fisherman at Holyhead. We grew up fishing the bay."

Though not completely the truth, it wasn't a lie, either. The two of them did have an uncle who was a fisherman and they did go out many times, but neither was much of a sailor.

"Are ye handy with those bows?" the captain asked, eying their weaponry.

"We both recently were archers in the prince's service, and I can shoot an Englishman betwixt his eyes afore he ever hears me," Hywel said with a wink.

"And yer brother?" Ferguson asked.

"This one?" Hywel patted Carys on the shoulder. "This one has always been a better shot, though I win on distance."

Captain Ferguson nodded once. "I sail through the day, hugging the shore, then land at night. I make me way up the coast of Éire, then the Scottish Lowlands, Highlands, and the inner isles. Depending on how well the weather holds and the trading goes, I'll be gone three months or more. Does that suit ye?"

"Aye, it does, though we aim to stay in the Highlands. Will that leave ye in a bind?" Hywel asked.

Ferguson waved a hand in the air. "Nae. This fight with the English has taken all the lads I'd usually hire here, so I'll take the two of ye and be glad of it. We should be able to find more hands along the way."

He named their wages and duties. The ship was a single-masted birlinn with a square sail and ten oars, though there were only twelve hands plus the captain, leaving four oars unmanned. The work would be hard, but it would take them beyond Edward's reach.

Hywel and Carys shook hands with the captain then assisted the other men loading the boat, rolling barrels across the gangplank and stacking them mid-ships. Her height and the calluses she'd gained drawing a bow and swinging a sword helped Carys pass as an older lad. None paused to peer through her disguise. The dog, however, gave them both a good sniffing.

"Dewr likes to get to know her crew," the captain noted. "She's canny as a selkie and protects the boat. When we're a'port, she'll keep a weather eye on the ship fer us."

Carys smiled at the mix of Gaelic and Cymraeg the captain used while speaking. She'd traveled enough to have developed an ear for Gaelic, Erse, and a smattering of English. Ferguson's speech gleaned words from each.

A sturdy red-haired boy of perhaps fifteen summers, a splatter of freckles across his sun-burned nose, approached them with a friendly grin. He stuck out his hand in greeting. "I's Tully. 'Tis me da's boat. I love boats," he said in a manner more befitting a lad of four or five rather than one at the cusp of manhood.

Hywel shook his hand and gave the lad a warm smile. "'Well met, Tully. I'm Hywel and here's my younger brother."

Tully nodded vigorously, his smile widening. "S'times they call me, Stew. I ken how to make stew. I's thirteen summers, though da says I's big for me age."

Carys's heart immediately warmed toward the boy. Though it was plain to see he was simple, he had a good heart and a strong back. The fact Ferguson brought his boy along instead of hiding him away made her respect the captain more.

"Tully m'lad, leave them be to finish their work so we can shove off," Ferguson bellowed.

"Aye, Da," the boy replied, undaunted by his father's loud rebuke. Tully snapped his fingers and Dewr followed him to a bench where he took his place at an oar.

Once loaded, they pushed off and raised sail, catching the outgoing tide and morning breeze, leaving the small bay behind.

A large ship emerged on the horizon. "Bloody English," Captain Ferguson spat.

Hywel quickly recounted the events of the past month to the captain and crew.

"To oars," the captain shouted. "I dinnae wish to give the bastards a chance tae get close. The *Seabhag* can outrun their lumbering cogs any day. That's it, lads. Show the bloody English who rules these seas."

Carys sat on the bench beside her brother, grasped the oar and mimicked his movements. The oar wasn't terribly heavy and she was strong from her years with the long bow, but she doubted her ability to row for hours on end. They settled into a steady rhythm, moving the *Seabgag* swiftly across the water. One thing was certain, she would be stronger after this trip. With the wind and tide in their favor, they kept the English ship at a distance and ceased rowing once the cog abandoned the chase and made for port.

Hywel leaned over and whispered, "How'd ye fare?"

Carys shrugged. "'Tis nothing I cannot and will not do daily. I only fear not being able to keep up with you when we have to row for most of a day."

"Don't worry. Ye'll grow stronger as we go along, and the wind never ceases to blow this time of year. Besides, he needs the hands. Ferguson will see how hard ye work. By the time he realizes ye're a woman, we'll be either in Éire or Scotland. If he insists we leave, at least we'll be a few coins richer and farther away from the English."

Chapter Two

MacLean Castle
Morvern, Scotland

Birk shifted in his chair, steadying himself against the urge to dismiss the entire council arranged before him in the great hall. He resented being recalled to MacLean Castle like a disobedient lad. Managing the improvements to Dairborrodal Castle overlooking the Sound of Mull from a promontory on the Ardnamurchan Peninsula kept his mind off both the past and the future. With the elder council calling him to task once again, he could deny the future no longer.

"They look a right solemn bunch," Dugan noted quietly with a short nudge to Birk's ribs.

He and Birk both glanced up as a dark-haired woman approached the table, her rounded belly giving her a bit of a waddling gait. Rising to pull out the empty chair to his right, Birk seated his older half-sister carefully. She lowered herself to the chair with one hand pressed to the small of her back. The council rose to its collective feet, a short bow to Gillian instead of the words of rebuke Birk had grown accustomed to.

"They are solemn," she shot back at Dugan. She adjusted her sights on Birk. "And if ye would only come down from that ancient pile of stones on Ardnamurchan long enough to take a wife—and breed an heir—I wouldnae be drawn into this." She sighed heavily. "'Tis nae enough my husband is away on the king's business and cannae attend this council in my place, but I am still weeks away from delivering this bairn, and as such, my discomfort means little to these auld men gathered." She indicated the elder council with a curt nod.

Birk covered her hand with his in a comforting gesture. "I would not have agreed to have them send for ye, even if ye are the only other remaining MacLean. Though I mean no disrespect to Ma or Signy." He managed a grin at the thought of his other half-sister, completely unrelated to Gillian, who had lived with them for only a handful of years before marrying a man from the Isle of Mull. Despite her short time at MacLean Castle, she and Birk had been very close for she had treated him as the brother she'd lost to the Scot raiders who'd destroyed their village years earlier. Though their da, Alex, had been able to bring Signy home to his grieving soon-to-be wife, nothing had ever been heard of Sten, and a memorial stone had eventually been quietly placed in Hanna's garden.

Gillian sent him a pensive look. "They have grown more determined since Da passed away. I dinnae know how ye keep from dispensing with the lot of them."

The twinge of guilt he always felt when reminded of his da's passing bit then was gone. No matter how much he wished it otherwise, his da had lived long past the years given to most men, and the lung fever had not been an enemy he could defeat.

"Mayhap they will offer *ye* the lairdship. Ye already have two heirs growing nicely at home." He cocked his head. "And from the looks of ye, mayhap twins this time."

"Perish the thought—on both accounts. 'Tis unlikely they'd offer it to a woman, and I have enough on my hands, thank ye verra much." She frowned. "I can think of things I'd rather have offered me—a trip across the sound in a storm, for one. Which reminds me, we've had verra strong tides of late. I hope none of yer ships have been inconvenienced."

Birk shook his head. "Nae. I've none reporting damage or mishaps. Weather worry isnae new."

"And ye have good captains," Gillian replied, rubbing a hand across her belly.

"Is something bothering ye?" Birk asked, offering faint courtesy. Though he'd two bairns of his own, Rose hadn't invited his interest in the proceedings. As always, thoughts of his deceased wife inspired a frown and a swell of anger. At least he could face his daughters with the knowledge they were his and not another man's. They'd inherited their dark hair and slightly olive colored skin from him, and did not resemble their red-haired, pale-skinned ma at all.

As if Gillian sensed his train of thought, she patted his hand.

"How are my nieces? Did ye bring them with ye, or did ye leave them in that pile of rocks at Dairborrodal Castle?"

"Abria and Eislyn send ye their love," Birk said. "They are with their grandma if ye wish to see them." He tossed her a mischievous look. "You should ask her how she, the dowager baroness, managed to escape the council's summons."

Gillian smiled. "None dares insist Ma do something she doesnae wish to. And, of course, I wish to see the lassies. They are adorable." She tapped a fingertip on the table. "How is Abria?"

Her hesitation was slight, but Birk, ever-conscious of his youngest daughter's troubles, noticed. "She doesnae speak." The skin on his neck heated; his reply curt.

Gillian nodded, her happy smile fading to one of commiseration, offering little hope and less assurance. "She will in time."

"Her ma abandoned her when she was but a bairn. I fear the lass is scarred."

"She is yet a bairn," Gillian reminded him. "'Tis good ye allow her to spend so much time with ye. She shouldnae fear losing ye, as well."

Birk ground his teeth, a predictable response when his dead wife was mentioned.

Gregor MacLean's chair scraped the floor as he resumed his seat. "If my lady is comfortable, mayhap we could resume our talk?"

If Gillian caught the mild rebuke from the elderly man, she did not respond. Casting a beatific smile his way, she gave him her attention. "By all means, Gregor. Let us be about deciding my brother's future."

Birk stifled the urge to kick Gillian's chair. He, for one, did not wish to hear more demands that he marry again.

Gregor lifted a ragged piece of parchment. "The council has compiled a list of women who meet our approval as the next Lady MacLean." He waved a lad near and handed him the scrap. Birk stared at the offending page as it approached, his glare, he was fairly certain, standing a decent chance of igniting the parchment. Being of a particularly non-burnable element, it unfortunately arrived intact. He reluctantly accepted it and scanned the scrawled contents quickly.

His frown deepened. "Ye wish me to take *another* MacDonald wench to wife?" Birk cast the parchment away. It slewed across the table and landed in a platter of congealing mutton juices. "Because the last time worked so well?"

Gregor spread his hands. "Mairi MacDonald is a good lass."

Birk bristled. "She's fourteen! If I have more bairns, I'll breed my own—not marry one."

"Robena Balloch isnae a bairn," Gregor countered quickly.

"Nae. She's seeking her fifth husband. I dinnae care to land in *her* net."

"She's experienced," someone offered.

"Well-plowed," another quipped.

Birk sent a quelling look down the table and the wave of laughter choked.

Gregor bristled. "Ye cannae object to Seonag MacBrehon. Her father has ties to the MacDonnell laird."

A round of nodding heads drifted down the table.

"Aye. The MacDonnell clan wields great power."

"They have lands along our shipping routes," Gregor added.

It was true. There was little he could say against Seonag MacBrehon. He risked sounding like the bitter man he'd become to point out the young woman's timidity, her seeming lack of courage. She'd eaten at the MacLean tables often enough with her da, a brawny man who did a brisk business in Morvern in whisky and leather goods in the autumn when worn footwear was exchanged for warm, sturdier boots toward off the cold in winter. Her character was well known.

But to join with a woman of no mettle—what courage would a son of hers have? Birk suppressed a shudder. Assuming he had enough of an urge to sire a child on her.

"Enough. I will consider the will of the council. But I dinnae wish to discuss it further."

His pronouncement was met with silence and skeptical looks. He waved a hand, catching the eye of his steward. "Fill their cups and assure them of a bed. I will make myself available for any questions on the morrow."

I've had my fill for today. Gripping the armrests of his chair to force a hesitation, he barely managed to push his seat back without overturning it in unseemly haste. Belatedly remembering his sister's presence, he wheeled about.

"Might I escort ye to yer room?"

She lifted a delicate brow. "As much as I would love to put my feet up, I believe we should take a stroll about the garden."

Birk hid a groan, his chest near to bursting with the frustration building inside. He needed an outlet and escorting his pregnant half-sister about the garden did not appear promising.

"In this weather?" he asked, hoping to put her off.

"'Tis bracing. Hand me my cloak."

"Certainly," he gritted, forcing a congenial smile, though he feared it resembled naught more than a grimace. Her knowing grin confirmed his suspicion.

She took his arm. They strode across the hall through the lingering council members who edged out of his determined path. Disapproval and disappointment lit their eyes, dragged the corners of their mouths downward. Birk answered with a brisk nod.

He and Gillian reached the walled garden his mother had spent the early years of her marriage creating. After spending the first half of her life as a minor Norse lord's wife on the Isle of Mull, she had fled the isle after her family and village were destroyed. She married Gillian's father, Alex MacLean, and, after giving birth to Birk a year later, embraced the beauty of the Scottish landscape by creating this marvel of sturdy Rowan trees, spring and summer blooming flowers, and pebbled pathways.

Around the first bend stood a slender stone Birk had brought her when he was twelve, the smooth sides crossed with peculiar symbols carved into the rock's surface. He'd found it nestled in a small copse, half-buried in thorns and twisted vines, as he trailed a buck through the brambles. Presenting it to her as a memorial stone for the son she'd lost years before, he'd meant to soothe the sadness from her eyes. She'd given the stone with its ancient carvings a place of honor in a bed of pretty white flowers, and it ruled the entrance to the rest of the garden with a benevolent eye.

"Ma is half-superstitious about that stone." Gillian nodded to the weathered rock, topped with snow and glistening with frost. "I remember when ye gave it to her."

Birk spared the rock a glance, a frisson of unease rippling across his shoulders. Gillian was quick to notice.

"Does it affect ye?"

"Nae. Rather, 'tis the first time it has done so." He frowned. "'Tis only a stone."

"Ye know better," his sister chided. "It belongs to Sten."

"That's ridiculous." The hair on the back of Birk's neck rose, as if sensing the presence of his long-dead half-brother. "I dinnae come out here to indulge yer womanly prattling."

Gillian halted, drawing her hand from his arm, surprise on her face. "Ye have changed, Birk MacLean," she accused. "I felt sorry for ye when Rose showed her true colors, but even with her dead, ye have grown more bitter, not less."

Rage bunched his muscles, flamed across his skin. Heat crept up his neck. He held onto his ire, using it to fuel his self-righteous anger. Fingertips pressed into his forearm, weight increasing until he lifted his gaze and met Gillian's worried eyes.

"Birk, she's gone. Why do ye allow her to torment ye so?"

His wrath subsided like a billowed sail losing the wind. It clung to him but failed to rise. Gillian was right. He brushed a layer of snow from a carved wooden bench across the path from the stone and Gillian sank with a sigh to its supporting comfort.

"I did love her," he admitted, surprised to hear the words. He didn't want to remember his boyish infatuation when he'd first met the voluptuous, spirited Rose.

"I thought 'twas an arranged marriage," Gillian replied.

Birk nodded, seating himself on the bench abruptly, as if he no longer could count on his burning rage to fuel his movements.

"'Twas. But I secretly hoped Da would agree. He wasnae interested in her da's offer at first, but I was already infatuated with her." He shrugged. "I dinnae know if she'd been instructed to do her damnedest to ensure the alliance, or if she was attracted to me in the beginning, but during the sennight she and her da were here, she taught me a few things I'd never dreamed of as a lusty lad."

He risked a glance at Gillian, hoping she did not condemn him for his youthful transgressions. Her shoulders shook, not, apparently, with indignation, but, if the twitch of her lips was to be believed, with humor.

"What?" Irritation sharpened his voice. "I confessed having swived a lass in manners I'd not imagined, and ye laugh?"

"Oh, Birk," Gillian cried, abandoning all attempts to rein in her laughter. "Ye fell for the oldest trick in the world and fell hard. Ye always were passionate in whatever ye did. None out-sparred ye on the training field. Ye brought back the heaviest buck, the largest brace of hares. It doesnae surprise me ye felt so passionate about yer wife—may God have mercy on her soul. She doesnae deserve yer sacrifice, ye know. Ye dinnae have to keep her memory alive. As passionately as ye loved her, ye hate her just as much—or more."

She tilted her head, compassion on her face, in the touch of her palm on his cheek. "Let the anger go. 'Tis stealing yer bairns from ye. They love ye yet are cautious in yer presence."

Her observation shook Birk to his core. "I would give my life for my bairns," he growled.

"I know that, and they do as well. But they need laughter, brother. Laughter and fond memories. I have those with our da," she added, the sheen of tears in her eyes before she blinked them away.

"Do ye think that is why Abria—" The words fouled in his throat. He did not wish to be responsible for his daughter's affliction. His fingers clenched, fisting on his thighs. "Why she doesnae speak?"

"Nae." Gillian's pronouncement was firm. "She has heard too many hateful rumors about her ma. I know ye try to shield her from them, but bairns have big ears. She was but two summers old when her ma ran away. All know Abria was a difficult baby, and she and her ma nearly died at her birth. 'Tis my belief she has heard it said she was the reason her ma fled. Either her ma dinnae wish to risk her life with another bairn, or raising Abria was too difficult. It doesnae matter. I suspect Abria fears ye will hate her if ye learn the truth."

Birk leapt to his feet. "It isnae true! None of it. Why would she believe such a thing?"

"She is a bairn," Gillian reminded him. "Reason doesnae enter into it. I'd hoped she would grow out of it, but ye say she remains mute."

New anger hammered in Birk's ears. Grinding his teeth, he paced before the bench.

"Ye have done yer best to include her," Gillian said. "'Tis not yer fault."

Birk shook his head, his sister's kindness falling on deaf ears. He should have heard the rumors, realized what they were doing to Abria. But the whispers confirmed his wife was a vain, self-indulgent woman, lacking in morals, with no interest in raising bairns. The pitying looks, the sympathetic gestures—all had fed his sense of betrayal, the justice in Rose's death.

He halted abruptly. "I will change everything," he vowed. "If I feel rage, I will hide it. If I hear rumors, I will stop them. And I will hire a nurse who will play with the girls and brighten their spirits."

"Very noble, and 'tis certain Rose's auld nurse, Ina, is a gloomy thing," Gillian agreed. "But what of *yer* life? Will ye agree to the council's charge and marry?"

A frown threatened to take charge, but he halted it with supreme force.

"Nicely done," his sister quipped, missing nothing.

"I will marry," he said. "But a woman of *my* choosing. I cannae stomach a weak-willed woman. She must have a caring heart, loyalty." He considered Seonag MacBrehon's timid behavior. "She will be capable of defending herself. Her actions will inspire respect and approval."

"And she must be beautiful," Gillian added, her voice solemn.

It took Birk a moment to register his sister's laughing skepticism.

"Where do ye expect to find this paragon of virtue?" she asked, her eyes dancing.

He shrugged, humor restored. "Not on the list I was given today."

A rustle of leaves announced another's presence. Birk schooled his face into a bland expression. A woman strolled down the path from the far reach of the garden, her russet cloak lined with plush fur. Silver glinted in her blonde hair. Her green eyes glowed, peace smoothing the lines of her face. The pair of lasses at her side were her exact opposite, possessing the dark, slanted eyes that bore evidence of their Armenian great-grandmother, their tresses a mass of thick sable curls. Their cold-pinked noses peaked out from the hoods of their cloaks.

Birk smiled at the pair, his exact images down to the slightly dusky hue to their skin.

Love and compassion gripped him in a stranglehold as he peered at the smallest of the children. Abria. Her name meant strength, but her eyes reflected the fragility of a troubled child. He squatted before her, draping his hands to dangle at his knees, neither reaching nor refusing her.

"How're my bonny lasses? Is yer amma taking good care of ye?"

Hanna's hand whitened as Abria's grip tightened.

Her sister sent her da a reproachful look. "Abria doesnae like the big dogs, but the garden is much better."

Birk held his half-smile and slid his gaze to Eislyn. Her quickness to shield her younger sister was admirable, but it had given her a sharp tongue and allowed Abria to hide in her sister's shadow.

"I thank ye for noticing," he told Eislyn. "What do ye like about the garden, Abria?"

"She likes—"

Birk lifted a finger, silencing Eislyn's response. He waited patiently, hoping Abria would break her silence. The child turned her face to Hanna's skirts and did not speak.

Clenching his jaw, Birk counted to ten before slowly rising. "I will let ye help with the new gardens at Dairborrodal, aye?" His words laced with entreaty, he had to be satisfied with the partial appearance of one of Abria's eyes, as though his promise provoked interest.

"And what would ye like to help with, Eislyn?" he asked. Though his greatest concern was with Abria, he could not let his older daughter feel slighted.

"I should help with the weapons," Eislyn announced. "I wish to continue my lessons, and there is no blacksmith or armorer at Dairborrodal yet."

Gillian elbowed Birk. "Spoken like a true MacLean. She takes after her amma."

"She comes from quite a lineage of warrior women," Birk agreed. "And 'tis remiss of me to not keep up yer lessons."

He lifted his gaze to his ma, noting the steel barely hidden beneath her serene façade. "How do ye fare this fine day?"

"I am pleased to spend it with my granddaughters, and understand your concern, though I have not yet reached my dotage," Hanna replied with a faint nod to Abria. "This one has my gardening heart, the other will make a fine shield maiden."

"I will," Eislyn declared. "Amma has agreed to teach me to throw a blade. She says ye are much too busy with clan 'fairs." She shrugged, a puzzled look furrowing her brow. "I dinnae know we were having a fair, but I want to go!"

Birk laughed. "She means clan politics, *leanbh*," he said. "Dinnae fash. Mayhap we will have a fair close to harvest time. I will speak to the steward and have him look into it. Will that do?"

Eislyn nodded vigorously. "Aye! And a dagger-throwing contest?"

"We will see. Though at seven summers, ye are a bit too young to compete."

Her scowl told him he would hear more on the subject. "Let's go inside and find something warm to drink. Would ye like that?"

Eislyn nodded vigorously. Abria cut her gaze from her da to her sister, her thumb lodged in her mouth. She pressed closer to Hanna.

Dugan appeared at the entrance to the garden. Abria disappeared behind Hanna. Biting his tongue at his daughter's continued fears, Birk merely swung about to face his captain.

"A word, Laird?" Dugan murmured.

Birk met his urgent gaze and drew in a breath sharp with the tang of winter. He glanced over his shoulder. "Mayhap yer *amma* and Auntie Gillian would see to the hot drinks?"

The women nodded, concern etched on their faces, and gathered the two lasses, bustling them past the men, their voices pitched unnaturally high with forced jollity. Birk folded his arms over his chest, belligerence returning as he guessed the council was not finished with him.

Dugan slanted a look at the retreating forms, then shifted his attention to Birk.

"Laird, there has been trouble at one of the crofts."

"Not pirates?" Birk asked, startled to find the problem not where he'd imagined.

"Nae. Raiders inland. A lad brought the report. They killed his da and left the lad for dead. Ran off with the cattle and a side of pork."

Birk's blood boiled. "Where is the lad?"

"In the hall. Awaiting the healer."

Birk surged forward, long stride quickly overtaking his ma and Gillian. "Take Abria and Eislyn to yer solar," he barked as he swept past. Startled, his mother halted and put a hand out, catching his sleeve.

"Do ye need my help?"

He shrugged from beneath her touch. "Nae. I will speak of it to ye later."

Hanna's eyes narrowed, but Birk did not apologize, even though he knew she was the last person who required sheltering from life's harsher truths.

He burst into the hall where a small group clustered, distress thick enough to almost touch. The group broke apart at his approach, baring a young lad of perhaps twelve summers to Birk's view. A jagged gash, bound together with a rag and crusted blood, marked the lad from crown to jaw. His dark eyes burned hot and large in his pale face.

"Do ye know who did this, lad?" Birk asked, blunting a bit of the authoritative rumble of his voice as he attempted to reassure the boy.

The lad shook his head. A grimace snatched at his lips, whitening with pain. "Nae," he croaked. "I've nae seen the man before." He measured Birk's body with his glance. "Yer height he was, and broad. Dark as night his long hair was."

Birk grunted, exchanging a quick glance with Dugan over the lad's head. It was not the first time a thief of long dark hair and unusual size had been reported. The soldiers had given him the nickname *Colin Dubh*. Nothing else was known about him. He attacked crofters, stole their livestock and food, and left dead any who resisted.

Birk ground his teeth. "Get the lad food and clean clothes. Tend his wounds and find him a place to sleep. I will speak to him again later." He brushed past Dugan who wheeled about and matched his pounding stride.

"Gather enough forces to scour the land. I want no bothy, croft or cave left unexplored. I willnae have this devil on my lands."

Dugan gave a curt nod and peeled away to gather his men.

A powerfully built man with the remnants of shockingly red hair planted himself before Birk. "I heard ye refuse to name a wife from those presented to ye today," he growled. "Seonag is a bonny lass, and well brought up." James MacBrehon grabbed his daughter's arm and dragged her between Birk and himself. "Whatever ye want, my lass will provide it for ye."

Seonag risked a look at Birk but jerked away as if struck as his eyebrows snapped together.

"Can ye tend the lad's wounds?"

Seonag glanced at her hands, the long fingers unmarred by work. Fury at the lass' ineptness overtook Birk. He stepped closer.

"Can ye wield a sword? Rally troops to rid my lands of this scourge?"

She shook her carefully coifed head.

"Bah! Then find another man to work yer wiles on. 'Twill not be me."

James shoved his daughter behind him, chest puffed out in righteous anger. "Ye will rue this day, Laird MacLean!" he proclaimed. "Ye dinnae deserve a wife to care for yer needs. Ye seek naught more than a warrior to fight yer battles—a woman like yer ma!" He pointed his nose into the air. "A Norsewoman when yer da could have had the pick of sweet Scottish lasses!" He jabbed a finger in Birk's direction.

"Ye're just like him!"

Birk's fist arced through the air. Bone crunched beneath his knuckles and blood spurted from James' broken nose. Not satisfied with the warning, Birk brought his other fist up, connecting firmly with the point of the other man's jaw. For a moment, James stretched up on his toes. His eyes flew open wide an instant before they blanked, and he crumpled to the icy path.

Stepping over the fallen man, Birk continued to the hall, not sparing a speechless Seonag a second look.

Chapter Three

Aboard the Seabhag

"Put yer backs into it, laddies," Captain Ferguson bellowed over the cold, whistling north wind. "We need tae make land afore nightfall."

They'd had a cloudy but mild day for their crossing of St. George's Channel. As the vessel plowed through the waves, the chop sent sea spray over the bow, misting all aboard, making the mixture of exertion, stinging gusts, and frigid moisture bracing.

Carys had long ago removed her cloak, leaving her jerkin and leather cowl. She'd wrapped her hands in strips of wool to protect them from the biting cold and abrasion from the wooden oar. The wintry breeze held steady all day, pushing their craft through the water with ease. Considering their load, Carys was impressed with the *Falcon's* speed. Ferguson did not exaggerate his ship's prowess. The captain allowed the crew rest between rowing sessions, but kept a brisk pace to ensure the *Seabhag* made port in Éire by the end of the day.

"Drop the sail," the captain ordered as they approached the docks, gliding in under oar. "That's it. Easy now." Ferguson manned the rudder as he coaxed the *Seabhag* into a slip at the port of Wexford. The coastal village appeared to be no bigger than the hamlet they'd left early that morn. Like many ports in southern Cymru, Norsemen and native people mingled over the years as the legacy of Viking settlements spread across the land.

"Wyn, secure the ship for the night. I'll pay the dockmaster for our berth and be stayin' at the inn if ye need me." The captain rubbed the back of his neck. "Lads, Wyn's in charge and will see tae yer supper. With any luck, I'll be back on the morrow with a few buyers. Nae wanderin' off. There'll be plenty of chances for shore leave in the days ahead. Remain here and guard our cargo."

Dewr waited by the rail for her orders.

"Dewr, stay with Tully," Ferguson commanded. With a wag of her tail, the dog trotted to a spot next to the boy. She plopped her furry rump on the boards, ears pricked forward, as other sailors secured their vessels for the night. Her head peeked over the rail.

Wyn supervised the securing the enormous woolen sail to either side of the boat, adjusting the massive wooden spar holding the sail so it pointed fore and aft. Once they raised the mainsail spar a few feet, the sail created a tent tall enough for them to walk upright down the middle of the ship. Though they had nothing to cover the ends, they would be mostly dry and protected should a squall blow through.

Wyn opened three barrels aft of the last oars near the helm. "Gather round, men. Each gets a ration of salted pork, biscuits and ale."

The crew formed a line and reached into one barrel for a wooden tankard, then filled it from a large tapped cask. When it was Carys's turn, she selected from a stack of wooden bowls in the barrel along with the tankards suggesting hot meals in the future. This eve's cold fare would do well enough, but as they traveled farther north, their bellies would crave hot food to ward off the wintry chill.

The twang of salted meat blended with the faint nose-wrinkling scent of the murky water sloshing against the dock. Carys buried her nose in her mug, inhaling the crisp aroma of ale.

Carys and Hywel strode toward the bow of the ship where they had stowed their gear. Wrapped in their cloaks and blankets, they settled in to eat. The salted pork tasted fresh enough, and the biscuits were sizeable pieces of unleavened bread made of flour and water—meager fare but filling. The ale was surprisingly good and held a hint of wildflowers. She and Hywel ate in silence, enjoying a moment of peace. The cries of gulls, paired with the sea lapping against the ship, wrought a calming effect.

Ferguson's rotation for the watch and clean up meant all shared in the shipboard chores except the captain. Hywel and Wyn had first watch. Carys had second along with another. She and her brother would both sleep during third watch.

"How fare ye?" Hywel asked on a whisper.

"Fine. Though I'm a bit sore and fairly worn thin."

"Do ye still agree with my decision to leave Cymru?" he asked, seemingly uncertain of himself, something Carys wasn't used to hearing from her brother. She sought to reassure him.

"What else could we have done, Brother? Wait for Longshanks to march into our village and burn us out? Anyone identifying the soldiers who fought with the prince will be rewarded. Double the reward for the capture of those of us with noble blood. The same for the traitors who showed the English how to cross the Irfon River and flank us at Orewin Bridge. If we had stayed, we'd live as outlaws in our own country until captured. Ye're right. 'Tis time we left home and made our way elsewhere."

Hywel nodded, his shoulders relaxing. "What do ye hope to find in Scotland?"

Carys stared at the few stars visible and thought about how best to answer. "Peace. I think I'd be content simply with peace. Mayhap a small village where my skills would be accepted. Mountains, streams, forests and a place to settle amongst quiet people. What about you, Brother? 'Tis ye who gives up yer birthright by fleeing to the Scottish Highlands. What do ye hope for in the mountains and forests of Caledonia?"

Hywel quirked a smile. "A small patch of land to build a home and raise a few sheep like Da. Find me a lass to take to wife who'll give me lots of children and keep my bed warm at night. What else would a man wish for?"

Carys shook her head. "Ye men are all alike. I assume ye expect her to cook and clean whilst ye tend a few sheep and bring home the occasional deer?"

Hywel's smile lit up the night. "Why, of course. 'Tis what good husbands do."

Carys's mood plummeted at the reminder of what she'd lost.

"Worry not, sister mine. With Da gone, 'tis my duty now to find a man worthy of ye, and I swear to do so." Sincerity rounded her brother's eyes.

"I don't know if I want another husband, Hywel. My dreams of having a family of my own died with Terwyn. After fending for myself these past months, looking out for ye as much as I have for myself, I'm not certain I need a man to care for me."

"I understand yer grief, Carys, but ye are a young woman, and men find ye pleasing to look upon. Ye are of noble blood. Even in Scotland, that will be valued. There will be offers and expectations for ye to marry nae matter where ye settle. Allow your sorrow to have its way, then we will speak of it again. Ye are too young to give up yer dreams. Besides, who else can make me an uncle?"

The words from the old woman in Aberswyth rose in her mind. Carys swallowed against the fear drying her mouth.

Hywel patted her arm. "I won't force ye to marry until ye are ready," he said.

"'Tis not that, Hywel. 'Twas a brief encounter I had whilst fetching the meat pies."

Carys told the tale of her moments with the old seer, and the thoughts and fear she'd had since.

Hywel frowned as he considered her words. "She said there was naught to be done?"

"Nae, only that by my leaving did I push my own death farther into the future."

Hywel shrugged and flashed a smile. "We've placed ourselves in plenty of danger these past few months fighting for our royal cousin. Though we didn't win, I wouldn't change aught I've done, including boarding this ship. When our time comes, it comes. What can be done to change it? The Almighty will do what He wills."

She nodded reluctant agreement, though her heart still ached. "Let me take yer watch," she offered. "I am far from sleep."

"Are ye certain?" Hywel asked.

She knew he could sleep anywhere, at any time. "Aye. Ye'll sleep like a babe and I'll wake ye in three hours so ye can take my shift."

Carys walked the length of the ship and settled in the bow. Dewr left Tully's sleeping form and curled up next to Carys, tucking her nose beneath her tail. Carys smiled and scratched behind the dog's ears, earning a few laps from Dewr's rough tongue before the dog sighed and buried her nose against the bitter night air. Carys welcomed the additional warmth of the dog's body as she stared at the night sky. A light fog rolled in, reducing the countless stars to a few faint twinkles of light.

Three hours into her watch, Dewr raised her head, a rumbling growl low in her chest.

Carys placed a calming hand on her. "Easy, girl. What'd ye hear?"

Rising to her knees, Carys silently crept to the edge of the ship and peered into the darkness. Though not yet midnight, Wyn appeared to be asleep at his post, slumped against the stern, unmoving. Man-shaped shadows stalked the pier toward their boat.

She counted ten, though the fog didn't allow for a sure tally. Reaching for her bow, she placed one end against the hull and bent it backward to secure the string. She then slowly drew four arrows, taking care to make no more than a whisper of sound.

Silver reflected off the short swords the men carried from what little moonlight pierced the evening gloom. They quietly picked up the gangplank and made to bridge the short distance between the *Seabhag* and the dock.

Carys nocked an arrow, rose and fired, striking the first man under the arm as he held the wooden walkway overhead.

"To arms! To arms! We are under attack!" She cried.

She fitted and fired another arrow, hitting the second man who held the gangplank aloft. Dewr helped sound the alarm, barking loudly enough to wake the dead. The catwalk clattered onto the wooden dock as the men holding it collapsed. The remaining thieves retrieved the fallen platform and dropped it into place with a loud bang, no longer caring about noise.

Carys's remaining arrows found a home in two more brigands. She dropped her bow, picked up her javelin and climbed to the edge of the rail. She leaped the distance, landing at the end of the dock, water on either side and behind her, enemies in front. Grasping the butt of her javelin with her right hand, she guided it with her left, braced firmly with her left foot forward. The robber nearest her drew a wicked seax the length of her forearm, hefting the blade in the manner of a seasoned fighter.

The man feinted, testing Carys's reaction. She ignored his move and drove the shaft of her javelin with her right hand toward her left until they met, darting her javelin forward then snatching it back in a lightning-quick move. The small leaf-shaped blade sliced into the thief's throat. He vainly grasped his pierced flesh with both hands and dropped to his knees, eyes wide in disbelief as his life's blood poured onto the pier.

The rest of the ship's crew had awakened and joined the fight. Hywel wielded his short sword and dagger while Wyn fought another robber. Hywel killed his man then helped Wyn finish his foe. Once it was apparent their attack had failed, the remaining thieves ran. Carys hurled her javelin, striking down one more, the last two fleeing into the night. Carys retrieved her arrows and javelin from the fallen men, then searched them for anything of value.

Hywel crossed onto the dock and assisted her as they'd done many times over the past year. The rest of the crew stared, some still half-asleep, mouths agape. Carys gave Hywel a grim smile as she nodded toward the crew. These were sailors, not warriors.

Wyn directed the rest of the men to follow Carys and Hywel's lead. After gathering weapons from the fallen, they dragged the bodies to the end of the pier onto the shore where they discovered two watchmen dead, their throats slashed. Carys pulled the hood of her cowl over her head.

The first mate appeared shaken and indecisive from the attack and his grisly discovery.

"There's nae need to disturb the captain, Wyn," Hywel said. "We did what he ordered before he left for the night. We guarded the ship. If ye wake him now, there's naught to be done that cannot be done come morn. Besides, he'll have lost sleep and likely be in a foul mood. If anyone is to get a good night's sleep this eve, I prefer it to be him."

Several of the men grinned, and Wyn nodded with a faint smile that fell far short of any humor. Carys chuckled at her brother's ability to ease even the most difficult circumstances. He'd make a fine bard.

"Agreed." Wyn appeared to regain some of his confidence. "'Tis time for second watch. Good work. Get some sleep, ye've earned it." He sent a flickering glance and nod to Carys. She nodded in return and quirked a smile, knowing he'd failed completely as first mate by falling asleep during his watch. She returned to the ship, accepting Dewr's enthusiastic greeting.

"Good job, lass," Carys murmured as she rubbed the dog's sandy-colored head. "Ye're the reason none of us are injured and the boat rests safe and secure. I don't know what Ferguson feeds ye, but I'll see to it ye're rewarded an extra ration."

Dewr strolled beside Carys, wagging her tail as they headed toward the front of the ship, passing Tully along the way. The lad grabbed her in a fierce hug as powerful as it was unexpected.

"Ye saved me da's boat. Ye saved me," he said with what looked too much like worship in his eyes for her comfort.

"Aye. Ye can count on me to keep ye safe." Carys had no idea why the reassurance slipped out. She patted his shoulder as he let her go.

Tully grinned and nodded, his flame-red hair bobbing in the torchlight.

The rest of the crew eyed her with respect, some touching their forelocks. *If they only knew they owe their lives to a woman and a dog.* She gave a light shrug. *They shall soon enough. We shall see how long their respect lasts.*

Carys spread her blanket on the hard deck, then wrapped her cloak about her. Dewr tucked in beside her once again. Replaying the last half hour in her mind, she pondered her lack of regret over taking lives. Killing men, even the cursed English, had once filled her with soul-wrenching guilt. She'd lost track of how many lives she'd ended—with another six tonight. Knowing they'd have slaughtered the crew and stolen the ship justified her actions. Upon reflection, she meant every word of her vow to Tully. She'd protect him as if he were her own. When sleep finally came, it was peaceful.

Ferguson's voice carried on the foggy morning air as he sang a Gaelic sea ditty. His song and the thump of his boots abruptly stopped. Carys rose and pulled the hood of her cowl low over her head. She strapped on her short sword, placing a dagger in each boot, one under each sleeve of her tunic, another at her waist, and one that ran along her belt at her lower back. The seax at her waist was new, thanks to their attackers last eve. She organized her possessions in case Ferguson decided to take offense at her presence and demand she and Hywel leave.

Wyn met the captain on the dock and retold their tale, wild gestures adding impact. Ferguson met Carys's gaze, motioning for her to meet him on the pier. Carys whistled for Dewr to follow, and the dog leapt to her feet, an action which caused the captain's brows to fly upward to his hairline.

Hywel strapped on his sword and joined her.

"Wyn greets me with quite a tale this morn." Ferguson frowned at his dog who remained at Carys's side, her tail wagging gently. "He says the ship was defended with no loss of cargo, nor any crewman injured, though two of the dockmaster's guards lay dead. Why was I not awakened?" he demanded with a scowl.

"What purpose would that have served, Captain?" Hywel asked. "Ye ordered us to guard the ship and cargo, and guard it we did." His engaging smile eased Ferguson's frown.

The red-haired Scot then pointed at Carys. "He says ye saw the bastards first. I'd have the tale from ye." The captain crossed his arms over his barrel chest.

Carys knew she'd be found out with so much to say, so she did not bother lowering her voice to affect a young male's tone. She patted the dog who sat beside her as if her allegiance had shifted.

"Dewr heard them afore me, Captain. I spotted them in the fog, strung my bow and woke the men as I fired."

"How many?" the captain demanded.

"I saw ten, though two made their escape," Carys replied.

"Wyn tells me he and yer brother each killed a man, yet only two got away? Who killed the rest?"

Carys pulled her cowl back. "I did, Captain."

"St. Finnian's holy cock! A woman?" Ferguson's eyebrows leapt skyward in disbelief. His shock turned to humor as he broke into laughter. Dewr danced around him on the dock barking, enjoying his mirth.

Carys scanned the crew for their reaction. Most seemed bemused while two grew stormy, their hands fisting.

"There shouldnae be a woman aboard," one growled, obviously displeased by her deception.

"Bad luck?" bellowed Ferguson. "The way I see it, the two females aboard saved the lot of ye and yer sorry male arses. Wyn here says he was takin' a wee nap. If neither of these two lassies had been here, I'd have arrived this morn to a stack of corpses foulin' the dock, including my son's, and the *Seabhag* and her cargo long gone."

"Any sailor worth 'is salt knows 'tis bad luck to have a woman on board," the man insisted, arms crossed over his broad chest, a scowl twisting his features.

The captain strode to within a hand's width of the sailor who lost some of his bluster in the face of Ferguson's intimidating presence.

"Well, now. I see yer mam raised ye to be ungrateful as well as disrespectful. Ye're released from service. Get yer gear and get the hell off me boat. I dinnae need ye."

The sailor shot a murderous glare at Carys then fetched a canvas tote from under one of the benches. He stalked off the boat and spit toward it once he reached dock.

Ferguson chuckled at the man's impotent gesture. "Any other fools who dinnae wish to sail with these two lovelies, 'tis the time tae say so. I'll nae have dissention aboard me ship."

The other man who'd glared at Carys when she dropped her cowl retrieved his gear and disembarked without a word.

"I'm sorry I lost ye two oarsmen, Captain," Carys said.

Ferguson grunted and waved away her apology. "Bah. 'Tis better to know the quality of the men aboard me ship afore we sail any farther. Besides, I found six others tae join us. Just leave yer hood off so they can see ye plain when they arrive."

Hywel bumped her with a shoulder. "I told ye, Sister. Once Ferguson learned of yer character and skills he'd be daft tae throw us off."

She managed a smile and nod. Mayhap they'd make it to Scotland after all.

Once the sun had fully risen, the new crewmen arrived while the rest of the crew unloaded the cargo the captain had sold. Ferguson pointed her out before the men boarded. Each man glanced her way and either shrugged or simply boarded. It appeared they didn't have the same beliefs as the men who feared superstition and had forsaken the safety of a well-defended ship.

Chapter Four

MacLean Castle

Birk slammed his fist on the table. His mug skittered on the boards. The men facing him jolted at the sound.

"This is *not* acceptable."

Dugan bowed his head. Birk knew his captain was not to blame, but the loss of a ship—the second in as many months—was not to be borne. Surging to his feet, he paced the length of the single table. Late in the evening, only a few servants lingered in the hall. A sleepy lad struggling to stay awake to tend his laird's needs covered his yawn behind his fist. Birk stomped past him. Dugan and the six other soldiers leaned wearily over their mugs, the failure to rescue the crew from the most recent attack weighing as heavily as the exhaustion from the frantic three-day hunt.

Birk pivoted on his heel. "Is this somehow tied to Colin Dubh?"

Dugan shook his head. "Nae. He seems to limit his raids to crofts—anything on land. The pirates appear to be a different force."

"What ships are due here in the next sennight?"

Dugan consulted a smudged parchment on the table before him. "The *Alacrity*—"

Birk waved a hand dismissively. "She's too well armed. Even should they come upon her unawares, the pirates willnae stand a chance against her."

"Agreed. But I would still suggest sending an armed ship to escort her through the strait. A show of force would make the pirates think twice about challenging us."

"See to it," Birk snapped, his ire still smoldering. "Anything else?"

"She's not one of ours, but a friend—the *Seabhag* is overdue her usual visit. They could be late for a number of reasons, not the least is the war between Edward and Wales."

"My reports say Dafydd has succeeded his brother as prince." Birk halted, sending Dugan a piercing look. "I wouldnae care to have a brother who played both sides of the crown."

"'Tis said Llywelyn's head still resides on the gate at the Tower of London," one of the soldiers offered. "Dafydd stirred up more than his share of trouble for his brother over the years."

"I heard he is on the run from Edward," another added.

"Longshanks has a far reach," Dugan grumbled. "There is no place he willnae search to rid himself of the man." He shook his head. "God have mercy on his soul."

"The devil will be taking Dafydd's soul," a soldier replied.

"Dafydd's soul may be up for grabs, but 'tis not our problem," Birk growled. "With our ships moving all over the world, they are clearly a target for pirates. This is our issue, not the troubles of the Welsh."

"I will set a watch for our ships," Dugan sighed, the strain on his face evident.

"And we will see what can be done about Colin Dubh," Birk added, disdain for the outlaw's actions twisting his lips into a scowl. "I willnae tolerate abuse of my people. He can either turn his hand to an honest trade or take himself across our borders. If he attacks again, he will forfeit his life."

* * *

Aboard the Seabhag
Off the Isle of Mull

"The bloody bastards are still gainin' on us," Ferguson shouted over the wind and the splash of ten oars slicing into the ocean in unison, propelling the *Seabhag* forward as if the hounds of hell were on their heels.

They weren't the hounds of hell, but pirates, the second band they'd encountered on their journey. The langskip closing on them had sixteen oars with plenty of hands to row, and a ferocious dragon mounted onto its prow. After their first encounter with the sea devils, Carys had prepared a dozen fire arrows, wrapping them in hemp twine an inch or so from the head then soaking them in a mixture of lamp oil and pitch. The lamp oil allowed the arrows to ignite quickly and the pitch made certain they continued to burn.

The raiders had drawn close enough this time to count heads. Close enough to shoot.

"*Now*, Captain," Carys shouted as the ship's bow crashed into another wave.

"Go!" he ordered.

Carys leaped from the bench and grabbed their bows while Rabbie left Tully on the starboard side bench to take Hywel's place at the oar they'd abandoned on the larboard side. Carys sprinted aft, Dewr on her heels and Hywel right behind, her soft-soled boots slipping a bit on the water-slick deck. They each clutched a handful of prepared arrows and made for the lamp Ferguson kept near the rudder.

The captain glanced over his shoulder. "May the good Lord be with ye both, as we've met our match. We cannae outrun them, and they outnumber us by a dozen or more."

Hywel tossed the captain a reckless smile. "Ach, dinnae fash, Captain. Me wee sister and I will have this riffraff off yer stern in nae time a'tall," he said mimicking Ferguson's brogue.

"Aim high for the rigging," Carys instructed, ignoring her brother's rash banter.

If they could catch the sail afire near the top where it attached to the main spar, the pirates would either have to let it burn or lower the sail to extinguish the flames. Either would be enough to allow the *Seabhag* to escape as they would be faster with both sail and oar than the other craft under oar only.

Hywel's first arrow sailed harmlessly over the top, missing altogether.

Nocking an arrow, Carys lit it with Ferguson's lamp. Drawing back on the bowstring, the burning portion resting just beyond her archer's bracer, she drew a breath, took aim, and released her shaft. The arrow buried itself in the main spar high above the ship, contacting wood, rope and sail. Carys waited breathless until smoke appeared.

The pirate crew ignored her shot, pulling harder on their oars as flames leapt above their heads. Carys fumed. If they did not slow the marauders down, there would not be enough time for her fire arrow to do its work.

"Hywel, the helmsman!" she shouted.

Hywel drew his bow and fired, striking the helmsman in the chest. The impact caused the man to push the rudder starboard, sending their craft larboard and away from the *Seabhag*. As another man took the dead man's place, Carys noticed a familiar cask at their stern.

She whipped her head around. "Do all captains keep their whisky close at hand as ye do?" she demanded.

The red-headed Scot tilted his head and frowned. "Aye, all I know do—tae keep the vermin from drinkin' it dry."

She turned to her brother. "Hywel, hand me a bodkin and shoot the helmsman again."

A crooked smile settled on his mouth as he drew a plain arrow and another for her. "What are ye about, Sister?"

She returned his smile, knowing he and the rest would enjoy her plan if successful. "The helmsman, if you please, my lord."

Hywel dispatched another helmsman. Carys drew her bow in the same instant. Allowing for the predictable lurch of their craft, she waited for the next man to right the ship then released her arrow. The long and narrow point on the bodkin was designed to slip through English chainmail, piercing the gambeson and flesh beneath. She needed this one to punch a hole through the oak cask resting at their stern. The arrow struck, though she couldn't tell if it had penetrated the small wooden tun.

Hywel had taken to picking off oarsmen in an effort to slow them down. The smoke from Carys's fire arrow billowed and flames crackled, fed by the gusting wind.

Carys lit another fire arrow. "The helm once more, Hywel."

The helmsman staggered backward, an arrow in his gut, giving Carys the opening she needed. Following the flight of her fiery missile, she thrust her hands in the air in triumph when the flaming arrow struck the cask next to the bodkin. The spilled whisky ignited, engulfing the stern in flames.

"Aye!" the crew shouted as the fire drove the pirates to abandon their oars to put out the growing inferno.

"Saint Peter, will 'ave his hands full dealing with these poxy rats in nae time," Ferguson bellowed as they gained distance from the burning ship. "Take a wee break, ye've earned it. Double rations for all once we make land."

A cry of victory rang out as the *Seabhag's* crew raised their oars from the sea and took a much-needed rest.

Carys looped an arm around her brother, a broad grin across her face.

Hywel matched her grin. "That was inspired, Sister. What made ye think of such a thing?"

She shrugged. "Our captain keeps his whisky aft as a stool and to make sure nae a drop is drawn without his permission. It seemed logical others would do the same." She tossed her brother a wicked grin. "And it burns a nice blue flame."

Carys stared at her handiwork. The enemy ship listed aftward as it sank, flames remaining on the water as the alcohol burned. Though land was visible to the east, she knew none would survive the frigid waters long enough to swim the distance. She searched her heart for guilt and found none. The words of the old crone echoed in her head.

Death follows ye like a hound.

She dismissed the morbid thought, knowing these men brought their demise upon themselves. Though she'd aided them to a watery grave, the path they'd chosen would meet a bloody end sooner than later.

She gazed at the heavens. "God, have pity on their souls," she whispered.

"'Tis a terrible waste of good whisky if ye ask me," Wyn quipped. He touched his forelock as he smiled at Carys. She dipped her head in acknowledgment, her smile returning, heady with the knowledge they'd again cheated death.

* * *

Birk grunted acknowledgement as an aide whispered in his ear. He dusted his grimy hands on his trousers and rose as his guest entered the walled garden, his full height towering over the sturdy Scotsman whose shock of red hair never ceased to amuse Birk.

"Captain Ferguson," he exclaimed, a wide smile creasing his face. The captain matched his greeting and clasped Birk's forearm in welcome. Birk gave him a clout to his shoulder, pained as always to find the man as solid as he appeared.

"Come inside. I'll have someone fetch ye a mug of my best whisky."

Captain Ferguson glanced about the garden area, a nod to the ladies present. "I dinnae expect to find a man of yer reputation planting flowers," he commented. "Though I am not at all surprised to see ye in the company of such lovely ladies."

"I will introduce ye to them if ye will swear to never discuss my reputation in their hearing," Birk countered.

The captain inclined his head. "Yer secrets are safe with me, m'laird."

"Might I present Ladies Abria and Eislyn, my daughters?" Birk settled a hand on Abria's shoulder in gentle reassurance. She edged closer to her sister but did not shrug away from his touch. Eislyn sank into a pretty curtsy with only the faintest bobble. Birk's eyebrows shot up.

Where had the lass learned that?

"'Tis my great pleasure," Captain Ferguson assured them, sending an encouraging smile to the youngest lass. She responded with a wide-eyed blink but did not answer. He lifted his gaze to the three women waiting a step behind the girls. "I count myself fortunate to be in yer presence again, my dear Lady Hanna," he said, a cocky grin on his face.

Hanna inclined her head, an answering smile playing about her lips.

"I believe you remember my daughters?" She indicated Gillian and Signy with a tilt of her head.

"Indeed, I do, for 'tis rare such beauty graces a single space, or that a man such as I is granted such a vision."

He reached for Hanna's hand and she supplied it, her smile broadening as he placed a brief kiss on her knuckles.

"Pretty manners for a ship's captain," she taunted lightly. "Yer compliments grow more fulsome with each passing year."

"Years in which my lady doesnae age," Ferguson vowed.

Hanna laughed. "I've known men with loftier titles who could learn from yer kindness," she replied. She waved her hand at him and Birk in a shooing gesture. "Out of my garden. Be about yer manly business elsewhere. We will send refreshments. I will be happy for the time to relax and speak with my daughters."

Birk shook his head at Ferguson and Hanna's well-entrenched verbal parries and draped an arm over the shorter man's shoulders.

"She fears we will trample her delicate flowers," he quipped as he steered the captain toward the hall.

"Yer ma is a gracious lady," the captain noted. "But not a woman I'd ever cross. She raised yer sisters well, and yer daughters are lucky to know her." He halted beside a small table equipped with a couple of flagons, a set of mugs, and an assortment of bread and sliced cheeses. A nearby platter boasted only a few crumbs and a stain of what might have been berry juice. Birk grabbed a hunk of bread, nodding for Ferguson to do the same, and filled two mugs with cool ale. Collecting their items, they strolled down the broad, hard-packed path which led through the village to the dock.

"What has kept ye, my friend?" Birk asked. "We expected ye a month or more ago."

Captain Ferguson heaved a great sigh and tilted his head. "'Tis been a hard haul," he confessed. "Ye no doubt heard Edward has taken Wales."

"Word has reached us of Prince Llywelyn's brother's duplicity," Birk agreed. "And that the prince was betrayed by people of his own tongue at Orewin Bridge. I would not wish to be Dafydd this day."

Ferguson rubbed the back of his neck as though sensing danger. "Aye. I've heard Edward is hunting him for initiating the rebellion. Cannae say for certain why the prince backed him when the English clamored for his head. Dafydd is a right black sheep." He scowled. "Edward's war cost me a number of oarsmen." He brightened. "Even in my haste to leave the Welsh port, I gained a couple of crew members who've been a boon. Poor souls, hoping to find a new home away from Edward's reach. Let me tell ye about the pirates."

Birk led the way to the wall above the portcullis. Though raised to be a merchant as his father and grandfather before, Birk's veins ran thick with the blood of Vikings and Scottish warriors, and he chafed at being closed inside a chamber. Here, above the sprawling village of Morvern, a forest of ships' masts bobbed in the distance, the screech of seagulls rising above the tramp of booted guards along the castle wall. It wasn't battle, but it was better than the closure of a stone room.

The Alacrity is due to make port. Where is the search party? He squinted, sharpening the lines of the ships' masts against the low-hanging clouds. No. He would know the *Alacrity's* lines even at this distance. She remained absent.

"A woman, did ye say?" he asked Ferguson, the man's excited chatter making its way through his thoughts. "Is it not bad luck to have a female aboard ship?"

The captain popped the last hunk of bread into his mouth and chewed. "Not this female. I'd thought of her as Hywel's younger brother until she dispatched nearly a dozen rascals who tried to rob the ship our first night out." He swallowed and his bushy eyebrows snatched together above his bulbous nose. "Damned watch had fallen asleep. If not for my dog and the lass's quick actions . . . .."

Birk gave a slow nod. "Yer lad. Is he with ye this trip?"

"Aye." Ferguson's look grew bleak. "For all his faults, I love the lad. He's a good 'un. I would have been fair mistraucht to lose him."

"Tell me more of the pirates," Birk commanded. "I have lost two ships to their thieving, and vow 'twill be the last."

"Och, the lass dispatched one crew to hell, she did," the captain rumbled approvingly. "Seemed a mite disturbed afterward, but she dinnae shirk when the time came to defend our ship and crew. They were a slipshod lot at best, eager to challenge us for our cargo." His lips puckered pensively. "The other crew, though . . . they would have been a different matter . . . but they dinnae catch us."

"How were they different?" Birk asked, his interest piqued.

Ferguson rubbed his bristled chin. "They were better organized. Two ships—they worked together and would have cut us off from escape had the wind not changed in our favor. And they apparently had a strong leader. Once the lead ship cried off, the other followed." He shook his head. "I dinnae wish to fall afoul of them."

"Ye shall have an escort should ye wish it," Birk assured him.

"That would lift a great burden," the captain admitted. "Mayhap until we reach the entrance to the strait. Though the bastards came at us near Oban and we mean to pass in the opposite direction, beyond Kilchoan."

"Headed north on yer regular route?"

"Aye. I've a bit of trading to do before summer's end."

"I hope ye can remain here a bit. Ye are always welcome."

"Yer hospitality is legendary," Ferguson replied. "But we're behind schedule, no thanks to Edward or the pirates. We will linger another day and be on our way with the next tide."

"Then we will speak of business," Birk said, rising to his feet. "I have a store of whisky that will interest ye."

A broad grin split the captain's weathered face. "My laird, ye are a man after my own heart."

Chapter Five

Three Days Later
The Sound of Mull

"Drop the sail afore the mast snaps and drags us under," Ferguson shouted over the squall screaming in from the north, catching them off-guard. The wind whipped first in one direction, then another, threatening to drive them onto the rocks of the shores on either side of the sound. The captain swore as the ship lurched and shuddered, tossed about in the furious waves.

Wyn and Tully scrambled to the mainsail blocks and untied the rope at the cleats, releasing both lines, sending the waterlogged sail and spar tumbling to the deck, barely missing the oarsmen seated on either side of the mast.

"Row toward shore. We'll have tae roll with the waves if we're tae have a chance," Ferguson ordered as he pushed the tiller away, sending the ship shoreward.

Carys watched helplessly, hands clenching her rain-slicked oar, as another wave crashed over the side of the *Seabhag* taking men and cargo with it. Screams and hoarse shouts rent the roar of the storm, none daring to leave their post to search for those who were instantly lost beneath the roiling waves. The remaining crew pulled at the oars, one side rowing forward, the other backward in the struggle to target the bow toward shore.

"Heaven help us," Carys prayed, knowing the speed at which they traveled would splinter their ship. Her words doubled as a plea for the souls of those now lost to them. She gripped the oar more tightly and huddled over the bench, hot tears of despair scalding her cheeks.

Before the *Seabhag* finished her turn, a massive wave swept over the boat, sending more of the crew overboard. The powerful frigid sea yanked at Carys to claim her as for its own, but she hooked both arms and legs around her bench and gripped with all her strength. Denied its quarry, the sea retreated.

"Hywel!" Carys shouted, unable to see her brother through the stinging spray.

She rose from the bench, stumbling as the surging ocean again rocked their craft. She worked her way aft, searching for Hywel.

"Lass, what'er ye doin' here?" Ferguson demanded.

"Hywel. I can't find Hywel," she shouted over the wail of the storm.

"I'm sorry, lass. There's naught to be done but ride this devil out." Ferguson looped two ropes to the tiller, one from the starboard and one from the larboard side, keeping the rudder aimed toward shore. Carys realized if Ferguson were lost, the ship would continue the journey without him.

"Take Tully and Dewr and rope yerselves to the mast. There's nae more tae be done and I dinnae need to worry about me boy. Dewr's too light tae stay aboard if a wave hits her. Make several turns with the rope, but dinnae make a knot as it would mean yer death should we capsize."

Carys glanced at the dog who shivered, leaning against Tully, and the boy who clung to his da, eyes wide with fear. He was as scared as she.

Carys bent, bracing herself against a rowing bench. "Come, Tully," she coaxed the frightened boy and dog. "Let yer da work while we stay out of his way."

Tully and Dewr each took a tentative step toward Carys, then fell in behind her as they staggered midships toward the mast. Taking an end of one of the many coils of rope sprawled across the deck, Carys made three wraps around herself, Tully and the mast, then pulled Dewr to her chest. Lifting an edge of the sodden sail, Carys covered them, providing shelter from most of the deluge. The three of them shivered together while the storm raged. The *Seabhag* creaked and groaned with the effort of holding together at this speed. The rise and fall of the waves sent the contents of Carys's supper onto the wooden deck. The old crone's prophecy flooded her mind and she fervently prayed for all the souls on board, naming each man.

Carys, Tully, and Dewr huddled together for what seemed like an eternity. An abrupt lurch of the ship jerked her painfully against the rope holding her to the mast, and the splintering crack of wood filled the air. The ship hesitated then heaved forward again, water swirling about Carys's feet. The boat wrenched to a stop, accompanied by the soft scrape of sand and gravel. Carys flung the sail off and unwound the rope. Dewr rose and shook excess water from her coat. Tully remained crouched, hugging the mast, his eyes tightly closed.

The squall blew southward down the coast, leaving as quickly as it had arrived. The golden halo of the afternoon sun peeked from behind the remaining clouds. The cry of sea birds punctuated the end of the storm.

Carys's heart sank as she turned in all directions. The craft had indeed run aground, and the rocks they'd hit lay a few boat lengths off shore. However, not another soul did she see, neither aboard ship, nor washed ashore. The drenched rocks glittered in the fitful light, black and forbidding—and unforgiving.

Carys dropped to her knees with a wail. "Why God? Why have ye taken everyone and everything from me?" She rocked back and forth, propelled by grief. Afternoon darkened into evening as despair emptied her soul.

Once her tears were spent, Carys curled into a ball, staring at nothing, feeling nothing.

Minutes or hours later, Dewr's warm, wet tongue roused Carys from her stupor. She slowly pushed upward, her body leaden. Sitting against the mast, she considered what to do next. Tully lay sleeping, still clinging to the mast. The Almighty had chosen to save them, but why?

She rose to her feet and again glanced about. They'd wrecked on the end of a peninsula near the mouth of a narrow bay to the south, and a much wider one to the north. Large rocks barely submerged off the point made entering either inlet dangerous. The great Caledonian Forest Hywel had told her of loomed majestically beyond the rocky crags.

Grief threatened to take her again at the thought of her dear brother. She steeled herself against the bitter bite. She needed to rouse Tully, salvage what they could, and leave this place before pirates or other scavengers spotted their wreckage.

She bent over the boy and gently shook his shoulder. "Tully. 'Tis time to wake. The storm is over."

The boy blinked a few times as if to gain his bearings. "Da?" he asked.

"I'm sorry, but 'tis only the three of us now," she answered, her own deep loss echoed in Tully's eyes.

After a few moments, he rose and took in the wreckage. "My Da will be verra angry when he sees his boat."

She didn't have the heart to correct him. "We must to gather what we need before the bad men come looking for the wreckage."

He tilted his head with a confused expression. "Pirates?"

"Aye, pirates. We must be gone afore they arrive. Help me take what we can."

He nodded once and fell in behind her.

Carys took a quick inventory of what was left onboard and of what stores they'd require to survive. The sail was constructed of large woolen squares. Using her boot knife, she made quick work of cutting two squares free, then folded them and tossed them overboard onto the beach. She gathered several lengths of rope.

"We can use the wool for a tent, mayhap for a nice pallet. Rope is always handy," she told Tully. Dewr thought it a game, inspecting each item Carys picked up and watching as Tully threw them over the rail.

Carys cut away some of the cargo netting and gathered a small fishing net. She filled her bag with the rest of the salt pork, then grabbed Hywel's pack, along with their bows, arrows, and javelins, which had been laced together and bound beneath their bench, adding them to her pile.

"Stew," Tully said as he heaved the smaller of the two pots over the side of the boat.

"Aye, yer stew pot," Carys answered.

Two bowls, mugs and spoons went over next as she made her way aft. Rocks had torn a huge hole in the larboard hull, almost shearing the boat in half.

"Easy now, we don't wish to fall through," Carys said as they carefully picked their way among the shattered boards.

Lifting the aft hatch, Carys gathered the carpenter's tools that lay scattered in the compartment. As she felt around for any others, she encountered another box.

"What have we here?" she whispered.

Grasping it by the rope handle, she slid the small but heavy chest to the opening and lifted it onto the deck.

"That's my da's," Tully said, his voice low with a mixture of awe and dread. "We're nae to touch it."

Realization dawned as she knew what this must be.

"Yer da said I could take the chest to keep it safe and use the coin to pay for yer care."

Tully considered her words, his brow furrowed before nodding reluctant approval.

Opening the latch, Carys lifted the lid and saw more silver coins than she'd ever seen in her life. Moving them around with her fingers, a few hints of gold winked underneath. She shut the chest, then carried it through the hole in the hull and laid it next to their collection on the beach.

After going back for the tools, she stuck a hatchet in her belt.

"We'll need to make a sled, Tully. Ye and I cannot carry all this without one."

"I's strong. I can help."

At the edge of the forest, Carys found what she was looking for. Using the hatchet, she felled three saplings as big around as her arms. She made quick work of lopping off the branches, then created lap joints in the two longer poles to rest three cross pieces she made from the third sapling. Tully held it in place while she tied the parts together. Though it was rough work, with the wool and rope it should prove plenty sturdy.

"What'd ye think, Tully, Dewr? Does it look like 'twill hold?"

Dewr barked and danced around their creation, sniffing every inch.

Tully grabbed the sled and moved it around. "'Tis strong."

"Does it pass inspection, my lady?" Carys asked with a bow to the dog.

Dewr tilted her head.

"I can pull it if ye like," Tully offered.

"How about I start and then we take turns?"

He smiled broadly. "Aye."

Carys stepped between the two long poles and dragged it to the beach. Using the remaining wool and rope, they wrapped the tools and supplies, then tied them to the frame. Once everything was secure, she laid the sled down and they both walked to the shore once more. Tully stopped aft of the *Seabhag* where the rocks had torn away much of the vessel. Carys stepped to the water's edge. No sign of their crew or her brother caused her heart to lurch anew with the pain of loss.

"God, please accept my beloved brother, Hywel ap Pedr, a prince of Cymru, into your arms." She lifted his gold signet ring to her lips and kissed it, then drew the chain holding all three rings from her neck. She walked to the sled and placed the rings in the chest. Standing between the poles, she lifted them then walked into the forest.

"'Tis our new home, Tully. Let's see what she has to offer."

* * *

MacLean Castle

Birk stalked the length of the room, his cloak swinging heavily across the tops of his boots as he pivoted on his heel, retracing his steps. He counted his strides in his head, giving himself an opportunity to calm before his next words. ... *eight, nine, ten* ....

"Is there none among ye who can give me an answer? None who has heard where the bastard hides?" He pinned each man with a challenging stare.

The assembled lairds glanced at each other, shaking their heads. Keir MacKern shoved back in his chair. Though he was the only man in the room not a clan chief, all knew he spoke for his father, Bram.

Rising to his feet, Keir captured their attention. "He is known as Colin *Dubh* for his dark hair and skin." He fisted his hands on his hips, swaying slightly, mesmerizing each laird. Though five years older than Birk, the dark copper braids framing each side of his face held no trace of gray.

"Some name him Colin *Mor*, for he is a great hulk of a man." Keir faced Birk, his glance measuring him from toe to crown as if for comparison. "'Tis rumored he is a MacKinnon, though even his own laird wouldnae claim him." His stance eased and a sigh settled about the room, such was the mesmeric hold Keir wielded over them.

The man gave them no time to settle into complacency. "He robs the crofters, slaughters them for defending what is theirs." The pace of his voice quickened. "He shows no mercy, grants no quarter."

The lairds leaned together, grumbling, nodding, tension building once again as Keir's voice vibrated with anger.

"The man has preyed upon the weakest of our people for many months. Those we are sworn to protect, he attacks with impunity. Staining *our* souls with each death."

Keir swung about, startling the men. "And yet none can stop him? No one has the wit to do more than chase him from one man's border to the next?" His voice thundered, dripping scorn. With a toss of his head, he turned his back on the assembly.

"My laird." Keir's voice smoothed, respectful, his eyes cast downward. "How might we help ye catch this man who plagues us all?"

Birk snorted, impressed with the show. Trust Keir to work the men into a frenzy then shame them into action with the mere cadence of his words. Were he not a laird's son, he would make an admirable—and useful—bard. Birk picked up Keir's question.

"See to yer borders," he barked. "Increase patrols. Follow no set pattern as ye check on the outlying crofts. Notice smoke as it rises through the trees. Can ye speak for it? Do ye know whose fire it is?" Birk's eyebrows shot together. "Run him down. Make no place safe for him."

"Have ye considered a reward?" James MacCain asked. Tall and spare, his frame spoke of the hard life he led. Birk wondered again at his sister's obvious infatuation with the stern man. With the evidence of their affection growing in Gillian's belly, though she boasted nearly seven years Birk's senior, and the fond look on her face when she spoke of her husband, he had no reason to doubt their strength as a couple.

His nod severed his thoughts of Gillian and her husband and returned him to James' question. "An excellent suggestion. I will put up twenty silver pennies." He glanced about the room. "Anyone care to add to the purse?"

The men glanced at each other. "I will add to it, though I cannae match yer offer," Ian MacInnis said. His worried gaze met Birk's. His small holdings would soon be destroyed if Colin Dubh continued his predations unchecked.

Birk granted him a curt nod of approval as the others belatedly took up the challenge.

"The purse is heavy enough the man might turn himself in," Keir noted quietly to Birk.

"As long as someone does, 'twill be enough," Birk grunted. He grabbed his cup from the table and downed a gulp of strong ale, one eye on the lairds as they spoke among themselves.

"My father wishes to know if ye've enough whisky to fill the latest order," Keir continued in a different vein. He wrinkled his nose as Birk shoved a mug at him. "I've better if ye'd care to retire to a private room."

Birk gave his near-empty mug an appraising glance and decided Keir had the better suggestion.

"Yer da always fills the orders," he replied. "And with a wee bit extra for sharing." He set his mug on the table and motioned to the door with a jerk of his head. "'Tis wise of him to allow the captain the luxury of good spirits."

"Good spirits make for good relationships," Keir quipped as he tossed his cousin an impertinent grin. Anger slipped from Birk as anticipation of an excellent glass of whisky crowded out his temper. His lips parted in feral answer to Keir's smirk, his eyes narrowing in rare humor. He tossed an arm about the smaller man's shoulders, ignoring Keir's pained look as the weight of his well-muscled arm dropped. Keir jerked his chin to the entry to the room and Birk's humor fled.

A man hesitated in the doorway before crossing to Birk's side.

"My laird," he murmured, his face pale.

Birk's heart stuttered, but he gave no outward sign. "Aye?"

The man stepped closer. "Word of the *Seabhag*, my laird."

Dread unfurled through Birk. The ship had not been seen since the squall two days before. The suddenness and brutality of the storm had prompted Birk to send out a search party for Captain Ferguson's ship.

"Speak."

"Wreckage of the ship has been found on the shore west of Kilchoan." He sucked in a breath. "There is no evidence of survivors."

A muscle in Birk's jaw twitched. He fisted his hands at his sides, strove to contain the grief the man's words struck. He nodded and the man scuttled quickly to the door.

Silence echoed. Birk's vision dimmed.

Shite! Murdoc Ferguson, dead in the storm. And Tully.

Bleak helplessness filled him. There was nothing he could do. The weather was fickle, uncaring. A treasured friend lost along with his son and crew. Birk's mind traced the memory of Ferguson's pride in the woman he'd hired, who'd saved his ship more than once, a woman who asked nothing but fairness in return. One who willingly gave of herself to benefit others.

A woman of rare ability.

His skin crawled, itching to release the fury building within. His fingernails dug into his palms, the pain doing little to distract him from his deep loss.

He pivoted tightly and stalked to the door. With barely enough sense to choose weathered wood over unforgiving stone, he rattled the doorframe with a blow of his fist.

Pain exploded up his arm, burst from his knuckles in a white-hot blast, jolting his grief-mingled anger into something he could manage.

Birk focused on breathing. On Colin Dubh. An enemy he could destroy.

His return to the meeting was slow, his fury echoed in the apprehension of the assembled lairds.

"Find him," he bit out, spitting the words as if laden with bitter wormwood. "I dinnae care what it takes." His breath came in slow heaves. "I dinnae care what it costs."

Chapter Six

MacLean Castle
Two days later

The cry of a new-born infant instantly snared Birk's attention. He scrambled to his feet as the healer's apprentice slipped into the room.

"Yer sister is well," she murmured, her face drawn, shoulders drooping.

Birk exhaled a sigh of relief. Gillian should have returned home weeks ago, but complications he, as a man, did not understand, kept her beneath the close watch of his ma, the healer, and midwife. Despite their care, the babe had insisted on arriving a bit before the date predicted by both Gillian and the midwife. The pains caught them all unawares just after the morning meal.

He and James exchanged looks in the instant before James lunged up the stairs, Birk on his heels. They careened around a curve in the hall, knocking a serving lass askew as she rounded the bend, her hands filled with bloody linens.

"Pardon, lass," Birk murmured, grabbing her by her shoulders and setting her on her feet. Noticing her kerchief canting to the side, he shoved it atop her curls and gave her a pat on her head that shifted her knees, then bounded after James who had gained the length of the hall.

"Da!"

Birk quickly joined his daughter at Gillian's doorway. Eislyn fairly danced with excitement, Abria standing quietly at her side, a thumb in her mouth.

"She's ever so beautiful!" Eislyn exclaimed, giving away the baby's gender before Birk had a chance to ask. He gathered his daughters beneath his hands and guided them into Gillian's room.

James stood near the window, the babe tucked in the crook of his arm, experienced after fathering two other bairns. But the look on his face gave away the awe he experienced anew, the tender look turning this fierce warrior into a gentle man.

A pang swept through Birk. Rose had never invited such depth of feeling. Bringing a child into the world had been the price she paid for the caresses she craved. He shrugged off the sense of intrusion and glanced from James to Gillian.

"How are ye, Sister?" he asked, surprised to find his voice husky with residual worry. Gillian sent him a tired look, her face pale and drawn.

"Naught to fash over," she said, reaching for his hand.

Hanna stepped to his side and leaned her cheek against his shoulder. "Yer sister is a brave lass. A bairn at her age added silver to my hair," she teased.

"At my age! Pah!" Gillian blew off her stepmother's concern. "'Tis the wee ones ye should be concerned with," she added with a wink at Eislyn and Abria.

"It happened so quickly, I had no idea these two had remained in the room," Hanna explained.

"Auntie was reading to us," seven-year-old Eislyn piped up. "And then she got a tummy ache."

Birk lifted an eyebrow. "Aren't they a wee bit young to assist at a birthing?" he drawled.

"We werenae in the way, Da," Eislyn assured him. "But . . .." She bit her lip and glanced away. Abria sidled closer to her sister.

Birk hunkered down, bringing himself closer to eye level with Eislyn. He gently took a hand from each girl. "Ye can tell me," he said, running his thumbs over the backs of the soft hands. He trembled to think what it was about the birth that troubled Eislyn, feeling woefully inadequate to the job of educating his wee daughters in the finer points of womanhood.

Eislyn narrowed her eyes then glanced at her grandmother. Birk followed her gaze. Hanna shrugged.

"What is it, *a leannan*?" Birk urged Eislyn's confidence with a gentle tug on her hand.

Eislyn glanced about, clearly uneasy with the attention—something quite unlike his normally outgoing lass. Birk nodded solemnly and managed to keep his mirth buried.

"The bairn," she began. "The bairn in Auntie Gillian's tummy . . .." She glanced over her shoulder and Gillian nodded sagely. Eislyn turned wide eyes on her da. "It came out here," she announced with a vague gesture with her free hand. She leaned closer to her da. "And it broke Auntie's hoo-ha."

Birk's mind blanked. "Her *hoo-ha*?"

Eislyn nodded vigorously. "Aye. I dinnae know it could stretch that big!" She paused, tucking one edge of her lower lip between her teeth. "I think it hurt."

Birk swayed on his heels, his remnants of self-control rapidly slipping away. "What does yer auntie say?"

Eislyn ducked her chin, clearly unwilling to discuss her dilemma with her auntie. Birk glanced at his sister, and for a moment paled to see her rigid form convulsing silently on the bed.

"I think yer auntie will recover quite nicely," Hanna managed in a slightly strangled voice. "'Tis the way of things for a woman's, er, *hoo-ha* to stretch a bit when she gives birth." She patted Eislyn's head. "She will be right as rain in no time."

Eislyn quirked a brow at her grandmother, then nodded slowly, apparently skeptical of the reassurance. She peered around Hanna's skirts to Gillian who, to Birk's relief, had ceased convulsing and regarded him with a grin, tears of mirth sparkling on her cheeks.

Hanna shook her head. "I fear your lassies have a new appreciation for bairns and how they enter the world," she admitted. "'Twas not my intention to involve them, and I will correct her misconception at an appropriate time. They were as quiet as wee mice and I did not notice them in the room once Gillian's labor began." She waved a hand vaguely. "I dinnae know where their nurse is."

"Somewhere in MacLean Castle?" Gillian choked, still struggling to withhold further mirth.

Birk gave her a warning frown. "Likely 'twas no harm done," Birk replied, turning his attention back to his ma, even as his twitching lips traitorously threatened to betray him yet again.

Hanna nodded. "Do ye still plan to travel to Dairborrodal Castle?"

"Aye. In a day or two. Repairs are proceeding, and I must see to the crofters in the area. Colin Dubh evades us yet." He shrugged nonchalantly. "And hunting is good in the area."

"Legends of a fine stag, if I am not mistaken," Hanna teased, a twinkle in her eye. "I think it would be an excellent idea to take Eislyn and Abria with ye. Gillian will be abed for some time—not because of her hoo-ha," she stumbled on the word, "but because the bairn came early and there were complications. She needs peace and quiet, and the girls need more time with their da."

Birk considered Hanna's words. Eislyn, bored with the adult talk, had wandered back to Gillian's bedside, Abria as ever at her side. The pair clung to the bedclothes, Eislyn chattering excitedly, her young voice rising and falling cheerfully.

"Mayhap 'tis time to give them a puppy," Hanna suggested.

Birk took the blow with only a slight grimace. He'd promised the girls a puppy more than a month ago—under extreme coercion from a tearful Eislyn when she'd decided she and her sister would be grievously harmed if they were denied the love and loyalty of their own dog. Birk had little use for dogs as pets. A braw hunting dog was functional, a thing of deadly, muscular beauty. Wee furballs that cavorted at yer feet, piddled in the hall, and yipped unceasingly were little more than annoyances, certainly with little or no other function. He'd hoped his daughter had given up on the idea.

As if reading his thoughts, Hanna smiled. "Talk of Gillian's bairn will wane, and Eislyn will pick up the battle for a puppy once again."

"Battle," Birk agreed. "One I am doomed to lose."

"Teach her to fish, or perhaps sail a wee boat," Hanna suggested. "It might serve to distract her for a time."

"And if it fails?"

Hanna gave him her best advice. "At least teach the wee beastie to pee outside."

* * *

Ardnamurchan Peninsula
Three months later

Carys sat with her back to a tree next to the stream that spilled in front of their cave, the waterfall concealing their home of the past few months. The aroma of rabbit stew made her smile and her stomach rumbled hungrily. Tully certainly knew his way around a cooking fire. His skills with a pot and hers with a bow had ensured they wouldn't starve.

She gazed into the dark sky. The stars appeared close as the moon's glow waned, giving way to their beauty. Dewr lay next to Carys, head on her lap as Carys absently scratched behind the dog's ears. Carys wondered how she would have survived since the shipwreck without her companions. Even with Tully and Dewr and the life they'd carved out for themselves in the forest, she longed for a home of her own rather than living in a cave. The land provided most of what they required, but she'd found herself calling on the crofters in the area more and more, to barter game she'd killed for oats and honey or simply for a home-cooked meal. If she was honest with herself, she needed to be around others more than she'd realized.

Tully was a sweet boy, but all their time alone weighed upon her, giving her mind ample opportunity to recall her husband's death and the terrible storm which claimed the lives of all aboard the *Seabhag,* especially her beloved brother. Tully had all but stopped asking when his da would return, which saddened her as he lost the hope of being rescued and reunited with his family. He'd told her about his mam, a couple of younger sisters and a brother. Though he knew their town was on the coast, she wouldn't know where to begin to look for it. Carys wasn't sure why the Almighty chose to spare them, but she felt certain it wasn't to live out their days in a cave.

"Hywel was right, girl. We're not meant to live alone." Dewr pushed her head into Carys's hand in response. She accommodated the demanding beast by scratching her head. "'Tis the thought of loving and losing again that scares me witless." A sense of hollowness in the pit of her stomach proved the accuracy of the statement.

Dewr licked her hand, brown eyes seemingly full of understanding.

"Ye know better than most since ye've lost yer home and master as well. Perhaps Fergal and Lorna will adopt us. Young

Gorrie has taken a liking to us since I made him a bow and started teaching him to shoot."

She'd made friends with the crofters when she killed a wolf that had been stealing sheep. Instead of payment, she'd asked for Fergal's vow he and his family would take care of Tully should anything happen to her. She'd been fearful they'd reject the boy, but after a few visits at their home, she realized they treated him as one of their own. He helped Lorna cook supper the times they stayed. Tully had been overjoyed when Carys made him a gift of the wolf's pelt and he slept on it each night.

Dewr perked her ears and whined.

"What is it, girl?" Standing, Carys caught the scent of smoke and spotted a distant fire the direction of Fergal and Lorna's croft. She slid down the hill and darted into the cave.

"Stew's almost ready," Tully said, a grin on his face.

"It smells wonderful. Save me some," she said with forced cheerfulness to avoid worrying the boy. "I need to go to Fergal and Lorna's, but I'll be back shortly. Dewr, guard Tully."

Dewr trotted over to Tully and plopped her furry rump on the ground next to him, tail swishing gently.

"Good girl," Tully said as he patted her head.

Grabbing her bow, quiver, and both javelins, Carys stepped into the night. She found the trail and loped along, using the wan moonlight to guide her. A distant scream pierced the night goading Carys's trot into a run. The light from the fire grew as she neared. Cautiously, she approached the croft away from the fire to preserve her sight. Four horses stood near the wattle and daub home. A man held Gorrie from behind, a knife at his throat. Fergal lay on the ground unmoving. Another man had thrown Lorna to the ground and lifted his plaid, his intentions rising clear from the junction of his legs. A third man stood by, laughing at the scene.

Laying her javelins aside quietly, Carys drew a bodkin arrow and aimed at the man who planned to violate Lorna. She let the shaft fly. The pointed tip penetrated his skull, exiting part way through the other side. The man crumpled at Lorna's feet like a banner on a calm day. Drawing a second arrow, this time a broadhead, Carys aimed at the devil holding Gorrie. At twelve summers, the boy hadn't yet gained his full height, and was held by a much taller man. The wide tip sliced cleanly through the villain's throat, causing him to release Gorrie and grasp the arrow. He staggered backward, gurgling as blood spilled down his shirt and onto the ground.

Carys drew another shaft and aimed at the third man who shouted something in Gaelic she didn't understand. He'd drawn a short sword and turned toward the forest searching for the threat.

Idiot. He gave up his night vision by standing near such a large fire.

Aimed midline and to the right, the arrow sank into the muscle of the brute's chest. He lurched forward then fell. Dragging to his feet, he staggered toward the horses. Carys tracked his progress with the tip of an arrow, but a fourth man shoved the door aside and charged out of the cottage like an enraged bull, drawing a sword so huge it required two hands to wield. Not wishing to waste an arrow, and seeing the third man fall again, she turned her attention to the swarthy man coming toward her. The fiend was the largest man she'd ever seen. His long black hair lay matted against his skull as if he never bathed, the exposed skin of his body covered in hair, much like a bear. She dropped her bow and picked up a javelin. Taking a step forward, she hurled her weapon and struck him just below the breastbone, driving the point into his lung muscle.

The strike knocked him back a step. He bellowed then plucked her javelin with a grunt and tossed it aside.

Gorrie had taken up the knife from the man who'd held him and approached from behind the mountain of a man.

"Gorrie, see to yer mam and leave this one to me." Carys's command rang crisp in the night air.

The lad hesitated but did as he was told, helping his ma to her feet and away from the dead.

"Show yerself! Or are ye too craven to face a man in battle?" the giant bellowed.

Grasping her remaining javelin, Carys stepped from the forest and strode toward her foe with a confidence she didn't feel. She spotted Fergal, still as death, blood covering his head.

"Craven? Ye attack good people in their homes, fire their barns, and ye name *me* coward?"

The man spat on the ground. "This is MacLean territory. There arenae good people here, only those who need killin'.""

"And yet, 'tis yer men who met their deaths this night," she countered as she lowered her hood and glanced about.

A malicious smile that would make the devil proud twisted the giant's lips. "A woman?" he mocked. "Aye, a situation I'll soon remedy after I gut ye, then tup ye as ye take yer last breath."

Chapter Seven

Ardnamurchan Peninsula, same night

"Shite!" Birk struck the pommel of his saddle with a blow that shifted the horse beneath him. Bran tossed his shiny black mane and champed his bit, using a front hoof to paw the ground.

Birk swiveled in his saddle, noting the desolation of the small croft. Moonlight shone on charred timbers no longer red with embers. Bodies stiffened in death's rigor, awkward bundles as the soldiers attempted to move them. A thin trail of smoke, easier smelt than seen, curled into the air from the haphazard pile of blackened wood that crowned crumbled rock walls. A solitary cow lowed softly, her udder swollen and pendulous, long past her milking time.

"He keeps one step ahead," Dugan spat, leaning his forearms on the pommel of his saddle. "The bastard boasts no man alive can kill him." He nodded to the bodies being lowered into shallow graves. "He proves his boast over and over, whilst we do little more than give proper burial to these muckless souls."

"He will boast one time too many," Birk growled. Bran shook his head and shied a step away as an errant breeze covered them in the stench of death. Birk dismounted and shoved his reins at Dugan who accepted them with a dubious look at the pitch-black stallion, his coat blending with the night. Bran sank to his haunches, backing away as he tossed his head in the air, stretching the reins taut, nearly jerking the leather from Dugan's hands.

"*Staund*!" At Dugan's command, the horse settled, ears pitched forward as he took a mincing step forward. "Ye great daft beast," he grumbled.

Birk strode across the moon-dappled grass. He halted at the still open, hastily dug graves and peered down at the bound bodies of the deceased. His men had wrapped them in old woolen cloth, the colors faded beyond recall. But he knew the man and woman who faced the dark sky, an elderly couple who ever had a kind word for friends and strangers alike.

"I will avenge ye," he muttered, sucking in great breaths of outrage. "Colin Dubh's blood will quench the land he has despoiled. I will slay him with my own hand. This I swear."

Another gust of wind blew tiny particles of dust and stone into the air, swirling it with smoke and a subtle hint of rain. Storm clouds raced in from the sea and large rain drops splattered the ground, grieving for the dead.

"Laird!"

Jolted away from the sight of his men rapidly scooping soil atop the graves, Birk spun about. Dugan dug his heels into his mount's flanks and raced to Birk's side, tossing him his reins. Bran skidded to a halt.

"Look!"

Inland rose a plume of smoke, a shade darker than the clouds. Dread struck Birk's heart. Colin Dubh's signature of destruction hovered close to Dugan's parents' croft.

Birk bounded into the saddle. He set his heels to Bran's ribs and signaled four soldiers to join them. "This will be the last night the bastard draws breath."

* * *

A wary eye on her menacing adversary, Carys retrieved her javelins. Slipping quickly to one side, she assumed a fighting stance, left hand and foot forward, her javelin in both hands, and waited for the beast to attack. A freshening breeze swept inland from the coast, and the moon dimmed behind swiftly racing clouds.

The Highlander swung his massive sword, forcing her to skip backward to avoid his strike. Once the blade swung past, she lunged forward and struck with her spear, the small leaf-shaped blade cutting across the muscle of his forearm. As she withdrew, she dropped the tip to his thigh and pushed downward, dragging the edge along his lead leg, opening a long slice.

Blood darkened the ground. The man's eyes sparked—rage, pain, surprise. But his steps did not falter.

While he was bigger and stronger, she was swifter. As her assailant recovered from his swing, he raised his sword high. The blackguard swung downward in a vicious attempt to cleave her in two. Carys slipped to one side before his blade arrived. Her short lance darted out and sunk into his flesh a few inches above his manhood, where the body stores water. Backing away, chest heaving, she awaited his next assault. A few more swings, and the huge man's breathing labored. Whether from exertion or his wounds, she knew not. He bled from several cuts while she remained uninjured. She needed only to outlast the beast and blood loss would do its work.

The colossus bellowed a war cry then lunged for her anew. Stepping to the other side, she avoided his charge and stabbed him again, this time in his side. He raised his sword once more and she leaped farther left, using all her might to drive her point into the hollow of his arm below the shoulder as he held his deadly steel aloft. She skipped away and behind as his arm fell limp to his side. Taking advantage of his pause, she again drove her javelin deep, this time into his back above his left hip bone.

The beast roared then dropped to one knee. Carys withdrew her weapon and drove it in again above his hip on the other side. Blood gushed from both wounds as the hulking brute attempted to stand.

With a booted foot, she pushed him over. He stumbled and twisted, landing on his back, eyes blinking.

"Finish it then, ye Satan's spawn," he growled.

Carys kicked his sword away, knowing the importance of a warrior dying sword in hand, denying him this last comfort. "I'd rather watch ye die knowing a woman bested ye."

Standing over him, Carys held her weapon at the ready and watched the life leave his eyes. Once his eyes filled with the fog of death, she turned her attention to the living.

"Gorrie, Lorna, are ye well?" she asked.

"Aye, but they've killed my Fergal," Lorna wailed, pulling her fist from her mouth. Her cries, stifled whilst Carys fought, rose in the night.

Carys strode to his side and felt his neck. "His heart still beats. Help me move him inside so we can tend his wounds."

She and Gorrie lifted Fergal and carried him to the bed while Lorna fetched bandaging cloths. Gorrie then hurried to heat water. They cleaned and bound his wound, a jagged cut which appeared bad, but likely bled worse than it was. To her relief, she'd felt no changes in the shape of Fergal's skull, nor observed any clear liquid that foretold death.

Once they had done as much as they could, Carys turned to Gorrie. "Come, let us see what we can do about the barn."

He nodded and followed her outside. The structure's roof was a loss, a few rafters jutting awkwardly from the stone building. The charred beams glowed with unspent flames, but at least the fire showed no sign of spreading. Carys removed the arrows from the dead and gathered her javelins.

"We need to move these bodies. I don't want yer mam to have to look upon these men again."

"Aye. 'Tis good thinking," he said, darting a glance at her then downward.

"What is this?" she asked, sensing Gorrie's frustration.

He hung his head. "Ye killed all those men yerself and I dinnae help."

Carys gave a sad smile and put an arm around his shoulder. "Aye, but ye did as I asked and protected yer mam so I could concentrate on the last devil and not worry about ye."

"I should have been at yer side fighting. Instead, I was as scared as a bairn and couldnae move."

Carys placed a finger under his chin and lifted his head until he met her gaze. "Aye. I was scared, too."

"Ye were?" he asked, his brow wrinkled.

"Of course. The bards sing about the glory of battle, praising the victor as if he were a hero. I've been in many battles and I've yet to see any glory, only blood, fear, and the stench of death. Tonight, we both did what was needed to make certain ye and yer family survived. Ye and yer mam stand hale and whole. Ye were smart enough to bide yer time and obey my command. We'll keep up with your training so ye can defend yer home against any who come around. Agreed?"

Gorrie stiffened his lip and nodded. "Aye."

"Good. Help me move these bodies away from the croft." They dragged the men in front of the barn, intending to burn them. She took a boot knife from the giant to add to her own collection of blades. As she did, Carys realized she had acquired most of her weapons from men she'd killed. Something to ponder another time. She removed one's short sword and sheath, then handed it to Gorrie, his eyes widening as she did.

"We shall include sword play in our lessons, but ye must promise me not to draw it without permission." She raised a brow and waited.

A grin split his face. "Aye, ye have my word. I'll do as ye say." His face grew solemn. "Ye saved us all," he said with a small voice.

Carys opened her arms and he stepped into her hug. The boy almost lost his mam, da, and his own life. He'd witnessed more death than a lad his age should.

"Aye. 'Tis what friends do," she whispered.

The sound of horses approaching interrupted them.

"Gorrie, go inside. I'll guard ye from the shadows."

The boy raced into the croft and shut the door while Carys grabbed her javelins, retrieved her bow, and melted into the darkness. She nocked an arrow and waited.

Six riders approached. She'd gotten lucky with the last four because they'd ruined their ability to see in the shadows and were over-confident, but taking on so many meant her death. One man jumped off his horse, drew his sword, then ran to the house.

"Da! Mam! Gorrie!"

Lorna and Gorrie met them at the door. Carys realized this was their older son they'd spoke of, the one in the service of the MacLean laird. A twinge of longing for family centered in her breast. Tears threatened to spill. She wiped her eyes.

"Tis only the fear of losing Gorrie and his family," she whispered.

Liar.

Not wishing to be seen, Carys slipped deeper into the shadows and made her way toward the cave, hoping Tully had saved her some supper.

* * *

Birk, steel in hand, spotted the bodies lying on the ground. The barn's roof had collapsed, and was mostly embers, their heated eyes winking red and gold in the night. He motioned for the rest of his men to circle the croft in case other enemies were near. Three riderless horses milling about suggested otherwise, but he would rather not take any chances. Birk kneeled and inspected the dead, recognizing the dark hulking form as Colin Dubh at once.

His eyebrows shot skyward as he contemplated the giant's wounds and wondered who he owed the bounty placed on the devil's head. Anger rose that the man had attacked Dugan's family—and Birk had not stopped him with his own hand.

Dugan joined him with Gorrie by his side, the youth telling some tall tale of a woman killing these men alone.

"Gorrie. Slow down lad and start over. Ye say a lass did all this?" Birk asked in disbelief.

Young Gorrie's head bobbed. "Aye, m'laird. Carys is deadly with a bow and killed three afore they kenned what 'twas about. Then she killed 'im." He pointed to Colin Dubh.

Birk toed the dead men.

"Three?" Only two bore evidence of arrow wounds.

Gorrie frowned. "I . . . I thought she killed three others. One held me, another stood by laughing as a man tried to hurt Ma, and . . . there are only two here."

Birk motioned two of his men to search the area, then gave his attention back to Gorrie.

"Tell me more."

"The fourth man—the big one—was inside the house and came charging out when the third man . . . .." He paused and glanced about, then sighed. "Her arrow caught 'im in the chest, but not so deep. He shouted somethin' fierce."

Each of Colin Dubh's henchmen had arrow wounds clear enough. Even with a man missing, Gorrie's story rang true, albeit far-fetched for a lass' doings.

"How did he die?" Birk asked a brow raised, pointing at their dead leader.

"She ran the monster through with her spear. He ne'er touched her with his big sword. She struck like a snake again and again, then danced away each time he swung," Gorrie boasted.

Birk frowned and nodded to Dugan. They rolled Colin Dubh over and spotted two gashes in his lower back. Though he bore several wounds, it was likely the two holes puncturing his kidneys took the fiend's life.

"Yer sayin' one woman did all this?" Birk asked, still reluctant to believe the lad's story.

"Aye, m'laird she did," Gorrie said with a nod. "We made a bow together and she's been teaching me to shoot. She gave me that one's sword to train me," he added, pointing to one of the dead villains, the other palm resting on the hilt of his new weapon. "One day, I'll join ye and Dugan at the castle."

Birk smiled and tousled the lad's hair. "We'll be proud to have ye. Run inside and help yer ma. Let her know we'll send a healer and be leaving men here to guard the rest of the night."

"Thank ye, m'laird," the lad said then returned to the croft.

Birk turned to Dugan. "Yer da?"

Dugan rubbed his chin. "Tis a nasty head wound, and no mistake. He lost a good bit of blood. We've both seen worse. Let's see what Auld Tess makes of him." He glanced about. "T'would seem we missed the fight."

Birk frowned and turned his attention back to the dead men, his anger simmering to disbelief. "Do ye believe Gorrie's tale about a woman?"

"It appears Colin Dubh's prediction was true. 'Twas no man who killed him," Dugan quipped. At Birk's glower, Dugan shrugged. "Da told me a sennight ago of a lass who lives in the forest. He says she killed a wolf that had been terrorizing the herd. Says she comes around with a simple lad and barters for supplies. They come for supper some."

Birk's frown deepened as he tried to make sense of this story. "Who is she? She's nae a MacLean?"

Dugan shook his head. "Nae. Da says she and the lad shipwrecked a few months ago."

Birk rubbed an ear, excitement rising. "Auld Murdoc Ferguson's boat?"

Dugan tilted his head. "Mayhap. I can ask Ma and Gorrie to describe the lad. There's nae mistaking Tully's red hair. We thought none survived that wreck. Mayhap we were mistaken."

Chapter Eight

Ardnamurchan Peninsula, 2 weeks later
Dairborrodal Castle

Squeals of excitement lifted the castle rafters. Birk uneasily straddled the line between the glow of pleasure from giving his daughters their hearts' desire and the grim knowledge of what lay ahead. Laird MacInnis stood beside him, arms crossed over his chest, beaming and nodding his head.

"I thought yer lasses might like the pup," he said, nudging Birk with an elbow. "I'd a mind to keep her for breeding, but her ma is still young, and this one needs a pair o' weans to play with." He grew solemn and leaned closer, giving his next words to Birk alone.

"Ye have my sincere thanks for bringing that bastard to justice," he murmured. "I left my portion of the bounty with yer man. The pup, her breeding notwithstanding, is only a shadow of my gratitude."

Accepting the gift for the spirit in which it was given, and realizing he had no further recourse, Birk grinned and clapped MacInnis on the shoulder, startling the smaller man. "Let's see how fast the wee beastie learns to piddle outside."

"She's the bestest puppy in the whole world!" Eislyn exclaimed, hugging the squirming ball of tan, black and white fur to her chest. Long pointed ears, a black button nose, and short stubby legs sprouted between Eislyn's arms, and a pink tongue flashed as the pup licked Eislyn's chin. More squeals.

"And what do ye say to Laird MacInnis?" Birk prompted.

Eislyn bounced up and down, hefting the pup higher on her hip. Her eyes shone. "Thank ye, Laird MacInnis!" she said, breathless with excitement. Abria gave a slight nod.

Birk sighed and summoned a benevolent smile. "What will ye name her?" he asked. "She's come from a long line of corgis in Wales. She deserves a Welsh name, dinnae ye agree?"

Eislyn's eyes rounded and her lower lip trembled. "I dinnae know Welsh," she confessed.

"Och, dinnae fash, *a leannan*," Birk said, dismayed by her response. "We'll come up with a grand name for yer pup. Laird MacInnis here may have a better command of the language than I do."

"I believe ye will come up with a name between the two of ye," MacInnis reassured her.

Eislyn's dark eyes sparkled with unshed tears. "I shall call her Wee Lass for now." She sniffed. Abria clutched one of the puppy's chubby feet and nodded solemnly.

"What would ye call the pup, *a nighean*?" Birk asked Abria gently, squatting before her.

Abria regarded him solemnly for a moment then dropped her gaze.

Holding his sigh behind his teeth to hide his disappointment, and, fighting to keep a slight smile on his face, Birk lightly touched his youngest daughter's cheek then rose to his feet. Eislyn set the puppy on the floor and, grabbing Abria's hand, pelted down the hall, puppy bounding at their heels.

Ian MacInnis sent Birk a sidelong glance. "She doesnae speak?" he asked, his voice low and sympathetic.

Birk tensed, bracing as if he expected a blow from the Almighty for what he saw as his inadequacy as a father. "Nae. Not since her ma died," he answered. "She was ill about that time, and we dinnae know if the fever took her voice, or if 'tis related to her ma's death. Mayhap the pup will put a smile back on her face."

"If so, 'twill make the gift all the more dear."

Birk took a deep breath. "More than ye could know."

* * *

"I am glad to hear yer da is doing better," Carys said, ruffling Gorrie's hair. She lay a brace of hares on a stump near the small cottage. "I know ye dinnae have much time to hunt now ye have all the chores, so I brought these. I'll dress them for ye and take them to yer ma."

"I'd appreciate that mightily," Gorrie sighed. "I dinnae understand how hard da worked to keep us all fed and the land cleared." He tilted his head, a wry smile on his lips. "I willnae complain about me chores again."

"I'm sorry yer da was injured. But he'll be back on his feet soon—in fact, I'm surprised yer mam has kept him abed this long."

"He helps me a bit, but gets dizzy and must sit a spell," Gorrie confessed. "But he's better every day."

"Good. Tully and Dewr are here to help ye and I will check on yer mam." Carys skinned the first rabbit, careful to keep the soft pelt intact, while Tully set off for the barn, hay fork over one shoulder. Dewr ambled at his heels.

Carys finished dressing the hares, then carefully measured her next words. "I am considering a trip to Morvern in a sennight or two. If yer da and mam can spare ye for a few days, mayhap ye can come along."

Gorrie perked up. "Och, aye! 'Tis where me brother Dugan lives! I told him ye'd kilt Colin Dubh all by yerself, and that ye were training me to be a warrior. Laird MacLean said he'd be proud to have me as a soldier when I'm older." Gorrie's voice cracked in his excitement, but Carys didn't stop to tease him about it.

"That was Colin Dubh? The one they call Colin *Mor*?" she asked uneasily, reflecting on the man's size and coloring. "I should have known. It happened so fast, and I only wanted to protect ye and yer family."

A shudder ran through her. She would never have chosen to challenge the man who had terrorized the area for so long. His viciousness was known far and wide and she was acutely aware how narrowly she'd escaped death. Inhaling a deep breath and releasing it with a sigh, she squared her shoulders. "Well, he shall not trouble us again, aye?"

Gorrie's eyes shone. "Nae. Not after ye kilt him."

Carys sent him a level look. "'Twas not easy, and 'twas not my first choice. Killing never is. I pray ye never find yerself in a place where taking a human life is easy, Gorrie."

Chastened, Gorrie dropped his gaze. "I want to protect people, not harm them."

Carys stuck the point of her knife into the stump and gathered the dressed hares. "Ye have a good heart, Gorrie. Ye do us all proud."

A grin crept back over his face. "If I had a sister, I'd want her to be like ye."

Carys swallowed past the unexpected lump in her throat, fighting the conflicting tides of warmth and cold that swept through her. Thoughts fled to Hywel and her eyes clouded with pain. "Ye are as a brother to me," she managed before her voice was swallowed up in unshed tears.

She slipped quickly away, measuring her tread to give herself time to gather her emotions. She missed her mam and da, her husband, and her brother. Grief was a treacherous beast, ready to ambush when least expected. She'd thought the memories had faded beyond such recall, but a powerful ache swelled in her chest, making it difficult to breathe. As much as she had come to care for Gorrie and his family, she didn't know if she could let them past the barriers she'd set around her heart.

By the time she reached the cottage, she'd managed, if not a smile, at least a less-haunted look, her face relaxed and tears wiped away. But she was thankful for the dimly lit interior of the stone building, as Lorna's keen eyes missed little. A single window lay open, allowing watery sunlight to pool on the dirt floor. Smoke from the hearth swept up through the thatched roof, creating a haze in the room.

Lorna glanced up as Carys knocked on the open door.

"Och, lass, 'tis good to see ye! Look who's here," she said, tapping Fergal's shoulder as she bustled toward the door. Her husband gripped his chair's arm rests and rose slowly to his feet. Carys set the fresh meat on the table and waited for Fergal to approach, not wishing to give him cause to stumble.

"We're forever indebted to ye, lass," he said gravely. "Ye have ever been a blessing to us."

Carys's stomach did a peculiar flip-flop and her breath caught in her throat. Bereft of blood kin she may be, but her idle longings for family seemed to be coming true. She swallowed twice before she was able to force words past her faltering tongue.

"Ye welcomed Tully and me when we knew no one," she replied, carefully sidestepping the issue of close bonding. "What manner of person would I be to sit idly by whilst ye and yer family came to harm?"

Fergal snorted. "There are plenty of lasses who daren't get their hands soiled, much less risk their life for another."

"Now, Fergal," Lorna chided, patting his arm as though hoping to halt a long-running tirade. "'Tis a shame to speak ill of the dead."

"I'll say no more. But ye, Carys, are always welcome here." He gave his wife a glance then cleared his throat. "Lorna and I've been talking. We'd like ye and Tully to live with us—not just a place for Tully should aught happen to ye. 'Tis no good allowing ye to live in the forest like ye do. We can add a room or even build ye a wee cottage." He hobbled to the door and pointed to a spot not too far distant. "There. Ye'd have a place of yer own, but close enough Lorna and I can keep an eye on ye."

Carys's head spun. Fergal's words and Lorna's excited encouragement buzzed about her. Her heart cried out equally against the potential for heartbreak and for the nurturing bonds of family. Her head assured her it was better to live among friends than alone. Her heart wasn't so certain.

She raised her hands in a sue for peace. "I am overwhelmed. Though I am very appreciative, might I think on yer offer? And speak with Tully, of course." She paused. "I promised Tully I would help him find his way home, though I do not know where his family lives. I had considered a trip to Morvern within the next fortnight to search for anyone who knew his da and where I might look. May I give ye my answer when I return?"

Fergal and Lorna exchanged glances. "We'd be pleased to help ye. And there is nae need to rush yer decision. As long as ye know ye are needed—and wanted—here, 'tis enough."

Oddly deflated now the need to make a decision had passed, Carys smiled. "I told Gorrie I would help ye around the house today. In the morn, I will see about adding to the larder before I leave for Morvern."

"Stay the night, then," Lorna insisted. "Ye can leave for the hunt with a warm meal in yer belly and our thanks for yer trouble."

Carys grabbed the empty bucket next to the door and escaped outside.

It would simplify things to share chores. Having others close by to talk to would be nice.

Or would it?

Absently filling the bucket from a nearby stream, Carys sought to understand the reticence in her heart.

They accept me for who I am.

They do not truly know me.

They are full of kind words and praise.

When would this change to urges to find a husband, start a family?

I am at peace in the forest, and yet, the solitude often overwhelms me.

Living near Fergal and Lorna would be a different kind of peace.

She grasped the wooden handle and hoisted the bucket from the stream, knocking it lightly against her shins. The slight pain jarred her thoughts to the truth.

I am afraid to love. Can I join Fergal and Lorna and Gorrie and keep my heart safe?

Carys nodded firmly though her heart raced. *Yes.*

* * *

The sun had scarcely added its pearly strands to the dawn sky when Carys and Dewr slipped from Lorna and Fergal's barn the next morning, a bundle of warm oat cakes in Carys's hand. Both Tully and Gorrie had insisted they accompany her, but she needed the time to herself and had only promised they could join her if they were awake when she left. A slight grin creased her lips. Both lads were at an age where rising before dawn was nigh impossible. Their gentle snores silenced abruptly as she gently closed the barn door. She flipped her fingers in invitation to Dewr, and they flitted like ghosts through the pre-dawn gloom.

The trees' dark shadows slipped over her like a protective shroud, hiding her from the view of her quarry. On the edge of a small glen she bagged two hares busy nibbling dew-bright grasses. Morning mists swirled about her as she crossed the burn and headed deeper into the forest.

An hour later, a brace of fat grouse also dangled at her belt. She now had enough to feed Lorna's family for several days, but Carys expected to be a week or more on the road to Morvern and back. Rays of early sunlight shone through the dense foliage, alighting on hillock and stone. Dewr growled softly. Something moved ahead. Carys waited, motionless, eyes scanning the woods to catch the movement again.

Sun beams glinted off the most impressive rack she'd ever seen on a stag. His ears twitched, seeking sound. Slowly he turned his head, regally surveying his land. Water gurgled over the stones in homage at his feet. Power rippled through his great muscles as he gathered himself and leapt the small stream. Setting Dewr to follow at her heel, Carys dropped to a crouch and scurried through the underbrush, in awe of the magnificent beast and feverish with the thrill of the hunt.

As she ducked and dodged through the forest, she sent up a quick prayer to the *bean sidhe* who cared for all such faerie cattle.

"Guide this hart before my arrow," she chanted beneath her breath as she halted and nocked an arrow. Dewr leaned against her, her excited tremble shuddering up Carys's leg.

The stag stood just at the edge of a glen, his coloring blending well with the leaves and trees, making him nigh invisible.

Move a bit more so I can see ye better.

In absolute silence, she waited. An ache grew in her arm from the tension on the bowstring. Long moments passed like hours. She scarcely dared to breathe. Step by hesitant step, the beast entered the clearing. Sunshine warmed the glen, the green grasses a contrast to his sleek, red hide. He dropped his head and nibbled a fern.

The tip of her arrow pointed to his cheek, and she swiftly drew her aim up his neck and shoulders to a spot slightly behind and above his elbow.

"Fly true," she breathed as she loosed the arrow.

* * *

"There's the proud beastie," Dugan whispered.

Birk lay on his belly and peered over the top of a rise. They'd been on the trail all morn of a hart big enough to feed the clan and now had him in sight. The stag stood at the edge of a field, grazing. Heavy antlers dipped as he ate.

"Dinnae I tell ye he was a fat laddie?" another man asked, a grin on his face.

"Aye, ye did. Good work. Fan out and dinnae let him see ye," Birk ordered.

They stood down wind of him, so he'd not catch their scent. As each man rose to a crouch, bow in hand, the stag stumbled toward the woods, then collapsed.

"What the devil?" Dugan took a step toward the edge of the ridge.

Birk placed a hand on him. "Hold," he ordered. He lowered his hand. "Down."

They all squatted and waited.

A black-haired figure strode out of the forest, dog at her side. She'd slung a long bow over her shoulder and drew a hefty dagger.

"M'laird, yer supper!" Dugan quipped, clearly torn between indignation and amusement, an arched brow querying Birk's next move.

"Shhh. Watch," Birk commanded.

The lass couldn't have boasted more than a score of years, yet she'd killed the deer they'd been hunting all morn with one shot. A smile grew across Birk's face.

"What're ye thinking, Laird? Ye get that look and I know ye to be up to nae good," Dugan said.

"I think I've solved my bride problem," Birk said. "That has to be the lass from Ferguson's ship. What better choice for the new Lady MacLean?"

Dugan frowned. "I dinnae understand."

Birk grinned at his captain. "She already defends our people and livestock. Yer ma and da like her fine."

"Aye, young Gorrie cannae shut up about her. But, Laird, the council will have a fit. If she's the one stranded from Ferguson's boat, she dinnae come from another clan. Clanless, she brings no alliances or dowry." He shook his head. "The council willnae approve."

Birk's lips twisted. "I'll nae have another spoiled laird's daughter to wife. Can ye see any of those women lifting a bow or sword to help our people?"

The men all chuckled. They knew as well as Birk the women brought before him the past few months were more worried about their own comforts than the well-being of the clan.

"Nae, Laird, I cannae," Dugan replied.

"Well, this lass has, and she's nae a MacLean yet."

"What if she says ye nae?" whispered another hunter.

Birk's smiled broadened. "She'll nae have a choice."

Dugan rubbed his chin. "What's yer plan? How will ye bring her in?"

"Tell me what the law is for poaching on MacLean land," Birk coaxed.

A ripple of surprise answered him.

Dugan frowned. "I dinnae like it. She deserves our respect."

Birk placed a hand on his captain. "Aye, she does. Howbeit, she has violated clan law. She isnae a MacLean. 'Tis our duty to take her in. Iain, take the men and bring her back. I dinnae want a single bruise on her, aye?"

"Aye, m'laird," Iain replied.

"Any harm comes to her, ye'll answer to me. If all goes well, she'll be yer lady in a sennight."

His declaration inspired a round of grins and nods.

"Dugan and I will head back to the keep. Dinnae name me laird. In fact, dinnae give her a name beyond The MacLean. I'll handle the rest."

Birk and Dugan crept back to their mounts, saddled up, and headed back to the keep.

"Laird, are ye certain about this?" Dugan asked.

Birk couldn't contain his smile if he'd wanted to. "Aye. I've nae been so sure of anything in a verra long time."

Chapter Nine

Her shot must have pierced his heart. Carys waited a moment, expecting the stag to bolt to his feet. Except for the sway of his heavy antlers as they listed to the side, the animal did not move. She strode warily to the deer, touching his shoulder reverently.

"A grand one, aye?" She murmured a brief prayer of thanks for a good hunt. The great beast would provide many meals for all of them, and Carys had several uses for the hide.

Laying her bow next to the stag, she drew a knife and moved to a cluster of small saplings. "We'll need to make a frame to carry this one back to Fergal and Lorna's," she murmured. "I fear 'twill take the both of us the rest of the morning to make the trek back."

Dewr sniffed the fallen animal, then turned to follow Carys. Suddenly, the dog's head jerked up, hackles rising as a growl issued from deep in her chest.

A shiver raised the hair on the back of Carys's neck. Had a wolf been attracted to the scent of blood? She slowly scanned the area, noting her bow and arrow several feet away, next to the stag. She gripped her blade securely.

"What is it, girl?" she whispered. "What does yer nose tell ye?"

Dewr erupted in a flurry of barks as five men rose from the underbrush, arrows leveled. Carys stared at them in shock that turned quickly to dismay when she noted their numbers.

"Lay down yer knife, lass," one called. "Ye'll be coming with us, now. Ye've been caught poaching The MacLean's deer."

* * *

Birk swung into his saddle, an ear to the scene unfolding behind him.

"She isnae likely to come willingly," Dugan remarked as he reined his horse next to Birk's big black stallion. "If she suspects the penalty for poaching is death, she'll fight."

"She'll fight anyway," Birk replied, his fingers restless on the reins.

A shout went up, but the words were unintelligible. Birk flinched. Sounds of men crashing through the underbrush rose. Birk winced. Dugan and the other two men exchanged looks.

"What if she escapes?" Dugan wondered aloud.

Birk scowled. "She's one lass against six men." He glared at Dugan. "*My* men. They'll nae let a lass get the better of them—even *this* lass."

Another shout, followed by a flurry of disagreeable grumbles reached their ears. Birk's horse pinned his ears back and champed his bit. After a moment, Birk tapped him lightly with his heels.

"I dinnae wish her to lay eyes on me yet. We'll meet Iain and his captive at Dairborrodal."

Dugan shook his head and urged his mount after Birk. "Iain has to catch her, first."

* * *

"Dewr, find Tully," Carys commanded. "Go!"

The dog hesitated, then, at Carys's commanding sweep of her arm, bounded away. As quick as Dewr disappeared into the underbrush, Carys laid her escape plan. There was little she could do against six men, but she had been hunting these woods for the past three months and more and knew the trails as well as she knew the path to Gorrie's home from the cave.

Slamming her knife into its sheath, she dove for her bow and arrows before she darted to the side and into the trees. A shout went up behind her. She flew swiftly down the trail, then, choosing a slight gap in the bracken-littered forest floor, dropped to the ground and rolled off the path. She rose to a low crouch and scurried deeper into the underbrush before halting at the edge of a ravine with a rumbling burn below, the sound of its rushing white waters rising to her ears.

Darting behind a large tree, she rose to her full height, back pressed against the bark as she peered around the trunk, looking for her attackers. Her breathing calmed and the roaring water became part of the noise of the forest. A twig snapped.

Carys stared over her left shoulder, the direction she'd taken from the path. A hand clasped her right wrist and yanked her from behind the tree. She immediately dropped to a crouch and bent her elbow toward him, breaking his grip. Bounding upright, she cupped her fist in her opposite hand and slammed her elbow into the point of his chin. The blow forced him up on his toes and Carys drove her foot into the side of his knee. He yelped and staggered forward, completely off-balance. With a helpful nudge with her boot, she sent him tumbling over the edge of the ravine.

The sound of his cry and plunge down the rocky embankment brought a shout from the others. Carys bounded away again, left hand outstretched before her to protect her face from low branches as she raced through the underbrush. She circled back to the glen, hoping to find the horses the men had left behind. Slipping over the edge of the ridge on the other side of the glen, she spotted six horses waiting patiently. Carys skidded to a halt.

Six? Her mind cast back. She'd seen five men earlier. One horse squealed in ill-temper and kicked at its neighbor. A mild ruckus erupted, then settled. Carys quickly recounted the horses. Six. Had one man remained behind?

A shout, undoubtedly meant to alert the others, came from near the tethered horses. Wheeling about, Carys fled back into the trees. Booted feet hammered the leaf-covered ground, pounding bracken and other small plants as they chased her, choosing speed over stealth. She wove through the trees, seeking darker reaches of the forest. Birds shrieked and burst from the trees near her, betraying her to her hunters. Carys dodged a large trunk, rounding it in a quarter-circle, seeking to mislead the men behind her. The feint gained her a few moments' time, but a cry announced they had her in view again.

She grasped a low-hanging branch and swung up into a tree. Her bow, slung across her back to free her hands, caught on another, sturdier branch. Her foot, boot soles worn smooth, slid over loose bark. She scrambled to catch herself, scraping away flesh from her fingers and palms as the limb slipped from her grasp. With a grunt, she fell.

Air blasted from her chest in a gasp as she hit the ground flat on her back. Shadows and light sparkled before her eyes as she fought to remain conscious. Her mouth gaped open like a landed fish, but only a trickle of air made its way into her lungs. The scent of decayed leaves and old leather filled her nose. Booted feet tramped next to her head.

Hands grabbed her arms and wrists and dragged her to her feet. Her legs would not support her, and she hung between two men, her breath a thin shriek as it whistled in and out of her lungs. Suddenly, she gave a great heave as her air passages opened, and she shoved upward with all the force she could manage, then collapsed toward the ground, her legs tucked beneath her.

The grips on her arms faltered, and Carys jerked free and straightened. Men stood in an arc to her sides and before her, hands spread wide, awaiting her next move.

"Dinnae make this hard on yerself, lass," the leader admonished. "Ye are well and truly caught. Give up."

Carys managed a grimace. "I imagine poaching carries a worse punishment than a chase through the woods." She shook her head. "I will not come peaceably."

The man nodded, a look of respect in his eyes. "I suppose ye willnae." He glanced at one of his men. "Disarm her."

Carys snatched her knife from its sheath, the blade winking as it wove gently back and forth before her. The first man who reached for her drew back a bloody hand, his palm sliced from wrist to fingertip. A murmur of displeasure rose from the men. Carys quickly counted the men arrayed around her.

Five. *Saint Winifrede save me! Where is the sixth?*

She could not risk searching for the last man and could only hope he'd remained behind to guard the stag and mayhap their horses. She sprang to her feet and feinted to her right. The man closest pulled back, then lunged toward her. But Carys was no longer there. Whirling about, she dodged the tree and branches at her back and leapt forward—and crashed into the solid wall of the sixth man's broad chest.

His arms encircled her as she spun around, yanking her back tight against his chest. Her hand holding her knife flew open and she lost the blade in the scuffle. Using the force of his grip, Carys flung herself backward, lifting both knees to her chest, meeting the rush of her would-be captors. With a determined shove, she sent the nearest man reeling and staggered the man who held her. She bent her neck forward, then flung her head backward as hard as she could and was rewarded with a loud crunch, a warm spatter against her cheek, and the giant's bellow, but he did not release her.

His arms tightened and Carys fought against the restrictive bands. Hands fumbled with her legs as she thrashed.

"Halt!" a stern voice ordered.

The men came to ragged attention and the giant's grip eased. Carys sucked in a deep breath and blinked to clear her vision. Before she could send her cocked elbow into her captor's ribs, a meaty fist tapped the point of her chin, and she slumped in a ragged heap in the large man's arms.

* * *

Birk paced the parapet, his eyes fixed on the forest to the north. Waves crashed on the shore to the south, beating against the base of the castle's wall. Pausing only long enough to solve a dispute over Eislyn's use of a boat in a nearby cove and to change into a fresh leine, he'd traversed the castle and bounded up the stairs. With thoughts of his daughter swirling through his mind, he stared out over the wall and wondered what kept Iain.

But, Da! I want to learn to sail!

I thought ye had enough to do with a puppy to train.

Abria spends more time with her than I do. I want to learn to sail!

I dinnae think Abria liked dogs.

Da!

Hoping the woman he was determined to marry would take the task from him, Birk hastily promised sailing lessons for Eislyn.

Where is Iain?

Horses moved away from the forest along the trail to the castle. Excitement—or perhaps trepidation—rose. Had he done the right thing? He was about to put an end to the question of marriage—but was this the right woman?

Of course it was. She was everything the others were not. Brave, loyal, fierce. He admired her skills with bow and arrow and her kindness to the people she lived near. She would make any man a fine wife.

He didn't know her name.

Whirling about, he stomped down the steps, timing his descent to mingle with the crowd that gathered as Iain and his men rode through the gates. He'd chosen his clothing to blend in, not wishing to be labeled as the laird until he'd taken stock of the woman and noted her reaction.

The men dismounted, dragging their captive from the back of one of the horses. Birk halted in surprise. Fully half the men sported obvious wounds. Kern's hand was wrapped in a length of bloody bandage and Oran's nose was misshapen and swollen, the front of his leine stiff and dark with what appeared to be a quantity of dried blood. Brody limped noticeably. Birk cut his gaze to Iain who caught his look and shrugged.

The woman staggered behind Iain, hands bound, black hair hanging loose about her face. Birk jerked his chin to the southern tower, an imposing edifice of thick stone built into the wall of the castle. Its fortified room on the upper floor boasted a single narrow window that overlooked the sea nearly a hundred feet below. With a curt command, Iain sent his two uninjured men to convey the woman to the tower. Birk waited as Iain approached.

"I said no bruises," he growled in a tone meant for Iain's ears alone, brows lowered in displeasure.

"She may have one or two," Iain admitted. "But none were intentional, and my lads fared far worse."

Birk tilted his head. "How are the men handling it? They arenae usually on the receiving end of such abuse from a lass."

Iain shrugged. "Oran and Brody will survive the ribbing from the other men. Kern may lose the use of his hand. He approached her whilst she still had her knife."

Birk grunted. "Ferguson said she was a warrior. Mayhap a few hours alone in the tower will settle her."

"She did warn us she wouldnae come peaceably," Iain replied. "But none of us thought she'd actually make use of the knife."

"Ferguson's tale seemed a wee bit fanciful. I thought mayhap he had embellished the story. He spoke of six ruffians dead by her hand when they attacked his ship in port and a pirate ship sunk because of her strategy and skill. He said she escaped Wales ahead of Longshanks and is rumored to have fought his army for two years." Birk rubbed his chin. "She has seen more strife than most women her age."

Iain's brows shot up. "A fair tale, but I will add she's tough and doesnae back down from threats nor challenge."

"She is but a woman," Birk growled. "Once she is wed, she will find her place in the household. As long as she warms my bed and gives me an heir, I will call it a bargain well met."

He nodded with satisfaction. "I willnae breed a bairn on a flighty wench—no lad of worth would come of it. But this woman has enough strength and bravery to give me a house full of braw lads."

"Do ye still plan to bring her into the clan, then? It seems, begging yer pardon, but, after a contentious lady like yer late wife— rest her soul—ye would seek one who wasnae likely to defy ye so often. Mayhap one who would be a real ma to those bairns of yers, teach them to be proper ladies, not train them to be warriors."

Birk's gaze drifted to the door at the foot of the tower. "I dinnae want Eislyn and Abria to become proper ladies." A grin threatened the tilt of his lips. "She is exactly what this clan needs."

Chapter Ten

Carys stumbled into the room as a shove from a large masculine palm between her shoulder blades propelled her forward. One of her captors sliced the rope from her wrists with a sweep of his knife, then followed the other man from the room. The heavy wooden door slammed shut. She peered about the stone chamber. Aside from a pallet on the floor and a bucket in a far corner, the room was empty. Air blew crisp through an arrow-slit, much too narrow to consider an escape route. She rubbed her arms in an attempt to erase the feel of strong hands manacling them, then, unable to help herself, tested the door. It was securely latched.

"*Ffwl!*" she spat. *Fool. Caught doing nothing more than providing food to hungry people.*

She stormed about the cramped space, her boots thudding across the wooden floor. "MacLean deer! MacLean *people!*" she snarled, targeting the absent laird. "*Twmffat!*" *Idiot.*

Carys leaned against the window, the aperture scarcely wide enough to sight through with more than one eye. Waves broke upon the rocky shore far below, an invitation to tempt death. A reminder of the ship's wreckage in another cove a fair morn's travel from here.

Tully.

Had Dewr reached him? Would he remember their arranged signal? For Dewr to return without her meant Tully should abandon the cave, take his belongings, and shelter with Fergal and Lorna. But what if Tully forgot? What if, because he was already at Fergal's house, he did not understand to swiftly gather his things from the cave before searchers found it?

And what if he did not remember the small chest of coins they'd buried?

Carys peered down into the frothy churn of water about the boulders at the foot of the castle, measured the width of the window with a hand splayed within its opening.

"'Tis a fair drop."

Pivoting on her heel, Carys faced the man at the door, amazed he'd entered unnoticed. His bulk filled the entry and he ducked as he stepped inside. He fastened the latch behind him, the click echoing in the nearly empty room, reminding Carys she was trapped.

She glanced up from his hands, now hanging peaceably at his sides, to his face. Dark eyes peered at her from beneath half-lowered lids, thick brows pulled together above his slightly arched nose as he studied her. His nearly black hair hung loose to his shoulders, a bit of curl softening his wide forehead and hard, chiseled features. She was startled to realize her head would likely reach no higher than his shoulder, for she was tall for a woman, and had found it easy to pass for a man. This giant would have been a more familiar figure stepping from a Norse longboat, had his coloring been the pale blonde of that race. She surreptitiously checked his hands for signs of an axe or sword.

A hint of metal glinted from his wrists and at the top of his boot, doubtless hidden sheaths with daggers. Carys's fingers itched with the need to somehow gain one of the weapons.

And do what? Doubtless the man was an accomplished warrior. His light step and sure balance told her as much. Relieving him of one weapon left him at least two more, and likely others she had yet to discover.

"A short sword at my back, two dirks in my belt, three throwing blades at wrist and boot, and a *sgian dubh* in the other boot," he said, as if reading her thoughts.

Carys shrugged. "I do not like being a prisoner."

"Killing me willnae get ye released. 'Twould be another feat to fight yer way down the stairs and out of the tower. Plenty of men would be anxious to stop ye before ye traveled far."

"I wish to be released." Every muscle thrummed with the urge to flee. For more than two years, she'd remained a step ahead of an English prison, aware a princess of Cymru would not simply be discarded as unimportant. She'd spent every waking moment—and many that should have been spent in much-needed rest—avoiding capture. Being a woman in the hands of an enemy held its own special peril. Fear roiled like an angry snake in her belly, sending the acrid taste of bile to her mouth.

The big man crossed his arms over his broad chest, bulging forearms corded with heavy muscle and overlaid with dark, crisp hairs. Carys was impressed, despite herself. With a mental shake of annoyance, she discarded the urge to touch him.

"Ye have been brought here on a serious charge," the man said with a frown, his voice rumbling deep and ominous.

Carys matched his stance, not bothering to hide her disgust. "Feeding the hungry should not be a crime."

"'Tis the fact ye poached on land that doesnae belong to ye." He tilted his head. "Ye are a stranger to our shores. Why did ye not present yerself to the laird's man when ye arrived?"

A myriad of emotions flushed through Carys, diluting her anger. Loss. Homesickness. Grief. Loneliness. She quickly tamped them down, shoving the sentiments into the deep space inside where she hid them away. She set her jaw stubbornly. What kind of honor did the MacLean laird have if he punished those who fed his people? He sounded no better than Edward and the cursed English.

"I did not see the need. I asked nothing from the clan—neither food nor lodging. Or protection."

The man gave a short nod. "Tell me how ye came here. There was rumor of a shipwreck, yet no survivors were found."

Carys's eyes narrowed. "You must not have searched very hard," she scoffed, though she knew she'd covered her tracks well. Once away from the foundered *Seabhag*, she'd not returned, nor allowed Tully to do so. Precisely because of the fear someone would stumble upon the wreckage. She had not wanted to risk anyone discovering a well-worn path to the cave they called home.

The man shrugged. "'Tis possible, yet the captain was known to us and an effort was made to discover what happened to him and his lad." His gaze pierced her. "Do ye know if any others live?"

"The men were all lost," she replied curtly, not placing thirteen-year-old Tully in the same category. She clenched her fists, digging her nails into her palms against the threatened return of grief.

Her captor studied her at length. "How is it a woman came to be a hand on the ship? Did they not object? Sailors are a superstitious lot. A woman is said to bring naught but doom to a ship."

"They welcomed me after I foiled an attempt to rob the ship whilst at harbor one night," she answered with a tilt to her chin.

"Ye earned their goodwill?"

"Is it difficult for you to imagine I could be an asset?" Temper flared, warming her skin as it crept from her chest up her neck.

"Women have their place," the man agreed.

Carys snarled.

"Mayhap ye are an uncommon woman. Ye gave Iain's men a bit of trouble. Have ye skill with more than a knife and bow?"

Exasperated with the inquisition, Carys flung her arms wide. "I have no more answers for you. Tell me my penalty for slaying your laird's deer—which I am certain you have gathered for yourselves—and let us be done. I will waste no more time on your land."

He arched a brow, though in arrogance or anger she could not tell.

"The penalty for poaching the laird's stag is death."

Even as he said the words, something rose inside Birk, shaming him for his duplicity. The woman did not cower from him, did not dissolve into tears meant to sway his opinion or rebuke him for his brutishness. Her eyes flashed and a flush stained her pale cheeks. Two thin streaks of crusted blood, remnants of her flight through the forest, slashed across one side of her face, and the dark stain of a recent bruise blossomed beneath her chin.

Her face was too slender, her eyebrows too straight for classic beauty, but it was the force of her nature that called to him. Tall and willowy, her body nonetheless quivered with power and life. Not calm and poised as one raised to be a lady, but agile, strong—and fierce.

Birk bit the inside of his lip to hide his pleasure.

"I could have yer sentence reduced—mayhap erased all together. 'Twould save yer life if ye agreed."

The woman shifted her balance slightly forward. Would she attack? Did she actually believe she could win against him?

"'Tis not what ye think," he drawled, one hand raised to pat the air, signaling her to settle. To his surprise, the action seemed to infuriate rather than calm her. He scowled. "I may be strong and intimidating, but I dinnae force women to my will."

Her challenging glare softened to one of belligerent disbelief, but she did not reply. Birk's small store of patience abruptly dried.

"Marry me. The charges will be dropped. There isnae penalty for a MacLean to hunt our lands."

Her chest rose and fell, breaths deepening as her jaw set firm.

Frustration warred with anger. "Will ye do naught to help yerself? Do ye have naught to say?"

In a lightning move, she gripped his outstretched hand, surprising him with her strength. Her other hand snatched the throwing knife from the sheath at his wrist. She leapt beyond his reach, the blade held lightly between her fingers, positioned slightly behind her ear.

"*Cer i grafu*," she snarled.

Birk ducked to the side as she released the blade. He swept one leg out, catching her off balance. Plucking the blade from where it protruded from the doorframe, he yanked the door open and left the room.

Dugan's footsteps matched Birk's as he thundered down the stairs.

"I take it she dinnae agree to wed ye." He danced lightly to the side as Birk whirled.

"She hasnae the sense to help herself," he growled.

"I dinnae think commanding her compliance would work," Dugan mentioned. "Did ye not think to try a more inviting approach?"

Birk grunted. "What difference should that make? *Invite* her to live? Sparing her the hangman's noose should be incentive enough."

"What is her name?" Dugan's voice softened, pointing to Birk's failure to attend to anyone's process but his own.

"Shite."

"I dinnae think that is a common name among the Cymry, so I'll ask yer indulgence to believe ye dinnae ask."

"I dinnae have time for nonsense. The council has hounded me for too long and even Dairborrodal isnae safe from their meddling. The castle nears completion and I have business in Morvern in a fortnight."

He shoved his fingers through his hair, battling against Dugan's rebuke. "She is a woman. She should know her place."

"She has been a soldier," Dugan countered.

"Then she should know how to follow orders."

"Yer lady has survived battle, killed men. She has likely given orders, been asked for her advice. She bested Iain's men—though six were at last enough to subdue her." Dugan raised his eyebrows. "I dinnae believe she will meekly follow orders, my lord baron. She is made of sterner stuff."

Birk braced a shoulder against the wall. "What would ye suggest?"

* * *

Carys picked herself off the floor, not bothering to batter her fury against the closed door. It would be a futile act with her energies best used elsewhere.

Marry him? Who does he think he is? His clothing and bearing do not suggest he is an ordinary soldier. Nor the gaoler looking to make an easy conquest of a helpless prisoner.

She paced the room.

He spoke with authority. Mayhap the laird's commander? Steward or his magistrate?

Carys halted, leaning next to the window on the far wall. Fresh air whistled through the gap, its fingers cooling her ire.

Could the penalty for poaching truly be death? And, if so, why would this man offer marriage to commute her sentence? Such an action was incomprehensible. He'd shown her no warmth, no interest in her well-being or future beyond marriage. Why would he bind himself to her? What flaw kept him from marrying a woman of his own clan? His own choosing?

An image of the man flashed before her. Tall, stern, unyielding. Her late husband Terwyn had been none of those things. He'd matched her for height, treated her with respect and kindness. Their marriage had been no burden. Carys flinched. Marriage to this MacLean brute? He was strong, obviously skilled with weapons— he'd dodged the blade easily enough. But she'd learned how to protect herself without relying on a man, and her skills were honed through the necessity of war and the struggle to survive.

Mayhap she should agree to this man's offer, then use the opportunity to escape since she could see no way out of this tower. Carys quickly discarded the idea. The MacLean chief might be lacking in honor, but as a daughter of Cymru, hers remained intact. Any vows she made she'd keep, unlike her traitorous countrymen who'd betrayed their prince at Orewin Bridge the dark day that sent her and Hywel fleeing their homeland.

Was her life about to come to a violent end swinging from a hangman's noose?

Death follows ye like a hound.

The auld woman's words sent shivers down Carys's spine.

I dinnae wish to die. The choice was taken from Hywel. Why is it being offered to me?

Chapter Eleven

Birk opened the tower room door, the faint creak of salt-laden metal hinges alerting the prisoner. Her dark eyes pierced him as he directed a lad inside. The boy placed a small folding table near the window, adding a tray of sliced meat, a bowl of raspberries, and a chunk of warm bread, redolent with yeasty fragrance, and a dish of fresh-churned yellow butter. With a short bow to his laird, he hurried from the room. Birk reached behind him, his gaze steady on the Welsh woman—recalling what Captain Ferguson had known of her history—and closed the door.

She glanced quickly at the portal, telling Birk she knew it wasn't latched.

Without correcting his apparent lapse, he strolled to the table and set a three-armed candleholder on its surface. The flames leapt about, disturbed by the rush of air from the narrow window. He then placed a flask on an empty corner and waved a hand invitingly over the small feast.

"Eat," he commanded.

She swept her glance to the table then back to him. "Are you so certain I will accept your offer?"

"I am. There would be no reason to feed ye if ye were bound for the gallows."

The woman continued to stare at him, steady, fearless. . . and unwilling to back down even one inch.

"Eating doesnae signify yer answer, neither aye nor nae," he grunted. "Ye must be hungry, and I wish to know ye better."

"And if you do not like me after you get to know me? What then? Will you stand by your offer? Or send me to the hangman?"

"Ye cannae have it both ways," Birk replied, his voice rumbling low with exasperation. "Ye cannae ask me to honor my offer *and* refuse to accept it."

She strode to the table and, choosing several of the dark pink fruit, popped them into her mouth. She chewed then swallowed. "I dinnae say I would refuse."

Birk's ire rose, but he recognized not a woman's prevarication, but a warrior's first steps into negotiating a surrender. She lifted her chin, daring him to take the next step in the critical dance.

"The first thing I would like to know about ye is yer name."

The statement clearly startled her, but the flicker in her eyes settled into a light twitch of her lips.

"Carys." She lifted a brow, inviting him to respond in kind.

"Birk."

She edged around the table, keeping him in sight, never turning her back to him. Taking the flask, she sniffed then tilted it to her lips. She emptied half the flagon of ale before setting it down. Picking up the small loaf of bread, she tore a thick wedge from it and topped it with a slice of meat.

"Besides a wife, what do you stand to gain from this?"

"I have two wee daughters who need a ma."

Her eyelids flickered. Interest? Birk knew of her rumored kindness to his clansmen. Did she like children? She seemed to like Gorrie, and he was clearly besotted with her.

She tapped a toe, revealing agitation. "And allowing a criminal to raise them is your solution?"

Birk shrugged. "As ye said, feeding the laird's people shouldnae be a crime."

She took a bite of the meat and bread, apparently giving him the point. "Ye live here?" She indicated the castle with a nod of her head.

"Aye. Part of the time. I have been known to also reside at MacLean Castle."

Carys swallowed the last bite and brushed her hands on her trews. "How old are your daughters?"

"Eislyn has seven summers, Abria, four. And I will confess I gave them a wee puppy the other day." His grimace elicited a faint smile from Carys.

"That doesn't sound so bad," she said. "Little girls love ponies and puppies."

His frown deepened. "Eislyn wishes to learn to sail and wield a knife."

Carys's brow quirked upward. "She sounds like a wise lass not to have to rely on a man."

Could it be this easy? The woman shows interest in a wee lass with a knife? Dugan's suggestions have merit, then. How long would I have treated her like a prisoner before it occurred to me to play to her strengths? At least I havenae lied to her. Not directly, that is. For some reason Dugan believes she will want the truth from me. Not endless posturing and sweet lies.

Thank Saint Andrew for that!

"I have an errand to accomplish before I can accept your offer. Will you trust me?"

Birk snapped his attention back to Carys, wary. "What is this errand? I will see it is done."

"Nae. I wish to do it myself. I cannot agree to your terms if I do not see the task through."

"If ye were hanged, ye wouldnae accomplish yer goal, either," he pointed out.

She drew her shoulders back, defiance sketched in her posture. "There is someone who would wish to know my fate—and I, his."

Birk flinched. Had she formed an attachment with a lad in the area? A broken betrothal was a complication he did not relish. Howbeit, if a single visit solved the issue, it couldn't be much of a commitment.

"Are ye spoken for?"

Carys's eyes flashed. "I am widowed this year past. There has been no man in my life since Terwyn died at the hands of the English."

Another piece to the puzzle of Carys. No wonder she wandered so far from home. Naught to keep her in Wales once Edward swept in.

Then her errand must be to return to Lorna and Fergal. It was plain there was an attachment between her and Dugan's family. He must keep her from them at all cost. They would know him by name and could be trusted to enlighten Carys of his true title—and his deception—within moments. As Baron of Morvern, he could easily drop the charge against her with no need to secure her alliance. He would have no hold over her. Seizing her for violating an ancient law had been to secure her and force an immediate marriage. To avoid the messy process of convincing family and council to accept a woman with no dowry or clan alliance.

If Carys refused to marry him, his plan was lost and he'd grown weary of searching for a woman he wished to marry, of the eager—and not-so-eager—women thrust at him for inspection. No. It must be this Welsh woman with the pale skin, black hair, and eyes as stormy as the gales that blew down the Strait of Mull.

Carys struggled to keep her hands from fisting and exposing the anger churning beneath her breast. The man gained everything from marriage and left her without even the ability to see her previous responsibilities were met. This was no convenient step away from the hangman's noose, but one straight into the darkest trap. At least the hangman was honest in what he offered. All the acceptance she'd reluctantly gathered to support this mad scheme scattered like startled grouse at the first sign of a predator.

"I will not walk into this and lose every freedom I have fought hard to possess." She advanced a step, clenching her fists tight, shoulders bristled forward. "You hold the upper hand with your outrageous law, but if you expect blind obedience from me, I will gladly face the noose instead!"

His brows plunged together. He opened his mouth, but a loud thump sounded at the door a second before it opened. A man Carys did not recognize stepped inside.

"Pirates," he murmured, his voice low and urgent.

A common enemy.

"I can fight," Carys stated, stepping firmly toward the door. Birk's outstretched arm blocked her path.

"No need."

She bristled. "Do not presume I will retire meekly when I can be of assistance," she warned. "I will not live beneath the heel of your boot."

Birk appeared before her in a swift, silent move, scarcely a hand's breadth away. "Fight whom ye will, so long as it isnae me."

"Do not give me reason," she countered, tilting her face upward to meet his hard gaze.

His breath, warm and heavy, betrayed some emotion in him. Carys's heart sped, not from the threat of pirates, but from his overwhelming maleness. He was a formidable foe—and would make a passionate defender. Or lover.

She swallowed the urge to retreat. With a brisk nod, he broke their impasse, turning his gaze to the man at the door.

"Add her terms to the marriage contract."

The man startled. "Aye."

Birk swung about, booted feet striding to the door. He hesitated, then glanced back at Carys. "The pirates cannae breach the castle walls. But they can wreak havoc in the village."

"I have fought pirates. I will fight at your side or there is nothing between us."

His eyes hardened, as though attempting to gauge her intent. "Dinnae betray me."

Carys lifted her chin. "My word is my honor." She sent the messenger at the door a haughty glare. "Add *that* to the contract."

Birk drew a dagger from his belt. "Ye will need this."

He handed the blade to her, hilt first, then plunged through the doorway, not waiting to see if she would follow or fling the dagger at him. She slipped the weapon into the sheath at her boot and descended the long stairs at his heels.

The bailey was awash with men, their movements concise, hurried yet controlled. Men who knew their jobs well and awaited orders. Birk conferred with the man who'd brought the news to the tower then turned to the stair leading to the parapet. Flames danced smokily at the ends of torches set on the wall, a macabre evening dance.

The door to the hall flung open and two small girls burst into the yard. A puppy bounded at their heels, its tailless rump bouncing.

"Da!"

Birk whirled and advanced on the pair. "Where is yer nurse?" he demanded.

The girls halted, the younger ducked behind her sister. Their dark hair marked them clearly as Birk's daughters, his alarm confirmed it.

"Ina is screeching under the table," the elder declared with a toss of her head. "She's too afraid of pirates to fight."

The younger hid her face in her sister's dress, trembling visibly. Carys's heart skipped a beat in sympathy for the child.

Birk dropped a hand on the taller girl's shoulder. "Ye must take Abria and go inside. 'Tis not safe here."

"Amma taught me—"

Birk cut her protest short. "No. Now is not the time."

Steel rasped on leather as swords were checked and daggers thrust into sheaths. Horses neighed, sensing the tension. Smoke drifted on a breeze as fires were lit on the parapet. Anxious cries flared as other doors in adjacent buildings opened, spilling more soldiers into the yard. Birk's daughter's high-pitched argument sent Carys spinning back into a memory she'd thought lost.

Mam! The word was but a whisper through lips paralyzed with fear. Men on horses stormed past, breaching the walls of the peaceful village. Too late the castle opened its gates to the villagers. Too late did Llywelyn's man dispatch soldiers to halt the raid.

Though related to the prince, Carys and her family did not share quarters in the castle, and this morning, as seven-year-old Carys slipped out of their cottage at the first hint of dawn to feed her new pony, raiders swept through the small town, seizing or destroying all within their grasp.

The pony, frightened by the screams of horses and people alike, and crazed by the billowing smoke from ignited thatch, jerked and plunged at the end of his lead, the far end held in his owner's tiny hands and wrapped about her slender wrists. He darted from the shed, pulling Carys behind him. She stumbled after him, her strides lengthening impossibly until she fell on her face, unable to release the rope.

He raced down an alley and into the market area. Shying violently to one side, he at last broke free, leaving Carys face down in a pile of debris.

She sat up slowly, her hands and wrists red with painful rope burns. She wiped her nose on her sleeve, a combination of snot, dirt and tears. A different odor assailed her. Sickly, cloying, much like the smell of a freshly killed and gutted deer. Carys peered around her, her gaze finding a bundle of what appeared to be rags—or a dropped basket of clothing. But who would be washing laundry this early in the day?

She crept closer, a flutter in her belly sending warnings she only partly heeded. Reaching the rags, the odor intensified. Hand trembling, she lifted the corner of what might have once been a smock, recognizing the pretty embroidery along the hem as belonging to the baker's oldest daughter.

Older, more experienced in war and death, Carys clearly knew what she'd seen that day, but she still quaked with the horror in her seven-year-old self. A second mouth blossomed red and black beneath the young woman's jaw. Her clothes were a jumble about her, distorting her slender figure.

Mam! Carys had crept into a dark corner, drawn her knees to her chest, and waited to be found, prayers merging with her sobs. The nightmares had lasted for months, to be eventually replaced by other harsh realities of life.

Why now? Why remember this raid when so many years and wars had passed?

Birk's daughter's voice trembled, pulling Carys back to the present. There appeared to be no one to take the children in hand.

She cast an impatient look at Birk. She was a warrior, not a nursemaid. She fingered the knife he'd given her, running her thumb over the roughened hilt. It would be but a moment's effort to take the girls inside the castle and find their nurse, though the woman seemed incapable of protecting the wee ones. And there were things no child should see.

Carys moved beside him. "I will take them."

He sent her a startled look, relief warring with wariness. Would he turn his daughters over to a stranger? Even one he'd proposed marriage to not an hour earlier? Kidnapping and ransom—not to mention using the girls as hostages for Carys's escape—would not be unheard of.

"They will be safe with me." She lifted her chin. "Upon my honor."

The elder girl's attention diverted and her sister peeked from behind her skirts. "Who are ye?"

"I am from Cymru—or Wales, you might say—come to tell you and your *corgi* a story of pirates," Carys replied breezily. "Come with me."

She gathered the girls and turned to the tower. She glanced at Birk. "Set a guard at the door and do not worry about us."

"Where are we going?" the older child asked, stooping to pick up the puppy. "And how did ye know she's a *corgi*?"

"*Corgi* simply means *small dog* in Cymraeg. I have seen many in my country."

The girl clasped the pup to her chest, struggling with its wiggly weight. "Do ye speak Welsh? 'Cause Da says she needs a Welsh name."

"I do," Carys replied, deftly plucking the dog from the girl's arms as she guided them swiftly to the stair. She sent Birk a final reassuring look, then scooped the smallest girl in her other arm, settling her on her hip.

His gaze met hers in a long, assessing stare. With a snap of his fingers, he sent a warrior with a limp to her side. Recognizing him as the man she'd tumbled down the side of the ravine, Carys raised a brow, inviting his loyalty, refusing hostility.

"I am Brody," he grunted. "Ye are a fair hand in close combat. I willnae make the same mistakes with ye again."

"I am honored to meet ye, Brody," Carys replied, unable to suppress a grin at his admission.

Brody's curt nod of acknowledgement passed for formal acceptance. He swooped the other child into his arms and plucked a torch from a sconce as she continued her excited chatter about the puppy, her amma, and pirates.

Behind them, the protesting creak of the portcullis shrilled over the rattle of horses' hooves on the cobble stone entry way. Carys noted the generous placement of soldiers along the wall and at the foot of the stair before the tower door closed behind them.

To the last of her breath, they would be safe.

Chapter Twelve

Some hours later, a triple knock sounded at the door. Two rapid taps followed by a slight hesitation then a single rap. The heavy wooden panel muffled the voice requesting entry, but Brody seemed to recognize it nonetheless, and rose stiffly to his feet. Carys noted the large knife in his hand as he hobbled to one side of the portal, opening the door with a cautious nudge.

The man who had alerted them to the pirates stuck his head inside the room. After giving Carys and the girls a swift glance, he spoke to Brody.

"They are wanted in the hall." He turned and disappeared down the narrow stairwell.

"It appears the pirates have been routed from the village," Brody said, giving Carys a brief smile.

Grateful for the news, she waited for Brody to hoist a sleeping Abria to his shoulder, then rose and woke Eislyn, motioning her to follow. Mindful of the puppy's stubby legs and the steepness of the stairs, Carys tucked the furry round body beneath her arm. Eislyn thrust her somewhat grubby fingers in Carys's hand, grasping tight.

Most of the night was past, and after the initial wave of excitement had waned, Carys had entertained the girls by telling tales, inventing games, and eating from a tray that arrived from the kitchen. After a time, Abria had curled up in Carys's lap and fallen asleep, surprising her. Carys had been uncertain how to respond. Her heart melted at the trust in the child's action while her head warned against the tug at her emotions.

I cannot let them too close. Life is too uncertain. Better they learn now to be self-sufficient.

She remembered Brody's surprise when Abria had left her sister's side to lean against Carys's shoulder, and the unexpected frisson of longing as the small hand touched her hair.

I left my chance for children buried beneath Welsh soil. What would it have been like to have Terwyn's child? Would marriage to Birk include children? He has no son. Surely, he desires a son as all men do.

The thought of birthing a son brought a seed of excitement she quickly squashed.

"A bonnie lass," Brody had drawled, his voice hushed and matter-of-fact. "Everyone's favorite for all that she hasnae spoken since her ma died."

The child had then crawled into her lap, laid her head against Carys's chest, and, tucking her hands beneath her chin, dropped off to sleep.

I seem to have an affinity for dogs and children.

Eislyn slipped on the stair, her grip on Carys's hand averting a tumble. She sent Carys a worried look. Carys squeezed her fingers.

"The shallow steps make it difficult for pirates, too." She smiled at Eislyn's nod. "I think the tower would be a safe place for you and your sister should you ever need it. But, mayhap we need to find a nurse who doesn't abandon you."

Eislyn nodded vigorous agreement. "I'm braver than Ina. She tells lots of scary stories. But she is verra old, and mayhap has forgotten how to be braw."

"'Tis generous of you to say so," Carys said solemnly, wondering why the woman would frighten the girls with troublesome tales.

Eislyn tipped her head back, a mischievous twinkle in her eyes. "I dinnae expect Ina could manage the stairs any better than the pirates. Mayhap Abria and I will use the tower whenever we're in trouble."

They arrived in the bailey as the first rays of sun lightened the sky. Horses stamped tiredly in the yard, awaiting lads to lead them to the stable. A few soldiers lingered, clustered together as they spoke. There was little urgency; the men's voices a moderate rumble, their stances relaxed.

Mayhap the pirates gave scant trouble. Carys was startled to find she cared that the men of this clan were whole, uninjured. That it mattered to her that none died.

Ahead, the door to the hall opened, Birk framed in the entrance, arms crossed over his chest.

Mayhap this is where the true trouble lies.

Tired, and frustrated with a mostly fruitless rout of the pirates, Birk waited impatiently to see his daughters. And the woman to whose care he'd entrusted them.

Six men could scarcely bring her in. Why did I believe two wee lasses and one lame soldier would keep her here?

A voice in his head nagged him. *She has honor.*

Brody entered the feeble light of the sunrise, Abria in his arms. Birk quickly glanced past him, seeking Carys. Her dark brown trews and jerkin blended with the shadows. Her pale face glowed behind the partial curtain of her raven's-wing hair. Eislyn pattered at her side, fingers tucked trustingly in Carys's hand.

Relief and an emotion he couldn't identify swept over him. Tightness almost like a hunger pang centered in his chest, holding his gaze on the woman he meant to marry. She caught his look and returned it with a silent questioning tilt of her head. He stepped away from the door, gesturing them inside.

Awaiting the children's arrival, Ina stood a few feet away, hands clasped before her, head lowered. Her eyes lighted on the girls and she gasped, clucking indignantly.

"My poor wee lambs!" she exclaimed, reaching for the child in Brody's arms, casting a resentful glance toward him. The man's eyes narrowed, his mouth drawing taut with displeasure. Abria woke. She gave Ina a swift, horrified look then buried her face in Brody's chest, arms tightening in a choke hold about his neck.

Eislyn slipped behind Carys, pausing to peer around her legs.

"Come with me," Ina commanded, changing her tack and holding a hand out for Eislyn's compliance. She set her lips in a severe line, giving her hand an insistent shake when the child did not comply. Ina took a step closer, brushing against Abria's sleeve. Abria tore her face from Brody's chest with a small whimper, drawing away from the woman's touch. Spying Carys only a few feet away, Abria leaned to one side, arms outstretched, begging the safety of Carys's arms.

"That will be all, Ina," Birk growled, surprised then furious to see his daughters' responses to the auld crone. Far from showing the grandmotherly love he'd envisioned when he'd allowed his dead wife's maid to care for the children, it appeared her care bordered much too close to negligence—if not outright abuse.

Flashing him a dark look, the woman dropped her arm and, in a swirl of tattered skirts, departed the room, muttering beneath her breath. He'd warned her against revealing his title, but he didn't believe her half-hidden words were an inability to forego the polite formalities. More likely imprecations against his lineage.

Carys's gaze followed the old woman. As she disappeared through a distant doorway, Carys shifted her attention to Birk.

Purplish stains beneath her eyes attested her near-exhaustion, and Birk realized she'd likely had little rest since she'd been brought to Dairborrodal Castle the day before. He didn't want to acknowledge her efforts beyond those required to keep his daughters safe, but again he was struck by her willingness to sacrificed herself to help others. When was the last time someone had gone out of their way to help *her*?

"My thanks for caring for Eislyn and Abria," he said, moving closer. "It appears Ina was a poor choice as a nurse. They are good lasses and deserve better."

Abria's waving arms succeeded in gaining Carys's attention. Setting the puppy on the floor, Carys accepted the child into her arms. Just as she settled Abria on her hip, the child wriggled down, chasing after the puppy that collapsed onto the floor beneath a bench with a thump and a sigh, obviously anxious to return to its rest. Abria curled about the pup's body, eying the adults from her chosen spot on the floor. Eislyn hurried to join them.

"Why did you choose Ina?" Carys asked. "The girls do not seem to like her."

"She was their mother's maid, and I thought she would care for them as she had Rose." He rubbed the back of his neck, striving for civility though he chafed at being asked to explain himself. "Their grandma, my ma, often has the care of them when we are at MacLean Castle, but she was unable to make the journey with us to Dairborrodal this time."

Carys's gaze lingered on him a moment longer. "Tell me of the pirates," she invited, changing the subject.

Birk settled on the bench next to his daughters, and Carys and Brody took seats close to the table. Eislyn leaned against his legs. A sense of well-being enveloped him, making the long hours they'd spent chasing the elusive pirates worthwhile. He gently ruffled his fingers through the hair on the top of his eldest daughter's head.

A serving girl approached with a tray, stifling a yawn, and poured warm ale into mugs. She set them on the table and left.

"We have had trouble with pirates—not that 'tis unusual. Bands of them show up from time to time." He nodded to Carys, watching her face with a keen gaze. "Captain Ferguson—whose ship was lost in a storm a few months ago—related a tale of a sailor of his who put to rout pirates with a few clever tricks he'd not seen before."

Birk noted the wary look Carys gave him but did not force her to admit she was the sailor he referred to.

"We were glad to know of the end to those pirates," he continued. "But there is another band we seek. They strike without warning and appear where least expected. We believe the same band has been operating in and around the strait for twenty years or more. 'Tis possible they were related to Colin Dubh."

This time Carys's eyes widened, betraying her knowledge of the man.

"Ye killed him."

She gave a slow nod.

"How many men were with him that night?"

"Three. I shot them with my arrows. Two died instantly. One . . .." She frowned. "He took my arrow in his chest, but I did not watch him die."

Birk grunted. "There were but two when I arrived. If the third man escaped, he could have carried the tale with him."

A look of horror swept across Carys's face.

"Dinnae fash. They were raiding villages long before ye interfered."

"'Tis unlikely he saw me. I stood in the shadows and wore my hood pulled low."

"Good. I will set a patrol along the coast." He sighed. "Again. We have searched but have been unable to locate their nest. 'Tis

130

possible someone shelters them and encourages the raids on those loyal to the King of Scots, for even with the Treaty of Perth, allegiances are uncertain."

"There is something driving them other than greed?" Carys asked.

"'Tis possible. Though it has been some years since the king of Norway ceded the Isles to King Alexander, old grievances yet simmer." Birk shrugged away his annoyance at her persistence. "But they prey upon my land and I willnae give in to their demands. I will see my people safe from such scoundrels if I must chase the devils to hell myself."

He peered at his daughters, struck anew at how precious they were. "They deserve a life free from such fear, as do all children," he added, eying Carys, recognizing her life had been anything but free from unending strife and fear that might have disabled another, less hardy spirit.

Carys nodded. "Aye. There are many things we would attempt for our children."

Birk leaned forward, hands clasped, forearms resting on his thighs. "'Tis clear the lasses learned to like ye this night. They did not fear being in the tower?"

Carys's face softened, yet she drew back, caution in her eyes. "They were happy enough to hear stories of Cymru and nibble the food your cook sent up." She clapped her hands on the bench on either side of her legs. "I must seek a bed for a few hours' sleep. Is the tower room your preference?"

"She can sleep with us, Da," Eislyn said, scooting forward to peer up at her father. "She isnae afraid of anything, and Abria and I willnae bother her."

"Ye like Carys, aye?" Birk tilted his head, curious to see the Welsh woman's reaction. Her cheeks pinked then blanched.

"She knows Cymraeg, Da," Eislyn reported as though this were of vast importance.

"Did she help ye choose a name for yer wee pup, then?"

"Och, I dinnae know," his daughter replied breezily. "I think Abria should choose. 'Tis more her pup than mine."

I would give half my life for Abria to speak the dog's name aloud. Birk shook his head gently. "Mayhap ye should help her make the decision. I'm certain she will like whatever ye choose."

Eislyn worried her lip through a gap between two lower teeth where she'd lost a baby tooth just the week before. "Carys told us *banon* and *maelona* mean queen and princess," she mused. "I like those for names."

"Her name is *Tegan.*"

A voice Birk hadn't heard in more than two years piped softly from the floor at his feet. His blood ran cold then heated his body in a rush as he realized Abria had spoken. Tears sprang to his eyes and his hands trembled. He swallowed hard, forcing his voice to remain calm.

"*Tegan* is a beautiful name, Abria. Is it Welsh?"

Slowly he allowed his gaze to drift to his youngest daughter, cautious lest he startle her. Eyes seemingly too big for her thin face stared at him, fathomless dark pools glistening with tears. Her lower lip trembled slightly. Birk gently curved his lips into a soft smile, begging her and all the saints for another word.

God, please dinnae let her retreat from me again! Whatever miracle has been wrought, dinnae take it from me.

Abria's gaze slid to Carys who gave an encouraging nod. "Do ye remember what *tegan* means?" she asked.

"Pretty," Abria whispered. She grasped the puppy tighter in her lap, pulling the unresisting furry body against her chest.

"*Rydych chi'n ferch ddewr*," Carys murmured soothingly. "You are a brave *and* beautiful girl. 'Tis a pleasure to hear your voice."

Memories crashed through Birk's heart of a time misspent in anger and impatience, of two wee lasses perplexed at the whims of their mother's love. Overwhelmed by the change wrought in the past hours, he struggled to find his voice.

His eyes met Carys's, her face swimming in his watery gaze. "Ye have no idea . . .."

A lump rose in Carys's throat. She'd watched Abria all the long night after Brody's revelation. Poor lass, bereft of her ma and trusting none but her sister, and mayhap her grandma when she was available. Not a sound had the child made, not through tales of mermaids or dragons, nor in response to the morsels on the tray sent up from the kitchen.

Only Abria's silent crawl into Carys's lap had broken the child's long hours of reticence. It had warmed Carys's heart to have the small body press trustingly against hers. It reduced her to tears now to hear the sweet tentative voice.

Judging by the look on her da's face, and the shock on Brody's as well, she was not the only one so affected. Eislyn hugged her sister.

"I like Tegan. 'Tis a good name."

Abria didn't answer, her chin propped atop the puppy's chunky head, a pointed ear brushing either side of her face.

"I should grant ye yer freedom for the miracle ye've wrought," Birk said, his voice hoarse. "But even at sword point, I wouldnae give ye up." His face grew grim. "There is still the matter of our marriage."

A prickle of fear slid down Carys's spine. *What would Hywel counsel? Marriage to a man I do not know, in reparation for a crime I did not knowingly commit? 'Tis no way to start a marriage. I do not know how to trust him, much less build a relationship with him.*

She was reminded of her boast to her brother. *I do not need a man for my life to be complete.* She glanced at Eislyn and Abria, their eyes round with expectancy. *But I do need family, and mayhap love. Would a son to help replace the men I've lost in my life be too much to ask?*

Her gaze shifted to Birk, the planes of his face unyielding, the tilt of his chin proud. But his eyes—his eyes flickered with insistence. He wanted her to agree.

But did he want *her*?

"Grant me the ability to finish my task. I have sworn a promise and will not rest until I see it through," she countered.

He's admitted knowing Captain Ferguson and Tully. Mayhap he knows where to look for Tully's mam. And 'tis possible I can find a way to meet with Gorrie and help supply food for his family and continue his training. Dairborrodal Castle isn't so far away.

Birk's jaw clenched, a ripple of muscle stretching the skin taut at his temples. Something kept him from releasing her. He warred with his thoughts and his brow lowered. Finally, he sent Brody a curt nod.

"See the lasses to their room. I will find someone to stay with them."

He rose and motioned Carys to join him. "Ye and I must talk."

A sliver of hope lit in Carys's heart. It seemed a small thing, but the fond murmurs of her mam and da late in the evening hummed in her ears. A smile tempted her lips. This could be the start of a new life. A son of hers would not only be an heir for Birk, but an heir of Wales. She would not let the prince's lineage end with her.

Hywel would be pleased. Whether the child ever returned to Wales or not, the prince's bloodline would prevail.

Carys could almost see her brother's face, a grin of encouragement as she fell into step with the man who would soon claim her as wife. Hywel would want her to live.

Chapter Thirteen

A rhythmic pounding caught Carys's attention as she and Birk entered the bailey. Birk paced slowly, hands loose at his sides while Carys searched for the source. Mists swirled from the ground as the sun peered over the castle walls. Premonition ran chilled fingers up her spine.

A tall post, leaning slightly with the weight of a cross piece near its top, loomed dark against the pale morning sky. Two men at its base hammered a support in place.

Carys whirled on Birk, anger flaring, loose strands of black hair snapping in the wind. "A gallows? You had a gallows erected?"

Birk motioned to a coarse wooden bench next to the smith's shed. It leaned against the newly repaired wall of the smithy, though no fire burned in the forge.

"That isnae what I wished to discuss."

"Wish it or not, 'tis standing in your bailey," she snarled. "Discuss it or not, it is meant to remind me of my fate, should I not agree to this marriage." She waved a hand at the new construction.

"Or, mayhap there are other miscreants in this castle soon to meet their fate." Birk countered her furious gaze with a steady look. "I wish to speak of your request to return to the forest. Howbeit, if ye would rather discuss the gallows, we can waste time there." He sat on the bench, his casual manner infuriating her further.

"Tell me the truth," she demanded, flinging a hand toward the edifice. "Is that meant to influence my decision? Remind me of what little choice I have in the matter?"

One dark eyebrow quirked upward. "I am not in the habit of looking for ways to frighten women."

"Choosing the gallows over you does not frighten me overmuch." Carys folded her arms across her chest, not only to keep from slapping the calm arrogance from his face but to shield herself from his gaze. She inspected his robust form from head to toe, his seated position doing little to minimize his tall, muscular build. He radiated power and authority, his body purely male, perhaps even attractive. At least, some women might think so.

Carys wasn't certain what she thought. Had she not been so completely furious with him, she might have agreed there was something about him that compelled a need to touch him. A deeply rooted need to turn her life and body over to a man who could so clearly protect her and give her strong children. A need as old as time itself, ingrained in her bones.

Skinned knuckles and the white scar that traced over his forearm did not bespeak a cautious nature. He was bold and strong. And arrogant.

"I would wager you are quite used to frightening everyone around you into doing what you wish. I will tell you now, lest there be confusion between us, I will not bow to your tactics. If I marry you, I will not say *aye* when I mean *nae*."

To her surprise, his arched brow dropped slightly, mirroring a tiny upward flash of the corner of his mouth. He settled his hands on either side of his hips on the bench.

"Tell me what else ye expect from this marriage," he invited, his voice pitched low.

"Before you threw the promise of death into my face," Carys retorted bitterly, outraged to realize her thoughts of a new life had been sadly misplaced, "I had thought to use my position to help a few people I know. I could have done it on my own, but kicking air from yon rope will do nothing to help."

"I have asked ye before to speak to me of yer plans," Birk pointed out. "Ye are right to think I could be of help to ye."

"Ye would help me? Or keep me in your debt?"

Birk sighed. "Carys, tell me."

The line of his jaw was implacable, the tilt of his head commanding. But Carys could find no anger. Frustration hooded his eyes, alleviating some of her ire.

The captain befriended this man. But did he like him? Did he trust him? Or did he trust him just enough to trade? Can I trust him? What choice do I have?

"'Tis true you knew Captain Ferguson?" she hedged, seeking the truth of what he offered through a circuitous route.

"Aye. He berthed his ship at the port at MacLean Castle whenever he sailed up the coast." Birk leaned forward, forearms resting on his thighs. "Shall I answer some question for ye only a friend would know?"

She eyed him warily. Birk held her gaze.

"He has a son named Tully, whom I have met. He is a likeable lad, for all he's a wee bit simple. The captain and my . . . laird's family have a long history. He particularly was kind to Hanna, the auld laird's wife. She was grieved to hear all aboard the ship were lost. Can ye tell us otherwise?"

Carys considered the man before her. He was clearly used to intimidating people and getting his way. It was likely rare anyone gainsaid his decisions, and the MacLean laird probably never received complaints from the people of the village. Did the villagers *like* him?

His daughters clearly loved him.

She could do worse than trust the instincts of children. Dear God, the children. The words of the crone echoed.

Death follows ye like a hound.

"My brother and I fled Wales after Prince Llywelyn was killed near Orewin Bridge. Our family was gone, my husband dead in the fight with the English as well. Captain Ferguson needed hands for his ship and signed us on. Tully was on board."

The matter-of-fact wording did not dull the sense of loss that hummed through her. She swallowed hard. "A storm struck as we exited the Strait of Mull, blowing us back onto the rocks some distance from here. Tully and I and his dog were the only survivors. I promised the lad I would try to get him home."

Sympathy and disappointment weighed heavily. Birk was glad Tully lived, but he sorely regretted the final confirmation his old friend had perished. He paused a moment, reflecting on his last conversation with Ferguson.

She's a rare lass, and no mistake. She and her brother will do well, wherever they land. And I'm not afraid to say I'll miss them.

What would the captain say to know Birk had for all practical purposes kidnapped the young Welsh woman and held her against her will? Would he applaud his choice in bride, or deride his chosen path? The answer was obvious, but Birk was reminded again what awaited him if he allowed Carys to slip through his matrimonial grip.

"I am sorry for the loss of yer brother," he offered, pitching his voice low as he might to soothe a frightened filly.

Carys's stance altered. Her hands, tucked beneath her arms folded belligerently over her chest a moment before, now gripped tight, as if holding some incredible force inside. Her body, already slim, seemed to draw in on itself, her shoulders slumped slightly forward. Grief flashed across her face, raw and bitter.

She turned away, stumbling. Birk was on his feet in an instant, uncertain where his sudden desire to protect her sprang from. She stiffened as his arms encircled her, then eased into his embrace as he drew her close. He turned her face into his chest.

Her sobs tore at his heart. Though Rose's tears had been prettily designed to bring him to heel, Carys's grief was real. And he had no idea how to soothe her.

"If I thought a pretty ribbon or bauble would ease ye, I would scour the village shops." He touched her hair lightly. "I cannae even bring a foul villain to justice and lay him at yer feet in retribution. 'Twas a storm, an act of God, that tore yer brother from ye. And I learned long ago railing against the Almighty doesnae alter His plans."

He sighed, uncomfortable at being so powerless. Neither brain nor brawn would help Carys. He had nothing to offer but himself, and the knowledge humbled him.

There is naught in me worthy of her. Even Rose found no reason to stay. But, God help me, I cannae let Carys go.

Hesitantly, he stroked her back as hot tears dampened his leine. Strangely, his heart warmed at their touch.

What do I have to offer her?

"I will send for Tully. We will help him find his way home."

Her shudders lessened, and after a moment, she slipped away, turning so he could not see her face. He gave her time to compose herself, gladness blending with a touch of pride to see her shoulders straighten. When she faced him, her eyes still shone with tears, but they also sparked with intent.

"I will keep the promises I have made to both Tully and Gorrie. We will discover where Tully's family lives and return him there. I will continue to instruct Gorrie in both the bow and the sword until such time as he is capable of continuing his training with the MacLean captain, or he decides to remain on his da's farm. And I will see the family is fed." She sent him a mocking look. "I will no longer be poaching."

Birk considered her words, a bit taken aback by the passionate demand.

"It may not be possible for ye to continue Gorrie's training." He raised a hand as she bristled. "If ye are unable to assist the lad, a suitable replacement will be found."

"You will not deny me the opportunity to train him," she stated flatly.

"Nae. But yer time willnae always be free for the lad. Ye'll have two wee lasses to care for, and their care will come first." He waited for Carys to accept his reminder. She gave a small nod.

"Eislyn has some skill with a blade," he continued. "Her grandma has promised her further lessons. Mayhap ye will consider Eislyn as yer pupil as well. And," he added, suddenly remembering promises he'd made, "she wishes to learn to sail."

"I can help her."

"Then it is agreed?"

"What of Tully?"

"That request I will grant in full. 'Tis not right for the lad to remain separated from his ma and sisters. If we discover he has no kin left alive, he will have my permission to live here."

"He has a place with Lorna and Fergal," Carys said. "They accepted us and promised to care for him should something happen to me."

"They are good people." He tilted his head. "Ye must be the lass who killed the wolf as well as the men who attacked their croft. There was a bounty on Colin Dubh's head. It is yours."

A hint of amusement crossed her face. "Strange to change from facing the noose to accepting payment for killing an outlaw."

The irony in her words stirred a rumble from Birk's chest. He grinned, wondering at this woman who could stir both his ire and his humor in short order. She also stirred other, more demanding emotions.

"There is one more item to consider from marriage," he said, disappointed when her gaze turned wary.

Her chin rose defiantly, but the lines of her body stiffened. "I have been wed before. I know what to expect."

Birk stood. "I want an heir. A lad with yer courage, yer capacity of care for others. Will ye give me a son?"

"I am also aware there is no way to predict whether a child will be a boy or girl," she replied crisply. "There is naught we can do to change *His* plans," she tossed back at him.

"If our first child is a lass, will ye give me another?" He loomed over her, not hiding his height or strength. He wanted her knowing full well the man she would accept. "I want ye willing in my bed, not shrinking from my touch."

Her breast rose and fell, betraying the turmoil beneath. Carys met his gaze, then looked away.

"What is different this time?" Birk asked. "What makes ye recoil from a second marriage?" His curiosity ate at him, punishment for whatever lack Rose had found in him that had sent her to the arms of her lovers—and to her death. Anger swirled with frustration, feeding on the humiliation of the loss of his wife's fidelity.

"When I married Terwyn, I knew he cared for me. He gave my cloak to his mother and sister to sew a seal skin into its lining. They offered it to me out of love and acceptance into his family." She returned her gaze to his, eyes now clear. "When he came to me on our wedding night, I *wanted* his touch."

"Is this beyond our resolve?"

"I'd known him for years. You, I do not know, nor is anyone I trust able to recommend you. You ask me to passively accept marriage to a man I know little about. And while 'tis true my first marriage was arranged, this one is by my choice."

Carys cast a quick glance over her shoulder where the gallows pierced the morning sky then back at him. Birk gritted his teeth, knowing his tactic did as much to draw her in as push her away. Should she come to their marriage bed cold and unwilling, he had no one to blame but himself. Dugan was right. If he wanted a willing lass, he was going about it the wrong way.

There was nothing to be done about it now. If he could find a way to bed her without worry she'd cut his throat during the night, he'd consider his deceit worth the effort.

She lifted her chin.

"Nae. If you will honor your promises, I will honor mine."

Chapter Fourteen

Carys settled gratefully into the tub.

Ah-h. The word was almost inaudible. The pleasure of hot water in a tub was so much better than a perfunctory splash in a cold stream. But was the luxury worth her freedom? Water lapped about Carys's shoulders and lavender-scented steam drifted from the surface. Her knees rose like twin mountain peaks from the glistening water, dark gold in the firelight.

Her freedom was no longer in question. Tonight, though released from the tower into a much more commodious room, she was still a prisoner. Tomorrow, her freedom would be within the boundaries of matrimony. A different kind of prison altogether.

The thought threatened to chase away her contentment induced by being thoroughly clean and warm for the first time in weeks, perhaps months. Carys pushed deeper into the water and closed her eyes, drifting beyond the squalor of war and life aboard ship.

Hywel's face came to mind, his easy smile and the way he drew her into whatever mischief he was about. His promise to see her settled well echoed in her memory and tears fell unbidden at her protest against marrying, against needing a man to protect her. How wrong she'd been. Men ruled the world, and she needed this one to save her life. While she was willing to acknowledge Birk's offer did indeed save her, she found herself unable to muster any gratitude.

A giggle woke her. The tepid water rippled gently against her legs, her exposed knees frigid. A tiny splash sent sparkling droplets into the air. Carys rolled to face the doorway, careful to keep below the edge of the tub.

Two pairs of mischievous eyes met hers. Eislyn clapped a hand over her mouth, a chunk of bread clasped in the other fist. Abria flung another piece of bread toward Carys, crumbs scattering like dandelion seeds in the wind. Tegan yipped and raced to the tub, her short legs giving her little purchase against the wooden slats. Her black button nose and enormous pointed ears appeared over the edge then disappeared with a clatter of toenails on the floor.

Carys's heart did a somersault.

"What brings the two of ye to my room?" she asked, giving her tone a slight growl.

"Da says we can see ye whenever we like, 'cause ye are living with us now," Eislyn asserted, ignoring Carys's mock scold.

Abria's eyes widened and Carys immediately softened. "I don't mind you coming here, but mayhap you could learn to knock first."

"We did!" Eislyn piped up. "Twice!" She giggled. "Ye were asleep. In the tub!"

Abria glanced at her sister and added her soft titter of glee.

"Then give me a moment's privacy whilst I towel dry," Carys instructed. "I'm freezing!"

Flinging the bread onto the tray, the girls fled across the room and bounded onto the tall bed. Tegan circled the carved posts, yipping excitedly. Carys grabbed a thick square of linen from the back of the chair where a maid had left it to warm—hours ago? She quickly wrapped it around her as she stepped from the tub, then bent to prod the embers back to life.

"Don't the two of you have a new nurse?" She asked glanced over her shoulder to the bed where the two mischievous pairs of eyes peered at her from the pile of blankets.

Eislyn sat, tucking her feet beneath her. "We dinnae need a nurse. Da says ye'll take care of us now."

"Indeed? What else did your da tell you?" Carys rose and twitched a shift from a peg near the door. She dropped it over her head, letting the linen fall to the floor, then added a heavy robe over the top. She knelt beside the bed and, laying her palms on the edge, propped her chin on the backs of her hands. Tegan snuggled against her thigh, head across her lap.

Eislyn gave her a solemn look. "Da says ye'll be our ma." Her brow furrowed. "Ye willnae leave us, aye?"

Carys's heart broke. "Is that what happened?"

Eislyn nodded. Abria burrowed deeper into the quilts. Carys decided asking further questions would only cause more hurt. She would ask them of Birk.

"Your da has asked me to marry him," *rather than hang*. "And that means I will be your ma, though I don't mean to replace her. You must feel free to speak of her if you wish."

Both girls watched her quietly. At last Eislyn nodded. "I think ye will be a good ma. And I will try to be very good, also."

"Though I prefer you mind your manners and be polite, whether you are good or not makes no difference to me being your ma. You will have grumpy days, and I will have them as well. But I will still be your ma, and you will be my daughters. Do you understand?"

Eislyn nodded slowly. "Aye." Her voice was slightly skeptical, but she appeared to accept Carys's word.

Carys turned her attention to Abria. "How does that sound to you, *fy merch*?"

"What is *fy merch*?" Eislyn asked.

"It means *my daughter*," Carys whispered past the lump in her throat. Abria's eyes sparkled with tears and her lower lip trembled.

"Will you be my daughter?" Carys murmured, uncaring that her heart had opened wide and enveloped both girls.

"Yes." Abria's soft answer brought tears to Carys's eyes. Moving the puppy from her lap onto the floor, Carys rose and joined the girls on the mattress that crackled beneath her weight, sending the faint scent of moss and lavender to her nose. She gathered both girls in her arms and hugged them close.

After a moment, Eislyn tugged free. "Can we sleep here?" She glanced about the bed then patted the mattress. "It's softer than ours, isn't it, Abria?" Her vigorous nod encouraged a similar response from her sister.

Carys canted her head to the side. "You don't snore, do you?"

The girls giggled.

"Or kick?"

Eislyn fell to her back, paddling her feet in the air, Abria mimicking her an instant later.

"You won't tickle me during the night, will you?" Carys demanded as she fell upon the girls, poking their ribs and tummies. They shrieked with laughter and rolled away. Carys dropped to the mattress and peered up at them.

"You won't wake me at dawn?"

Eislyn shook her head, gasping for breath. "Nae!"

Tegan planted her furry forefeet on the edge of the bed and barked. Carys rolled over and stared at the pup. Tegan yipped again.

"Whose turn is it to take the dog out?"

* * *

Birk raised his head slightly as Dugan dropped to a chair next to the hearth.

"I thought ye'd be pacing the floor," Dugan remarked.

Birk grunted.

Dugan leaned over and sniffed a flask on the small table between them "Drinking—the night before yer wedding?" He shook his head. Picking up the flask, he swirled the contents. "Planning on getting drunk?"

"Join me, won't ye?" Birk asked in parody of a request, his teeth showing in a grim smile.

"Not likely," Dugan laughed. "Not enough whisky left in the flask to warm my belly. And 'tis no good trying to drink ye under the table. I learned that years ago." He settled back into his seat. "Are ye having second thoughts?"

Birk grunted again and stirred himself, setting his mug on the table with a thump.

"Nae. She's th' lass I'm goin' tae marry," he replied, slurring his words. "But I've dug a hole deep enough to bury the whole of the castle in."

Dugan raised a brow. "Aye? Ye dinnae take my advice, then?"

Birk shrugged. "I couldnae have her thinkin' I'd release her. And she dinnae think marryin' me was much better than facin' th' hangman."

"I'm guessing building a gallows dinnae make the best marriage proposal."

With a flick of his wrist, Birk sent the mug and flask crashing to the floor.

"Ye should've listened," Dugan said. "A lass likes to be wooed. A woman like yers doesnae like to be told what to do."

"Bah! I'd rather fight pirates!"

"Ye will have enough time for both. There's been no word on those who struck the village last night. They grow bolder, laird. Or mayhap angrier. There remains unrest between the Norse and Scots. Raids on both sides to gain land and plunder."

Birk roused from his personal woes, pricked by a curious thought. "Could the pirates be Norse marauders?"

Dugan shrugged. "There is a difference?"

"These could be acting to stir up unrest. They are better organized than the typical ilk I've seen. Ye raise a valid point, Dugan."

"'Tis been rumored they berth near Islay. MacDonald aligns with the Norse king."

"We align with the Norse when it's prudent. MacDonald has been known to kiss King Alexander's arse."

"More like thumb his nose," Dugan chuckled.

Birk stared into the embers on the hearth. Their pulsing glow caused his eyes to blur, heightening the dulling effect of the whisky.

"What do ye suggest?" he asked, his voice husky with a plaintive tone. "I dinnae really know her, yet I know she is the wife I need. If I release her, she would never return to me."

"Would that not be a good test? If there is an attraction between ye, she will give ye another chance."

"There can be no second chance," Birk replied. "There is no MacLean heir. Gillian's lads are braw, but they are MacCains and neither is interested in the merchant business. Signy's lad will follow his da on Mull. My da wouldnae wish his enterprise to fail."

"Being head of the largest fleet of merchant ships on the western coast of Scotland is something a lad should be born into," Dugan agreed. "None of the other lasses will do?"

Birk's muscles tensed. "I want Carys."

Dugan pushed his feet out, slouching in the chair. "Then ye have yer work cut out for ye. I hope the priest says an extra blessing over ye tomorrow." He sighed and closed his eyes. "And mayhap a wee prayer for when yer ma discovers ye wed without *her* blessing."

* * *

Lightning streaked the sky and thunder rumbled, shaking the foundations of the castle. Torrents of rain poured from the roof tiles, creating a roaring sound almost too loud for speech to penetrate.

Carys eyed herself in the silvered glass. Her gown—her wedding gown—had been borrowed from another woman at the castle, though the maid sent to her this morning had been reluctant to name the donor. The simply cut design was nonetheless of a wool so fine it was almost weightless.

Green. The color reminded Carys of the majestic pine and juniper trees that lent their bracing scents to the winter air of the Welsh mountains. A hint of blue caught her eye as she turned before the glass, inspecting herself from all angles.

The neckline swept wide across her shoulders, nearly baring them, and someone with a fine hand at embroidery had wrought tiny red and silver flowers at the borders of sleeve, neck and hem, shimmering like rowan berries in frost. Narrow sleeves belled at her wrists, the cloth draping halfway to the floor. No servant's dress this. What would her station be once she wed? Was Birk captain of the guard? The steward? 'Twas certain, he was no lowly man-at-arms.

The silent maid tied strands of silver ribbon in Carys's hair, twining the long ends in with the dark waves that hung nearly to her waist. Carys twisted a strand of hair behind one ear. The maid clucked her annoyance and pulled it back to frame her face, winding it about her finger to form a long curl before patting it in place.

It looks fine, but I doubt I could draw a bow whilst garbed thusly. Carys kept her sigh to herself, feeling poked and prodded like a mare at market. The cloth tightened as she tentatively flexed her arms. She gripped the soft flared skirt and lifted the hem from the floor, exposing the dyed-to-match chemise.

"Ye look like a faerie princess." Eislyn's adoring look gave Carys pause. She caught the child's gaze in the mirror and smiled.

"You are lovely," Carys said in all sincerity, noting the pink, freshly scrubbed cheeks and rumple-free gown of lightweight blue wool. Abria crept next to Carys and tucked her fingers in Carys's hand. Her simple dress of deep burgundy echoed her pinkened cheeks.

"I am quite privileged to have such lovely ladies at my side today," Carys said.

Abria flinched and shuffled closer as thunder rumbled.

"Don't mind the thunder." Carys spoke lightly, seeking to banish the girl's fear of the sound as well as her own apprehension of the possible portent of such weather on her wedding day. "'Tis but a warning for us to remain inside whilst the rain waters the trees and crops."

"Ma died in a storm," Eislyn stated bluntly.

A shiver shook Carys. "What happened?" The question slipped out before she thought better of it. Who asks a child how her mother died?

"She got on a ship and left us. Da dinnae know about it, and he was angry when he found out. A bad storm sank her ship and she died."

Carys dropped to her knees before the girls.

"My brother was also killed in a storm only a few months ago. I know how you must feel."

"Was it your fault?" Eislyn asked. Abria crept beneath Carys's arm.

Carys cupped each girl's face in her palm. "Nae. Storms are never anyone's fault."

"Do ye miss him?"

"Very much. I try not to think about it often. And when I do, it hurts for a while. So, I try to remember how much he loved me. It helps a bit."

A rap at the door sounded and Carys rose, a hand on each girl's shoulder. Birk strode into the room, his gait slightly awkward, his shoulders stiff. She perused his face for a hint of his temper, noting fine white lines at the corners of his eyes. His mouth drew down at the corners, matching his stormy look to the weather raging outside. Was he in pain? Or aggrieved over their marriage? Did it matter?

He came to an abrupt halt, eyes widening as he stared at her. Carys stifled the ripple of pleasure—or perhaps mockery—to know he was taken aback by her appearance. The gown transformed her from bedraggled poacher to, if not quite the princess she was, at least a woman facing her wedding day.

"Da! We're getting married today!" Eislyn burst at the seams with excitement.

"So it seems," he murmured, a slight wince crossing his face. His brow furrowed.

Carys was at a loss. Mistrust churned in her belly. Whatever gripped Birk in worry did not bode well at all.

Chapter Fifteen

Birk's head throbbed. His back ached from spending the night sprawled in a chair, and his damned vision seemed blurred. He blinked his eyes repeatedly, uncertain of the sight before him.

When did the rough warrior woman who slew men and lived alone in the forest become the beautiful woman in the steward's wife's best gown?

His daughters clung to Carys on either side, staring at him expectantly. He gave his head a slight toss to clear it and winced at the painful result. He frowned—and would have groaned if the prospect of such an utterance wouldn't have unmanned him. He couldn't remember the last time he'd gotten roaringly drunk, but now clearly remembered why he hadn't continued the practice.

"I am blessed to have three lovely ladies at my side today," he remarked, relieved when the throbbing eased. Abria tilted her head, her large, dark eyes wide. Slipping her hand from Carys's, she crossed to Birk and nested her palm in his. Whether from sympathy with the pain creasing the corners of his eyes, from acceptance, or perhaps love, her gesture warmed his heart and formed a lump in his throat. He gently squeezed her fingers. Her hesitant smile banished the last of his drink-induced bad mood and he faced his bride with half a grin.

"My lady?" Giving Carys a slight bow and the bend of his elbow, he indicated she should join him. After a moment's hesitation, Carys stepped to his side and accepted his arm.

Her touch, light as it was, sent crackling waves of shock racing through him. His cock bumped against his sporran, profoundly interested in the woman at his side. A harsh reminder of the previous night's indulgence drummed behind his eyes as his heart pounded. It was going to be a long day. And perhaps a longer night. He'd not yet decided how to approach the future with a woman capable of killing him once she discovered his ruse.

Without a word, he matched Abria's tiny stride through the hall, careful not to set his feet down too firmly lest he jar his brain loose.

I cannae imagine what drove me to empty a flagon . . .. He paused thoughtfully. *Two flagons of whisky. She's a bonnie lass and 'twill be no hardship to sire a dozen lads by her once I convince her life with me is better than living alone in the wilds.*

A smile tugged one corner of his mouth. Reassurance buoyed in his chest, overriding the apprehension that had driven him to consume the better part of a small cask of whisky. He'd coerced his bride—given her no choice, actually—and the thought continued to needle him, adding to his headache. Though she'd vowed to embrace the hangman's noose rather than the bonds of matrimony more than once, she'd clearly seen the error of her ways and was only moments away from sealing her life with his.

He cut a glance at her. Waves of glistening blue-black hair cascaded down to her hips, pulled back from her crown in two slender braids twined with silver ribbon and held at the back of her head by a silver clasp. The green gown hugged her figure to her waist then fell to the floor in sweeping folds. Silver and red embroidery winked at her neckline, framing creamy skin rising from her softly rounded breasts.

His fingers twitched, as did his cock. He imagined the weight of her breasts against his palms. He swallowed, mouth dry. It wouldn't do to show himself over-eager before the priest. It had been difficult enough to talk the man into the precipitous marriage but promise of a new chapel to replace the one likely original to the castle and sadly in need of either repair or replacement had helped.

They crowded through the door and into the hall leading to the laird's study. Built on the same level as the great hall, the spacious room overlooked a plunging view of the ocean from one wall, as well as the road to the village from another. A young girl with a cheerful grin on her face gently steered Abria and Eislyn to a corner of the room. Birk led Carys to his desk, halting a few steps away. A piece of parchment lay upon the surface, held in place by an inkpot on one corner and a thick, leather-bound book at the other. The priest eyed him across the expanse, arms folded, hands hidden within the sleeves of his long brown robe and resting atop his round belly. The steward and his wife stood on either side of the priest, witnesses for the ceremony.

The priest turned his attention to Carys. "If the bride will give me her name, I will complete the contract."

Lifting her chin a fraction, Carys avoided Birk's gaze.

"Dinnae fash. He's been well-compensated for overlooking the irregularities of the wedding."

She blinked. "You bribed a priest?"

"Nae. Compensation comes after he performs the ceremony. Bribery would indicate payment before he does as I ask. I am not that foolish."

Carys squared her shoulders and addressed the priest.

"Carys Wen, filia Pedr."

Nodding, the rotund priest carefully inserted her name in the proper place on the document, with a bit of help in spelling from the bride.

Birk dropped Carys's arm and stepped boldly to the desk. He plucked the quill from the stand and, dipping the tip in the ink, scrawled his name at the bottom of the parchment. With an instant of uncertainty, he handed the quill to Carys.

To his surprise, she waved it aside and approached the desk. Splaying her fingertips upon the wooden surface next to the parchment, she studied the contract.

She can read? Birk's breath left him in a small whoosh. *Shite!*

Her shoulders stiffened and she ran one blunt fingernail over the parchment as if clarifying what she saw. Whirling, she pinned him with an enraged look.

"You lied to me?" She blinked furiously and drew a deep breath, stuttering once before she found the words she sought. "You lied to me! You aren't the steward, or the captain of the guard, or even the head gaoler. You bastard! You're the chief of Clan MacLean!"

Aware of the small crowd avidly listening to every word, Birk folded his arms over his chest. "I dinnae lie to ye. Ye dinnae ask."

Her eyes blazed. "You skirted the issue," she accused, jabbing a finger beneath his nose. "You skirted it as you would maggots on a rotted carcass!" She flung her hand toward the marriage contract. "You didn't think I'd be able to read the contract, did you? As laird, you could pardon me without thinking twice, yet you insisted I marry you. Why? Can you not find a woman willing to marry you? Is the bribe of being Lady MacLean not enough?"

Her chest heaved, fury radiated from every inch. Birk surveyed her laconically. "Are ye finished? Have ye run out of spite?"

"Spite?" Her voice squeaked up the scale, eyebrows punctuating her indignation less than an inch from her hairline. *"Cer i grafu!"*

Birk's eyes narrowed. "Ye've said that to me before, and I dinnae think it means *I do*."

"It doesn't," she bit out, clearly angry enough to spit nails.

His head throbbed again. Harder. "Sign the contract, Carys," he growled.

"Ye willnae force the lady," the priest protested.

A whimper from the corner of the room silenced Birk's response like a deluge of frigid water.

Carys froze, her anger instantly dashed by the sound of a child's distress. Painfully aware she and Birk were the focus of the small party in the room, something akin to shame slid through her as she met two wide-eyed gazes. Abria shoved a thumb in her mouth and hid behind her temporary nurse's skirts.

This is why Abria does not speak. She has witnessed too much strife and does not know how else to respond. The realization the child had been witness to her parents' problems tore at her heart. Letting her shoulders relax, she approached the girls with slow, careful steps. She sank to the floor before them.

"I am so sorry, *fy merched*. I am so sorry I've hurt and frightened you." She gave each of the girls a solemn look and placed her hands in her lap. "I do not wish to spoil our friendship. 'Tis true your da and I are not in accord." She firmly refused to cast a glance his way as a shadow fell over her shoulder.

Abria glided forward and curled against Carys. Eislyn took position at Carys's shoulder and whispered into her ear.

"Ma ran away after she and da fought," she confided. "And then she died."

There must be more to the story than what they can tell me. He is infuriating, but surely not so much a mother would leave her girls.

Birk's hand clasped her shoulder, fingers tightening briefly— pledging unity? Agreement? Apology? There was not enough force in his grip to think he tried to warn or intimidate her. She laid her hand over his.

"Only God knows when 'tis our time to die, little one," she said, giving the girls a soft smile. "But I will not run away." Once again, the crone's words of death echoed in her mind. Carys caught the gaze of each precious girl and swore she'd not let the prophecy haunt her or her new family. She knew but one way to approach life, and it was to not worry about events over which she had no control.

Birk's grip eased. Did he not believe her capable of keeping her word? With an effort, she kept her opinion behind her teeth. If that was his experience with women, she would not add to it.

"Return with your sister, *bychan*," she urged, giving Abria's arm a reassuring pat. The child rose reluctantly then rejoined Eislyn and the older girl who met Carys's appraising look with an easy smile.

"My name's Margaret, my lady. The weans are safe with me."

Brody and another man Carys recognized but could not name, stood in the doorway, arms crossed over massive chests, feet braced apart. They also gave her a slow nod and she hid a smile to think of anything less than an English army attempting to breech their protection.

Birk's hand appeared before her, palm up, offering assistance. She placed her hand in his and allowed him to raise her to her feet. They faced the silent, stricken pair on either side of the desk.

"My steward, Archibald, and his wife, Elspeth."

Archibald nodded his head. "My lady."

Elspeth bobbed a curtsy. "My lady."

Noting Elspeth and she were of a size, Carys realized who had loaned her the wedding dress. "I thank you for sharing your beautiful gown with me on such a special occasion."

The woman's cheeks pinked. "The honor is mine, my lady," she replied.

Yielding to Birk's slight tug on her hand, she sighed deeply, then joined him again at the desk and added her signature to the document. Her hand bobbled slightly as she replaced the quill.

I am tied to these Scots now, and this man in particular. The rest of the ceremony is only a formality. I have signed my life over to him.

Two years of fighting for her life ran hot through her veins.

God help him if he betrays me. The MacLeans will need to choose a new chief.

The priest's words droned around her, and she belatedly closed her eyes for prayer when she caught the priest's disapproving frown.

This is not the marriage into obscurity and peace I envisioned when Hywel and I spoke of our retreat into Scotland. If I had to marry—if that is the path chosen for me—I would have wished for a simple crofter. A man of the land with an appreciation for wealth that comes from hard work, care, and, if not love, quiet companionship.

She stole a look at Birk. *I'd had my fill of court intrigue and betrayal in Gwynedd. Enough political posturing to last me beyond my lifetime.* She sighed softly. *And I find myself bound to a Scottish laird. 'Tis clear he needs not only a mother for his girls, but an heir as well. And mayhap an advisor, one familiar with the deceits of men who thirst for power.*

His left hand clasped her right forearm, turning her palm up. His ceremonial blade, hilt encrusted with red and green stones, nicked her wrist just above the faint scar marking her binding to Terwyn.

Birk placed his own slight wound against hers and the priest bound them together with a narrow strip of cloth.

"I, Birk Alexander MacLean, take ye, Carys Wen, filia Pedr, as my wife. In the presence of God and before these witnesses I promise to be a loving, faithful, and loyal husband to ye, for as long as we both shall live."

His gaze as he urged her to reply bore into her, yet he remained utterly still. As if a weight had lifted from her shoulders, Carys found the words came easily to her lips.

"I, Carys Wen, filia Pedr, take you, Birk Alexander MacLean, as my husband. In the presence of God and before these witnesses, I promise to be a loving . . .."

Birk's lips twitched. Carys stared at him. His brows lifted slightly, rounding his eyes into mock innocence.

". . . faithful, and loyal wife, for as long as we both shall live. I will respect you, your beliefs, your ways, and your people. *Mi gerddaf gyda thi dros lwybrau maith.*"

He tilted his head, question in his eyes. Shyness crept over Carys.

"I will walk with you over many paths," she translated.

Birk placed his free hand over their bound ones, approval in his eyes. "And I will walk with ye, respect ye, and learn yer ways."

His profession startled a small smile to Carys's lips. Perhaps he wasn't as unreasonable as he seemed. And it was as good a starting place for their marriage as she could ask for—under the circumstances. Marriage to a Scottish laird surrounded by barbarous Vikings to the north, marauding pirates to the west, and the evil bastard Edward to the south. Had she jumped from the boiling pot into the fire?

Chapter Sixteen

There was no wedding feast, giving rise to more questions in Carys's head.

Was feasting not traditional in a clan this small? Or did he seek to draw as little attention to their union as possible?

Supper was a small affair in a private dining room only a few feet away from the laird's study. Two lasses, craning their necks in an attempt to get a look at their chief's new bride, served the platters of venison, vegetables, and bread, then left the room.

The few present at the ceremony seated themselves at the table amid silver candelabra and snowy linens. No more than the requisite witnesses needed to legitimize their union. A wide margin—a different world—separated this wedding from her first. She'd gritted her teeth against tears as she pledged her life to Laird MacLean, trying not to think of her dead husband, her father, and her brother who'd always championed her. She now felt . . . empty, as if she were bereft of any identifiable emotion. A welcome relief after the tumult of the past hours.

Carys's step slowed as she surveyed the rich accoutrements. Trenchers of bread sat inside fine china bowls embellished with gold trim. Mugs of pewter set with semi-precious stones clustered about the base of a matching pitcher, beaded with droplets of water. Delicate eating knives with ivory handles graced each place setting, and heavily embroidered cloths lay next to each bowl. The MacLeans were a wealthy clan to afford such finery. She'd not seen such since Llywelyn's court.

Birk sent her a questioning look as she came to a near-halt, and she covered her awkward lapse by urging the girls to their seats.

"But we want to sit with ye in yer chair!" Eislyn argued as Carys pointed to two chairs at the head of the table.

"I do not wish to muss the gown Lady Elspeth so graciously allowed me to borrow," Carys said, noting the frowns of disappointment as the girls climbed into their seats. Touching the back of her chair, she saw a flicker of impatience in Birk's eyes. He drew her next to him and faced the assembled group.

"I thank ye for your attendance at my wedding. I present Lady Carys, now Lady MacLean."

Carys managed not to wince at the title. She may not have found the obscurity she desired in her new home, but she would not cause dissent. At least she was well-prepared for this role, whether Laird MacLean knew it or not. He likely thought it a compliment to name her lady. Little did he know it was beneath her. He wasn't the only one with secrets.

She managed to eat despite the growing knot in her stomach. As she'd told Birk, she'd been through a wedding night before, and knew what was to come. But she and Terwyn had known each other, attended gatherings and banquets together. He hadn't been her equal in rank—few were—but he'd been of noble blood. They'd spent time getting to know each other better other during the days after their betrothal had been announced. His teasing, forbidden kisses had tempted her to more.

There was nothing forbidden about Birk MacLean. *Forbidding* would better describe him.

His rough approach to life told her he got whatever he wanted, most likely without regard to how it affected those around him. It was now clear he was liked as laird, judging from the way his men responded to him the night of the pirate attack, and from the easy manner the five men in the room displayed, jesting with one another as they ate. His daughters and the other women in the room showed no fear of him. Perhaps a bit of awe from the serving lasses, and it might be as well to see they served elsewhere in the future, not at the side of the man they unabashedly ogled. Carys noted he seemed oblivious of their fascination.

The tension in the room was because of her. She noticed the sidelong glances, the brief hesitations as they caught her gaze. It had been a long time since she'd been on display. No one here knew her, and they plainly wondered why their laird chose to wed a woman he'd claimed from the gallows.

She wondered the same.

"Ye cannae have my pasty!" Eislyn shouted as she lunged forward in her seat.

Carys whipped around in time to see Eislyn snatch the last pie from the platter, beating her sister to the treat. Abria slumped in her chair, lower lip pushed forward in a pout.

"Girls." Carys's low voice carried her warning to their small ears.

"Margaret, 'tis time the lasses bid good-night," Birk announced meaningfully. He dipped his head in the girls' direction, a slight frown on his face.

"I'm sorry, Da," Eislyn said rather unconvincingly. "Abria wanted my pasty."

"And what is a better way to tell her nae?"

Eislyn poked the pie. "Take it before she finishes hers?"

"That is one way. What is a better way to speak to yer sister?" Birk asked, one brow raised.

"Sorry, Abria," Eislyn piped in a cheerful voice. "That one's mine."

Carys stared at Birk, uncomprehending his calm correction. It was a strategy her mam had used when she and Hywel were children, but such was at complete odds with the man who had repeatedly lost his patience with her during the past two days.

Birk nodded. "That is fine. Have Margaret stop by the kitchen and wrap a pasty for each of ye to eat later in honor of yer new ma." He tilted his head at Carys. "She willnae be joining yer mischief this day."

Something rippled in Carys's belly. It wasn't revulsion, for she found the man—as infuriating as he was—compelling. Thoughts of Terwyn had filled her with warmth, a sweetly eager anticipation. This burned like banked embers rousing to a breeze, twisting her insides into complicated knots, demanding and urgent as fear, though she had no desire to flee. It was impossible to understand. Having spent the last two years of her life relying on her gut instinct for survival, Carys found this new sensation disturbing.

The girls wiggled down from their chairs and at their da's prompt, stood beside Carys's chair. Holding hands, they both executed wobbly curtsies before bursting into giggles and fleeing the room, Margaret on their heels.

There was a scuffle of chairs on the stone floor as the remaining guests rose. Late afternoon sunlight angled low through the window and the knot in Carys's stomach tightened. Dropped lower. Tingled. Throbbed.

"Good e'en, m'lady, Laird," they said, curiously eager to leave rather than stay and harass the newly married couple.

"You must not hurry away," Carys said, anxious not to be left alone in Birk's company.

Birk stood, his feet braced as though expecting an onslaught. The wedding party filed past, short bows for the laird, curtsies and sidelong glances for Carys.

Brody clapped Birk's shoulder. Birk winced. "God's blessing on ye both. That and a wee bit of warm buttermilk with some salt and pepper to cure yer hangover." He sent Carys a broad grin and confided, "His sour attitude isnae about his bonnie bride."

Birk aimed a clout at Brody's head, but the man laughed and ducked as he followed the others from the room. The door clicked shut.

Silence surrounded them.

Birk grabbed the decanter of wine and poured the blood-red liquid into two heavily embellished silver goblets, offering one to Carys.

"*Slàinte mhath.*" He tipped the goblet to his lips and drank.

Carys ran her fingers over the intricate chasing near the rim and dipped a fingertip in the liquid. "Drunk? And in front of all our guests. 'Tis a fine way to begin a marriage. This *was* your idea, if you'll recall."

Birk set his goblet down with a thump of metal against the cloth-covered wood.

"I dinnae wish to remarry at all. 'Tis not about ye."

Carys pushed her drink away, furious with his lack of courtesy. "Well, a drunkard rarely has a stiff cock," she observed caustically. "Mayhap one of us will get a good night's sleep. At least no one will be expecting bloody sheets on the morrow."

"I am nae so hung over as that," he growled.

"Oh, I'm *certain* I'm relieved to hear it," Carys purred, heedless of the warning gleam in his eyes. Brody was likely right. Her husband's bad mood was probably more about his sore head than his marriage—though she rather doubted he'd have gotten roaringly drunk the night before if he hadn't been marrying her on the morrow.

She had to admit the thought irked. A lot.

"A woman has expectations, you know."

Birk's eyes narrowed. "Expectations?"

Carys folded her hands on the table and leaned forward, resting her breasts on the arc of her wrists, deepening the valley between them as they swelled above the gown's modest neckline. Birk's gaze dropped. An ironic smile twitched Carys's lips. Men were so predictable.

"Expectations of her wedding night," she said, drawing her words out, voice husky. Birk's attention wavered. Carys rose, abandoning her moderate display, and, placing the fingers of one hand on a heavily muscled shoulder, paced slowly to his other side. She drew her fingertips lightly across his back to the other shoulder and feathered them down his arm.

He twitched.

"I've been there before, as have you," she murmured, sending an appraising look up and down his body, deliberately baiting him, not knowing how to tame the wildness rising unexpectedly inside. "Terwyn was kind and considerate." She lifted a limpid gaze to Birk's. "Are you?"

Fire raged through Birk's veins, stoking his desire. He was irritated with his bout of over-indulgence the night before and its lingering results, but he was even less pleased his wife of fewer than two hours nagged him about it. What he'd meant as a salute to their marriage, a way to break the awkward silence between them, had rolled right into a nasty supposition he would be unable to consummate their marriage.

She must not have married much of a man before, if she believes a wee bit too much to drink will render me incapable. As blood pounded through his cock, smithies set up shop behind his eyes, reverberating agonizingly inside his skull. The meal he'd just eaten swirled uneasily in his stomach, but he manfully ignored the protest, rubbing his temples to ease the hammering.

Carys's touch lit his skin, sizzling across his shoulders and down one arm. He quivered with the effort to remain still, silent, wondering at the mood she'd taken. And where it would lead.

Damn her for comparing him with her dead husband! And twice damn her for forcing him to abandon his pledge to remain calm— Dugan had insisted 'twas the only way to soothe her ruffled feathers. His hackles rose.

Kind and considerate? In the face of her blatant challenge? His blood boiled.

"Nae," he growled, grabbing her arm in a vice-like grip and pulling her close. Her scent assaulted him in a delicate wave of lavender and spice. Her eyes blazed, dark and stormy. Fine blue lines pulsed in her neck and temples beneath translucent skin.

She would be the death of him.

He loosened his grip, knowing there would be finger marks on her arm when he peeled the gown from her body. "I willnae be compared to yer dead husband. I willnae be challenged on what I can or cannae do."

She did not shrink away, and once again he was reminded that this and no other woman would suit him.

"Where ye are concerned, I dinnae know why I cannae keep my temper. I am not known to be hack-handed around women. Blunt, mayhap, but not a brute."

"Then why did your first wife leave you?"

Her words struck with the subtlety of a stormy wave off the North Shore. No one ever dared ask him of the troubles between him and Rose. His clan had turned its head, likely believing the worst of him—and her. Carys only had to listen to the gossip certain to begin as soon as they arrived at MacLean Castle. Rose's loose proclivities were well known in that place.

"We dinnae suit," he gritted out.

"You have already stated you aren't remiss in your husbandly duties. And that you aren't a brute around women," Carys replied thoughtfully. "What else would drive a woman to leave her daughters behind?"

Birk stared at her in disbelieving silence. Her gaze showed interest, and she did not appear to taunt him. But he did not owe her an explanation. And damned if he'd show how much her question opened old wounds, scars barely covering the belief there was something within him lacking the ability to keep a wife, that he'd driven her away.

"She was a wee slip of a thing. I likely frightened her." He gave a dismissive wave of his hand.

"Then 'tis fortunate I am neither wee nor easily frightened," she retorted with a huff of disbelief.

Birk's gaze traveled across her face, noting the dark lashes that framed her eyes like the kohl his aunt had often used. Carys's nostrils flared slightly, a flutter that reminded him of a skittish mare. Silky black hair escaped from the braids framing her face and slid sensuously over her shoulder.

Birk's infirmities fled.

"*I* am, howbeit, a verra large man." He slipped a hand behind her, his fingers splaying across one green-clad buttock. His other palm cupped the back of her head, fingers tangling in her heavy mane.

"With verra large appetites." His mouth claimed hers in a kiss borne of the need to test her, to taste her, to seek some guidance of her response to him. He pulled her full length against him, curving her body into his, grinding his cock against her, groaning as the contact threatened to tear him apart.

Carys grabbed his leine in both fists and yanked it from his belt. Sliding her hands beneath the cloth, she raked her fingernails down his back. She pressed closer to him as though to reach him better and her tongue played furiously with his. Her teeth scored his lower lip, nipped painfully. Her fingers dug into the flesh of his back.

Caught unawares by her response, Birk shoved her backward over the table, dishes clattering as they slid across the surface. His forearms braced unsteadily on either side of her shoulders, cock nestled in the vee between her legs. He panted lightly as he struggled for some measure of control. A candle stick crashed sideways.

"Are we fightin' or lovin'? Cause I dinnae think well when my cock's this hard."

Something caught between anger and laughter rumbled from Carys's throat, and she rucked his leine up further, exposing his belly.

"I'm not certain," she admitted in a hoarse whisper.

"Do ye want me to stop?"

He ran a hand roughly over the swell of her breast, pleased with the hard peak that strained the cloth of her gown. Her skin flushed pale pink and she squirmed beneath him.

"No."

Chapter Seventeen

"Do ye want me to toss ye over my shoulder and carry ye to bed, or would ye rather I take ye on the table amid the supper plates?"

Carys's heart raced, her breathing deep and ragged, her mind slow to register the fact she lay on her back—the handle to a platter digging into her side and a spilled drink pooling beneath her ear—where anyone could interrupt them. She gathered her wits long enough to answer.

"How far is your bedroom?"

Birk chuckled, the sound resonating through her, fanning the passion raging through every inch of her body to new heights. He drew back and grabbed her hand, hauling her to her feet. Carys's muscles moved with the speed of winter-chilled honey, sweet, tantalizing—and entirely too slow.

With a grunt, he hoisted her over his shoulder and strode to the door, a hitch in his gait as he adjusted the swing of his sporran.

"Put me down!" Carys hissed, landing a well-aimed fist on one of his ears. He yelped and dropped her to her feet, sliding her the length of his hard body. His mouth met hers as her face drew level, crushing against her lips, bending her back over his arm. She answered his powerful kiss with moans of pleasure that spurred his hands to frantic exploration.

Her breasts tightened with an exquisite ache as she pressed them into his palms. She leaned against him, inhaling sharply as he rolled the hard peaks between his fingertips. He pushed her breasts upward, exposing their crests above the neck of her gown and bent over her, lavishing the skin with his mouth and tongue.

Carys countered by sliding one hand up his muscular thigh, fingers finding the warmth between his legs. His sac filled her palm and she squeezed gently.

He broke away, panting, sweat on his brow. He glanced about the room, then, grasping her hand again, dragged her to a door in the corner. Flinging it open to reveal a narrow passage of stairs winding upward, he pulled her behind him, her feet flying to keep up as he took the steps two at a time.

They burst into a large bedroom, walls covered in faded tapestries, a fire laid on the hearth. Birk kicked the door closed and drew his dirk.

Carys stared at him in surprise. He reached for her gown. She slapped his hand away.

"You destroy this dress and *you'll* answer to Elspeth on the morrow."

Birk grunted and shoved his blade beneath a pillow and quickly shed his clothing. With nimble fingers, she loosened the laces and pulled the gown over her head. She blinked to find Birk scarcely a hand's breadth away.

His desire for her thrust between them, standing bold from a nest of black hair. It bumped against her belly, demanding her surrender. She stared for a moment then lifted an eyebrow.

"I will not compare you to Terwyn again," she commented, a smile rising from purely feminine approval. She gently encircled his cock with her fingers, closing her fist about it. Hard and silky smooth, the heat of it scorched her palm. Her core melted in answering fervor. A moan escaped her lips. She wanted him inside her, wanted to burn in the flames he promised.

She tightened her grip, pleased with the groan wrung from his chest.

"If ye dinnae remove yer chemise, I cannae swear it will return to its owner in one piece."

His voice a rumble of barely leashed passion pushed her heart rate even higher. She scarcely knew this man yet he owned her. Body and soul, she was his to do with as he pleased. Everything about him was overwhelming, from his towering height to his enormously swollen cock, his raging self-confidence, and the passionate fire blazing from his eyes.

A voice in her head urged her to run, but an instinct older than time rumbled approval at her new mate. He was worthy of her, and law bound their union.

She pulled the fine shift over her head and sent it floating through the air with a flip of her wrist. Her hair swirled about her in a black curtain. Birk's chest heaved, muscled bands rippling burnished gold in the fire light. Thunder rumbled and lightning rent the sky. The scent of rain rode through the open window. Carys's skin fairly crackled with anticipation.

If she was his, then he was, by God's will, hers.

Birk caught the gleam in Carys's eyes as she leaned closer. A fresh surge of blood tightened his cock almost beyond endurance. He'd dallied with few women after Rose died, and they'd simpered before him, praising his attributes. A balm to his sense of inadequacy after finding his first wife hopping from one bed to another. An outward appearance only that did nothing to touch his scarred soul.

Carys met his nakedness boldly with her own, stirred him beyond arousal to a beast he did not recognize—and she did not back away. Her hand on his cock drove him mad, each finger as it shifted its grip sending bolt after bolt of desire straight through him, reverberating, building.

He growled a warning. A wedding night should woo the bride—Dugan had insisted. But his bride was no shrinking virgin, and her passion threatened to surpass his. He slipped his fingers between her thighs, finding her hot and wet. He swept her into his arms, carrying her the few feet to the bed. Releasing his cock, she laced her arms about his shoulders as he laid her amid the bed coverings. With a grunt of impatience, he seated himself between her legs and plunged deep.

Her gasp stopped him. He lay atop her, panting with the effort to remain still. His cock throbbed painfully, threatened to explode before he could complete the act.

She would be the death of him.

She inhaled deeply and wrapped her legs around his waist. With a hitch of her hips she pulled him deeper.

"Don't stop," she breathed. Her fingernails dug into his upper arms. She gripped him tighter, grinding herself against him.

Birk drew back, against the restraint of her legs, gasping at the feel of her just before he pulled free. His strokes intensified, unable to resist the frenzy of Carys's response. He hurtled over the edge, her passion meeting his.

The furor died away. His arms shook as if he'd just finished a day of heated battle and could scarcely lift his sword. He rolled to the side and pulled Carys against his chest, burying his nose in her scented hair. Between one breath and the next, he was asleep.

* * *

Carys woke to the unaccustomed feel of a soft bed beneath her. The fire glowed contentedly on the hearth, giving the room a faint red glow. She stretched, her muscles aching, but it was a glorious ache that brought a satisfied smile to her lips. She reached for the large bulk of warmth next to her, gratified to feel him swell beneath her questing hands. She went eagerly into his arms, seeking the place where they were equal, where they were one. Groaning as he filled her, meeting his urgency with ardor that quickly spiraled out of control, she exploded into a thousand particles of light.

Birk shouted, gripping her tight. He rode her to the end of their passion and lingered over her. He drew away as if reluctant to leave. She hooked her heels behind his knees, savoring the feel of him a moment longer.

"Ye are a rare lass," he murmured, settling next to her.

"I am nothing special," she replied. "What happens between us is rare."

He chuckled softly. "'Tis not every man who finds a virago in his bed."

"I admit this is beyond my experience as well. But this is not all there is to marriage."

"'Tis a sight better than I've had before," Birk declared, yawning mightily. He rolled to his back. "Our bargain is well-met. I am content."

A settling snore drifted from his pillow.

Carys considered smothering him with the down-filled square.

You are content? Pleasing you in bed is the extent of our relationship? She inhaled sharply, grinding the breath out between clenched teeth.

He bargained my life for an inspiring bed-partner. I suppose I should be grateful he included marriage in his proposal. She snorted. *The bed sport wouldn't have lasted long had he been less honorable. He sleeps so deeply I could rifle his rooms for loot, dress, and eat my fill before coming back to plunge his own dagger into his black heart.*

She flounced onto her side, presenting her back to him, and pounded her pillow into submission. A large hand lazily fondled the curve of her hip and passion flared anew. Steeling herself against its onslaught, she let soft tendrils of longing curl within. Birk patted her buttock as his breathing evened, and his hand slipped to the mattress.

* * *

Light streamed in through the window. Bleary-eyed, Birk stared at the tiny dust motes dancing on sunbeams. Memory jolted through him.

Saints' toes! What a night! His cock shot to attention, eager for more bed sport. He groped for his wife, encountering only cool, bare sheets. He sat up, scratching the back of his neck as he noted the empty bed, the fire untended on the hearth. A tray of bread and a mug sat upon a low table. He listened for sounds behind the screen in the corner. A bird chirped outside the window.

Damn! He wasn't ready to leave his bedchamber. He wanted his wife. In his bed. Beneath him as he pumped into her.

With a frustrated growl, he swung to his feet and snatched his leine from the floor. He dragged it over his head, shoving it past his erect cock. He splashed a bit of water from the ewer behind the screen over his face then did his best to hit the chamber pot.

Striding to the table, he drained the mug, wincing at the bland taste of watered ale. He ignored the bread and dragged a pair of trews over his hips, settling himself uncomfortably within the snug fit. His mood thoroughly soured, he pulled on his boots and stomped from the room.

Laughter drifted from the hall below. He stood at the railing and spied a cluster of people at the head table. His wife, in brilliant yellow wool, entertained the small group with a tale that brought rippling amusement to his ears.

My wife! She should be attending me! Not entertaining the rabble.

He clomped down the stairs, boots loud on the stone. Smoking green tendrils of jealous possessiveness wound through him, twisting his face into a scowl, further darkening his mood.

The little knot of people quickly dissolved at his approach. Carys remained in her seat, calmly eating from a platter of fruit, cheese, and oatcakes. She poured a stream of golden honey over the cakes. Meeting his gaze, she lifted a bannock to her mouth and took a bite, running her tongue over her lips to catch an errant drop.

His balls tightened as he remembered the ingenuity of her tongue the night before.

He grabbed a handful of oat cakes. "Couldn't find ye this morn," he remarked. "Ye're looking well."

"A mixed bag, is it? A complaint and a compliment in the same breath. I must have done something right."

"I wanted my wife. I got cold watered ale and stale bread."

"You slept late. I had better things to do than wait on you."

"Better things?" His eyes narrowed. "I remember ye were quite satisfied last night."

Carys glanced about from beneath her lowered brow and took a sip. "This is hardly the place to discuss private matters. Cool your heels, m'laird. 'Twill be evening again soon enough."

She rose and, collecting the tray, strolled from the room, gathering a trail of serving lasses and the interested gazes of several men-at-arms who lingered over their meal. Jealousy dug its barbed claws into his belly.

"She's already made friends," Dugan noted as he slid into the chair next to Birk. He set his mug and trencher on the bare wooden boards and dug into the steaming porritch.

"She's my wife!" Birk growled, burying his face in his mug.

Dugan looked up, startled. "Aye. Was that not the plan?" He shrugged. "A fair waste of time and effort if it wasnae."

"Exactly my plan," Birk retorted, taking another swallow of cider.

"Dinnae tell me ye mucked up yer wedding night," Dugan clucked, shaking his head.

"My wedding night was fine."

"*Fine*? Laddie, ye willnae please yer wife with *fine*."

"My wife is well pleased." Birk slammed his mug down, tired of Dugan's ribbing.

Dugan pointed a bannock at the kitchen doorway. "Aye. And already handling Cook with sweetness and tact, charming the serving lasses into a complete cleaning of the hall and upper chambers, and has yer weans eager to begin lessons in another hour or so." He shrugged. "Doesnae sound to me like a woman who cannae stay out of her husband's bed."

Birk rose to his feet, his chair's legs clattering on the flagstones. Catching sight of his daughters crossing the room, he unclenched his fist. Grabbing the pitcher of cider, he emptied its contents into Dugan's lap.

Chapter Eighteen

Carys stood in the kitchen doorway, ostensibly viewing the redesigned garden, when it was the fresh breeze from the sea she craved. The heated skin of her neck and cheeks slowly cooled, as did the racing beat of her heart.

Damn the man! He will not know how much I longed to run my fingers through his hair, press against him and demand he take me upstairs. She exhaled slowly. *I cannot let him know how much he affects me, for it feeds his overweening ego too much. He thinks to keep me only as a broodmare. Well, I desire children as well. At least the creating of them will be no hardship. It seems our marriage begins and ends in the bedchamber.*

Carys shook her head grimly. *I will likely have a pair of weans on my hip before the first two years are out.* She stepped to one side as a lad entered the kitchen, hefting a large woven basket laden with vegetables freshly picked from the garden. She surveyed the contents with a critical eye then smiled at the boy who gave her an anxious nod.

Whether my laird realizes it or not, he has married a woman well versed in running a castle such as this. I am capable of adding improvements he likely never thought of. A smile crossed her face. *Won't he be surprised?*

"M'lady."

Carys turned as she realized the voice addressed her. The cook, an ample woman with a pleasant face and a spotless white apron spread over her light woolen gown, wiped her hands on a towel at her sash. "We take our main meal at noon unless there is a banquet.

If this meets with yer approval, I have a moment to share the menus with ye."

"Everyone appears well fed," Carys said. "That schedule is one I am familiar with. I am certain your menus are impeccable, though I would like to confer with you."

Cook, obviously pleased with Carys's response, drew a ring of keys from her sash.

"What shall I call you?" Carys asked.

"I answer to Cook most of the time." Her brisk manner gave way to a small smile. "No one ever asks, but me Christian name is Ava."

"Well met, Ava. Let us see what you say grace over." Carys raised a hand suggesting Ava lead the way.

Carys spent the next hour on a tour of the kitchen and store rooms, pleased at the cleanliness yet puzzled by the low quantities of food.

"Laird MacLean only ordered the rebuilding of Dairborrodal Castle less than a year ago. 'Tis not his main residence, and unlikely to house more than a handful of people and men-at-arms when he isnae here," Cook confided. "But dinnae fash. We'll have everything as it should be by fall, with a fair amount from the gardens and hunters put by to carry us through winter."

"I see," Carys replied slowly. "Where is his regular residence, then? And do you know how long he plans to remain here?"

Cook gave her a startled look. "I know ye married hastily—we all know." She waved a hand vaguely about the room. She pursed her lips, brows lowering. "And we are every one of us loyal to the laird. I willnae gossip, but men dinnae always tell the women what they need to know. I will tell ye I have been asked to prepare foodstuffs for a return journey to MacLean Castle on the morrow."

Carys forced a slight smile. "Thank you, Ava. I do not indulge in gossip and appreciate your loyalty. By the way, which direction to MacLean Castle?" she asked innocently.

"Why, south along the coast a half-day no more, m'lady," Ava answered.

"My thanks again. I will see to Laird MacLean's and the girls' preparations."

Cook nodded approvingly and returned to her duties.

Carys crossed the hall and entered the stairwell at a thoughtful pace. She'd won over the most important member of the staff at Dairborrodal Castle, but the woman apparently was not part of the staff where the family would be living.

MacLean Castle? A niggle of memory took shape. A bustling dock with a large keep overlooking the bay, and a flourishing village between. Captain Ferguson had left them to barter with the merchants on the shoreline while he spent the afternoon meeting with the laird.

Laird MacLean, of course. Her new husband.

So, he was no mere chief of this rubble—albeit a rubble under obvious reconstruction—and a few scattered crofts beyond, but an affluent laird in charge of a busy shipping port off the Strait of Mull. An important and strategic holding for commerce and in times of war. And vast lands beyond. Gossip had been free among the sailors, though she'd been so tired she'd paid little heed. What had she missed?

Travel to MacLean Castle on the morrow? The knowledge still rankled. He'd promised to take her to see Tully settled with Lorna and Fergal whilst they sought his mam and siblings, and to fetch the rest of her belongings from the forest. Either he'd forgotten his promise—unlikely—or was not a man of his word—and she was not willing to believe that. Whatever his reasoning, she wouldn't be put off any longer.

Adjusting once again to her altered life, she climbed the stairs and entered the girls' room. She planted a cheerful smile on her face when she wanted to wring the truth from her husband and discover why he planned on breaking his word to her about Tully's welfare. She spent half an hour or so encouraging Eislyn's penmanship and promising her an hour after supper to teach her how to wield a knife. Carys then gave Abria a hug and petted Tegan, assuring Margaret of the evening hours alone—or however she chose to spend them.

Farther down the hall, she opened the door to Birk's bedroom— now hers as well. She spied the trews and tunic she'd worn two days' previous—had it only been two days?—cleaned and mended, hanging from a peg. Making a mental note to thank the maids for their care, Carys quickly exchanged her kirtle and surcoat for her worn clothes, more familiar than expensive finery after two years as a soldier in Llywelyn's army and the last few months aboard ship and living off the land.

She slipped her feet into her boots, grateful she'd not discarded them as she awaited a new pair. Her thick woolen cowl and sturdy leather bracers followed. Flipping open the lid to the chest at the foot of the bed, she grabbed her belt and sword then slung her bow and quiver across one shoulder. Daggers slipped into each boot and one at her belt.

Finding a bay gelding in the stable with long legs and bright eyes, Carys quickly tossed a blanket and saddle over his back and slid a bridle over his head. She dashed through the gate beneath the watchful eyes of two soldiers on the wall, hearing no voices calling to her to halt. A weight she'd not realized she carried fell away as she breathed deeply of the midday air. Within minutes, she was enveloped by the shadows of the forest.

Birk could not contain his good humor—restored after a bout of sword practice in the field behind the bailey. He pulled his leine over his head and scratched an armpit, then draped the sweat-soaked shirt over a fence rail. He shoved his head beneath the water in a rain barrel, surfacing with a shake of his head to good-naturedly accept the ribbing from Dugan and the men.

"Ye dinnae get a prick from her dirk during the night?"

Birk spread his arms wide and turned to show his unmarred torso and arms. "I'm the one who did the pricking, lads."

Brody shook his head. "I'd be afeard to take a lass like her to bed. Too likely to wake up missing parts."

"Not if ye use them right, eh, Dugan?"

"Yer parts or the lass's?"

Birk pounded Dugan's shoulder. "Och, she's a bonnie one. No doubt about it," he grinned, lounging back on a bench, his legs sprawled before him. "I'll need a wee nap to keep up with her wild ways."

"She fell for yer charms, did she?" Brody laughed as he limped up to the water barrel, performing a like ritual and slinging fine droplets from his shaggy mane. "We noticed ye were quite the laggard this morn."

"His lady wasnae so affected as our laird. He dinnae limp down the stairs until nearly mid-morn. She was already up and seeing to her duties." Dugan elbowed Birk. "Mayhap we should take it easy on ye, auld man."

"She'll be back in my bed by sundown," Birk boasted. "I've a thing or two to show her."

"That's good to know, Laird. Considering she was up afore ye, mayhap she wasnae impressed with what ye showed her last night," Dugan suggested.

Chuckles rose to laughter. Birk scowled as Dugan's lighthearted words unintentionally drew blood.

Iain approached, gripping the pommel of his sword in its sheath. He jerked his chin over his shoulder at a guard lingering on the edge of the yard. "I dinnae think she'll be back by sundown if she's the lass Alain saw ride through the gates a bit ago."

Birk roused, leaned forward, eyes narrowed. "What?"

Alain took a hesitant step forward. "A woman riding a bay horse, m'laird," he offered.

"Are ye certain 'twas my wife?" Birk demanded.

Iain raised an eyebrow. "There are precious few women at Dairborrodal, as ye know. And fewer with the audacity to steal a horse and ride alone into the forest."

"She's a braw lass, m'laird," Oran chimed in. "And 'tis nae stealin' now that she's Lady MacLean."

The men grinned.

Birk stormed to his feet. "Where the hell was she headed?"

Alain stood frozen. "The forest."

"Bah!" Birk kicked over his bench and snatched his belt and scabbard from the hook on the wall behind him. He slid the blade a few inches out then slammed it back into the sheath and buckled it about his hips. "I want four riders with me. Find yer horses."

Dugan, Iain, Brody and Oran hastily refastened their weapons and tossed the ends of their plaides over their shoulders, leaving their leines to dry on the boards. They called their reluctant horses from the pasture, grabbing saddles and headstalls from stable lads who rushed to do their bidding.

Birk swung onto Bran's back as the beast snatched a final mouthful of grass. His men mounted and filed in behind as they galloped through the gate and rode into the forest.

Before one of the men thought to ask where to look for the errant bride, he reined Bran toward the north in the direction of Fergal's cottage.

Dugan's suggestion that Carys wasn't as impressed with their wedding night as he was twisted in his gut. Why else would she leave the day after he granted her freedom? No matter what she thought, she belonged to him now. He'd either convince her to return with him or he'd tie her up and sling her over a horse himself.

Chapter Nineteen

Carys slowed her horse to a stop near the edge of the beach, not wanting to risk a broken leg on the scattered rocks. She tied his reins to a low branch and proceeded to the cave on foot, careful to watch for signs of intruders, hoping Tully had remembered to get his belongings and remain with Fergal once Dewr returned.

She hoped the dog had made it.

Crouching behind a large boulder, she surveyed the area near the waterfall, the rush of water drowning out any audible signs of people, knowing they were not likely to hear her, either. After several minutes spent scanning the area, she was satisfied no one had discovered her and Tully's home, and she slipped behind the curtain of water. Tully's pot lay on its side near the back of the cave, evidence of his turmoil when she did not return from her hunt. His small cache of belongings was gone, as was the collection of tools they had brought from the ship.

She'd had little in the way of possessions that she didn't carry with her, but she rolled up the weathered blanket she used for sleeping, tucked it beneath her arm, and gathered her javelins. She left Tully's pot, deciding it was too bulky to bother with and, hopefully, not needed. With a cautious tread, she exited the cave.

Once again, she peered up and down the beach. Determining she was still alone, she paced off the required steps behind a large boulder sitting askance beneath a weather-beaten tree. Kneeling, she used her oldest dagger to scrape away the rocky soil until she encountered the chest of coins. Beset with memories, she opened the top and peered at the contents, her brother's ring sitting amid the silver and gold coins like a glowing ember, linked on the chain with her own wedding band and the ring she'd taken from the English soldier.

She quickly strung the necklace over her head, tucking the rings beneath her cowl. Removing two leather bags from her belt, she dumped the coins inside and drew the drawstrings tight. She stood, gripping the heavy bags tightly as she made her way back to the patiently waiting horse, leaving the empty chest beneath the tree.

Carys tied the bags with leather straps behind her saddle, wrapping the bundle with the blanket so it would pass silent and unremarked. Mounting her horse, she reined him onto the faint trail through the woods to Fergal's and Lorna's cottage.

Dewr's warning bark rent the air on her approach. Tully and Gorrie looked up from splitting kindling for the hearth. Dressed as she was, it didn't take either lad more than an instant to recognize her. They tossed their tools to the ground and ran toward her as she rode into the yard.

"Carys!" they shouted, clambering about her like excited puppies as she drew the horse to a halt. Dewr joined their antics, dancing in circles, equally glad to see her.

Her heart swelled as tears sprang into her eyes. She hadn't realized how much she'd missed Tully, how much she'd worried over him. Alighting to the ground, she gave both lads a tight hug and a clout to the shoulder.

"We knew ye'd come back!" Gorrie declared, face beaming.

Carys grabbed her horse's reins beneath the bit and ruffled Dewr's ears as the dog bounded about her feet. "You did?" she teased. "I only knew it myself a couple of hours ago. How'd you know?"

Both boys fell silent, their gaze drifting to the house where Lorna and Fergal stood, Birk and Dugan on either side.

To the left of the house, beneath a tree, five horses waited, tails swishing at the occasional fly. Three men squatted in the shade a few feet away, watching silently.

Carys laid a hand on Tully's shoulder. "Be a good lad and fetch your belongings."

"Are we leaving?" the lad asked, a puzzled look on his face.

"Aye," Carys replied. "We're going to help you find your way home."

* * *

Birk stared at his wife as she rode into the yard. The lads and dog greeted her excitedly, leaping about as she dismounted her horse. Her gaze cut to the house and he knew he'd been spotted. He stepped from the doorway and crossed the yard.

"A little bird told me ye left the castle unattended—and without permission."

Carys tossed her head. "You should question your little birds. There should have been an entire host of soldiers on my heels." She cast a look at the three men waiting in the shade. "Last time you sent men after me, it took six to bring me in."

Furious with her flippant attitude, he grabbed her arm—and found the tip of her dirk at his belly. He deflected the point with a quick turn to the side, presenting his sword scabbard and thick belt instead of his less protected belly.

"Put the knife away, Carys," he murmured, his voice low and threatening. "I willnae have ye scarring my leathers."

"If a scratched scabbard is all that bothers you, mayhap I should point out 'tis unlikely we've conceived a child as yet. Even with as much effort as you put into your marital duties last night, I wouldn't gamble on it so soon."

Birk eyed her dirk again, his stomach clenching to note the wicked gleam of the slender blade and the ease with which it could slip past his guard if he didn't control the situation—and his temper. He took a step back, drawing a deep breath.

"Why did ye leave the castle?" he demanded. He dropped her arm, satisfied when she slid the dirk into a sheath at her belt.

"When did you plan on fetching Tully?" she countered. "Sometime along our journey *south* to MacLean Castle? We are a bit too far *north* to make that practical."

"I would have seen to the lad," he growled. "I gave ye my word."

"I have taken care of it and retrieved some belongings of mine I did not wish to leave behind. And I thought mayhap I'd encounter a deer along the way. Seems 'tis no longer poaching to feed my friends now I've become a respectable member of Clan MacLean. There was no need to come after me."

"Ye dinnae have permission to leave," Birk pursued stubbornly. He knew they were the center of rapt attention, yet he could not help himself. The blow to his gut to learn his wife of less than a day had left the castle—left him—had been too much. He would not believe her faithless as Rose had been, yet the old, deep hurt would not let it go.

"I was unaware I needed your permission. 'Twas not in the marriage contract. I did read it, if you'll recall," Carys replied archly. "Where did you think I'd gone?"

Birk's lips thinned, refusing to speak to her of his dead wife. Yet she must have guessed, for her eyes narrowed and her chin tilted.

"I gave you my vow—only yesterday. I do not know how things are done in Scotland, but in Wales, we honor our promises."

The barb struck home. He'd forgotten to bring Tully to the castle. It wasn't a promise deliberately broken. He was known as a man of his word. No one could dispute that. And yet, in short order, his new wife had reduced him to a man who appeared to make false promises—and who allowed past memories to cloud his judgment. He reined in his anger. He would not be accused of being a brute on top of not keeping his word.

Tully slipped to Carys's side, sending Birk a wary, unfriendly look. He tugged Carys's sleeve. "We dinnae have to go with him, do we, Carys?" He stepped closer as if reluctant for Birk to hear him, though he did not lower his voice.

"We could live here with Lorna 'n Fergal. And Gorrie. I like Gorrie."

Birk's ire rose. The one thing that had kept him from losing all sense of proportion was the knowledge that if Carys had left him in truth, at least she had not left in the arms of a lover. Tully was obviously someone she cared for, and the idea she'd been willing to set her marriage aside to help someone else reminded him all too much of his dead wife.

Help someone else. The realization drew him up short. That was certainly unlike Rose. Wasn't that one of the reason's he'd married Carys? Through rumor and his own knowledge, Carys Wen filia Pedr was a woman who unselfishly helped others. Selfishness was something he abhorred. He needed time in the saddle to think this through before he made more of a muck of the situation. He could play the gracious laird and lay the angry husband aside—for now.

"Things are a bit different, Tully," she told the lad. "I go with Laird MacLean. You, however, have a choice. You are free to remain here with Lorna and Fergal and Gorrie, or you can come with me to MacLean Castle. If you wish, we will help you find your mam. The decision is yours."

Tully fidgeted, clearly uneasy with making a decision. "What will happen to Dewr?" He glanced about, looking for the dog. She lay a few feet away, ears alert, intent on the people in the doorway.

"I'm certain Laird MacLean will allow her to come with you," Carys replied, sending Birk a questioning look.

"I apologize," Birk said, pitching his voice low with contrition, catching the startled look in Carys's eyes. "I havenae introduced myself, though I met ye once aboard the *Seabhag*. I am Birk, the MacLean chieftain. I knew yer da and was very sad to hear of the shipwreck."

"Da died," Tully said. Sorrow flashed across his face, but quickly cleared. "Ye know Gorrie's brother!" He turned adoring eyes on Dugan.

Dugan shrugged lightly, clearly confused to find himself a hero in Tully's eyes.

"I've told Tully lots about ye," Gorrie admitted as he stepped up to the group. "I will be a warrior like ye one day."

Dugan gave his younger brother a smile. "Do as da asks and build those muscles, aye?"

"I promised Carys I'd see to continuing yer training—while ye help yer ma and da." Birk added his provision, hoping to soften the hard, accusing look on Carys's face. The grin on Gorrie's face sealed the gamble. Carys's lips tilted slightly and Birk hid his sigh of relief.

"When my wife assures me ye are ready, I will send for ye."

And I will remember this promise.

Fergal and Lorna clutched each other, concern—or possibly dismay—on their faces. They were clearly approaching an age where they could not care for the croft on their own. Laird MacLean had taken one son and now promised to take the other as well.

"I will see about finding a lad to help Gorrie with the chores," he said. "If he proves acceptable, mayhap he could make his permanent home here."

It was a compromise, and one that didn't entirely meet with the couple's approval. With two healthy lads of his own, Fergal had little love for giving his life's work into another's hands. It was plain Lorna already grieved the loss of her sons.

"'Twill be some time before Gorrie is ready to take up soldiering," Carys soothed. "He may yet meet a lass and decide to raise sheep instead of a sword." She rumpled Gorrie's shock of hair as his face flamed.

"Aye." Lorna allowed a small smile. "Ye cannae predict what's in a man's heart."

Carys helped Tully stow his meager belongings behind the saddle on Brody's horse. Keeping the two leather bags hidden beneath her blanket, she draped them, one on either side, across her horse's withers. She mounted and helped Tully up behind her with Birk's assistance. The lad gripped her about the waist within a tight hold, his knees and legs pressing hard against the horse's flanks, causing him to prance nervously.

"Loosen your grip, Tully," Carys murmured. "He'll settle when he realizes you aren't about to fall off."

Tully eased his hold slightly, only to tighten it once again when Carys urged the horse forward.

"'Tis much like being on a boat. You know how different being on a boat is from being on land, aye? Sit comfortably and let the horse rock beneath you."

Alternately soothing the horse then Tully, Carys finally managed to get the lad settled. The ride to Dairborrodal Castle was a long one, but a gait faster than a walk was beyond Tully's skills.

"I understand ye've charmed quite a few of the servants at the castle," Birk remarked.

Carys raised an eyebrow. "I do not believe vexing them is a good way to run a household."

Birk was silent a moment. "Where did you learn to run a household of this size?"

Carys made a deprecating sound. "You know so little of me, yet I know your cook's name is Ava, and your stable master likes his whisky a bit too much." She cast a look over her shoulder. "He was fast asleep when I saddled my horse."

Making a mental note to replace the stable master, Birk attempted a different approach. "Would ye tell me of yer family?"

Carys shrugged. "We were caught up in Prince Llywelyn's fight with King Edward. There is nothing left for me there." She turned her head aside, and Birk allowed her a moment to compose herself. As a gambit to get his new wife to share her memories, he'd failed badly.

She cast a look his way. "I also know you have a sweet spot for your girls. You may appear tough and difficult to get along with, but they are your pride and joy."

"Difficult?" He glanced at her in surprise. "I am the epitome of tact and graciousness when 'tis warranted. I admit I have a short supply of patience, however." He tried for a long-suffering look. She quirked one eyebrow.

"I have much to do and dinnae like having my time wasted," he protested.

"Aye," she replied softly. "A man with all of Clan MacLean to see to, as well as a busy shipping business and port, has little time to indulge in political posturing. You are a blunt man, Birk MacLean. You know what you want, and you get it. But you keep your schemes close. What do you have in mind when you marry an unknown woman from a distant country, one whom you could have as easily pardoned? And why did you choose to hide your identity?"

Birk eyed her steadily, returning her thoughtful gaze.

"I could ask the same of ye, lass. I remember the name ye gave the priest. Carys Wen, filia Pedr. I know this means yer da's name was Peter. What does Wen mean?"

A flush lightly stained her cheeks. "*Wen* means *fair* in Cymraeg. Much like your word *gael*."

"Where did ye learn speak Scots Gaelic?" he asked, believing a Welsh woman far more likely to be familiar with English.

"Umm," she replied vaguely. "We lived near the coast. There were people of many countries in the village. I pick up languages rather easily."

"Good to know." He eyed her thoughtfully, noting the blue-black sheen to her hair, her pale skin that glowed with delicate health—even when he knew there was nothing delicate about her.

"Carys the Fair?" He grinned as her lips thinned, daring him to tease her. "I suspect an ode has been written to ye, has it not?"

She slipped him a haughty look. "And the best minstrels Cymru has to offer have sung it in the highest courts. You'll not hear better any place in Scotland."

Birk turned thoughtful, for he had an uneasy suspicion her reply was only partly in jest.

Chapter Twenty

The hall erupted in chaos as Carys and Birk stepped inside the long room. Eislyn raced across the floor and flung herself dramatically at Carys.

"Ye left and dinnae tell us!" she wailed, gripping Carys about the knees. Tegan's yips of protest added to the din.

Carys silenced the pup with a snap of her fingers and lowered the bags of coins to the floor, covering them with her blanket. She glanced at the distraught girl, then to her sister, who hung back, eyes wide as she peered from Margaret's side. Kneeling, Carys gathered Eislyn in her arms, motioning Abria close. After a tiny hesitation, Abria joined them for a reassuring hug before Carys sat them at a nearby table, nudging the bags and blanket beneath the bench with a push of her toe.

"All is well, *fy merched*," Carys soothed, drawing her palm over Abria's head and smoothing strands of hair from Eislyn's face. "I went to make certain a friend of mine was well, and the ride back took much longer than expected. He has been a brother to me these past few months."

She turned and motioned to Tully, who hovered in the doorway, rocking from one foot to the other in an agitated manner. He brightened and, at Birk's prompt, hurried to Carys's side.

"Eislyn, Abria, I'd like you to meet Tully." She linked the boy's arm through hers. "Tully, these are Laird MacLean's daughters— now my daughters as well."

He clenched his fists and ducked his head, giving the girls a slight nod.

Eislyn tilted her head. "Can he talk? Is he truly yer brother? Why is his hair so red?"

"He and I became family because we worked together when we had no one else." Carys squeezed Tully's arm. "I am happy to call him my brother." She tousled his head. "I do not know why his hair is so red."

"Can he be *my* brother? I think his hair is nice." Eislyn asked, sliding from her seat to approach Tully. She gently touched his sleeve. "I like my sister, but I'd like to have a brother, too."

Tully flinched, but did not draw back, and he stopped swaying to stare at Eislyn. She stood barely taller than his waist, a slim contrast to Tully's bulky build.

"That is entirely up to you and Tully," Carys replied. "Tully's mam and family live far from here, and our task is to find them and see he gets home. I do not know how long he will be with us."

"He can still be our brother while he's here," Eislyn declared. "Mayhap we'll have a baby brother by the time he leaves."

Carys's eyes flew open wide and she caught Birk's mocking grin. She struggled to form a reply but was saved when Dewr slipped between Tully and Eislyn, shoving her nose into the girl's hand. Tegan yipped excitedly, her canine territory invaded by another dog. The corgi's stumpy tail wagged furiously. Eislyn jumped, her startled look turning to one of pleased surprise.

She glanced at Tully. "Is she yers?"

At Tully's slow nod, she threw her arms about the dog's neck and buried her face in her ruff.

"Dewr," he said. "Her name's Dewr."

"Dewr means *courageous* in Welsh," Carys supplied, thankful for the distraction. "She is a very brave dog."

Eislyn turned to her sister. "Look, Abria. A new dog *and* a new brother!"

Abria reached a cautious hand to Dewr's thick coat. The dog's entire body wiggled with pleasure.

Carys shook her head. "As it is too late to be discussing the family tree, mayhap you can take Tully to the kitchen and introduce him to Cook. If there are any boiled sweets in her cupboard, ask if she could spare one for each of you. Then bring Tully back and we'll see him settled in for the night."

All three children perked up at the enticement of the coveted treats. Catching the whiff of anticipation, the two dogs flanked the trio as they hurried from the room. With an apologetic smile, Carys motioned Margaret to follow the children.

"I'm very sorry . . .." she began as the young woman passed.

Margaret shook her head and waved as she left the room. Carys breathed a sigh of relief.

"I did not know how the girls would react. Tully usually makes friends without much difficulty, though it hasn't been an easy time for him of late. He seemed anxious, but I believe he will be fine."

"I'm not certain how ye accomplished it, but ye have them eating from yer hand," Birk said, a brow raised.

"They're eating from Cook's hand," Carys corrected. "'Twas generous of Eislyn to name him brother."

Birk shrugged. "She'd hoped Abria would be a brother, though she accepted her from the moment she was born. A good thing—" He broke off, face flushed, a scowl twisting his lips downward.

Carys glanced about, but their presence no longer seemed cause for concern, and the room was mostly empty of servants and listening ears.

"Why? What happened? I have already caused the girls harm by absenting myself today. I should not have left the castle without telling them. I need to know what other behaviors to avoid so they can grow accustomed to me and not fret over things so much."

Birk rubbed the back of his neck, clearly unwilling to continue the conversation. "I dinnae wish to speak of it, for it tweaks both my ire and my pride. Howbeit, if ye believe it would help my lasses adjust to ye and our new life, I will soon tell ye what I can." His frown deepened. "Dinnae press me on it."

It was a start. And more than Carys had expected. She offered a soft smile to indicate her appreciation and changed the subject.

"Where would you prefer Tully bed down until we can make firm plans?"

Birk perched one hip on the edge of the table. "Would he be more comfortable in a room on the family's floor, or in the barracks with Dugan?"

"Why don't we give him the choice? Having Dewr with him will help."

"Ye dinnae suppose he expects to sleep near ye?" His brows plowed together and Carys hid a laugh at his obvious consternation. A tingle of awareness blossomed low in her belly and a sigh slipped out before she could stop it. She bit her lip.

In an instant, the people lingering in the hall did not matter. Birk's blood thickened and he shifted his position on the table. He wanted his wife, wanted to hold her in his arms, feel her skin against his.

"'Tis time for the bairns to find their beds," he rasped, his throat dry.

"I told Margaret she could have the evening to herself," Carys said, a breathy, apologetic tone to her voice. "'Tis difficult to watch the girls without help of some sort."

"Ye thought to stay with them this night?" Birk held his rising temper in check. They *were* his children, after all, and he should appreciate his wife's concern. But he wanted Carys in *his* bed tonight—and every night.

"Nae. Only for the evening—which we missed." She tilted her head. "If 'tis any help, I had not planned on being gone so long, nor had I intended to abandon our bed."

"Nae, it doesnae help," he growled, tempering his response with a sigh of resignation.

"'Twill take longer to put the girls to bed," Carys mused. "They are that excited. But 'tis important they get a good night's sleep and prepare for travel on the morrow."

Birk gave her a blank stare. "Travel?"

Carys frowned. "Do we not leave for MacLean Castle in the morn?"

King Edward's balls in a vice! He'd forgotten. Only this morning he'd been anxious to announce his marriage to the elder council and bask in their consternation when they realized he'd married a penniless woman with no family from Wales, on the run from Edward's army. He rather relished regaling them with the qualities his new wife possessed. Generosity, ferocity, selflessness—and beauty. He did not desire her for her connections or what monies or land she might bring him and cared not that she had none. He wanted her. And now he found he did not want to share her.

"We will stay here. For a time." He cleared his throat. "We must see to Tully."

Carys raised a brow. "You did not seem to find him particularly important earlier today." She stepped closer. "What has changed?"

"Ye ask a lot of questions," he muttered, not expecting to deflect her curiosity, but he gave a half-hearted try.

She laughed. "How else shall I discover things? You are quite close-mouthed when it comes to information, *Laird MacLean*."

So, she hadn't forgiven him that bit of neglected information. And yet, it puzzled him that it would appear to disagree with her to be a laird's wife. All the women he had dealings with would have given their front teeth to be married to him. Their eyes fixed on his money, his power, the status his wife would have. They appeared before him in their finery, posing prettily in fine wools and silks, hoping for satins, brocades, and velvet. They glittered with modest jewels about their necks and upon their fingers, knowing of the treasures his aunt had brought with her from the Holy Land. Pigeon's blood rubies the size of a robin's egg, pearls set in delicate gold filigree, emerald necklaces weighing as much as a small sword. The MacLean treasury was vast—and well known.

Carys wore the leather trews and tattered shirt in which he'd first seen her. A heavy woolen cowl, once dyed black and now faded to a mottled gray, graced her neck. Leather bracers adorned her arms, scuffed yet oiled and cared for. Her fingers were bare, not even a wedding band from her former husband. Had she traded it for coin when hunger had urged practicality over sentiment? He realized he'd not placed his own ring on her finger, an oversight he needed to address. The world needed to understand she was now Lady MacLean and belonged to him.

Black hair swept back from her forehead, revealing skin so pale it shimmered. Nothing about her shouted wealth—or avarice. To look at her, she'd seen much hardship—and endured.

Yet, there was a grace about her, something about the way she boldly met his gaze that did not bespeak life as a crofter. Her skills with weapons was something no peasant woman, no matter how pressed by war, would know.

Carys Wen filia Pedr. Who are ye?

She sighed. "I suppose you have your reasons and will tell me in time. At the present, I am tired and wish a bath. Would you see to the children for half an hour?"

Guilt at dodging her questions forced him to agree. Cook would soon send the weans from her kitchen and with Margaret away, someone would have to mind them until bedtime. Birk eyed the lengthening shadows falling through the narrow windows and sighed.

"I'd rather assist ye but see the merit in not allowing the bairns to run about unattended. Mayhap ye will scrub my back once they are abed?"

Carys flashed a smile full of shy challenge that intrigued him. Could it be for all the passion she shared with him last night, she experienced something different with him? He sent her a wolfish grin.

"Shall I teach ye something new tonight?"

Her cheeks flamed and Birk's loins tightened. Her gaze remained steady, but he read mischief, not embarrassment, in the sparkle of her eyes.

"You are an intriguing man, Laird MacLean," she answered, her tone lightly mocking. "So very willing to assist a young woman such as myself."

"Not *any* young woman," he growled, exchanging his teasing for indignation. "My *wife*."

"Aye. I am your wife." She stepped close and kissed his brow. "Though I fear I am less than appealing in my current state—"

He grabbed her upper arms and dragged her against his chest, covering her mouth with his, silencing her words. She tensed, then, with that magic that beguiled him almost into incoherence, softened and sagged into his arms, molding herself against him. Her breasts, nearly hidden beneath tunic and cowl, pressed against his chest. Her slender hips fitted between his thighs, grinding against his cock.

Blood leapt hot through his veins. He wrapped his arms about her and broke the kiss to nuzzle her neck. "Yer *current state* is tying me in knots. I dinnae know what to do except hold ye and take ye to bed and not let ye go. I dinnae like sharing ye."

"I think 'tis best to continue this in private," she sighed, tilting her head, exposing more of her neck to his lips. "Once the girls are abed and Tully is settled, and . . .."

Birk nipped her neck with his lips, pushing the cowl aside to breathe her scent.

"Oh!" She breathed out, a whisper of sound. Whisky did not intoxicate him half as much. He tugged at her tunic—and she stepped back, gently forcing his hands down.

"My presence is enough of a shock to the people. Let us not give them something more to gossip over."

Birk's breath came harsh as he fought past the fog and became aware of the darkening room around him, the quiet footsteps marking the passage of people seeking their beds. As if to punctuate his need for awareness, Eislyn swept into the room like a small storm.

"Da! Cook knew Tully's da! She cried over Tully and gave him an extra treat!" She continued her prattle as she lunged across Birk's thighs, clambering into his hastily arranged lap. Abria, Tully, and the dogs followed, piling about Birk's feet.

Carys drew a few steps away, gathering her blanket and two small bags from beneath the bench. She hefted her belongings as if they were unexpectedly heavy and Birk wondered if she'd fall asleep in the tub. She waggled her eyebrows.

Her laughter floated back to him as she drifted toward the stairs.

"Och, sweets and excitement right before bedtime. Whatever was I thinking?"

Chapter Twenty One

Carys startled as a hand rested heavily on her shoulder. Strong and broad, the palm stroked across her back, fingers digging gently into muscles lax with sleep. There was no accompanying bid for her to rise, to face a day of toil and fear, of daily struggles and sorrow. The demand was deeper, triggering a familiar warmth in her belly. Her breath deepened as she fought her way through to wakefulness.

Her eyes flicked open, registering not the walls of the cave or the snow-flocked trees of Wales, but new landmarks she was growing to learn. Heavy curtains draped the soft bed beneath her, open to sunlight on the hearth from the unshuttered window, and the scent of fresh bread.

Her stomach rumbled.

"I expected a different hunger." Birk chuckled in her ear. "But I can accommodate either." He moved from his reclined position next to her, muscles rippling across his shoulders and back. The heat in Carys flamed to life.

She gripped his upper arm and pulled him back to the mattress. He fell across her, arms braced on either side to keep from landing atop her, and grinned.

"M'lady has a different plan?"

His voice, silky smooth and seductive, spiked her pulse. She twined a fingertip in the crisp hairs of his chest.

"If you've no objection," she murmured, tracing the line down his belly, drawing a finger past his waist.

Birk sucked in a rumbling breath and lowered his mouth to hers. "No objection at all."

* * *

Birk had considered his plan to remain at Dairborrodal Castle a sound one. He could answer most questions which arose at Morvern from this distant seat. Keeping his private life separate from that of his other obligations had become important to him. It appeared the privacy would not last.

He scowled at the leather bag stuffed with missives. Concerns, requests, items requiring his signature. Council news. Council requests. Shipping manifests and invoices.

They would have to return home soon. No later than the end of the sennight.

He leaned back in his chair, rolling the quill between his thumb and forefinger, idly noting the tiny drops of ink spattering the blotter.

A serving lass appeared through the partially open door and silently placed a flagon of ale on his desk. She turned to leave the room.

"Find Dugan for me, will ye, lass?" Birk murmured, scarcely giving her a glance. Rising to his feet, he moved to the open window where the occasional thud—sounds of knife practice to his trained ear—punctuated the normal sounds of the castle. His gaze met the slender form of his wife, clad once again in leggings and tunic, next to a diminutive replica of herself—right down to the dark hair and leggings. Carys mimed the action of throwing a dagger, blade balanced between thumb and first two fingers. Eislyn mimicked her perfectly. Birk grinned.

Late afternoon sun strayed through gathering clouds promising an evening shower, glowing warmly on Carys's leggings, emphasizing the curve of her bottom. Birk's grin slid into a surge of lust for his wife. His attention broke reluctantly as Dugan entered the room and took the chair in front of his desk.

"I see the messenger delivered his packet." Dugan nodded at the bag. "Ye dinnae slit his throat, did ye? Shall I dispose of the body?"

"I dinnae kill the lad," Birk groused, leaving the much more interesting sight outside his window for the issue at hand. Nighttime approached and he could wait. Probably.

"Though it crossed my mind," he added. "I liked Dairborrodal when it was a refuge from Rose and her harping. I like it even better now and dinnae wish to return to Morvern."

"But duty recalls ye?"

"Aye. There are disputes to settle and a ship to have refitted, another to be unloaded and sent on its way." He stuck the quill in its pot and leaned back in his chair.

"'Twill be no hardship to see the *Már* is ready. She was taking on supplies last week when ye changed yer mind about going back to Morvern." Dugan rose. "'Twill be good to be home. I think yer ma will like yer new wife."

Birk sent him a sour look and Dugan laughed. "Ye cannae keep yer hands off her! I dinnae know how to describe what is between the two of ye, but 'tis nae the shyness of newlyweds. 'Tis a fierceness, and we have all noted it."

Satisfaction softened Birk's scowl. "Nae, she isnae shy. And I willnae apologize for touching my wife."

Dugan shrugged. "I respect yer choice. At least she hasnae turned ye into a blithering idiot. Or gutted ye in yer sleep."

Birk narrowed his eyes, unsure if Dugan jested or not. He could certainly think of a few times when the need to take Carys to bed had overridden any other judgement. Howbeit, he did not think he could complain, and, surprisingly, neither had she.

"Nae. I still draw breath and am not yet an idiot."

A shout from the walls silenced the sounds in the bailey, only to explode in a flurry of movement and bellowed commands. Birk's chair clattered to the floor where it spun about once before it stilled. He was at the window in a trice, his heart racing. Carys and Eislyn stood motionless, the child pulled tight against Carys's body, her arm across Eislyn's chest, locking her in a protective position. The line of her body tensed, her gaze fixed on the massive gates as they swung slowly closed. Birk followed her line of sight and saw an arrow driven into the ground, still quivering from impact.

An instant later, a cloud of whistling iron-tipped rain poured over the wall.

Shoving Dugan aside, Birk raced from the room. The doorway to the keep was filled with people hurrying inside, but he fought against the screaming surge and met Carys, Eislyn tucked against her body, as they joined the mad dash to safety. He paused for a heartbeat, his gaze sweeping the pair for injury. Finding none, he pivoted about and plunged up the stairwell to his chamber.

He quickly donned a padded tunic—aketon—and tightened the ties across his shoulder, chest, and waist. Stripping away his sword belt, he added a leather hauberk, then repositioned his belt over all.

He pounded back down the stairs only moments later. Dugan paced the yard, a large shield his only concession to the stream of arrows that continued to bombard the castle.

Arrows bristled in the turf like the widespread fan of a capercaillie's tail. A scattered few splayed across the cobblestoned area before the door of the keep. Birk pulled one from the ground, inspecting both fletch and tip. The short, straight feathers on the end told him they'd been crafted specifically for distance and speed, not accuracy. Perfect for shooting over castle walls.

The men on the ramparts returned fire to the as yet unknown enemy beyond the gates. Birk took the stairs to the outer wall two at a time and found Iain on the parapet closest to the gate.

"Who are they?" Birk rumbled, sidling past a soldier refitting his bow.

"I am not certain," Iain replied. "I havenae seen more than a line of archers. They step from the shelter of the forest, fire, then vanish. My men have dispatched several." He nodded to shapes dimly outlined by the fading sun.

"I dinnae want them to disappear into the forest. There is no sign of a siege tower. I will take twenty men and scour the area."

"Laird? I'm not certain we can protect ye . . .."

Rage exploded beneath Birk's skin. He clenched his fists. Iain was right. It was likely they would ride into either a volley of arrows or a similar trap. He recalled the terror on Eislyn's face.

"I willnae calmly accept their attack, nor will I allow them to escape. Gather the arrows from the yard and send them back to the bastards. At this distance, accuracy isnae expected. Just keep them away from the gate."

His shouted commands rose above the heightened commotion. Men raced for the stables. Others put their shoulders into opening the gates, the sound of metal twisting beneath the heavy wood grating and shrill.

Birk dug his heels into Bran's sides. The warhorse squealed and leapt forward, twenty horses with armored riders on his heels. A cry of challenge rose from the men on the wall, tribute to those who rode out to meet their enemy. Arrows sailed overhead, giving Birk and his men some protection as they charged toward the trees nearly two furlongs distant. The shafts fell short of the woods, but it was enough to force the enemy into hiding.

The arrows ceased. With a shout, Birk pulled Bran to a halt, rolling the stallion back onto his massive haunches. Around him, his soldiers mirrored the maneuver, forming a seething mass of horseflesh—and chaos.

A dozen archers rose from behind boulders and slender trees. Birk sent his horse bounding back up the road, luring the enemy from their hiding spots. Three nocked their arrows and Birk released his soldiers from their apparent retreat to charge the exposed enemy.

The rout was over in a matter of minutes. Two of Birk's men strode the field despite injuries—one a shoulder wound, the other with a broken shaft in his thigh. The wounds did not appear life-threatening, and the pain would register once the battle fervor cooled. All but four of Birk's men now scoured the surrounding forest for any others who had so far escaped.

He counted eight dead among the enemy. Two would quickly add to the number, and another sat against a boulder, arm clasped tight to his side to stem the bright red blood oozing from a gash that parted flesh shoulder to wrist.

A slender form knelt beside the wounded man. Fire and ice roiled through Birk.

Carys.

He was at her side in three angry strides and came within an enraged breath of hauling her to her feet and demanding to know what the hell she was doing on the battlefield. She glanced up and rose, tearing a strip from the bottom edge of her tunic.

"I would recommend cutting his throat," his wife said, her jerky movements betraying her wrath. Birk's fury shifted into reluctant admiration. "But he may be useful to us." She quickly bound the man's arm then jerked him to his feet. Birk whistled up a soldier and sent him back to the castle with the prisoner. Carys swung up onto her horse's back, arching a brow at Birk. Rather than reply to her silent question, he left Oran in charge and rode with Carys to the castle.

* * *

Birk recognized the prisoner's dialect. His ma spoke in a similar manner when she was agitated, slipping back into her Norse roots.

"Why were ye here?" Birk asked as the healer laid out needle and thread on a small table next to the wooden chair. The prisoner, face pale with blood loss and pain, shifted uneasily on the hard seat. He favored Birk with a glower.

"Raiding," he spat.

"*Raiding* is what ye did in my village a fortnight ago," Birk returned, hoping to prod the man into admitting or denying the two groups were the same. "This action today had no aim other than to harry my people with the hopes of causing damage."

A strained grimace slashed the man's face as the healer plunged her needle into ripped flesh. "Reparation."

Birk studied him, eyes narrowed. *So, he doesnae deny being part of the raid.* "Explain."

Sweat broke out on the man's brow and he lost his arrogance as the needle plunged into his arm again. "Ye support the Scottish king."

Isn't that interesting? The Treaty of Perth has been in effect these past seventeen years and King Alexander's youngest daughter married King Eric of Norway, though she died this past April in childbirth. Are there still pockets of resentment on the Isles? Those who still pay homage to Norway?

"And ye killed Colin Dubh." The prisoner's voice rasped low, but his accusation was clear. They'd been here to exact revenge.

'Tis time to take my wife and daughters to MacLean Castle. None can harm them there. His gaze sought Carys. She stood to one side, mostly in the shadows, intent on their prisoner. Her eyes still burned with anger and he recalled the way she'd protected Eislyn with her body, carrying her to safety. Her fingers tapped the hilt of the dagger at her belt as though eager to put an end to the

interrogation. A large dark splash marred the front of her tunic, though from her behavior, Birk did not suspect the blood was hers. She stepped forward.

"*I* killed Colin Dubh."

Shouts erupted in the room. Carys stood firm, holding the startled gaze of the man before her. He scrambled to an upright position, his hand reaching for a weapon that was no longer at his side. Carys stumbled as Birk shoved her aside, away from the wounded man's reach. Furious with his interference, she shoved back. Catching him off-guard, he faltered.

"I will handle this." He growled low, for her ears only.

"Have I not earned the right to question him?"

"'Tis man's work." He glared at her, attempted to stare her into submission.

"So was killing this blackguard's leader, but I killed him and two others without a man's assistance," she shot back.

Gripping her sword's hilt, shoving it deep into its sheath lest she bury it in someone's chest, Carys stormed from the room, ignoring Birk's bark of command to return.

I will not be cosseted. I will protect what is mine, and his opinion of what is proper can go hang!

She choked back a sob. *I am responsible for the attack by the pirates. They came after me. 'Twas me they sought to punish.*

Anguish overrode her better instincts, keeping her from answering Birk's orders.

Death follows ye.

But I will fight for what is mine. My children. My family. My honor.

Footsteps pounded the stone behind her as she grabbed the doorframe and whirled about, landing nearly level with Birk's startled face. He stepped to one side, clearing the doorway. His glower returned, eyes dark, red spots of rage on his high cheek bones.

"Do ye have any idea . . .?"

"I have many ideas," she snarled.

"Ye are my wife, and I willnae . . .."

"*Ye willnae*?" she mocked. "I have had my fill of what ye *will* and *will not* allow." She advanced, forcing him into the yard. Stunned looks followed them, and she straightened abruptly. "Follow me."

Her march to the area between the stables and the high wall surrounding the castle settled her anger, forcing her into a place of quiet focus, her fury on full simmer. She faced Birk, hands flexing over the sword still at her belt.

He towered over her, using his height in an attempt to intimidate her. "A woman shouldnae be responsible for leading a rout of pirates."

She tossed her head, undaunted. "And yet, here I am. I have routed my share of them, and care not if ye do not like it."

Birk growled. "Nae. I dinnae."

"What did ye think ye'd get when ye married me, Birk MacLean? A warrior woman who would become a submissive fool and turned to needlework once I said my vows?" She shook her head at his foolishness. "I thought ye possessed a keener wit than that. Mayhap I err."

"I expect ye to do as ye're told—as any good soldier!" he shouted.

Carys's laugh rolled bitterly. "What do ye fear? That I will be injured and cheat ye of an heir? 'Tis easily remedied. Another wife shouldn't be so difficult to find." She shrugged. "Or, mayhap ye are uncomfortable around a woman who speaks her mind—and has the skills to back up her words?"

"Ye are fearless—and foolish. A woman cannae fight against a man and win."

Carys stepped slowly to the side, loosening her shoulders as she circled him. "Have I not proven myself? Were Colin Dubh and his followers not evidence enough?"

Birk frowned, clearly not pleased with the memory she stirred.

"Or the pirates who attacked the *Seabhag*? Mayhap the thieves at port when Hywel and I first signed aboard Captain Ferguson's ship? Or Longshanks' soldiers who invaded my country and killed my family?" She continued her steps, watching him move, angling first forward then back, forcing him to avoid her advance.

Birk braced his feet in the dirt. "Ye cannae win against me. Put away yer anger and come inside."

"Ye doubt me? Then meet me with steel."

She slipped her sword from its sheath, her heart rate increasing to fighting speed at the *shush* of steel against leather. Birk's scowl deepened. He flexed his hands then drew his sword, the reluctant lines of his body sliding forward into battle readiness.

Carys eyed him carefully, mindful of the length of his arms, the stretch of his legs that increased his reach. She was not quite as tall as he, but slim and quick. His muscles made him a daunting adversary, but fighting was not always about power.

Her steps light, she continued her slow circling, weaving her hands gently back and forth in front of her body. Birk moved only enough to remain facing her, conserving his strength, giving nothing away.

"Fight me, then," he commanded, drawing his guard close. Carys did not fall for his ruse but kept her distance. He lunged forward, aiming for the sleeve of her leather tunic. She flicked her arm back, avoiding his half-hearted attack. She would teach him to never underestimate her again.

Swinging her sword, she rushed him, nicking his arm and shoulder before she spun about, dancing lightly out of his reach. Blood welled to the surface of each wound and surprise lit his eyes.

"Do not pamper me," she warned.

Birk crossed the ground between them in three ground-eating strides, forcing her back with a flurry of blows. She parried neatly, expending only the energy needed to avoid his attack, never meeting his blows directly. She noted he presented the flat of his sword only. He still feared harming her, and he did not appear to take her earlier attack seriously.

Her breath came harsher, but her anger was not sated. How dare he belittle her? How dare he insist she conform to his whims? If he'd wished a proper lady for a wife, he should have married elsewhere. She'd show him exactly what kind of woman he'd earned by his duplicity.

Birk took a step back, his guard relaxed, as if his attack should have proved his point. Carys realized several men had followed them to the yard, and now stood back, watching. Several had their arms crossed over their chests, disapproval etched on their faces. Others appeared speculative. She would teach them all a lesson this day about the grit of a Welsh woman.

"Ye yield so soon, m'lord? Surely, those wounds are no more than scratches," she taunted.

Birk's gaze hardened as he assumed a defensive crouch.

Carys used stuttering steps, changing the rhythm of her attacks each time, forcing Birk to block her strikes. However, he refused to counter attack. Did he think her anger to be as a gale at sea? Swift and blustery, but soon over? She drew her dagger, a blade almost as long as her forearm. Birk's only response was a tightening of his jaw.

"I concede ye have skills . . . for a woman. Cease this and let us discuss our differences in the privacy of our chamber."

Several men snickered at Birk's suggestion. Carys ground her teeth at the bawdy proposition, intentional or not. Birk's neck flushed. Carys ignored his hack-handed attempt at peace and drove straight forward for an attack. Standing his ground, Birk met her predictably by using his strength to meet her blade, then lunged forward in an attempt to off-balance her. Anticipating such a move from her hulk of a husband, Carys shuffled to the right, giving way to his shove. Not expecting her move to the side, Birk overstepped, stumbling once before catching himself.

His misstep provided all the space she needed. With the dagger in her left hand, she slammed the pommel into the back of his knee, driving his knee to the hardpacked soil. She then whirled about, placing the blade of the sword in her right hand on his shoulder, the edge against his neck.

"Do ye yield, Laird MacLean?"

Birk attempted to rise. Carys placed her dagger on his other shoulder, the smaller blade mirroring the placement of her short sword. This time, the edge drew a bead of blood as his movement broke the skin. Birk released a snort of surprise.

"I yield," he ground out.

Carys thought to make him say it louder, but teaching him not to treat her as if she were delicate was one thing, humiliating him in front of his men was another.

Soft metal clinked. Carys glanced up as a scowling Scotsman handed Brody a handful of coins. Brody caught her gaze and grinned.

Chapter Twenty Two

The *Már* slid through the waves, the rhythmic sway as familiar to Carys as the beat of her heart. The boards creaked beneath her feet and the sail snapped overhead. Sea-spray laden breezes whipped her hair. Music as faint as the thrum of a distant rain rose to her ears, the words a familiar ditty Captain Ferguson regularly sang. Hywel's face appeared on the periphery of her sight, smiling as though he approved of her return to the sea.

She turned instinctively to speak to him, but the vision vanished, leaving nothing more than a pang in her heart.

The girls tossed a rag ball with Tully. Dewr watched from a perch atop a hatch door, a pained look on her face as if undecided which required her attention more—the girls who shrieked and raced about the deck, or the puppy whose stubby legs carried her with awkward grace over the wooden planks.

Birk stepped beside Carys, leaning his forearms against the polished rail. She sent him a sidelong glance, curious how he would respond to her after the previous day's fight—and the night they'd spent in heated, intimate *discussion*. Her skin warmed in remembrance, tingled to anticipate his touch. She slowly brought her pulse under control.

Birk tapped his fingertips together. "How do ye like the lass?" He gave the ship a nod.

"She's a sturdy ship," Carys replied, the impersonal subject welcome. "And just the right size for a trip along the coast."

"Aye. I had her refitted with a large cabin and rigs for awnings for the weans." He straightened, patting the rail as if it were alive. "She's carried her share of cargo, but I have larger ships. This ship has good bones and will live out her years plying the coast from

Morvern to Dairborrodal and mayhap a few other small trips with family."

"Eislyn says *már* is the Norn word for seagull."

"Aye. Eislyn helped me rename her after I retired her as a cargo ship."

"Tell me about your family."

Birk stared into the horizon but did not seem displeased with her request. "I am the youngest of five children. My father married my mother a couple of years after his first wife died. My elder half-brother Donal and the twins, who died young, would have been many years older than I. Gillian, the youngest of his children by his first wife—who may or may not be at MacLean Castle when we arrive—is nearly eight years my senior."

"Does she often reside with you?"

"Nae. She has her own bairns and husband. She came to a council meeting several months ago and remained a bit after deciding travel in her delicate condition was unwise. I am happy to say she delivered a healthy lass a few days before I left for Dairborrodal. 'Tis likely her husband took them both home, though I daresay not before Hanna gave permission."

"Is Hanna your healer?" A healer held in much respect was a boon.

The right side of Birk's lips quirked upward. "Nae. She is my ma."

Carys pondered this, eyebrows drawn together in concern. A mother by marriage who lived with them and carried much influence? It did not seem a happy combination. She fingered her leggings—not the attire she'd wish for a first meeting with her mother by marriage, but she preferred practicality over formality when pirates were a distinct possibility during the voyage.

Birk brushed a strand of hair from her cheek, tucking it behind her ear where it lingered a moment before whipping free again. "Dinnae fash over my ma. She will like ye. In fact, ye remind me much of her. Strong, fair, kind. She lost her family in a raid by Scots and met my da as she fled capture. Someday I'll tell ye the story."

The anxiety over meeting Birk's ma faded slightly. "I would like that."

The backs of his fingers trailed down her cheek, lowering her unease further, thickening her blood, centering her pulse to a deep awareness of his touch. His palms drifted down the sides of her tunic, kept mostly out of sight beneath the folds of the cloak she'd donned against the brisk sea wind.

She leaned against him, turning to help shield them from the gaze of others, closing her eyes as the heat of him seeped through the cloth, lighting a fire in her veins. His mouth touched hers, capturing the moan that drifted from deep inside.

Birk nibbled her lips, cupping her cheeks in his palms. "I will take ye on a trip—just the two of us—and make love to ye as the waves rock beneath us." With a slow wink, he strode away to join the men at the helm.

Carys shuddered with need, wondering at the sensations he evoked in her. *Is there a difference between loving and wanting? He's naught like Terwyn . . .* She hesitated. *Do I wish him to be?*

Salt-laden air swept over her, refreshing, new. *Nae. I cannae say I completely trust him, but I cannae say I regret my decision to marry him—and the problems we have appear to be mostly behind us. Settling in as a laird's wife isn't what I envisioned for my life, but simple enough. I have not been a princess of Cymru since Hywel and I fled the massacre at Orewin Bridge. And I do not wish to be that person ever again.*

* * *

Dugan beckoned Birk near. "We are being watched."

With a leap made effortless with years of practice, Birk swung up onto the aftcastle, a steadying hand on the rail. Shielding his eyes from the sun, he peered over the horizon. After a moment, the form of a sailing vessel appeared.

"Twelve, maybe fifteen benches," Dugan noted. "That will mean thirty to forty men. And the mast is midship. The helmsman can steer fore or aft. 'Tis a Norse vessel."

Birk grunted. "They arenae close enough for worry yet. Keep an eye on them. We have another two hours or so before we reach Morvern. If they mean to attack, they will have to move soon."

Dugan nodded. "Aye. I'll put an extra pair of eyes to watching."

Birk leapt back to the deck. "I'll warn Carys."

She looked up when he approached, her expression hooded. Eislyn and Tully raced about, dodging the indulgent men on board and the few chests lashed to deck cleats. Abria waited patiently at Carys's feet, playing with Tegan who appeared on the verge of settling into a nap.

Leaning against the rail, he turned his back to Abria to lessen the chance she'd overhear. "A ship follows at the horizon."

Carys moved her gaze from him to the open water, the only indication she understood.

"Twenty-four oars?"

Birk wasn't certain if her words were statement or question, though she had better sight than he if she could make out the number of oars from this distance.

"Possibly, though I havenae counted. 'Tis a ship built for speed."

Carys's skin blanched and she shifted as though she'd received a blow.

"'Tis me they seek," she murmured, hand white-knuckled on the rail.

"Dinnae fash," he drawled, using his words to pull her back from whatever panicked her. "We will sort them out. Again. 'Tis likely they willnae come closer." He placed a palm over her hand, but she snatched away.

"You do not understand." She glanced wildly about, her gaze landing on Tully and Eislyn, and Abria sprawled trustingly at her feet. "Death follows me." Her voice rasped low. "I have brought harm to you and the children."

Birk eyed her askance. What could possibly have startled her? It was clear to him the man they'd captured a day earlier had no idea Carys had been involved in Colin's death. What else stalked his wife?

"Walk with me, Carys." His command brooked no refusal, and Carys's hesitation was slight. With a nod she appeared to calm and followed him to a deserted spot along the rail.

"Tell me what haunts ye."

This time he saw the struggle in the terse line of her shoulders, the rapid breaths that rose and fell beneath her cloak. Several long moments passed before she sighed deeply and spoke.

"'Tis naught but words an old woman spoke to me some months past. Pay no attention to my ramblings." Red spots rose on her cheeks, and had Birk not just witnessed her alarm, he would have dismissed the flush as a product of the brisk wind.

"This auld woman has a bit more hold over ye than I'd like. I wish to hear more."

She turned away, eyes again on the horizon, though whether she sought the ship there or a distant recollection, he couldn't say.

"The day Hywel and I left Cymru, an old woman approached me. She was gnarled and half-blind. We have much respect for our elders and I was compelled to listen."

Birk mustered as much patience as possible as Carys wrestled with the memory. He edged closer, bumping her shoulder with the length of his arm, giving her a bit of his warmth. The touch seemed to sooth her somewhat and she leaned against him as if her burden was too much to bear alone.

"She told me death stalks me. I asked how to avoid this, and she said it did not matter, though if I left Cymru that day, my death would move to some distant future." She tilted her head back and stared into the distance.

"The battle at Orewin Bridge was but a couple of days past, and I suggested this was what she sensed on me, but she insisted that was not true."

She turned haunted eyes on Birk. "Everyone around me has died since that time. The men on the *Seabhag*," her voice dropped to a whisper. "Hywel."

How to prove her brother's death was not her fault? He stiffened. As easy as proving Rose's death wasn't his fault.

Carys edged away. She'd misread him. He slipped a palm against the small of her back, gently holding her in place. Her body tensed but she stilled.

"Their deaths werenae yer fault, Carys Wen," he rumbled. "Death stalks us all and enters our lives when we dinnae wish it. Ye have protected far more than ye have killed."

"I do not wish to bring harm to you or the girls."

"Yer path brought ye to us for a reason—and I dinnae think 'tis for harm. I know ye care for the girls, and know ye are a formidable force against pirates." He stared down his nose. "Is this not true? Or was the beating ye gave me yesterday a whim of luck?"

She relaxed beneath his hand, then motioned toward the trailing ship. "Have Dugan ready the oars. The ship draws near."

She would have taken an oar, but the men seemed appalled when she moved toward a bench. Perhaps it was better if she remained topside. She herded Eislyn—ignoring her protests—and Abria into the small cabin with Tegan who'd roused with yips and barks amid the grim excitement.

Tully followed along, completely unaware of Carys's concerns.

"Carys can fight pirates!" he raved, causing Eislyn's eyes to widen. "I's seen her! She set their ship aflame—big flames that burned up their whole ship!" He swung his hands wide in a sweeping gesture. Abria giggled nervously.

"She shot their whisky," he confided. "With a big flaming arrow! I seen it light up—whoosh! Da said she sent them poxy rats to argue with Saint Peter." He grinned.

Carys rolled her eyes and hastily changed the subject. Hoping to keep Tully from potential danger yet give him a purpose, she extracted a promise he'd protect his new sisters and left him and Dewr in the cabin as well, pretending she did not see the slightly open door through which concerned faces peered. She'd ensure they closed it when necessary.

She joined Birk at the rail. One hand rested on the hilt of his sword, pushing his cloak aside. He met her gaze then nodded at the ship that appeared to have gained on them.

"She pulls less draft than the *Már*. I dinnae expect her to manage to get close enough to attempt to board, but they may think to fire a few shots in our direction."

Carys peered at the ship, its long, slender lines with high bow boldly stating its Norse heritage. "It skims the water," she remarked, appreciation for the ship overriding her fear for the children.

"A *Snekkar* or snake-ship. Almost flat-bottomed." Birk frowned. "And verra fast." He glanced over his shoulder toward the cabin. His frown deepened.

"But unstable," Carys noted.

"Aye. But the waters in the strait arenae as rough as open water."

"How long until we sight Morvern?" Carys asked.

Birk adjusted his gaze to the sky. "We should sight the harbor within the hour."

"They risk much plying the waters so close."

"Aye. But we carry much they desire."

Carys's heart rate sped. "I . . .."

Birk sent her a hard stare. "Ye arenae the only passenger aboard worth ransom."

Or worth killing. Cold fingers swept up her spine. The children—Tully's boast of protection notwithstanding—were completely helpless. And would make good hostages.

She pulled her attention from those things she could not change to the image of the ship drawing ever closer. A row of brightly colored shields ranged along the top of the rail, protecting the oarsmen from attack. Tension crackled along the planks of the *Már*. An eerie quiet reflected the anticipation of battle. The sails snapped overhead and water crashed against the prow. Oars dipped almost silently into the depths before pulling the ship forward, shedding the scent of brine as they raced above the waves for another bite at the sea. The deck planks rocked beneath Carys's feet.

A metal shriek stuttered as the wheel cranking the ballista mounted on the aftcastle tightened another notch. A seagull shrieked overhead.

A shout from above nearly sent Carys over the rail. She glanced up to see the lad on the mast pointing excitedly off their starboard bow. Following the line of his arm, she squinted against the glare of the sun. A second ship, built much like the *Már* only bigger, pricked the horizon.

"The *Alacrity*!" Excitement swept the deck. Apprehension drained from Carys. Whether by accident or design, help was at hand. The pirates would not face two ships at once.

She swept her gaze westerly. The *Snekkar* slowed its approach. Within moments, the gap between it and the *Már* increased noticeably. Moments later the *Snekkar* slipped from sight.

* * *

MacLean Castle loomed on the horizon, perched atop a cliff as both a beacon and sign of strength, as the *Már* eased into port. The village of Morvern lay between them, busy and full of vigor. Birk, immersed in conversation about the pirates, left the disembarkment of the children to Carys.

She checked the cart arranged for the girls—puppy snuggled between them—and then helped Tully climb into the back of the conveyance, feet trailing off the edge, a happy smile on his face. A weather-worn Scotsman took up the reins.

Carys mounted the horse held for her with Dewr standing alongside. Eislyn and Abria, impatient for their noon meal and on the verge of exhaustion after a full morning of shipboard excitement, fidgeted and whimpered. Birk showed no evidence he was ready to leave. As Carys took stock of the children, safely ashore and ready for the last short leg of their journey, relief swept over her, leaving a hollow spot where tension had coiled like a viper. Her muscles quivered, released from their strain.

Eislyn shrieked. Carys sighed.

"We'll go on without him," she said, giving the girls a bright look. "I doubt he'll be long, but I'm hungry. Aren't you?"

Like magic, the girls' whines became happy chatter. Carys put her heels to her horse's sides and set aside her lingering worries about meeting Birk's ma and the people of MacLean Castle. A dozen mounted soldiers hurried to catch up.

They wound through the village and approached the castle gates. Her stomach pitched and dropped as though still aboard ship. She frowned. She did not want to be nervous to meet Birk's ma, but her confidence waned as they approached the formidable castle. She smoothed a hand over her hair, noting the strands that had pulled loose from her braid, victim of the brisk sea air—and Birk's clever fingers.

Damn him. 'Tis too easy to allow him to distract me. Coupling—and an heir—is all he wants from me. 'Twill be all he gets. A pang of regret bubbled inside.

She glanced at the cart rattling its way over the cobblestones. All three children gripped the wooden sides, but none appeared discomfited by the bumpy ride. Dewr darted ahead through the crowd, then returned to the cart as if to check on her charges, her efforts ensuring she'd cover at least three times the distance before they reached the castle.

Carys smiled. *I have a family again.* Her heart rose in her throat, threatening to choke her, and she swallowed back the reminder of what she could have lost that day. She turned her attention to the fortress looming far larger at the end of the road than she'd imagined.

Laird and wealthy merchant? Very wealthy and for many generations if she'd any guess. A shiver slid beneath her skin. Such a man could draw the attention of kings. At least Edward Longshanks had not turned his acquisitive eye toward Scotland. Yet.

The girls' excitement rose in shrill shrieks and giggles as they approached the massive gates. They passed through the barbican, a stone tunnel so thick torches were required to light the way. Carys was further startled to discover the gates in the curtain wall were still a fair distance from the keep. The sweep of the yard included many buildings, some, like the smithy, instantly recognizable, others less so. Magnificent horses, very different from the ponies she was accustomed to, grazed in a paddock beyond a low stone building with a slate roof. The stable.

Abria half-stood in the little cart. She cried out when Eislyn pulled her back to her seat. The corgi pup yipped. Carys drew a deep breath. She could scarcely scold the girls for being excited to be home.

The double doors of the keep opened, and a tall woman, hair pulled neatly back beneath a long white cloth, appeared on the top step. The cart rumbled to a halt and Abria and Eislyn rose, impatiently awaiting help. Carys dismounted, and the man driving the wagon handed the girls down to her. Abria hopped from foot to foot, snatching her puppy from the man's grip. Eislyn beckoned them to follow.

Carys walked at Abria's side, a hand on her shoulder, her other tucked in Eislyn's as the child pulled her forward. At the bottom of the steps the girls tore free and rushed to the top, wrapping their arms about the woman's legs.

"Amma!" Eislyn shrieked.

The woman met Carys's gaze, her expression neither welcoming nor forbidding.

"Welcome to MacLean Castle, Baron MacLean's home. You must be my granddaughters' new nurse."

Chapter Twenty Three

A swirl of disbelief, anger, and frustration pulled at Carys. *Baron? His children's nurse? What other surprises await?* Her temper simmered, threatening to boil over. *If this doesn't drop me from a cauldron into a fire, I do not know what does.*

Words Birk's ma would likely not wish to hear about her son almost left Carys's lips, but Eislyn leapt to her defense.

"Amma! She isnae our nurse. We have a new ma!" She beamed at Carys. "Her name is Carys, and she knows Cymraeg."

Abria released her squirming puppy. Tegan sat at her feet, tongue lolling, round rump wiggling against the stone.

The woman stilled, the expression on her face wiped away for the moment it took to compose herself. "A new wife *and* a new puppy?" she murmured. A smile flirted with her lips, but something, perhaps uncertainty, seemed to temper her response. Her gaze slid up Carys from leggings to cowl to bedraggled braid, and Carys managed not to squirm.

"I apologize," she said, inclining her head toward Carys. "Birk did not inform us he'd married." Something flickered in her eyes—amusement? Anger? "My name is Hanna, my lady, and I am the *eldhúsfífl's* mother. On behalf of Clan MacLean, I bid ye welcome home."

Home? What a kind thing for Hanna to say. Tension eased in Carys's chest and she decided not to ask for a translation for *eldhúsfífl*. At least not with the children present. She returned the woman's slight nod. "I am pleased to meet ye. I am simply Carys."

Hanna arched a brow. "Ye are a baroness now, Lady MacLean, but I will be happy to call ye Carys. Did my son not explain his holdings to ye?"

"I thought he was a gaoler," Carys drawled, allowing her tone to show what she thought of Birk's deception.

Dewr bounded up, her bark interrupting the conversation. Tully dragged a chest to the foot of the steps and dropped it with a thud to the ground. He grinned broadly, looking from his new sisters to the woman at the door. Carys wrapped her arm about his shoulders possessively.

"This is Tully. 'Tis a long story, but he is as a brother to me, and the girls have adopted him temporarily. We are searching for his family."

"My da died," Tully stated matter-of-factly.

"Welcome to my . . . *our* home," Hanna said. She stroked a hand over the girls' heads. "Let us go inside. There is food waiting, and then, I think, a nap. I wish to know more about your new ma."

Abria slipped to Carys's side. "I like her."

Hanna paled and Carys caught her breath as the older woman's mouth dropped and she took a staggering step. A hand flew to her throat and she swayed like a ship's mast in a gentle swell. After a moment, Hanna broke her gaze from Abria and fixed an astonished stare on Carys.

"Oh, aye," she whispered, her voice raspy with shock. "I wish to know much more about ye."

* * *

Birk gazed beyond the dock, but the *Alacrity* was beyond his sight. Were the pirates bold—or vengeful—enough to attack the larger ship? He snorted. Let them try. The *Alacrity* was well protected and took pride in the ballistas mounted both fore and aft. The pirates' galley was too unstable to risk ramming tactics, and the *Alacrity* would take little harm. He sent a silent blessing for her fortuitous appearance that morn and safe travel beyond.

He returned his attention to Dugan and Iain who would send patrols.

"Have we heard from any clansmen? Word of attacks or even unexplained thefts? Any mention of sightings?"

A chill swept through him to think what could have happened had the pirates timed their approach even a little sooner. He recalled the agony of Carys's fear that she'd brought the attack on them for her actions against Colin Dubh. Rage roared through him. By God's teeth, he'd see the pirates routed one way or another.

"Nae." Dugan shrugged. "Mayhap a missing ewe or calf. Who's to say 'twas pirates, a wolf, or simply a beast yet to be accounted for?"

Birk ground his teeth. "I willnae wait for them to attack my people," he growled. "We must find their lair."

The men waited quietly as Birk drew a deep breath then settled a calmer line to his jaw.

"We will find them and put an end to this nonsense. Whatever pockets of resentment still exist in the Isles, I will have it settled—if need be, by the sword."

"The king is tolerant of those remaining who dinnae care for the change in rule," Iain pointed out.

Birk snapped his head around. "Tolerance be damned! I willnae subject my people or my family to these predations for one more day! They have crossed the line and will suffer the consequences."

Dugan and Iain nodded. Birk knew he set them a nigh impossible task. There were many islands and inlets more than able to hide the renegades, not to mention hiding in broad daylight among people who paid tribute to Scotland whilst harboring grudges against the Scottish king. He sent each man a hard stare. Impossible or not, he would have it done.

He glanced up, seeking Carys and the children across the pier. They were gone. For a heartbeat, he scanned the water beyond the dock, but a cart, three children, their driver and a horse couldn't have fallen in without creating a *stramash* of some sort. His gaze flew along the road through the village to the gates of MacLean Castle. The road wove intentionally back and forth, not allowing an enemy a straight path to the fortress. From the dock, he could not see through the village. But he had no doubt where Carys had gone.

Shite! His careful plan to introduce Carys to the clan—and his mother—had fallen apart. He mounted Bran, retrieved from the makeshift stall aboard the *Már* and kicked him into a slow canter, hooves clattering on the wooden planks before reaching the packed dirt of the road into the village. Ten mounted soldiers fell in behind him. He slowed as they reached the cobblestone street packed with people, then urged his horse faster as they approached the castle gates. Small carts and foot travelers gave way before him, closing behind his men-at-arms like water flowing around a large boulder.

He spied his mother before the keep's doors, one hand on Eislyn's head, the other at her throat. Abria and Carys stood at the foot of the steps.

His gut clenched.

He drew his horse to a halt a few feet away, tossing the reins to a stable lad who scurried across the yard. Battling down his concern, he reached Carys's side and placed a hand on her shoulder. She stiffened. Abria glanced up and held out her arms. Birk scooped her up.

"My Lord *Baron*." Carys's greeting slid like cold steel between his ribs. "Your mother has a meal awaiting us. Shall we go in? The children are hungry."

Without lingering for his answer, she swept up the steps, Tully on her heels. She nodded to Hanna who sent Birk a wide-eyed gaze that settled on Abria. Birk patted his daughter's back and followed the others inside.

A cheer went up from a group of soldiers gathered at one end of a row of tables. Servants paused, glancing at the door. A few joined the huzzahs while others doubled their industry. Abria squirmed to the floor, joining her sister as they bolted for the head table. Carys seated them and Tully, hands in their laps as they awaited permission to eat, bottoms bouncing eagerly in their chairs.

Hanna sat, waving Birk to the table Carys calmly took her seat to Hanna's right, leaving the large chair—the lord's chair—*his* chair—empty. Talk slid to an awkward halt in the room as all eyes turned to Carys who'd claimed Lady MacLean's seat as though her right. A speculative buzz swept the crowd.

"Please be seated, Birk," Hanna chided, her voice clear. "I wish to get to know your lovely wife better, and our meal is getting cold."

His eyes narrowed. They'd not been five minutes ashore and Carys had already drawn Hanna to her side. He trod forcefully across the boards to the table and yanked his heavy chair from beneath the table and sat. The room grew hushed again as he said a brief prayer over the meal. Before the chatter could resume, he rose.

"My apologies for not being available to escort my wife into the castle. 'Tis difficult to bribe children to remain in place a moment longer when food and their amma await."

The people stared at him in wordless astonishment. Birk ground his teeth and hid his scowl. "Carys Wen fila Pedr honored me by becoming my wife a little more than a fortnight ago. We will celebrate with a feast tomorrow night."

He returned to his seat and dragged a platter of sliced meat to his trencher. He added bread and cheese before taking a bite.

"Don't forget your vegetables," Carys murmured, reaching for a platter of roasted carrots. She placed a number of them on his trencher. "The girls need ye to set a good example." She gifted him with a brilliant smile, its effect marred by the arched brow challenging him to complain.

He grabbed a carrot and tore it in half with his teeth, eliciting a giggle from Eislyn, a hesitant smile from Abria, and a mimicking move from Tully. Carys smiled serenely. Hanna raised an eyebrow in reproof.

The girls' high spirits soon unraveled into bickering, emphasizing their need for a restorative nap.

Carys rose. "I will see to the girls."

"I have missed them. I shall accompany ye." Hanna stood. "Tully, would ye care for a bit of a rest, or are ye well enough here?"

Tully glanced at Birk. "I dinnae need a nap."

Birk nodded. "He is fine with me. Dugan or I will show him about."

Carys paused. "Then do not look for me before the evening meal. I will find my way back."

Birk bristled at her tone. What had he done? The woman who had melted in his arms whilst aboard ship, had once again erected a chilly barrier between them. And dragged Hanna behind it with her.

* * *

Hanna kissed each of the girls and tucked their blankets to their chins. "I wish to hear all about your new ma as soon as ye wake from your naps. Mayhap after supper?"

"Aye," Eislyn yawned, sleep already catching up with her. "She came to us 'cause of the pirates."

Carys's heart warmed. Eislyn had a warrior's heart, her sister the gentle one. Though Eislyn obviously cared a great deal for Abria, she was fiercely protective rather than nurturing.

230

"She helped me name Tegan," Abria added.

Hanna brushed a lock of hair from Abria's cheek. "I love hearing your voice." Her tone was light, but Carys heard the conflicting undercurrents of pride and pain. Hanna placed a kiss on each girl's forehead and motioned Carys to the chairs near the hearth.

Carys tucked Tegan onto a rug beside Abria's bed, though she knew where she'd find the puppy later. "We will linger a bit until ye are asleep," she reassured them, noticing their sighs as they closed their eyes.

Hanna stood silent a moment then turned her gaze from the girls to Carys. "Will ye join me?"

Carys perched on the edge of one chair, apprehension striking again as she realized she faced her husband's mother. Though Carys had taken a moment to change from her travel-stained leggings and tunic into a plain woolen gown, she didn't think Hanna would make the mistake again of judging her by outward appearances.

"I have so many questions," Hanna began. "But no matter who ye are or what your circumstances, I will never forget Abria's first words to me were of ye." She blinked her eyes rapidly. "When did this miracle occur?"

"A little more than a fortnight ago."

Hanna's bland questioning look told Carys she awaited a better answer.

"I had arrived at Dairborrodal Castle, and the village came under attack."

To Hanna's credit, she merely drew her lips into a hard line.

"I have fought—many times." Carys wasn't certain Hanna would understand. But the older woman nodded.

"Your clothing when ye arrived told me ye arenae merely a pretty face. There is sorrow and hardship behind ye. 'Tis possible we share a similar past." She favored Carys with a half-smile. "Mind ye, my allegiance is to my son, but I do not speak out of turn when I say Birk needs a strong wife. Tell me more of Abria."

Carys gave Hanna's words a chance to settle. It cheered her to know her new mother by marriage did not harbor unreasonable expectations of her son.

"Their nurse, Ina . . .." Carys paused when Hanna nodded thoughtfully. "Ina was nowhere to be found. Eislyn announced she was hiding beneath a table, but we did not have time to seek her out. Though I was on my way to lending a hand with the rogues in the village, I could not leave the girls unprotected."

Another thoughtful nod, this one accompanied by a low hum of approval.

"Birk sent Brody and me with the girls to the tower room. We spent a lot of time singing, playing games, and telling stories." Carys shrugged. "It comforted Abria, I think."

"We have spent two years comforting the child," Hanna disagreed.

"But I was a stranger yet vowed to protect her."

"Ye offered your life for hers, should it come to that. And ye wrought a miracle."

Carys opened her mouth, but Hanna shook her head. "'Tis the most precious gift, and I will not have ye tarnish it with your denial." She leaned back in her chair and laced her hands across her lap.

"Tell me how ye and my son met."

Chapter Twenty Four

Birk attempted to settle into the shipping business at hand in the solitude of his solar, but thoughts of his ma and Carys left him uneasy. He pushed away from his desk and stormed across the room.

I willnae leave either of them to weave tales about me—true or not. The time to tell Hanna how he'd met and married Carys in his own words was well past, but perhaps he could salvage at least part of the story. He did not expect her to lie, but the part of the story Carys knew was enough to put him in his ma's bad graces for quite a long while.

He grasped the latch as a knock sounded. Surprised, he jerked open the door, startling the man on the other side of the portal. Slim, with the wiry build of a sailor, skin burnished from hours in the sun, he bobbed his head.

"'E'en, m'laird," he said, fumbling in a leather pouch looped over his shoulder with a thin strap. Finding what he sought, he handed Birk a packet wrapped in oiled cloth. Birk accepted it and motioned for the man to join him in the solar.

"Thank ye, but th' wife will be lookin' fer me, and I'll no' miss one of Agnes' meals an' I can help it." He grinned. "Master Dawe said he'd be along shortly if ye have any questions."

"Be off with ye, then, and dinnae give Mistress Agnes reason to think badly of me."

The man bobbed his head respectfully before continuing on his way.

Returning to his desk, Birk opened the packet the dockmaster had sent and removed a scrap of wood about the size of his hand, planed very thin and gray with age. The surface had been wiped clean many times, but smudges of ink from previous use stained one corner. It did not take Birk long to decipher the writing. He smiled, pleased with what he'd discovered. Carys would be pleased as well.

* * *

Hanna offered Carys a mug of watered ale. "Tell me about yourself. What manner of woman caught my son's heart after rejecting numerous offers?"

Carys blinked. "He had women proposing marriage to him?"

That did not follow her opinion of him. Tall, broad-shouldered, built as a warrior, he doubtless set feminine hearts aflutter. But his curt dismissal of things—and people—that did not interest him should not make him the target of a large number of women.

She considered the hall below. She'd had little time to study its appointments, but she'd noticed the large tapestries, the vast display of weaponry on the wall behind the head table, some swords in shapes she'd never encountered before. The food had been excellent and plentiful, with golden candelabra and goblets marching across ironed white linen spread across the tables. The soaring ceiling had reached two—no, three—storeys high, and the doorway she'd entered from the outside had taken three paces to clear.

Baron Birk MacLean was a very wealthy man.

"There were ambitious fathers presenting their daughters," Hanna amended, possibly following a similar train of thought. "The council was eager for him to present an heir, and not inclined to consider either of his daughters as potential clan leaders." She shared a smile. "Men."

"Aye. Even in Cymru," Carys agreed.

"Ye fled Edward's army?"

Carys went along with Hanna's change in topic. "My brother Hywel and I fought alongside Prince Llywelyn ap Gruffudd after our parents were killed. My husband died in battle as well."

Hanna's surprise was evident as she tilted her head. "Ye were married before?"

"Aye. Briefly. Kings rarely consider the impact of war on families."

"'Tis the Lord's truth." Hanna subsided into her own thoughts.

"Hywel and I escaped Cymru after the battle at Orewin Bridge once the prince was killed."

"Some say the prince was betrayed."

Carys sent Hanna a startled look.

"Just because I live in Scotland does not mean I do not take an interest in other places." Hanna smiled. "Ye truly know so little about the man ye married?"

"I must confess, I believed I married a man of minor consequence, mayhap the captain of the guard, for there is no mistaking his commanding manner or his skill with weapons. I did not think him the gaoler for long." Carys sighed. "I came to these shores seeking refuge and mayhap a family of my own in time."

"Ye will find peace, and your family is larger than you know."

Carys turned a bleak expression on her new mother by marriage. "I was afraid of that."

Hanna frowned, her brow furrowed. Carys fluttered her fingers to stall the questions. "My brother died when our ship sank in a storm off the Ardnamurchan Peninsula this spring. Tully, the captain's son, and I, along with his dog, were the only survivors."

Hanna blanched. "I knew Captain Ferguson. He was a good man. I am grieved by his loss."

"He was not simply a business acquaintance, then? Birk mentioned he knew the captain."

"Nae. He was a family friend for all we only saw him when his ship docked here. I know little of his wife and children. He was full of tales of his travel."

"We mean to find Tully's remaining family and take him home."

Hanna appeared lost in thought, but her eyes saddened and Carys wondered what memories haunted her.

"His mother will be undoubtedly overjoyed to have her son returned to her." Hanna forced a slight smile. "Not all mothers are so fortunate."

"I am sorry for the loss I see in your eyes," Carys murmured.

Hanna patted her hand. "Not to worry. My son died defending our home. At least . . . nae, I will not speak more of it. It belongs in the past."

Carys did not press her, understanding the wretched misery of thinking on the things that occupied the holes in her heart.

"King Edward's political ambitions drove us here and killed Hywel as surely as if he'd fallen in battle. Marriage to a man with no title would have left me safely in obscurity from my past and from any who thought to finish what Longshanks started. Now I find myself brought to prominence I did not seek."

"Ye are well spoken," Hanna commented, her tone reflective. "And ye do not seem worried about running a castle of this size. Ye have lived this grand before."

There was no question in Hanna's words, and Carys merely shrugged. "Grander. From time to time."

Hanna nodded. "Ye are quite an enigma, Carys MacLean. I will enjoy chatting with you more. For now, I believe the girls are asleep. Let us see what my son might add to your story."

* * *

Birk placed the parchment-thin scrap of wood next to a slim, hide-bound book he'd left on his desk still opened to a treatise on use of lateen sails on a ship. The packet he'd brought with him from Dairborrodal sat square in the center of the desk. He perched one hip on the edge of the desk, his mind on Hanna and Carys.

She has apparently won Hanna over. Just like she did Eislyn and Abria. And Cook. And even the men she trounced rather than agreeing to come along peaceably. He shook his head, eyebrows lifting as he remembered the day they'd captured her. *As easily as she won me over.*

She is wild and willful, and completely at odds with the women the council wished me to take to wife. A smile broke across his face. He couldn't wait to see what the council made of his new wife. There were many reasons Carys was a better choice than MacBrehon's spineless daughter or MacDonnell's lass of only fourteen summers. And especially better than the sultry widow looking for her fifth husband.

It didn't matter that Carys wasn't bound to his clan by blood or alliance. What mattered was her heart and her courage. The fact that she set his bed aflame added passion to their union, something he'd not dreamed possible after his disastrous marriage to Rose MacDonald.

Birk shifted in his seat to ease the tightness of his breeches, his temper taking a turn for the worse. Hanna could see to the weans. He wanted his wife—who was spending too much time with his ma. His brow furrowed. Having both women under the same roof might not have been his best plan.

Hanna strolled through the open doorway without knocking, Carys only a few steps behind. Birk eyed them warily. Hanna lowered herself gracefully to a chair near the hearth and Carys chose a seat next to her. Their bond was apparent, and though Birk had to admit he preferred it to bickering or distrust, the back of his neck tingled with apprehension. He needed to give Hanna the reasons he'd married—and how—before the tale got out of hand.

Birk rose and stalked to the tray a servant had left on a corner of his desk. Hanna and Carys glanced up and he raised a mug in silent offer.

"Put it down, Birk. I am not here for refreshments."

Hanna's calm command only raised his level of unease. Birk sloshed a measure of whisky into the mug and tossed it back, sucking in a breath at the fiery bite that slid to his belly. He set the mug down with a clatter and strode to a spot by the hearth where Hanna and Carys did not have to turn to look at him—and immediately felt like a recalcitrant lad before his elders.

He leaned a shoulder against the stone. "I have . . .."

Hanna lifted a hand. "I am glad ye are home safe. I have missed ye and my granddaughters. But I am trying very hard to not tear a strip from your hide for your silence whilst at Dairborrodal—and your selfish audacity." Her voice rose. "Have ye any idea how hurtful it is to discover your son has married, without invitation to the wedding or any notice whatsoever? Or to discover my precious granddaughter who has not spoken in two years has found her voice again? Not a single word from ye to bring me joy of either occasion."

Tears would have been less effective. Her pain was clear, and Birk understood why. Sten, her son from her first marriage had died when Scots had raided their village, her last sight of him standing resolutely before the door of the long house with two of his friends, ten summers of age, determined to protect the women and children sheltered within. His body had never been recovered, but the entire village had been razed to the ground, a fitting pyre for their courage.

Hanna lived in Birk's home, cared for his daughters, had raised his half-sister as though she was her own daughter. She might rejoice over his marriage and Abria's return to normalcy, but he'd put off the lengthy explanation which would have required including news of his marriage—which he felt was best done in person—and he'd not included her. He winced. He hadn't considered the impact on his own mother.

Birk's reasons for not waiting to marry Carys when they arrived at MacLean Castle fled. He glanced from Carys to Hanna. "I humbly apologize for neglecting ye. Ye deserve better."

"I assumed she was my granddaughters' new nurse!" Hanna's hurt slipped into indignation.

"How did ye know I'd dismissed Ina?"

Hanna waved a hand in the air. "Och, she arrived here a fortnight ago, distressed over being replaced by *a woman his lordship has taken up with*."

Birk lifted an eyebrow. Carys grinned. "Ye at least did not accuse me of being his mistress when we first met."

Hanna shook her head. "The words that could have crossed my lips before I knew ye'd wed my son . . .." She glared at Birk. "Ye have a lot to answer for."

Birk's unease spiked. "Aye. I do."

"I approve your choice in wife, though not the way in which ye went about it."

Birk grunted. If she knew the entire truth, she'd like it even less. He wondered what Carys had said. Another glance at Carys's face told him nothing—except he was on his own.

"Ye know I cared not for being pushed into marriage. I had reasons to refuse each woman—lass—put forth by the council."

"Good reasons," Hanna granted. "But you must agree this is quite sudden, even shocking."

"I dinnae mean to hurt ye, Ma. I knew Carys held every virtue I valued in a wife, and I dinnae wish to bring her here to fall beneath the scrutiny of the council until after we were wed."

Carys's eyes widened. Her lips parted, but no sound escaped. She blinked as if uncertain whether to speak—her hands clenched.

"Ye thought so little of your ability to sway Gregor?" Hanna mocked. "They do not all follow his lead."

Birk's neck heated. His ma baited him, and he deserved it.

Hanna sent Birk a narrowed look. "She thought ye were a gaoler. Do ye wish to explain this to me? My son, Baron MacLean, Lord of Morvern, head of the largest shipping concern in Scotland—represented himself as a gaoler?"

"Not the best way to woo a wife," Carys affirmed, her expression guarded. "Though fairly original."

Birk folded his arms over his chest, refusing to be drawn into the discussion further.

Hanna sent him a look he immediately recognized—and refused to be intimidated by. "I will have the entire *true* story when I am not distracted by the attempt to neither scandalize nor alienate your wife. I will have ye know, Birk Alexander MacLean, that 'twill be some time before I forget I first greeted Carys as a servant—not as your wife. I pray I have her forgiveness, and I would hope ye have the wits to understand what position ye placed her in by your silence on the matter."

The room sparked with tension, then Carys inclined her head. "I harbor no ill-will toward ye, m'lady." Her gaze shifted to Birk. "My husband and I will no doubt have this settled between us in short order."

Birk ground his teeth. Ruled by a pair of conspiring women! And if Carys thought sending him from her bed—a common ploy of

Rose's when she was out of sorts with him—was the answer, he would set her straight before nightfall.

Hanna rose, the light of battle in her eyes. "Ye, my son, had best hope your tale is convincing. I would not have dreamed ye *hrafnasueltir*. If your father were still alive, he would be ashamed of your handling of this."

She left the room, her head high. Birk did not bid her stay.

The door closed behind her and the room was bathed in silent recriminations. Birk spoke first. "I have news of Tully's family, though it can wait if ye wish to speak of other things."

"As much as I could shoulder a bit of the blame since I did not await your escort from the ship, I will not since there should have been no reason for me to be forced to explain myself in my own home. A formal introduction, aye, but as far as Hanna was concerned, I, as your wife, did not exist."

She sighed. "I confess I am at a loss as to why ye married me, as much as I cannot fathom the deceptions ye have played along the way. But as I may never fully understand these things, I would have ye explain one thing before we speak of Tully."

Relief gnawed at Birk's desire to fight, to have the argument over and done with. She was right. He did not believe he could convince her of the many subtleties of his plan, nor his desire for her once he'd finally met her. Nor could he explain to himself the reasons he showed her only his passion—and not his admiration.

He hadn't wanted to address this. He'd wanted only to secure a wife he could more than tolerate—be proud of. He hadn't wanted to love her. Did he love her? He was convinced Rose had cured him of that foolish emotion years ago. He had no fear of falling into that trap again.

He eyed her warily. "What is it ye wish to know?"

"What is *hrafnasueltir?*

Birk's heart stuttered. *Coward.* The import of Hanna's words swept over him. Though she'd scarcely raised her voice, there was no doubt she was truly angry. His actions might have been important to him, but he had betrayed her.

"Raven starver. A man who is afraid to fight."

Carys gave him a puzzled look.

"Only a man who has the courage to fight dies on the battlefield. His body will feed the ravens. A man who does not fight willnae become carrion—and thus, starve the ravens."

Birk walked to his desk, feeling the heat of the hearth too much. "Hanna is Norse. Though a follower of the Christ, the auld stories were a part of her history—and mine. Ravens were a fearsome sight, hovering over battlefields, awaiting their chance at the fallen. To the Norse, ravens had the power of gods. They, along with the Valkyries, chose who would live or die in battle."

"One who ignores a raven must then be seen as a fool."

Birk gave a curt nod. "She isnae happy with me."

A slight smile played along Carys's lips, but she made no response.

She is amused? Birk narrowed his gaze then sat, willing to turn to less weighty matters.

"I received word of Tully's ma and siblings just a bit ago. They live in Kinlochkillkerran, on the eastern side of the tip of the Kintyre Peninsula. She owns a small tavern near the docks. 'Tis a busy port and I imagine she makes a bit of coin, though the work is undoubtedly hard."

Carys leaned forward. "How far is that from here?"

"By ship, mayhap two days. I have sent a letter regarding Tully's whereabouts to his ma. When Tully is ready, I will take him."

"I will go with ye."

It was on Birk's tongue to say nae, to remind her of her responsibilities to Abria and Eislyn. But she had an earlier tie with the lad, and he could not bring himself to demand she remain behind.

Chapter Twenty Five

Carys breathed deep. A mixture of happiness and sorrow washed over her. Once Tully left, her last tie to Hywel and their final journey together would end. Each time she saw Tully, visions of their voyage along the coast of Scotland filled her heart. Hywel had insisted this was the place and life he wanted, but now she'd never tease him again about being a difficult husband or know the heart-wrenching love of seeing his child for the first time. Had she chosen the forests of Éire and taken a different path, would they still be together? Carys shook such morbid thoughts away. God, not Carys, had control over who lived and died. She wondered—not for the first time—if she'd been better off not hearing the words spoken by the old crone all those months ago. Those prophetic words changed nothing of the bitterness of her losses.

Her gaze settled on Birk. What other secrets lurked beneath his scowl? She was foolish to think him a simple gaoler when they first met. Seeing him now, there was naught simple about him. But a baron? She still struggled to accept his lofty status, now hers as well. Carys readily understood why he chose not to present himself as nobility when they first met. But, why would a man choose a wife destined for the gallows?

Even more important, why would a *baron* choose such a wife? What attributes did he see that he'd not found in any other woman presented to him? His earlier revelation had stunned her. As had the realization he'd set up her capture for the sole purpose of forcing her to marry him. She wavered between furious and puzzled. Why her?

He married me because I care for his daughters and can—with God's blessing—give him an heir. There was more? She studied his face—the brooding dark eyes and tight-lipped frown. He did not appear anxious to reopen the discussion. And she wasn't certain she was ready to ask.

"Ye have ordered a feast for tomorrow eve," she said. "We could take Tully home mayhap a day or two later, if that is what he wishes."

"Pirates have been sighted near Oban, a couple of hours' sail from here." Birk faced her. "Are ye certain ye wish to go? We could take an overland route if ye prefer, though it would be more arduous."

Carys tilted her head. "Ye think to frighten me with tales of pirates?"

A reluctant smile lit his eyes. "Mayhap ye tire of fighting."

His observation took the wind from her sails. "Aye. I have had enough to last me the rest of my days. But I will not run from a fight. Nor will I allow fear to shape my choices."

His nod seemed to hold admiration behind it, though Carys thought it unlikely. Her fighting abilities could not be something he looked upon with favor. Such skills, honed in battles for her life and country, had thwarted him more than helped—her actions to keep the girls safe during the attack at Dairborrodal notwithstanding. Again she wondered what virtues she possessed that he admired. What characteristics had he had found in no other woman that had pushed him into his bizarre plot? She remained puzzled—and perhaps a bit intrigued.

"We will take the *Már*. 'Tis easier for her to slip down the coast than a larger ship." The right side of Birk's mouth tilted with a half-grin. "I promised ye a wee trip, and 'twill be only us and the crew on the return. They will be discreet."

Warmth settled low in her belly. Would spending two uninterrupted days with Birk open doors between them? Or close them?

"I will speak with Tully. I have no doubt he'll be overjoyed to know he is at last going home." She rose. "I believe I will indulge in a brief nap after I check on the girls. Hanna sent a lass the girls knew to watch over them."

"About the feast," Birk said, halting her steps toward the door. "By holding the gathering tomorrow, rather than tonight, most council members will have time to arrive."

Carys raised an eyebrow. They were wed. What could a few highly placed men in the clan do to cause Baron MacLean's unease? They had no power to undo what she, Birk, and the Holy Church had done. Any talk of her being put aside would not end well for anyone foolish enough to suggest such.

"They wished me to wed for power, alliance, and wealth. I wished to wed the woman of my choice. They will question ye—and they willnae be kind."

Her temper flared. He would not protect her from the meddlesome men? She was a princess of Cymru and above such interrogations. Howbeit, she could handle a few surly old men. Without doubt, conflicts within Clan MacLean could not hold a candle to the court intrigue she'd experienced back home.

"I willnae allow them to go too far," he added. "But they will have questions."

"Do not worry yourself," she seethed. "I have nothing to hide."

* * *

Carys peered tiredly over the crowd. Even before drink had gotten the better of them, they had been boisterous, overbearing, and rude. There was not a man on the council she would trust farther than a well-thrown blade. And she'd be certain to aim well. Gregor MacLean already topped her list.

The lairds loyal to the the MacLean had been polite—no, cautious. It was clear Birk's marriage had knocked them off-kilter. Some of Birk's family had arrived midafternoon with various responses to his announcement.

James Campbell, whose wife Gillian had remained at home with their infant daughter, had greeted Birk with the intent to bloody his nose, passing along his wife's indignant response to his marriage without Birk's older sister's knowledge. Hanna's watchful eye had thwarted near-disaster as she diverted him with grandmotherly questions about his bairn, her new granddaughter. Bram MacKern, laird of the neighboring Clan MacKern, and his son Keir, had welcomed Carys into the family, offering her a place of refuge should she tire of Birk's brooding. Carys had smiled sweetly— puzzled at Birk's reaction to their offer—and assured them she was content.

The feasting would likely simmer for hours yet, but Gregor had indicated he and the rest of the council would like a word with her and Birk. Favoring Gregor with an imperious look learned at her cousin's knee, she slipped gracefully to her feet, thankful the gown Hanna had loaned her had required only moderate adjustments. The soft wool was dyed a deep blue, offset with a blindingly white surcoat richly trimmed in silver embroidery. Embellished with a fortune in rubies anchored in the heavy shimmering thread, the exceedingly fine garment had forced her to reassess her opinion of the magnitude of Birk's holdings once again. The weight of the embroidery and stones reminded her of her infrequent days at Prince Llywelyn's court, and she resolved to put a stop to the murmurs swelling among the MacLean council.

It was Gregor's mistake to seat himself in the most comfortable chair in Birk's solar before Carys was two steps into the room. Instead of accepting the chair he indicated with a curt nod of his head, she glided serenely across the floor and halted before him, the tip of her dagger placed firmly beneath his chin. His ears and bald pate reddened as he fought to control his reaction. Clearly, he'd not dreamed he would be thwarted in his petty play for power.

Concern buzzed in the room. Birk folded his arms over his chest, feet braced comfortably apart, his stance effectively halting the two men who had started to Gregor's assistance.

Gregor dropped his furious gaze from Carys, sliding it from one man to another, a deep scowl on his face for their deep insult. How dare they assume he needed protection from a lass? After a moment, he rose to his feet, careful not to duck his chin against the glinting steel. He glared at Carys.

Her nostrils flared as if she scented something foul. "Had ye offered the courtesy due me, I would have given the better chair to a man of advanced years such as yourself. However, I will give courtesy only as ye define it, old man." She lowered the dagger and motioned for him to move.

He reluctantly abandoned his seat.

With a graceful settle of her skirts, Carys sat. Birk paused by her chair, placing a palm on her shoulder.

"Ye have made an enemy where he was merely a nuisance before," he murmured.

Her calm smile belied the fire in her words. "I am a baroness and will be afforded the privileges of my rank." She patted his hand. "An enemy who is wary is better than a nuisance who would plunge a knife into your back."

Birk shot her a startled look, then faced the men gathered. "This council bade me marry and produce an heir for the benefit of the clan. I present to ye my wife, Carys Wen, filia Pedr, now Baroness MacLean."

They'd heard the rumors—both true and false, for Carys had heard many of them herself—of Birk's new wife, and excitement rushed through the group with the swoosh of fire through dry grass. Carys schooled her face into a careful absence of expression, back straight, head held high.

After a moment, Birk raised a hand, and the murmurs faded to silence. "I will answer questions I deem appropriate. But let it be known, Carys is my wife by the grace of God and the Holy Church, and therefore subject to all courtesy due her. Any who finds fault with my decision is encouraged to take it up with me personally after this discussion." His glare landed squarely on Gregor.

Several men glanced at each other, but none offered to accept Birk's challenge. Carys suppressed a smile. Perhaps they weren't as short-witted as she'd first thought.

"She isnae one of the lasses we presented ye." Gregor's jaw jutted forward, face furiously red.

"I declared more than a month ago I wouldnae marry a woman from yer list." Birk's reply was final.

"Why her?" another man whose name Carys did not know asked.

Birk planted his feet. "Yer new baroness is fierce."

Ah—one of the virtues he espoused. Carys longed to know the others, but she was content, for the moment at least, to listen to him address the subject of their marriage to the council.

A wolfish smile full of approval for Carys's actions a few moments earlier aimed at Gregor as the word *fierce* rolled off Birk's tongue. "She dinnae seek me out for my wealth or position. She dinnae seek me at all. I sought her. I couldnae ask for a better wife."

Carys momentarily lost her composure. *I should have already asked him for his reasons. I had no idea of his standards—or that I had somehow met them.*

She lifted her chin, bringing her swirling emotions under control. Birk's hand, still possessively on her shoulder, squeezed lightly.

"She brings naught to the marriage," Gregor scoffed, unwilling to concede the point. "'Tis said she is a refugee from Wales. Shipwrecked, without family, and penniless."

"'Tis true she and one other were sole survivors of a storm off the Ardnamurchan Peninsula this past spring. As for family, the whole of Clan MacLean stands ready to support and care for her." His eyes lit as he canted his head, his gesture mocking. "Any who do not, will find themselves outside the clan. Where do yer loyalties lie?"

Carys's blood warmed. Her husband's position was crystal clear to all in the room. He allowed their questions, but he would protect her with his answers. She had forgotten what it felt like to have someone's firm support. Her chest tightened, but she set aside the unfamiliar sensation for reflection another time. Gregor shifted once again in his seat. It was clear he was not satisfied.

Birk reached beneath his tunic and drew forth a leather bag. He tossed it onto the desk where it landed with the heavy chink of metal. "As for wealth, she brings this. The bounty from several clans set on Colin Dubh's head. Forty silver pennies. Two witnesses watched her kill Colin Dubh and two of his men single-handedly. I saw the bodies. The bounty is hers as is the gratitude from all who suffered under the bastard's murderous ways."

Murmurs buzzed again, some in disbelief one lass could kill three men, while others spoke of respect, though all silenced quickly as Gordon stormed to his feet. "Forty silver pennies is naught. The pretty dress she wears means naught. Ye have married a woman who brings no glory or honor to our clan. Her children will be half-blood Scots."

Carys quickly grasped Birk's hand as it slipped from her shoulder, pulling him firmly back to her side. She accurately read the fury in his clenched jaw, the white lines in his red face, and his shoulders hunched forward a mere instant from pummeling the older man for his insolence.

He married me for my fierceness. Let this be the first test.

She drew the slender chain around her neck from beneath the borrowed gown and fingered the ring Hywel had given her. The crimson dragon edged with gold warmed beneath her touch. She opened the clasp and pulled the ring free of the chain, holding it for all to see. Bitter sweetness greeted her as it always did when she gazed upon Hywel's ring. As she grasped the proof of her lineage, the truth of her heritage fired her blood.

These interfering men know not who they challenge.

Carys stood tall and in turn locked gazes with those who questioned her fitness as baroness of Clan MacLean. For centuries, Cymru warriors had fought the Vikings, the Romans, and the English—and before them, the Picts. Their proud spirits filled hers to overflowing as she scanned the room.

"I bring no alliance to Clan MacLean, for my bloodline is nearly at an end. I am of the house of Llywelyn ap Gruffudd, Prince of Cymru, and as a princess, the blood of Prince Llywelyn runs through my veins. I add noble blood to that of Clan MacLean. Any man who dares doubts my claim may meet me outside with steel in hand."

A slow grin spread over Birk's face. She'd seen to it he knew of her skills firsthand. The tilt of his head told her he half-hoped someone in the council was foolish enough to accept.

Chapter Twenty Six

Carys stroked Tully's head, her fingers lightly feathering through his short-cropped bright red hair. He curled next to her on the wide couch in the women's solar, Dewr and Tegan at their feet. Abria and Eislyn sprawled beside him, clutching him tight, sharing his joy and grief. He was going home, and the anticipation was bittersweet.

Hanna's wooden knitting needles clacked quietly from her chair where a beam of sunlight crossed her lap.

Completely worn out by the emotional tumult of the past two days, Carys softly sang the lilting strains of a lullaby her mother had once sung to her.

"Dacw nghariad lawr yn y berllan
Tw rymdi, rô rymdi, radl idl al

O na bawn i yno fy hunan
Tw rymdi, rô rymdi, radl idl al

Dacw'r ty a dacw'r sgubor
Dacw'r ddrws y beudy'n agor

Ffaldi radl idl al, ffaldi radl idl al, tw rymdi, rô rymdi, radl idl al"

Abria sighed and snuggled closer. "I like it. What does it mean?"

"'Tis a love song," Carys replied. *"There's my love, down in the orchard. Tra, rymdi, ra, rymdi, radl, idl, al."* She smiled. "The last part is rather like singing *tra, la, la,* but much prettier, I think." She hummed the tune for a moment. *"Oh, how I wish I was there, myself. Tra, rymdi, ra, rymdi . . . ."*

"*Radl, idl, al.*"

The ragged chorus of the children's voices brought tears to her eyes. "*There's the house,*" she sang, "*and there's the barn; and there's the cowshed door open.*"

"*Tra, rymdi, ra, rymdi, radl, idl, al.*" They sang the nonsense words with her.

Eislyn giggled. Tully snorted. Abria ducked her head against Tully's tunic.

"Will we ever see ye again, Tully?" Eislyn asked, bringing a close to the song.

Tully pulled his head from Carys's shoulder and straightened, kicking his feet as they dangled an inch above the floor. "Och, aye," he assured them with a fervent nod. "I's gonna have a ship as big as Da's was. Then I can sail here any time."

Eislyn scooted to the edge of the cushion and slipped her feet over, matching their swing to Tully's. "I dinnae wish for ye to go."

Carys studied the children. Eislyn had adopted Tully as her big brother, not quailing at ordering the much older child around. He followed her faithfully, never objecting to her often imperious nature, but always quick to laugh and do as she asked. Though they'd been together less than a fortnight, their bond appeared unbreakable.

Abria eyed him, tears in her eyes. She was rarely far from Tully's side, hounding his steps like a puppy—eager to please and happy to be able to join him and Eislyn.

"I like ye, and Abria, too, but I have brothers and sisters at home." His breath hitched. "And, I miss my ma."

Eislyn turned and wrapped her arms about him. "I know," she said. "Sometimes I miss my ma, too." She sat back, folding her hands in her lap. "But we have Carys now, and I dinnae think of Ma as much. Ye will feel better once ye are home." Her matter-of-fact voice cleared the air of its sadness, invoking absolute assurance that Tully's reunion with his ma and siblings would right all that was wrong in the world.

And just that quickly, Carys saw the tension around the children ease. Smiles lit their faces, happy once again.

Abria popped up onto her knees. *"Ffaldi radl idl al, ffaldi radl idl al, tw rymdi rô rymdi . . .."*

"Radl idl al!" Eislyn chimed in, Tully's voice a chant as he pumped out the nonsense words.

They collapsed against the bolstered back of the couch, clutching their sides as they giggled and guffawed.

The door to the solar opened. Dewr and Tegan leapt to their feet and rushed forward. Birk managed one step inside the room before they circled him tightly, effectively halting him until they were acknowledged.

"Ye are well protected," he noted. "Get bye, lass. Aye, Tegan, ye are a good lass." He fended the excited dogs off with both hands for a moment, then put an abrupt halt to their antics. *"Staund!"*

Both dogs immediately dropped their paws to the floor, furry bodies quivering as they eagerly awaited his next command. The children clapped hands over their ears at Birk's bellow, grins widening as he then strode across to Hanna's chair. He leaned forward and kissed her cheek. She smiled.

"Ye learned that tone of voice from yer da," she said, lowering her needles to her lap.

"I should, I heard it often enough. Usually stopping me from one *stramash* or another." He moved to the couch and planted a longer kiss on Carys's cheek, smoothing a palm over her hair. He glanced at the boy next to her.

"Are ye ready, Tully? The *Már* is set to sail first thing in the morning."

Tully nodded. "I's ready. Carys helped me pack."

"And me!" Eislyn reminded him.

"Me!" Abria piped up.

Hanna sighed. "It warms my heart to hear them chatter so. And who knew Abria had such a lovely singing voice?"

"Singing?" Birk eyed the girls, letting his gaze settle on Carys. "Who is teaching the girls to sing?"

"Carys is, Da," Eislyn proclaimed. "But the words are in Cymraeg, and they sound funny."

Abria slipped from her seat and tugged on Birk's tunic. "Da, I'm packed, too."

Carys returned Birk's startled look. She hadn't helped Abria pack—or even suggested it.

He chucked her beneath her chin. "I am pleased ye accomplished this on yer own. Howbeit, ye and Eislyn will be staying with yer amma."

Howls of dismay rocked the room. "I wanna go!" Abria sobbed. "Tully needs me!"

"Please, Da! We dinnae wish to stay behind!" Eislyn grabbed Tully's sleeve as though to anchor herself to him.

Hanna rose, setting her knitting aside. The girls' eyes darted immediately to her, and their cries faded at the implacable look on her face.

"Do not worry, dearlings." An expectant look fell over the children. Hanna smiled serenely at Birk. "I, too, am going sailing."

* * *

Carys struggled to remain awake. For the second night at MacLean Castle, Birk was late to bed. The night before, he'd slipped into their chamber hours after she'd fallen asleep, waking her in the still hours, stirring the passion that seemed to lie just beneath the surface, always eager for his touch.

She found him less irritating to be around recently. Which of them had changed? She sighed. 'Twas far more likely she'd grown accustomed to his abrupt ways and decided to not let them bother her. His actions were not petty, he was simply used to getting his own way and clearly astonished when people or circumstances did not line up immediately at his bidding.

Hanna had something to do with that, Carys suspected. It was quite likely Birk was headstrong as a lad, but Carys could easily imagine and sympathize with a woman giving birth to a son long past the time she thought to bear children and raising him as she grieved the loss of her older child. Deep inside Birk was the gift of caring Hanna had obviously planted, sometimes hidden by the strong, unwavering man his father had shaped to be the leader of Clan MacLean.

She would like to have met Alexander MacLean.

A cool draft found its way beyond the curtained bed and Carys shivered. Weighing the discomfort of crossing the room to prod the banked coals into action against waiting for Birk to arrive and accomplish the chore, Carys wiggled from beneath the blanket and scurried to the hearth. Tucking her bare feet beneath her chemise, she perched on the warm stone and used a metal rod to poke the smoldering embers.

The door creaked softly open and Carys crouched on the hearth, fingers flexing to seek the balance of the poker, letting the tip linger in the hot coals.

Birk entered the room and pulled up short. He jerked his chin at the metal rod in her hand. "'Twill make a good weapon, heated like that."

She wasn't entirely happy with his attempt to enter the room so silently, so late. "'Tis a fine weapon, hot or not."

He nodded and strode to the chest at the foot of the bed. Dropping his cloak, he pulled off his boots and unlaced his trews.

"I thought ye would be asleep."

She motioned briefly to the crackling fire as she sank back onto the warm stone then returned the rod to its place on the hearth.

"I was cold."

Birk's eyes flashed and he paused briefly. "I needed to explain things to Hanna."

Carys hugged her knees to her chest. "Why don't ye explain them to *me*?"

He tossed his trews aside and placed his sword on the chest next to the bed, taking his time about arranging his weapons so they were within easy reach in the middle of the night.

"I'm not the only one with secrets." He sent her a sidelong look. "My shipwrecked poacher is a princess of Cymru?"

Carys could not tell from his voice if he was angry or pleased. Or perhaps simply frustrated she'd had knowledge to which he had not been privy. It didn't really matter. *She* was angry. "Och, and ye've been a paragon of truth? What bothers ye more? That ye threatened to hang a woman of royal blood? Or that my rank is superior to yours?"

Birk scowled. "Rank? This has naught to do with rank. I married ye because ye dinnae care about who I was."

Carys slipped from her seat at the hearth to stand before him, fists clenched in frustration. "Didn't *care*? I didn't *know*! And I will tell ye now, if I'd known ye were a bloody baron, I'd have sought the gallows!" She flipped a hand at him in annoyance. "I'm willing to bet *that* didn't make it into your chat with your ma."

"Interestingly enough, it did." Birk's eyebrows beetled together. "I now fear she may have me dropped overboard on the return voyage from Kinlochkillkerran." His face cleared and he sent her a mocking look. "Ye should have been there. Ye could have collected more Norse insults for me to translate for ye."

"I'm certain they were fervently meant. I have a few for ye in Cymru. Hanna and I could compare them."

Birk rubbed the back of his neck. "I had my reasons."

Carys's temper flared. "Aye. And they were *your* reasons, yet they affected us all."

Birk narrowed his eyes, stubbornness firming the muscles in his jaw. "I willnae be questioned. I acted in the best interest of the clan." His palm slashed sideways through the air. "I am finished."

Carys stepped closer, matching his mulish look. "Questioned? Or held accountable? Just because your council is out of control does not give ye the right to manipulate others' lives."

"Ye are a princess!" Birk exploded. "And I looked a bloody fool trying to convince the council ye are fit to be my wife."

She drew back and tossed her head. "Och, so the truth of the matter is appearances, is it? As long as I was a nobody ye rescued from—well, I do not think they know about the gallows, so mayhap ye liked them to think ye simply felt sorry for me and wed me because I appeared to be a woman capable of caring for your girls. As long as this was true, ye could lord it over those silver-haired men who shouldn't have their noses in your bed to begin with. Show them how their offers of noble ladies and wealth and alliance didn't mean anything to ye."

Carys stepped neatly to one side as Birk reached for her. "But I defended myself against them without your help. I'm not a peasant wench without a penny to my name, a woman in need of your protection. I am a princess of Cymru with a small fortune recovered from the wreck of the *Seabhag,* and a ring to prove my bloodline."

Birk's shoulders rounded, his chin lowering until his gaze burned directly into hers. "They bought my first wife from the MacDonalds as surely as if they'd exchanged coin for her. And a lot of bloody good it did me. She enjoyed my wealth, her status, and the attention from the men who swarmed to her side. After Eislyn was born, she stopped coming to my bed, and locked her door after Abria's birth. She spent most of her time taunting me with her list of grievances and bed partners."

His chest heaved, but he did not move closer. Carys eyed him with interest, scarcely daring to breathe lest he decide he'd said enough. She wanted to hear it all. She needed to know why her husband wanted nothing more from her than an heir. She had far more to give, and was heartily tired of being pushed aside as if her use did not extend past the bedroom.

Birk fisted his hands on his hips. "I was too big, too brutish, gave her no pleasure. She finally left me and fled with her lover to Stornoway, but their ship sank crossing the Minch."

His voice hollowed, as if all his energy had disappeared. "I drove her away. I tried to be the husband she wanted, but nothing pleased her. Least of all, me."

"I do not believe all the gold in the king's treasury would have made a difference."

A wry grin tweaked the corner of Birk's mouth but did not reach his eyes. "Och, my grandda brought home two sizeable fortunes when he returned from the Holy Land forty years ago. Rose had access to enough gold to last her lifetime and far beyond."

Carys tried not to show surprise at Birk's casual regard for such tremendous wealth. She doubted Prince Llywelyn—God rest his soul—could have boasted such. Her surprise at Rose's rejection of

Birk as a man did shock her. Though he'd earlier confided the woman had been small and he'd likely frightened her, the statement did not ring true to Carys's ears.

"'Tis not your fault Rose was discontented."

"Ye dinnae know that. I was her husband. I should have been able to satisfy her."

"If she merely enjoyed the outer trappings of her marriage," she replied, her tone a mix of tart and sympathy, "then she did not attempt to discover the man she'd wed. She was too concerned about wealth and position to try to learn who her husband really was."

His lip curled, challenging her statement. "Then who am I, Carys? Ye see before ye a man larger than all others around me. A man feared by many, obeyed by all. Only Dugan and occasionally Iain dare gainsay me. I am respected though not loved. Tell me who ye think I am."

Birk stared at Carys, his chest hollow, emptied by the words he'd spoken. Each thought of Rose gutted him, reminded him he was not fit to be a husband. Her scorn. Her accusations. Spoken enough times to make them true.

Carys, the woman he'd bound to him through deceit, gazed at him. Temper rode every line of her body. He knew she would not shout merely to bring him low. Nor would he receive empty platitudes filled with false flattery. After the beating he'd taken at Hanna's clipped tongue tonight, he wasn't certain he wanted to face Carys. Yet, he'd asked.

"Ye *are* one of the largest men I've met." Carys tilted her head, softening her stance. "Yet, I do not fear ye. I only have to look at your daughters, watch how ye deal with your soldiers and clansmen to see respect, not fear, in their eyes."

260

"Ye dinnae fear me *before* ye met the lasses," he scoffed. "You snarled something that sounded verra uncomplimentary in Cymraeg, and only wed me after *ye* decided to. I sometimes wonder how close ye came to saying *nae*."

"Fairly close." Humor lurked in her eyes and a longing Birk had never felt before centered itself in his chest. He lifted his hand, then dropped it, remembering how she'd avoided him earlier. She did not want his touch.

To his surprise, she moved closer. Rose had always backed away, leaving him cold and empty. That Carys would approach him whilst angry—or at least out of sorts—with him, intrigued him. She halted, eyes directly in line with his chest.

"I see a man large in size, but I also see a man with shoulders broad enough to accept and manage his responsibilities—and give his daughters shelter when they need him. Birk, ye have the skills needed to be a warrior and a leader. But ye dinnae give people credit or understand how your actions affect them." She tapped a forefinger against his chest. "I see a heart, but ye hide it away most of the time."

Birk's body flushed. Her words confused him. Her touch twisted him inside. "A warrior doesnae have a heart. I cannae give way to such notions. I am a warrior. I know battle." He snorted. "A warrior with a *heart*. What next? Picking flowers?"

Her eyes flashed. "Ye do *not* know battle. Fighting for your life, fighting *every day*. Not knowing who might betray ye, which of your friends will die next. Inhaling the stench of death so long, ye choke on a fresh sea breeze. Losing everything so ye are forced to flee to a foreign land. Ye are skilled, no one doubts it. But your people live in peace, notwithstanding the occasional brute who is eventually accorded justice."

He blinked, not only at the passion in her words, but also at the turmoil, brutality and loss she'd endured. The long years of battling Edward, loss of her parents, husband, and brother had left its scars. Her head nearly reached his chin, slim, pale—and so strong. Her shoulders slumped and he caught her hand before she could draw away. She flinched but left her palm in his. Slowly, he pulled her fingers to his lips and kissed each tip before releasing her.

"I dinnae understand everything ye have told me. I dinnae wish to be considered a brute, but 'tis what Rose called me, over and over until I believed it. I want to be the man ye see, but I fear I dinnae have it within me."

Carys offered a half-smile. "Let me help."

Chapter Twenty Seven

Birk wasn't certain how to answer. Was Carys about to take him to task for being the idiot his ma said he was? He'd lost enough hide from Hanna's tongue-lashing to look forward to enduring the same from his wife. He held his breath as Carys lifted her hand to his cheek, fought the damning words he could not get out of his head.

Ye are a brute, Birk MacLean, and I dinnae know why I married ye.

Hanna's accusation still stung.

I am your ma, and I still do not understand ye, elskan mín.

She had quivered with rage when he admitted his subterfuge with Carys, ensnaring her, forcing her on the path to marriage rather than the gallows.

Your wife is strong. I would have chosen her for ye, rejoiced to see ye wed. But I do not understand what compelled ye to act as dishonorably as ye did.

Hell, *he* wasn't certain any more. He only knew Carys would have rejected him as Rose had if he'd tried to court her honestly. Rejected him or fled, neither was acceptable, and both foretold the same result. He would have lost her before he'd even had a chance. He knew what he was. Despite Hanna's well-meaning reassurances to the contrary, Rose's petty spitefulness had confirmed the kind of man he was. A brute. Too big and too rough to be any woman's husband.

Carys's touch somehow calmed the beast in his mind, and he met her gaze.

"Ye now know I can be so much more than simply a woman who gives ye a son," Carys said. "I will always place the children above all else, but ye must not confine me to the bedchamber. I am intelligent, skilled in running a large household—and I fear very little."

She is a smart young woman who deserves your respect, my son.

"I wanted ye for my wife like I wanted no other, and I dinnae want ye to slip away from me into the forest." *And the less ye knew of me, the less ye'd see the brute in me.*

Her brows knitted together. "Tell me why ye thought I—a woman ye did not know—would be the best wife for ye."

Birk hesitated, shied from revealing too much. Telling Rose would have . . . Carys was *not* Rose. He did *not* want to re-create the marriage with his first wife. He wanted more. He wanted Carys.

"At first I thought to thwart the council," he admitted. "I wanted none of the women on their list—for verra good reasons. There were ideals I held close to my heart, ideals that I believed were more important than just a pretty face, an alliance, and the power it bestowed."

"Ye have said as much. I want to know more."

"There was no woman I thought could embody all of these traits. I wanted a woman who dinnae exist, a woman I couldnae have." He placed the backs of his fingers against her cheek, sliding them gently across the soft skin. The contact, the fact she did not flinch from him, urged him to give her more.

Ye will not win her heart if ye do not give her something in return, sonr min.

"I wanted a wife who was selfless, who placed the welfare of others above idleness and her next gown. Word reached my ears of a resourceful woman who lived on my lands, without family or home, giving help to those in need. Giving help to *my* people."

His fingers traced gently along the curve of her jaw, down her throat where her pulse beat steadily. He recalled the words he'd given his ma. *Selfless, generous, fierce.*

"And so fierce. I dinnae believe the tales at first. But I soon saw for myself, and I tricked ye into marrying me before ye knew me."

A smile flirted with her lips, sparkled in her eyes. "Such eloquence from a man who has much to offer, yet missed seeing the truth of the matter."

"Would ye have allowed me to court ye?" he demanded, still unable to believe she would have welcomed his advances.

"'Tis difficult to say. I am not a woman who must marry for protection or to have a roof over my head. And I do not desire wealth or power. Sometimes I see in ye . . .." She sighed and dropped her gaze. "'Tis possible I may have sent ye away and mayhap even traveled elsewhere had ye persisted. Ye are not who I imagined marrying."

His stomach clenched. She would not have found him worthy. "Might I suggest my way ensured ye married me?"

Carys laughed. The sound startled and amused him. "Might *I* suggest threatening a woman is *not* the way to engage her affections."

Birk tilted his head. "Do ye like me even a wee bit?"

"I will grant ye a wee bit." She arched an eyebrow and slid her gaze quickly up and down his form. "Mayhap more than a wee bit."

"Can ye truly manage something as large as . . .." He cupped one hand slightly below his waist then allowed it drift upward, moving her gaze from himself to the well-appointed room. "As MacLean Castle?"

"So that's what ye call it?" she drawled, tossing his double entendre back at him. "'Tis a solid edifice as I well know." She leaned against him, her thinly clad body hot against his chest. "I can handle anything the castle gives me, including your elder council which is *dim gwerth rhech dafad.*"

Birk eyed her narrowly. "I dinnae speak Cymraeg."

She shrugged and wrapped her fingers about his forearms, her thumbs caressing the sensitive spot inside his elbow with slow circles. "Worthless."

He grunted. "A lot of words to mean *worthless.*"

She flashed a grin, eyes dancing. "*Not worth a sheep's fart.*"

* * *

They were good together. The fact—in full evidence as his cock relaxed into sated dormancy—never ceased to surprise and please him. The cool air felt good on his sweated body and he stretched, careful not to disturb Carys who curled at his side. She sighed gently as she shifted against him.

He would apologize to her in the morning for being *eldhúsfífl* these past weeks. Hanna had been right to call him an idiot. He deserved every Norse insult she'd hurled at him, and perhaps a few Welsh ones as well. Apologizing was likely a good gesture, and though he didn't wish to enumerate all the ways he'd probably risked her displeasure, *eldhúsfífl* seemed to cover most of his sins.

"Share your thoughts?" Carys's breath teased the hair on his chest and he idly scratched the spot.

He remained silent for a moment, his first impulse to rebuff her attempt to entice him to speak his thoughts. *I want more.*

"Not the best time to think of my first wife," he admitted with a shrug, "but I was marveling at things I'll never understand."

Carys raised to an elbow and leaned against him, trailing a finger across his chest. "Oh? What do ye not understand? Other than this is not a good time to think of *her*."

Her touch distracted him from his doubts. Her voice remained calm, sleepy.

"'Tis difficult to speak of such things." He grunted, hoping to dissuade her from pursuing the topic.

"I understand. Who do ye usually talk to?"

"Och, no one wishes to hear such things."

"I do."

Birk sucked in a deep breath and released it slowly. Tested his words before he spoke them. Took a chance. Carys stroked his chest and Rose's influence vanished.

"I dinnae understand why marriage to ye feels so right when it began with deception. My first marriage began, well, better, and ended badly."

"I thought ye said the council bought her. Arranged it."

"Och, she seduced me, and I was besotted enough with her to be led like a sheep to slaughter when my da—with the council's urging—approached her da for an alliance."

Carys sputtered with laughter. "She seduced ye? How old were ye?"

Birk rubbed his chin, caught between embarrassment and humor. "I was but a wee lad—not even in my nineteenth summer. I'd bedded a few lasses before, but she taught me things I'd never imagined."

"Truth?"

He rolled to his side and, sliding one foot over Carys's leg, pulled her against him. His cock responded instantly to her closeness. "Let's make up a few of our own."

* * *

A summer squall peppered the Már with rain and a wind that chased the ship down the coast. Waves rose and fell, tossing the craft about like a child's toy in a loch, sending Eislyn, Abria, and Dewr inside the single small cabin to wait out the storm. Tully grasped the mast, conquering his fear like the very best of sailors. Birk braced on deck, arms folded across his chest, feet spread, knees slightly bent to absorb the roll of the boards, keeping a wary eye on the far shore.

Hanna and Carys stood at the rail, embracing the sting of salt water, already noting the clouds breaking up on the horizon. The sea settled grudgingly, and the deck subsided to its more accustomed roll beneath her feet. To her surprise, she still had her sea legs.

Carys eyed Birk, mentally running her palms over his broad shoulders, remembering the twist of muscle beneath her hands. *His* hands, working their wicked way over her body.

"Ye are completely sodden," Hanna remarked with a grin.

Carys startled. "Besotted?"

Hanna laughed. "With my son, aye, but what I said was, ye are *sodden*. Drenched."

"Aye. That, too." Carys wiped her hand over her cheek, brushing a strand of hair behind an ear. Her cheeks warmed despite the wind that chilled her wet skin.

Hanna moved closer. "I did not expect to see ye on deck during the squall. I thought 'twas only the Norse who relished Thor's antics."

"Thor? Are ye not a follower of the Christ?"

"Aye. But the old tales are life's blood to the Norse. Stories we tell our children. *Why does it thunder, móðir?*" she warbled in a childlike voice. "Thor is angry, my child." She smiled. "So many tales for a long winter's night." Bracing her forearms across the rail, she stared at the calming sea, and her voice dropped to an intimate level.

"The children will be on deck soon. Tell me, what keeps ye from walking away from my son after the way he treated ye?"

"Or plunging a dagger into his treacherous heart?"

Hanna gave her a startled look, then nodded slowly. "Aye. I admit I was tempted the other night when he told me how ye wed." She sighed. "Rose changed him. He grew up very aware of who he was, and who he was expected to be. Yet, he was my third child, born to a man I loved very much, and I . . .."

Carys placed a palm gently on Hanna's arm. "Your first son died in a raid. I am terribly sorry."

Hanna blinked rapidly and tilted her head away. "My last sight of him was sword in hand, his face so grim, so young. He and two of his friends placed themselves at the doorway to the great hall, protecting the women and children. He did not wish to be there—wanted to fight the Scots beside his father. I persuaded him this was as heroic as meeting the enemy on the beach—and hoped it would be far safer." She sighed and tilted her head toward Carys.

"In the end it did not matter. I escaped, and later discovered a few of the young girls—my daughter Signy among them—had been taken as slaves. Thankfully, Alex—Birk's father—discovered her and brought her home." She managed a wan smile. "She lives on Mull with her husband and daughter. I do not see them often, but such is the way of life. I am grateful she survived and lives a full life with a man who loves her."

Carys joined Hanna's study of the sea. Land drifted near as Birk allowed the *Már* closer to shore once the storm died away. Sun broke through the clouds as if in apology for the discomfort of the squall, sending brilliant rays streaking down, touching the bruised earth, sparkling on the rolling water. The scent of rain gave way to the tang of saltwater. A gull glided overhead.

"Alex was not harsh with Birk, but Birk understood he was the only surviving son, and was rarely satisfied with anything he did. He pushed himself far harder than necessary, and to be honest, I was relieved when I discovered he and Rose had begun meeting each other in secret. I'd missed his funny, teasing boyish nature that had died over the years. For a time, he was my son again, not the hardened warrior, driven to master every subject his da or tutor gave him."

"I know what happened," Carys murmured.

"No, I do not believe ye do. For even Birk will not see the truth and shoulders all the blame. After he and Rose married, they began bickering. Birk's father fell ill, and Birk took on the burden of the clan. He once again became driven, and unfortunately, Rose felt the lack of his attention."

"And acted according to her nature?"

"Aye. I tell ye this, not to demean her, but because I sense ye are nothing like her. Ye seem strong, tolerant, and very loving. My son needs ye to help him become the man he was born to be."

* * *

Tully danced about, his loping gait thumping the boards as they approached the harbor.

"There's Cap'n Anderson's ship, and the tabby cat that lives on the dock." He turned to Dewr. "Dinnae chase the cat, Dewr. He eats the rats," he confided to Eislyn and Abria.

Abria clenched Carys's plaide in one fist. "I dinnae like rats. I'm glad I dinnae bring Tegan."

Carys patted her head. "I do not like rats, either, *bychan*. And this was not a good trip for Tegan."

270

"I'm not so little." Abria frowned.

"Oh, so ye are picking up a bit of Cymraeg? Do not worry. Ye will always be my little one. It means ye have a special place in my heart."

Apparently mollified, Abria grinned. She released Carys's cloak and dashed off to join Tully, Eislyn, and Dewr who huddled excitedly near the rail as the ship drifted gently to the dock. Birk took Carys's hand and winged an elbow for Hanna.

"Shall we go meet Tully's ma?"

The children clattered across the planks as soon as Birk released them. Tully raced up the dock and headed unerringly toward a clapboard structure with a faded gull painted on a sign dangling above the door. Birk's soldiers surrounded the group, keeping dock workers, merchants, and sailors at bay. The hair on Carys's neck bristled at the rugged faces, leering grins that died quickly enough beneath Birk's scowl, and the smell of unwashed bodies emerging from newly docked ships.

Fouled water ran alongside the cobbled path to the town, and horses nickered in protest on the congested wharf. Men shouted commands and replies, words unintelligible to Carys's ears. A pair of women, skirts hiked above their knees, loitered next to a disreputable structure, eyes on the purses of sailors emerging from the dock. One blew a kiss in Birk's direction, but his scowl only deepened.

Tully drew to a halt at the door to the Thirsty Seagull and cast an excited look over his shoulder. "Ma's here! I's home!"

At Birk's nod, he burst through the door into a room boasting six tables and a row of benches beneath a grimy window that let in little light. Carys blinked to adjust her sight. A tall woman, a white cap on her head and an apron stretched across an impressive bosom, glanced up.

"Tully?"

"Ma!"

Tully wove around the patrons and halted a foot or so away from the woman, uncertainty in his stooped shoulders.

"Where's yer da? Ye shouldnae be back so soon. And get that filthy dog out of me tavern."

Dewr whined and sat at Tully's feet.

Birk stepped forward. "I am Birk MacLean. Ye are Mistress Ferguson?"

"Aye. I'm Captain Ferguson's wife. Name's Gavina."

"I sent a letter about Captain Ferguson. Did ye not receive it?"

The woman tilted her head, then grunted. "I havenae had time to hire someone to read it." She waved a hand. "I gots customers."

Birk motioned to a tiny table in a corner. "May we sit there?"

Gavina harrumphed. "I've got to set Tully to work. I can give ye a moment. Make it quick."

Carys and Birk followed the woman to the edge of the room. Hanna and two of Birk's soldiers corralled the girls. Tully dogged Birk's heels.

"Somethin's wrong," his ma challenged. "Tell me quick."

Carys stepped forward, her heart going out to the woman. "The *Seabhag* sank in a storm off the Ardnamurchan Peninsula earlier this spring. Tully and I were the only survivors."

Chapter Twenty Eight

Gavina's face twisted, but she squared her shoulders. "Murdoc's dead?" She glanced at Tully. "And left me naught but a simple boy and his dirty dog." She lifted her arms in exasperation. "He's my boy, but I's got six others to care for as well."

She shook her head. "Married almost ten years, with seven bairns and a run-down tavern to show for it. 'Tis a wonder we had so many, no more time than he spent here."

I know why he spent so much time at sea. Carys shuddered, enraged at the woman's insensitivity. Captain Ferguson had sincerely loved the boy, giving him the sense of family aboard ship where the other sailors treated him as a younger brother. Tully's da would never have allowed another to abuse the lad. Mayhap this was one reason he'd allowed Tully to sail with him.

Carys's gaze crossed the room and found three sets of eyes set in serious faces peering at them from behind the bar. Three young girls in tattered dresses and aprons that bespoke the work they'd been born into. It was impossible to determine their ages, but Carys decided they were the oldest of Tully's sisters, the eldest perhaps boasting, at most, eleven summers. Their gazes settled on Tully with some recognition—and little interest.

Carys motioned to one of the soldiers and took the two leather bags he held out for her.

"I recovered this from the wreckage of the *Seabhag*. Even after Tully receives his wages for fair work, the coin should see ye through the winter and beyond."

Gavina's eyes brightened and she reached a hand toward the bags. "That's a fair bit of coin."

Carys retained a small bag. "This one is Tully's. He worked hard aboard ship, and his da would want him to receive his share." It was far more than the boy's wages would have been, but Carys suddenly did not want his ma to get her hands on the entire treasure.

Gavina sniffed as though offended. "As ye wish, though I could put the money to better use than he will." Her eyes narrowed. "Well, give it here. I'll need to make special arrangements to manage that much coin. There's not enough time in the day as it is."

"Ye can have mine, Ma," Tully ventured. He leaned forward, as though longing for a kind word or gesture. It was clear to Carys that he rarely received tenderness of any sort from her.

"Tully," Carys murmured softly. "Ye have dreams, aye? Help your ma and your brothers and sisters, but put a bit back for the ship ye want someday."

"Ship?" Gavina's derisive laughter bowed Tully's head. "He won't be sailin' no ship. He's a hard worker, but he hasnae the head to run his own ship."

Carys gritted her teeth and reached blindly for Birk's arm. Taking a step back, she turned Birk to her. He glanced at his forearm where her fingers dug deep. She loosened her grip.

"He cannot stay here," she whispered, furious.

"I do not wish to leave him, either," Birk replied, his voice low. "But 'tis not our place to make the decision. He is *her* son. And I am not her laird." He placed a palm over her hand. "And we cannae save them all."

Carys drew a sharp breath to protest, but recognized the fire in Birk's eyes and the muscle that twitched along his jaw. With a short nod, he pivoted on his heel and approached Tully.

"Tully, yer ma has her hands full here. I know ye are the eldest and feel the need to stay and help, but I have an offer for ye that will allow ye to help her even more."

Carys's heart nearly broke when Tully's hopeful face lifted to Birk's. She clenched her fists to keep from slapping the woman who tapped her toe impatiently on the wooden floor.

"Work for me," Birk invited. "I will pay ye a fair wage. Ye can send a portion of what ye earn to yer ma."

Tully nodded once, then glanced at his ma, a cautious look on his face.

"Do as ye wish," she growled. "I'll not have ye moping about, wishing ye were aboard a ship and neglecting yer chores."

Carys sought even the tiniest bit of remorse in the woman's face, but greed glowed meanly in Gavina's eyes. Tully would likely never see any coin earned if he stayed with her, and she knew it.

Tully turned back to Birk. "Kin I sail?"

"Aye. I plan on keeping the *Már* fitted for travel, and there are a lot of jobs necessary to keep her afloat. Can ye use a broom and an axe?"

Tully's face brightened. "I's strong! I's a good worker. Da says so!"

"Are ye willing to swab decks and keep the ship in order and do whatever Captain Aklan requests of ye?"

"Aye!"

"The job is yers if ye wish."

Tully glowed with pride. Birk patted the lad's shoulder. Tully gravely shook his hand as he'd likely seen his da do many times to seal a bargain, then bounded over to Eislyn and Abria who sat with Hanna and Dewr some distance away.

"I's going home with ye!" he announced, his happy voice crossing the room. Eislyn and Abria squealed excitedly as they jumped up and down, hugging him. The three girls behind the bar disappeared from view.

"I am grateful to ye for allowing Tully to work for me." Birk gave a slight bow to Gavina, breaking her attention from Tully. She glanced at Birk, her gaze taking in his expensive, albeit wet, cloak, and the sword hanging from the heavily tooled leather belt at his waist.

"Ye fill his head with sailin' nonsense, but he's yer problem now. He's a boon ta me, make no mistake," she added, rubbing her chin. "'Twill be costly to replace him."

Birk handed her one of the leather bags. She hefted it once then tied it to her own belt.

"'Twill keep us from starvin' this winter, and mayhap the next," she muttered ungraciously.

"I will add a silver coin to whatever he sends to ye," Carys said. "And we will hear from ye no more."

"Ye cannae keep a lad from his ma!" she protested.

"I would not dream of interfering should he wish to visit ye," Carys said. "Should ye visit him, ye will quarter with him in his room, and your visit will not exceed three days."

"I wouldnae like to cut his wages for work not done whilst ye were there," Birk added, a meaningful look on his face.

Gavina scowled, understanding the hint she would not be welcome for long at MacLean Castle. Though it flew in the face of every tenet of hospitality Carys held, she was glad she had not made her home available to Gavina. She could not imagine housing the odious woman with Hanna and the girls, or the havoc such a visit could wreak.

"I must lock this away." Gavina draped her apron over the leather bag at her side, hiding it from casual view. "Help yerself tae dinner whilst ye're here. Family prices for ye." She gave Carys a pointed stare. "This time."

* * *

The children's excitement over returning home with Tully waned. Boredom settled in aboard ship with little to do, and Hanna quickly offered them a choice between swabbing the deck or listening to a tale she'd heard of a witch who brewed storms in the strait between two islands.

"'Tis but a short distance ahead between Jura, the island ye can see to the west, and Scarba which is an hour or so's sail away."

Birk grinned. His ma was a great *skald*, and he could trust her to keep the children enthralled for a bit, though he wondered, if she told the ancient tale of the whirlpool between Scarba and Jura, how she'd manage the part about the king's daughter's lost virtue.

"She is a remarkable woman," Carys murmured. She twined her fingers with his and leaned against his shoulder, trapping their hands between them. 'Tis clear the girls adore her."

Birk dropped a kiss on the top of Carys's head. "Hanna lost much in her fight with the Scots who raided her village. But she married my da and found her heart again. The girls adore her, also."

Hanna beckoned the children closer. "'Tis said a cailleach lives in a cave on the coast of Scarba . . .." The children circled about, rapt with anticipation for the tale.

Carys shifted her weight against him. "A cailleach is an old woman, aye?"

"Anything hooded, actually. A mountain shrouded in clouds might be referred to as a cailleach. A nun is often called a cailleach because of the hood she wears. But in Hanna's story, a cailleach is a witch who stirs the whirlpool between Jura and Scarba when she washes her plaide in the waters, creating a maelstrom that will send the unwary to the depths of the sea."

"A whirlpool? Truth? Large enough to sink a ship?"

"Och, aye. 'Tis worse just before winter and at any Spring tide combined with a westerly wind. A maelstrom like none other which rages for hours when the tide advances. Even on calm days the swells can rise dangerously when the corryvreckan is in spate."

"I've never heard of such," Carys admitted. She glanced over the bow. "We will not take the strait between the islands, will we?"

Birk chuckled. "Nae. 'Twould take something drastic to drive us to that route. We can be home at Morvern without inviting the wrath of the cailleach for trespassing her waters. But dinnae fash. 'Tis said the worst of her cauldron is when she washes her plaide and drapes it across the land to dry. Since she is the auldest woman, her plaide is completely white, and thus we get the first snowfall."

"Which should be several weeks away."

"Aye. The *Már* would likely survive a dip in the corryvreckan, but I'd rather not test the auld woman's wrath."

His interest in Hanna's story faded as the wind ripped Carys's black hair from her braid, sending strands dancing about her head. Her cloak winged from her shoulders despite the belt securing it about her waist. He wanted to snatch the leather thong from her hair and spill the silken mass over him. Glancing at the single cabin beneath the aftcastle, he made a firm note to create a second, or even third, cabin for privacy. They would be home before sundown. Perhaps he could keep his hands off her until then.

Carys stepped in front of him and, wrapping her arms about his waist, buried her face against his chest.

"Cold?" he asked. He slid his hands beneath her plaide and pulled her close.

Carys shook her head. "I want ye to hold me."

Birk's world spun. He didn't wish this moment to ever end, yet couldn't arrive home fast enough. He groaned. "Ye have broken me. Broken my fears, the lies I believed. Swear to me ye will never leave me."

She snuggled closer. "I honor my vows, Scotsman," she reminded him tartly. "But I also honor what is between us. I will not leave ye. More importantly, I do not *want* to ever leave ye."

He held her against him, breathing deep as he wrangled his body into a semblance of calm. His daughters' laughter rose and Tully guffawed at some silliness. Birk could not imagine a time he'd been so content.

* * *

"Ship ahoy!"

Carys released Birk to answer the captain's call. She crossed to the circle where children, one dog, and a padded, salt-streaked leather ball romped across the deck. She dodged an errant kick and caught the ball as it flew toward her head. With a warning that a ball overboard was a ball forever gone, she tossed it back to Tully. He batted it to the deck and chased it down, stopping it next to a wooden bucket filled with sand. Eislyn rushed to his side, then turned to Carys.

"Why are there buckets of sand on the deck? I count eight."

"I count lots," Abria piped up, joining her sister.

Taken aback, Carys struggled with her answer. "They are here in case of a fire," she replied carefully. *And to absorb blood to protect our footing during battle.* But this she could not tell them. A shiver of premonitions swept down her spine.

The children sent each other speculative looks that included the vast waters around them, then shrugged and returned to their game. Carys sighed thankfully and continued across the deck.

"Birk told me of the Corryvreckan whirlpool," she said as she reached Hanna's side.

"I'm certain ye have such tales in your land. The true story of the corryvreckan is a combination of Norse and Scots. I'll tell it to ye sometime when curious ears aren't listening."

Carys and Hanna glanced up sharply as Iain strode purposefully toward them. He stopped close with a glance over his shoulder at the children.

"Ye are to gather the bairns and secure yerselves in the cabin. Now."

Carys hesitated, scanning the horizon. The Isle of Scarba loomed just off the port bow, a largely uninhabited stretch of land to starboard. A gust of wind poured into the sail, shoving the ship down into an unexpected trough as the seas roughened, pushing them deeper into the narrow strait. Carys grasped Iain's arm for balance. Clouds thickened, darkening the sun. She regained her stance, bending her knees slightly to absorb the increased roll of the deck.

"I do not . . .."

The entire ship shuddered and groaned. Children's screams pierced the air as a spear landed in their midst. A slender ship, toothy dragon's head carved into the bowsprit, battle shields bristling along the rail, loomed over them before plunging down into the next trough to sink beneath the *Már's* bow.

Tully grabbed Eislyn and Abria. Sliding on the wet boards, he dragged them to the cabin. He struggled with the door, but before Carys could reach them, Hanna was at his side. Together they wrestled the door open and shoved the girls inside.

"Do ye know how to use this?" Hanna drew a dagger from a sheath at her waist.

Tully nodded.

She flipped the blade over and shoved the hilt at him. "Let no one cross this door who does not know ye by name."

Carys and Hanna turned to Iain. Hanna nodded grimly. "We are at your disposal." She glanced over her shoulder. "Tell your captain to keep us away from the witch's cauldron."

Chapter Twenty Nine

"They will attempt to run us aground."

Birk startled at Hanna's voice at his shoulder. "Ye shouldnae be here. Protect the bairns."

She laughed softly, a sound of defiance and challenge. "The women in your family are warriors, Birk MacLean. 'Twill serve ye well to never forget."

He glanced past her and found Carys at the bow, the Norse spear hefted familiarly in one hand, an instant away from being plunged back into the heart of the pirate ship. The deep gouge where it had struck the deck gleamed, a pale wound in the aged wood.

"Shite."

Hanna pointed to the approaching ship. "The langskip is light and fast. See how tall and narrow the bow and stern are? 'Tis also clinker built, and the midsection is quite wide. 'Twill be very fast and stable even in these waters. But they know our ship could withstand any force they tried against her. If they can drive her onto the beach, they can board and fight us on even footing."

"There is no *us* . . .. Ye and Carys . . .." He rubbed the back of his neck. "Shite."

"Your vocabulary is not improving, *sonr min*. Pay attention. We must avoid the shoreline at all cost."

"I know how the Norse fight. Ye dinnae need to tutor me in battle tactics."

A sailor dragged a long, deep chest across the deck. He unlocked it, opened the lid and dispensed weapons to the crew. Hanna slipped from the aftcastle to the deck, joining Carys at the chest. Birk ground his teeth as the startled sailor glanced up, seeking permission to arm the two women. Without waiting for his sanction, his mother and wife slipped daggers as long as their forearms into sheaths at their sides. Hanna plucked a short sword from the chest. Carys also selected a short sword and grabbed a bow and quiver of arrows from a passing soldier.

Brody handed the weapons to her without fuss. He knew Carys could fight. He'd learned of her skills firsthand that day in the forest, and again when she'd bested his laird in the yard at Dairborrodal.

I should be protecting them. Birk raked a hand through his hair, grudgingly recalling tales of Hanna in years past. With a grunt, he acknowledged the pair was far from helpless, and possibly better fighters than many of the sailors. He did not have time to worry. The pirate ship, larger than the one that had threatened them near Morvern, drew closer.

"This is not the same ship," Carys remarked as she stepped to his side.

He nodded. "And 'tis too far south. My men have scoured the coastlines from Dairborrodal to Oban and not discovered their lair."

"Mayhap the question is not, *why are they so far south*, but rather, *why was the other ship so far north*?"

Birk struck his forehead with the heel of his palm. "Shite!"

Hanna leaned close. "I've told him to improve his vocabulary, but I'm afraid my pleas fall on deaf ears."

Birk whirled. "Iain, who lays claim to Jura?"

"Angus Mor MacDonald claims much of these isles."

"He pledged allegiance to King Alexander, aye?"

Iain tilted his head. "Aye. But he fought with Haakon against the Scots at Largs."

Birk waved a hand in the air. "'Twas nearly twenty years ago."

"Scarcely eighteen, and there are Norse in the Isles who do not agree with his change of allegiance."

Birk gripped the rail as the *Már* plunged into another trough. He glanced at Hanna, her face pale, eyes fixed on some long-ago memory. "Enough to pillage the Scottish coast?"

"Aye," she murmured. "There are those who have not forgotten the treachery at Scottish hands."

Carys jerked her chin toward the approaching ship. "I would attempt flaming arrows, but the sail would not light for long with the spray kicking up as it is. And the angle is wrong for the ballista—most of the time, at least—to aim over their rail. The shields are well-arranged, and they take care to sail just out of our range."

Birk rubbed his chin, startled to realize he took Carys's observations—and Hanna's—seriously. But both women made perfect sense and their comments helped him make up his mind.

He turned to Captain Aklen. "Alert the crew. We have no option but to find wind and current to take us out of this strait. 'Tis too narrow and we could be too easily run aground."

"Ye mean to sail between Jura and Scarba? The strait there is narrow as well and we sail a flood tide. The full moon was last night and the cauldron will be boiling." He shook his head. "We could round Islay and head for the open sea, but their ship is fast and I dinnae know if we could outrun them. Mayhap we could aim for Crinan on the mainland instead. 'Tis not so far. There's a port there and the bastards arenae likely to follow us."

Birk shook his head. "This is a sturdy ship, but we must get out of these waters." He stared at the Norse vessel gliding easily across the waves, maintaining a steady distance. "We will head into the Gulf of Corryvreckan—and hope the westerly wind fails."

* * *

"He means to force the pirates to abandon the chase through the witch's cauldron." Hanna's voice stretched thin, her face strained.

"The langskip sits too high and they would be fools to challenge the whirlpool."

"Why do ye fear it so?" Carys followed Hanna's gaze—not to the following ship, carved dragon head riding high above the waves, but to the shore of Scarba as it slipped past, rocks at its base partly hidden by mist and sea spray.

"The tale is an old one," Hanna said. "A prince of Norway loved a princess of Jura. Her father would only allow them to wed if the prince showed the skills and courage to anchor his ship within the fury of A'Cailleach for three days. 'Twas an impossible task, but he would not give in. To secure his ship against the witch's wrath, he wove three ropes—one of hemp, one of wool, and one from the hair of a maiden of pure virtue.

"He sailed alone into the maelstrom as the tide rose. His ship struggled against the pull of the whirlpool, and the first night, the woolen rope broke. The hempen rope fell apart the second night, and the third night, to his horror, the rope woven from the hair of his less-than-virtuous princess also parted. His body washed ashore the next day, and he was buried in a cave nearby—as was his beloved who died of a broken heart not long after."

"Am I to understand few ships make it through the corryvreckan?" Carys asked.

Hanna turned bleak eyes to her. "If the cailleach is angry, none may pass."

Carys shifted her gaze to the rising sea, hearing the strain of the ship's boards as the current battled beneath them, forcing its way up the narrowing strait.

Mayhap the pirates will abandon the chase before we are committed to sailing through these waters. Her heart raced, a thready tattoo fluttering in her chest. *I prefer open battle to this.* Her thoughts turned to the children sheltered in the cabin. *Nae. They*

*must be protected. The longer we remain out of reach, the less
chance the pirates have to overtake us.*

"Waiting is not easy," she murmured. "I learned to endure it
whilst hunting Edward's soldiers in the mountains. Battle is
decisive, quick. But once committed, there is no turning back."

Hanna nodded. "We have bairns to consider. Running is our
best option. For now."

The waves leapt higher, pitching the ship about. The langskip
kept pace, its mast dipping and swaying as it danced up and down
the tossing seas. Clouds pulled tighter overhead and sunlight
dimmed. Carys tugged her plaide snug about her, noticing the new
sharp edge to the wind.

"'Tis growing colder," she remarked.

Hanna nodded. "Such a change in the weather bodes ill."

Carys gripped the rail as the sea fell away beneath the hull. The
Már tipped forward, sliding down the wave, leveling its mast like a
jousting lance. The sail fluttered as it momentarily lost the wind.
Birk shouted commands Carys could not understand and the rigging
creaked with strain. The ship righted itself and rotated slightly,
lurching as it once again caught the wind.

In tandem, the two ships entered the strait.

"Why do they pursue us?" Carys asked.

Hanna shook her head. "Much wrong was done to my people
and has not been answered for. And there is potential treasure to be
gained from capturing a merchant ship—especially a MacLean
ship."

The waves dropped and the seas churned. White-capped swells
boiled about them, and the current sent the ships bolting through the
strait.

"Hold to the south edge of the waters," Hanna murmured. She
glanced at Carys. "The strait is less than a mile wide. The waters are

shallower on the northern side and create standing waves that would dwarf the *Már*."

Carys nodded, her throat dry. This was no wind-and-rain storm. This was something created within the waters themselves.

The pirate ship fell back, clearly aware of the dangers of running parallel to the *Már*.

"I will check on the bairns," Hanna said. "I am of little help here."

Carys lingered a moment more at the rail, then followed Hanna to the cabin, her feet slipping on the wet deck. Tully's face loomed pale in the darkness of the small room, flanked by the anxious eyes of Eislyn and Abria.

"Are we gonna sink?" Tully swallowed hard.

"Nae. We are taking a route that is not pleasant, but I have no fear of sinking," Hanna replied. "I wondered if my granddaughters remembered how to keep the blue men from attacking a ship?"

Carys stared at Hanna. A story? Yet, Abria nodded vigorously as Eislyn scooted forward on her knees.

"Och, ye must answer a question with a rhyme," Eislyn replied, clearly no stranger to the tale of the blue men—whomever they might be.

"Good lass," Hanna said. "Do ye know the words, then? Here is my question. *O, ye of the Már, what do ye say, as yer ship sails over the sea?*"

Eislyn tilted her head. "*My sailing ship takes the shortest way, ye'd do well to follow me.*"

Hanna ruffled Eislyn's hair. "Excellent. We will finish when Carys and I return. Remain inside and do not let Dewr be afraid."

Abria grabbed the dog's ruff and pulled her close. Dewr licked the child's cheek. Dropping a kiss to each child's head in turn, Carys and Hanna closed the door securely and walked back to the rail.

"Another Norse tale?" Carys asked.

"Nae. Celtic. But it may keep them busy thinking up rhymes rather than reasons to be afraid."

Carys smiled. "Ye are a wonderful woman, Hanna. I am honored to be your daughter by marriage."

A loud pop sounded over the water. Carys jerked to one side, scanning the sky for a bolt from a ballista, even though she knew the enemy ship did not carry one.

"Look." Hanna pointed ahead. The white-capped water swirled about, boiling upward from the center of the eddies. Spouts burst upward, taller than the mast of the langskip that shied like a frightened horse. As the water shot skyward, another clap sounded.

Carys's heart raced, caught between fascination and horror.

The green water churned and roiled, slapping the sides of the ships with angry force. The Norse ship hit a wave broadside and slipped about, its bow reeling to the side. Caught in a large whirlpool, it pitched and yawed, caught in the relentless waves. The water swirled as if brewed in a giant cauldron, powered by a sea god's wrath.

Despite her eagerness to escape the pirates, Carys leaned against the rail, gaze fixed on the floundering pirate ship. Oars strained against the current and slowly the ship righted. It bobbed once more, then, instead of tipping to the center of the maelstrom, the langskip nosed away from the vortex. Now on the outer edge of the swirling sea, the ship caught the rushing current which shoved it out of the cauldron—and directly into the *Már's* path.

Birk's shout sent the *Már* yawing toward the shore where rocks held firm against the slap of angry waves. Carys's heartrate tripled, memory of the rocks that had broken the *Seabhag* rising in her mind. She wanted to close her eyes, but a macabre fascination held her gaze as the langskip slid past the *Már's* bow, close enough to read the determination on the faces of the pirates. Correcting the surge toward the shore, the *Már* came about, drawing alongside the langskip, forcing it closer to the rocks.

Birk's jaw clenched tight as the langskip slid gracefully around the giant boulders that rose without warning from the foaming surf. Her captain's sailing skills wrung Birk's reluctant admiration. He saw the rock as the waves receded before the langskip's captain did, and he watched in fascinated horror as the bow slid up the slippery rock and poised, keel out of the water, before plunging with bone-snapping force back to the waves.

Carys and Hanna raced up the steps to the aftcastle and joined him as the langskip broke up on the rocks.

The crack of fractured timber ripped through the crash of waves. Shouts from the foundering ship rose and fell, but there was no possibility of getting close enough to search for survivors. With the children to protect, Birk was hardly in the position to bring pirates aboard. If anyone made it to shore, it would likely be a long walk—or swim—home.

He ordered Captain Aklen to bring the ship out of the strait. The sail for home would cross a bit of open water, but the dangerous water was past. The ship swayed as her bow turned a bit to starboard and caught the westerly breeze. They would follow it along Scarba's coast and through the Firth of Forth, skirting a few small islands until they reached the Firth of Lorn and rounded the coast of Mull.

The last of the roil of the whirlpool died away as they turned north, entering the Gulf of the Corryvreckan. Jura lay aft, Scarba just off the starboard bow.

Straight ahead, appearing from behind an outcrop of Scarba's coast like a predator, lay a smaller langskip, its bow curled high above the row of shields that gleamed colorfully in the midmorning light.

They had survived the witch's caldron—and sailed into a trap.

Chapter Thirty

Peering from beneath the bladed palm of her hand, Carys flinched as the langskip sailed into view. Incredibly fast, it was inside ballista range before the cumbersome weapon could be brought into play. The *Már* rocked as Captain Aklen sent the ship reeling away. But the langskip was faster. Its nearly flat hull skimmed the waves, bringing home to Carys exactly why the Norse had ruled the Isles for so long.

She swallowed the fear that clogged her throat and snatched the spear from the deck. One hand tapped the bow slung over her shoulder, deriving a measure of reassurance from its presence. The pirates would attempt to board the ship. All weapons would be needed. The fight would be hard and fast. Her heart raced.

"I will protect the children," she stated.

Hanna nodded. "I will be in the cabin with them." Her eyes sparked. "None who enter will live."

Birk sent Brody down to the main deck with Hanna. Brody's stout form braced before the cabin door as it closed behind Hanna. He would allow none to approach.

The langskip's bow scraped the *Már's* side, a screech of challenge. The *Már* reeled to port, absorbing the strike, an attempt to put distance between them. But the shoreline was too close, and rocks threatened to send the *Már* to the same fate as the first pirate ship.

"They will board us," Birk said, his voice low, harsh.

The ship listed hard to starboard. Carys shifted her weight against the roll.

"I am sorry." Birk's jaw clenched, the set of his shoulders full of anger.

"We will do what we must. And apologize for naught."

The two ships' hulls grated together and grappling hooks thudded onto the *Már's* rail. Men raced about, releasing the hooks they could, but the pull of the pirate ship caused the metal tips to bite deep into the burnished wood.

Birk sent Carys a last look, and she read the regret in his eyes. Before he could turn from her, she rose on her toes and kissed him, needing one last touch to center her before the battle. Dropping back to her feet, she placed her fingertips on his chest.

"Go. May God be with ye."

Birk hesitated. "And with ye."

Without a backward glance, he left her on the aftcastle and bolted down the steps to the main deck, pausing to give orders before joining Captain Aklen, now at the bow. Carys drank in a final sight of him, dark head above those around him, broad shoulders accepting the command of a battle whose outcome was uncertain. Soldiers along the rails grabbed the buckets of sand and tossed their contents onto the deck, anticipating spilled blood that would create treacherous footing. A ripple of unease slid through Carys as she remembered the children's earlier innocent question. Had it been a premonition? Or mere curiosity?

She shoved the superstitious thought aside and faced the starboard bow where pirates clung to swinging, knotted ropes. Fingering the feathers on the arrows in her quiver, she selected one and pulled her bow from her shoulder. From her perch atop the aftcastle, she surveyed the deck below and marked her first kill.

Pirates boiled over the side of the ship despite the attempt to repel them. Carys nocked an arrow, setting it firm against the bowstring. She let it fly and instantly nocked another. The first arrow dropped a pirate to the deck who had escaped the line of MacLean soldiers at the rail. More pirates invaded the ship, but Carys held back, afraid of striking a MacLean.

The ship pitched, the wooden planks slippery with sea spray and blood despite the sanded deck as swords and daggers did their work. The men grappled, hand-to-hand, the fighting fierce. They swarmed the deck, shouts underscored by the clang of steel. The stench of death filled the air.

Carys searched the deck below her, using her arrows to help Brody as he defended the cabin door. Two pirates died, an arrow in each black heart. Another stumbled as the shaft slammed into his shoulder, giving Brody a chance to defend himself against a second attacker before delivering the killing blow. There was scarcely time to draw breath before each dispatched pirate was replaced by another, their battle cries and the shriek of steel on steel adding to the din. Carys nocked arrow after arrow, the deck around Brody fouled with bodies. He took a blow from a Norse battle axe. His right arm hung at an unnatural angle, blood dripping from his fingertips. He switched his sword to his left hand, hunched his shoulders, then straightened and met the next pirate.

Carys reached for another arrow but found the quiver empty. The spear lay at her feet and she exchanged her bow for the long wooden shaft, the throwing string caught in her fingers. She peered anxiously over the seething mass of men below her on the deck, painfully aware she had lost her position of power and safety once the last arrow had sailed from her bow. She could regain her ability to fight if she dropped to the deck, using the spear much like she would a javelin, but it would put her in the midst of the fighting.

Her body trembled with frustration, fear. Skilled she was, but not foolish. Hand-to-hand combat with this many men would not last long. She had one distance weapon remaining, one last chance to help. When the spear was gone, she would be left with only the short sword and dagger at her belt, and whatever time given to her before she ran out of options—and died.

She stared at the deck of the langskip, nearly empty, the last of the pirates clambering aboard the *Már*. How much longer could the MacLean soldiers repel the boarders? The dead and wounded massed on the deck, the fighting fast and brutal, making it difficult to predict the outcome of the battle. Her heart thudded against her ribs and she choked back agony for the children hidden away in the cabin below.

The scrape of wood behind her caught her ear and she whirled, startled to see a man she did not know levering himself over the port quarter rail. Blue eyes met hers, sparkling above a dark red beard. The blade of his short axe bit into the deck of the aftcastle, and an instant later he was on his feet. He was only an inch or two taller than Carys, but his bulk bespoke hours of hard work, and the easy familiarity with the axe caused her heartrate to double. He drew a long dagger from his belt and grinned at her.

On the deck below in the melee, or alone with this pirate, her time was near the end. Opting to use the reach advantage of the spear, Carys advanced two steps toward the pirate, away from the edge of the aftcastle. The pirate's grin widened. Extending his arm, he tapped the end of Carys's spear with the head of his axe, testing her skill and, perhaps, her resolve.

Determined not to allow him the first move, she lunged forward, driving her spear toward the Norseman's heart. He deflected her strike at the last second with his dagger, but could not avoid the bite of her weapon. He grunted and glanced at his arm where she had opened a long gash.

He bit out a stream of Norse with a snarl, likely a descriptive curse, but Carys did not invite translation. Buoyed by drawing first blood, Carys pressed the attack and thrust again. The pirate deflected her spear with his axe and spun toward her to close the gap. He swung his dagger with a sweeping backhand aimed at her throat. Carys ducked, his attack whistling just above her head. She took a sliding retreating step to her left, cutting his thigh as she drew the extended spear back to guard position. The Norseman narrowed his eyes and circled her, wariness in his gaze. She'd lost the element of surprise. He now realized she was more than a defenseless woman with a man's weapon.

The pirate feinted to draw her attack, but Carys stood her ground, not willing to give in to his attempts to bait her. She recalled her battle against Colin Dubh and how she'd outlasted him. The spear she held, however, was substantially heavier than her thin javelin. If she didn't end this soon, her arms would cease to wield the weapon effectively.

She thrust again. The pirate hooked his axe over the shaft of her spear and jerked the weapon from her hands. It clattered to the deck and rolled away, coming to rest against the railing. He lunged at her, his dagger flashing in his hand. Carys dropped and rolled to one side, narrowly missing being gutted. Warmth trickled down her belly, evidence he'd found flesh. She leapt upright then drew the short sword and dagger. She'd no option but to give away size, strength, and now reach to her foe. Even wounded, she was the quicker of the two—a poor consolation considering his advantages.

The warrior rose to his full height and strode confidently toward her, his axe raised. Carys crouched, ready to move to either side to avoid a blow she had no hope of blocking. He swung his axe in a diagonal strike that would open her from shoulder to opposite hip. Stepping to the side and slightly forward, Carys managed to move out of his reach. She took another step forward, just past him, and swung her short sword low before he could halt the momentum of his heavy axe. Her blade bit into the back of his leg and he staggered. He turned, reaching for her as he dropped his axe.

He shoved her backward and Carys fell awkwardly, losing her grip on her sword and dagger as she struggled to regain her balance. Landing hard, she banged her head against the side of the *Már*.

The Norse warrior picked up his axe and charged, showing no sign of his injury. Cornered against the railing, Carys lay helpless, her sword and dagger out of reach. He raised his axe for a killing blow, only a few steps away. Desperate, Carys tried to roll, but landed against the spear wedged between her and the rail. Bracing the blunt end in the angle between deck and rail, she brought the tip up as the Norseman lunged. Unable to stop his attack, he impaled himself, shock widening his eyes and mouth. His axe hit the wooden deck with a *thunk*, its arc carrying it a few feet beyond Carys's head. His massive body fell lifeless across Carys, driving the breath from her lungs. Pain streaked across her side.

Gritting her teeth against the stabbing ache in her belly, Carys shoved his body aside and staggered to her feet. She retrieved her short sword and dagger, then made her way toward the ladder, her steps faltering, her breath catching in great gulps as she tried to suppress the pain, shocked she still lived.

The sounds of battle had ended, replaced by the groans of the wounded. The once-orderly deck had become a scene of carnage. Brody remained standing below her, the cabin door shut. His arm dangled uselessly at his side. Carys scanned the deck for Birk and found him among the surviving men returning the dead invaders to the sea.

A small group of wounded, divided MacLeans to one side, pirates to another, lay midships, surrounded by armed MacLean warriors. A burning pain stirred her sluggish brain. Carys placed a hand against her middle. It came away sticky with blood.

Birk glanced about, seeing little of the ship, seeking Carys. The aftcastle was empty and he found her a moment later among the wounded—to his gut-wrenching relief, alive and on her feet. He turned back to the job of removing the dead. With a shove, the last body disappeared into the frothing sea. Birk dragged the back of one hand across his forehead, wiping away sweat that dripped into his eyes. He flexed his shoulder, the tug of a long gash hindering the move. He motioned to the wounded.

"I wish to know who they are." With a grimace, Birk left Iain to complete the task of minimizing the damage to the ship and crossed the deck. His step quickened as he saw Hanna wrap a length of cloth about his wife's midsection, and only managed through great presence of mind not to grab her into a fierce embrace.

"She has taken little harm, though 'twill ache from the bruising." Hanna knotted the bandage then tilted Carys's face from side to side. "Any other places?"

"Nae. I will be fine," she replied, her voice thin.

"Fine?" Birk buried his anger and relief but did not fool Hanna.

"Aye, she will be fine. At the moment she is sore and exhausted. I do not believe the wound requires stitching, though we must keep watch that it does not fester. The bandage should control the bleeding."

Bleeding? His hands itched to yank the knotted strips from her belly and inspect the wound for himself. His arms ached to hold her against him.

Carys pulled her cloak about her, shadows dark about her eyes, her skin pale and drawn. "See to Brody," she murmured. "He saved us all."

"I would be dead ten times over were it not for ye and that bow of yers." Brody grunted as Hanna prodded his arm that hung at an awkward angle. Sweat beaded his brow and color left his face. Birk knew what Hanna would do with the dislocated limb and left the job to her and two others. He touched Carys's shoulder.

"In a bit I will realize I almost lost ye today. I dinnae know what happened to ye on the aftcastle, and someday ye will tell me. For now, 'tis enough to see ye alive and on yer feet."

"I am relieved to see ye, also. There is still much to do. I will help where I can."

Birk gazed at her, taking in her slack-shouldered stance that spoke of her weariness, and the careful tuck of her left arm against her side to protect her injury. He palmed the back of her head and she sighed. He kissed her cheek.

"For now, let us see to the others."

Kern glanced up from the wounded who lay against the bow railing. He slid the palm of his hand over one man's eyes, closing them in the finality of death. With a shake of his head, he allowed the sailor assisting him—and looking only a heartbeat better than the man at his feet—to draw the edges of the sheet of canvas that had once been a hammock below decks over his still form—his own bed now a shroud.

Beyond the MacLean wounded, three pirates still breathed. With the enemy swept from the deck like so much detritus, Iain had set men to work with pails and brooms to scrub the blood from the boards. Debris from the second pirate ship floated past. A hole had been hacked into its side to scuttle it, the mast hewn to little more than firewood.

Birk and Carys approached the three pirates. A moment later, Hanna joined them. It was immediately clear two were beyond questioning.

The third man, body battered and bleeding, rolled his head slowly side to side. Hanna drew to a halt next to him. Her hand flew to her throat.

"Odin, Allfather!" she gasped.

Birk and Carys stepped to her side. Hanna wavered. He grasped her elbow, steadying her, then followed her gaze to the injured man.

"What is wrong, *móðir*?"

Hanna raised a trembling hand. "It cannot be, yet this man . . . he looks exactly like Torvald—my first husband."

Chapter Thirty One

Late afternoon sun slanted through the evening clouds. As soon as the deck had been cleared, Carys had taken bannocks and cider to the children, giving them full bellies to help reassure them all would be well. Exhausted from the fright, they had eaten sparsely then curled up on blankets to rest. Carys left them in the cabin, bidding them stay within a while longer. Birk consulted with Captain Aklen atop the aftcastle, and she missed his presence.

Hanna remained at the injured pirate's side, silent and withdrawn, clearly caught in a time when she and Torvald had lived together, raising two children on the Isle of Mull. A time before King Alexander set out to conquer the Isles and bring them under Scottish rule.

Carys stepped from the cabin, her heart aching for the older woman. She shared her sense of loss, but could not begin to imagine losing a child as Hanna had lost her son, Sten.

"We will question him as soon as he wakes." Carys laid a palm on Hanna's shoulder. "Ye should eat a bite. Brody will watch over him."

For a moment, Carys wasn't certain Hanna had heard her. Then, as if waking from a deep sleep, she rose, leaning heavily against Carys as though her strength had left her. In that moment Carys understood Hanna had outlived two husbands and was no longer a young woman herself, despite her active nature. Without comment, she lent the support necessary until Hanna straightened and regained her composure.

"'Tis uncanny, the resemblance," she murmured, glancing over her shoulder. "It should not affect me so, but . . .."

"Your heart does not forget," Carys replied soothingly.

Hanna drew a deep breath. "Alex's father was the great love of my life, not Torvald, but our life together was not without caring. He was stern and demanding, yet fair, and with him, I was blessed with two . . .." Her voice broke.

Carys squeezed her hand comfortingly.

The prisoner groaned and rolled to his side. Instantly, Brody and two other soldiers stepped close, hands on their sword hilts. The man flinched and placed the heel of his palm to his forehead. A pained look crossed his face and he twisted face-down, pushing feebly from the deck with his hands. He retched but spat only a bit of bloody liquid from his cracked lips.

"*Bikkju-sonr*," he growled, touching his fingertips to his mouth. He glared at the men towering above him, his gaze settling on Hanna who stood only a few steps away. Her golden hair—more silver now with age—fluttered in the wind. Her face reflected the same prominent brow, the same piercing blue eyes as the prisoner, bound together in similar ancestry.

"Ye are not Scots." He glowered. "Ye keep dishonorable company, *Amma*."

"I was born Norse but wed a Scot—whose vocabulary in the presence of women, I might add, was more respectable than yours."

He cocked an eyebrow. "I am sorry for your loss, *Amma*, but nothing good has come from Scotland in many years."

"Ye appear to claim fewer than twenty years, *ungr*. Much has changed in your lifetime."

"I would delight in discussing the times with ye, if these *swina bqllr* would permit me to rise. I am weaponless and pose no threat to them."

"Let this *murtr* sit," Hanna instructed. The prisoner scowled at Hanna then raised a hand in surrender to Brody's growl.

"I am not a *small fish*," he complained. He gasped and clutched his side. No one moved to help him. He sat gingerly on the deck then slumped slowly against the side of the ship, hand tucked beneath the opposite arm, body folded forward.

"Who captained your ship?" Hanna asked.

The man did not answer for several long moments. Finally, he drew a stuttering breath and stretched his legs one small movement at a time until they sprawled before him. He cocked his head.

"I did."

Carys narrowed her eyes. *Nae, he is no small fish, but rather someone who can answer our questions.*

Hanna lifted her chin. "Why choose pirating over honest work?"

He flicked his fingers in the air as if a stronger gesture was beyond him. "I have a home and honest work. 'Tis an honor to reap some satisfaction from those who destroyed my family."

"There is little strife between Scot and Norse these days, save that which ye create." Birk's gravelly voice startled those gathered around the prisoner. Carys jerked about, surprised she had not heard his booted step upon the boards.

"What is yer name?" Birk demanded.

The prisoner flushed, a sickly hue against his ashen skin. "Ye stand and lord over me as a coward would an enemy not downed by his own hand." He glanced unflinchingly at Birk, his lips tight, the skin around them gray.

Birk's eyes narrowed. "Yer name, or only the ravens will speak it."

"I am Haldor of Colonsay. By what name are *ye* called?" Haldor sneered as though speculating on Birk's honor. As though, without the women present—and with a lesser injury—he would give voice to Birk's presumed ancestry and character.

"I am Birk of Morvern."

Carys snorted lightly, well-versed in her husband's tactic of giving little information away.

"Of Colonsay?" Hanna interrupted. "That is very close to Mull . . .." Her voice trailed off.

Carys eyed her narrowly. What did the Isle of Mull have to do with pirates?

Haldor gave a one-shoulder shrug. "*Faðir* was born on Mull."

Hanna took a step closer. "What is your father's name?"

Birk placed a palm on her shoulder. She quivered as though she would shrug him off, but Birk's fingers curved, holding his hand in place.

"Answer her," he ordered.

Haldor coughed then gasped, clutching his side, his face twisted in agony. A trickle of blood appeared in the corner of his tightly pressed lips. "What does it matter? *Faðir* was captured in a raid as a young boy and sold into slavery. 'Twas many years before he was able to return home, only to find it in the hands of the Scots. He discovered those who sympathized with him, with the plight of the Norse despite the treaty signed by Scotland and Norway."

Hanna knelt beside him. "I beg ye, speak his name."

Haldor turned his gaze to her, his eyes dull, his breath shallow and forced. "His name is Sten of Hallstein. He is the son . . .."

"Of Torvald and Hanna of Hallstein."

* * *

Birk stretched his arm about Carys's shoulders and she settled against him with a sigh. Tully and the girls played a quiet game of sticks on the deck, near the shelter of the cabin. Their gazes drifted occasionally to the bow where Hanna and the prisoner sat. A spare cloak had been rolled and used as a bolster between his back and the boards, another draped over him to keep off the worst of the sea spray. Even with what comforts they'd accorded him, Birk knew the slap of the ship against the waves had to hurt like hell. Broken ribs needed stabilizing, not a ride against a choppy tide.

He tightened his arm about Carys. "I couldnae bear to lose ye as Hanna lost her family."

Carys traced her fingertips against his arm. "Neither of us will live forever."

"I understand that well," Birk replied. "And there are perils in everyday living. But I dinnae believe I could bear losing ye to something as senseless as a raid."

"'Tis why ye are glad I am skilled with the weapons at hand." Her voice, light and teasing, carried a bit of the dread that enveloped his own heart.

"'Tis the same with the children," she continued. "None are guaranteed long life—or even to grow to adulthood. And yet, it tears my heart to consider a life without their sweet faces."

Birk dropped a kiss to the top of her head. It pleased him he did not have to bend much to accord himself such a small pleasure. He liked this tall, confident woman he was blessed to call wife. This warrior who'd killed more than her share of pirates, protecting his children with her life.

"This has broken Hanna's heart. There is a wide gulf between grieving for a child thought dead and discovering he had been torn from her to another's purpose."

His daughters' faces rose in his mind, and it took all of his power to not lose control at the thought of them taken from him to appease a captor.

As though she felt his rising anger, Carys shifted away, and he carefully relaxed each muscle, letting his right hand fall from his sword hilt.

"I am glad Da found Hanna's daughter Signy not long after she was captured. I remember her a bit from when I was a wean, though obviously she was many years older than I. She was like a second mother, for a time. She wed when I was verra young and moved away. Gillian and I are much closer."

"She will be glad to know her brother still lives." Her whispered words cracked, and he knew she was likely grieving the loss of her brother all over again.

"I would give Hywel back to ye if I could," he murmured.

She turned her face into his chest and wept.

* * *

Eislyn nudged Carys. "He's our uncle?"

"Aye." How to explain to a child the complications of the relationship? It was easier to simply agree as he apparently was Hanna's grandson, and let time take care of the rest.

"I dinnae know I had a pirate for an uncle."

"Mayhap he will choose to no longer be a pirate," Carys replied. "'Tis what he does now with his life that is important."

Abria grasped Carys's hand, worry translating in her grip. Tully leaned against the rail.

"I see a ship!" he cried, pointing over the bow.

The *Már* glided gracefully into a beautiful, horseshoe-shaped bay. Sparkling sapphire water blazed like emeralds closer to shore. White-tipped waves lapped lazily at the sandy beach. Mountains rose on either side, protecting the bay and the longhouse in the low land between the hills. A langskip rested near the shore, its nearly flat hull perfectly crafted for the shallow water.

Men lined the bay, armed and alert to the ship sailing into their harbor in broad daylight. Others stood defensively near the longhouse. Smoke rose lazily from wooden racks draped with what appeared to be rows of fish. No women or children could be seen, but a leather ball much like the one Tully and the girls played with had been abandoned near the door of the longhouse.

Six men stepped into the shallow water as the crew dropped anchor several cautious lengths from shore. Birk requested a small craft lowered over the rail, then climbed aboard, flanked by ten soldiers, Hanna, and Haldor.

He set Haldor carefully at the bow.

Carys gathered the children together, arms about them protectively as the boat crossed the surf.

Birk hailed the men of Kiloran Bay as they approached the beach, though his words drifted away from Carys's ears. Two men replied and caught the bow of Birk's boat, holding it steady as another lifted Haldor from the craft. Carys winced as they set Haldor's feet in the water, understanding the agony he must feel as the waves pushed and pulled at his broken body. Slowly, determinedly, supported on either side by the Norsemen, he walked through the surf to the beach. Having apparently reached some manner of accord, Birk and Hanna, along with eight MacLean soldiers, followed.

Abria whimpered. Carys knew the children had to be exhausted, frightened by the wild race through the witch's cauldron and the terror as pirates boarded the *Már*. It alarmed her to see Birk and Hanna disappear into the longhouse, but she knew neither had undertaken the journey ashore lightly.

"I want to go home," Abria whined, pulling on Carys's hand. She plopped her bottom to the deck, jerking her palm from Carys's grip, and ducked her head.

Carys knelt beside her. Eislyn sat and hugged her sister. Both turned wide eyes on Carys, needing reassurance.

"Had we been closer to Morvern, we would have taken ye there before bringing Haldor to his home. But he is hurt very badly, and we wanted him to return to his family whilst he still could."

Abria sniffled. Carys's heart lurched at the sight of tears on the tiny face.

"Will he die?" She gulped. "Ma died."

"I know she did, *bychan*," Carys crooned, scooping Abria into her arms. "And I am very sorry. I think Haldor will live, if he gets the care he needs."

She stroked Abria's dark head, not mentioning the blood at Haldor's mouth that bespoke the possibility one or more ribs had punctured his lungs. She had seen too many men with similar injuries slide slowly into death despite the best of care.

The strain of worrying over Birk's and Hanna's safety exhausted her, and she coaxed the children to the shelter of the cabin's wall, promising them a story and an early supper of cold bannocks and watered ale.

"Brody will bring honey for the bannocks," Eislyn reassured a tearful Abria. "He likes us and knows we like honey."

Abria nodded and allowed herself to be led from the rail, seeking one last glance of the shore which still bristled with armed men, watching the ship rock silently at anchor.

The quiet seemed somewhat reassuring, though Carys knew it would take only one misunderstanding or flare of anger to turn the tables against them. Inhaling slowly to steady her voice, she began the story she'd promised, tweaking the tale to reflect the cove in which they harbored and the nearby mountains.

"Branwen was a beautiful princess of Cymry . . .."

"Like ye?" Eislyn asked.

"Mayhap." Carys smiled. "She married a king of Ireland, and though he treated her well, she was so homesick, she taught a raven to say her name, then released him to fly across the seas to Cymry. It landed on her brother's shoulder. He was the giant, Brân, and he immediately set out to rescue her."

She caught Tully's nod of approval and her heart filled to see he considered rescuing sisters a good thing. Abria scooted closer to Tully and he draped his arm protectively over her shoulder.

"I'd rescue ye, if ye needed, Abria," he whispered.

Carys smiled. "Brân departed so fast, he left a boulder from his pocket on the cliff where he'd been watching for ships." Carys nodded to the hills beyond the bay. A large boulder perched nearby as though placed just for her story. "And his footprint created a lovely beach."

"Did he find her?" Eislyn asked.

"He waded across the sea, dragging an entire fleet of ships behind him, and found her alone in her tower," Carys said. "'Twas not long before Branwen settled into her new home, with Brân's help, and she lived there happily for the rest of her days. Of course, her brother visited often."

Eislyn clapped her hands. "I like that story. Tell us another."

Movement on the beach caught Carys's attention. She rose, motioning for the children to remain seated. "I will tell ye another when I return. Here is a lad with yer supper. I must speak with Brody."

Carys slipped away, flinching at the anxious gazes between her shoulder blades as she turned her back on the children. Her attention riveted on the beach where the men, calm and watchful a moment before, drew together, a burr of noise drifting to the ship.

Something was wrong.

Very wrong.

Chapter Thirty Two

Birk halted just inside the longhouse door, giving his eyes a chance to adjust to the gloom. A double row of posts ran the length of the building, benches draped with sheep skin set between the pillars. The center aisle held two fire hearths lined with stones, the fires banked to embers. Smoke drifted up and disappeared through small openings in the thatched roof.

The outer aisles appeared empty until Birk's vision adjusted and he saw the women and children huddled at the far end. A door at the far wall stood slightly ajar, admitting sunlight—and an escape.

Simple lamps of hollowed stone filled with oil and a wick of twisted fibers sat upon a few benches. A woman hastily lit them, creating a surprising amount of light. The two Norsemen guided Haldor to a bench near one of the hearths. Two women lit more lamps, setting them close to Haldor's still form.

A woman, her fur-trimmed cloak announcing her prominence in the clan, streaks of silver in her bound hair betraying her age, approached Haldor. Her gaze searched his body, moving slowly, her fingers fluttering as though afraid to touch him. Hanna stepped to Haldor's side and laid a palm against his cheek.

The woman shrieked. "Do not touch him, *kerling*! He is mine." She rushed at Hanna, arms extended, eyes wild.

Hanna stepped to one side, grabbed the woman's forearm, and twisted it behind her back. It took an extra shove to halt the woman's movements, but she continued to shriek words Birk did not understand. His quick glance took in the stunned men who had entered the longhouse. Hands raised to sword hilts, angry murmurs grew. The partially open door at the rear of the building darkened as a broad-shouldered form filled the portal.

Hanna slapped the woman once, and her cries stopped as if cut with a knife. "I will pardon your grief, but I will not accept your insults." She released the woman, pushing her into the arms of the other two. "Is there not a healer among ye? This man needs care to ensure his ribs heal properly and the blood within his chest does not putrefy."

A woman, wizened and desiccated with the passage of time, jostled through the small crowd and dropped a leather bag onto the bench. Hanna held a consultation with her, each nodding as the healer assessed Haldor and his wounds.

Tension swirled through the room, rank with anger and fear. Birk flexed his fist, but took care not to reach for his sword. The man at the door stepped into the long room, advancing quickly to Haldor's side. He halted beside the bench and peered over the healer's shoulder, his gaze falling on the large dark bruise over Haldor's ribs. His breath caught on an inhale, but he quickly faced Birk.

"He attacked your ship?"

Hanna's body jerked and she stumbled to her feet, her face pale even in the lamplight. Birk stepped forward and placed a hand on her shoulder. Her gaze fixed on the man beside the healer.

"Aye," Birk replied. "We were chased out of the Sound of Luing and fled south. I dinnae know whose ship that was, for it cracked upon the rocks near the witch's cauldron."

The man's eyebrows rose.

Birk shrugged. "Haldor," he continued, motioning to the man on the bench with a nod of his head, "and his ship awaited us on the far side of the Corryvreckan."

Silence fell in the longhouse. Haldor moaned softly. The older man jutted his chin.

"Ye could have consigned him to Rán's net. None would have blamed ye."

Birk grunted agreement. "We sent many to the bottom of the sea, but Hanna," he nodded at her, "insisted we bring this one to ye."

The man narrowed his eyes and adjusted his gaze to include Hanna. "Why would she wish to save this man?"

Hanna lifted her chin. "He is my grandson."

He stared at her, face slack, stricken. "He is my son."

* * *

Carys breathed easier as the doors to the longhouse opened and Birk and Hanna stepped into the open. A man appeared at Hanna's side, lacking Birk's height, but matching him for breadth of shoulder. The three spoke among themselves, then strode to the beach.

The MacLeans boarded the small boat, the same MacLean soldiers returning with Hanna and Birk as had left more than an hour earlier, reassuring Carys further. A few minutes later, they bumped gently against the *Már's* hull. One by one they climbed the rope ladder to the deck, and she searched their faces for any indication of what had occurred in the longhouse. The few who caught her eye smiled briefly and shook their heads, leaving her to look to Hanna and Birk for answers.

Hanna spoke briefly to Kern who nodded and entered the cabin. Her shoulders lifted and fell as she drew a deep breath, then turned, favoring Carys and the children with a soft smile. Stepping away from the rail, she gathered the children to her.

"I am remaining here for a short time," she said, smoothing a curl from Abria's face.

Alarm raced through Carys. *Ransom*? She shook her head. Birk would never allow it and the Norse were not positioned to ensure Hanna's return to the beach.

The girls whimpered and Tully frowned. Hanna hugged each one.

"Many years ago, I was told my son," she glanced at Birk, "older than your father, had died."

Abria tilted her head. "Older than Da?"

Hanna smiled, though pain shadowed her eyes. "Aye. Older than your da, older than Auntie Gillian, though younger than Auntie Signy." She sighed. "I just discovered he lives here, and I wish to spend a bit of time with him. I will be home with ye soon."

"Is the pirate still our uncle?" Eislyn asked.

"Aye, though they may not be pirates much longer."

Eislyn frowned, clearly still not certain what to do with the idea of a pirate in the family.

Kern approached, Hanna's bag in his hand. She nodded.

"I want a hug and a kiss from each of ye," she instructed, "and a solemn promise ye will strive to be good children and do as Carys and your da ask." She tapped Eislyn's nose. "I will know if ye do not."

With a clamor of reassurances mixed with pleas for Hanna not to go, Abria and Eislyn threw themselves against Hanna. Tully hesitated, then stepped close, placing a palm on Hanna's shoulder. She caught his wrist and gently pulled him into the embrace.

Carys's throat constricted as tears sprang to her eyes. Joy for the return of Hanna's son and the unexpected boon of a grandson, tempered with sadness to lose the wise, caring woman who had befriended her. She consoled herself with the knowledge Hanna would return to Morvern at some point, and managed an understanding smile when Hanna at last rose to her feet.

Hanna dropped a final kiss to each child's head then accepted her bag from Kern. Stepping away from the children, she motioned Carys to her side.

Together, they strolled to the rail.

Hanna cupped Carys's chin in her palm, her gaze earnest.

"I will miss ye," she said. "But I am lighter of heart to know I leave my son and my grandchildren in good hands." She dropped her hand and peered over her shoulder where Birk awaited.

"Especially my son. No matter the manner in which he wed ye, his choice was a good one. Ye have brought a light to his eyes I never thought to see again, Carys. For that, I will be ever grateful."

Carys swallowed and tilted her head, one corner of her lips twitching upward against the pain of farewell. "Mayhap ye mistake light for the heat of frustration," she quipped, uncomfortable with the praise.

Hanna laughed softly. "Mayhap. Yet I see also a light of love and of pride in ye. He has always needed a strong woman at his side, and I will pray daily he not vex ye beyond endurance."

"I will take him beyond the practice field and remind him why he chose me," Carys said, finding her balance once again.

Hanna's eyes twinkled. "He told me ye bested him once," she confided. "He will not forget."

She wrapped her arms about Carys and Carys hugged her fiercely. "I will care for the girls. They are no less precious for not being born to me."

"I know. Ye will be a good ma to them."

Birk stepped close and Hanna and Carys moved apart. Hanna shifted her gaze from Carys to Birk. "I expect to receive word of a bairn soon." Her raised eyebrow lent a seriousness to her words.

"Ye will return in time to welcome him or her into the world." Birk's low voice betrayed his emotion at leaving Hanna behind.

"And I will strive to not vex my wife into picking up arms against me . . . again."

"Ye are a good man, Birk MacLean. Ye have not heard it enough, but yer da was ever proud of ye."

The muscle along Birk's jaw leaped. He folded Hanna into a tight embrace. "If ye dinnae feel safe, wanted, *loved*, send word. I will have Captain Aklen visit from time to time. I will expect to hear from ye." He released her reluctantly.

"He is my brother." A hint of awe touched his voice.

Hanna's smile lit her eyes. "Aye."

With a final wave to the children, Hanna stepped carefully to the ladder and disappeared over the side of the ship. Breaking their solemn huddle, Eislyn and Abria rushed to the rail, standing on tiptoes to watch as Hanna reached the boat and was rowed to shore.

* * *

The MacLean standard flew atop the castle, visible even from the mouth of Loch Aline, announcing the impending arrival of Baron MacLean. Carys leaned against Birk, his arm about her waist, rocking gently with the swell of the tide as the *Már* approached the dock. The beat of his heart thudded beneath her ear, the rumble of his voice a pleasurable hum.

"Sten and I will meet again soon. I mean to offer him a position in MacLean Shipping."

He hesitated as if seeking Carys's approval. She nodded. "'Twould give him purpose beyond hating Scots and pirating. And 'twould put his seamanship to good use. He was surprised to learn Hanna lived?"

"Aye. They will have much to discuss. I know little beyond what he disclosed in the short time I was ashore, but it seems when his home was raided, he and the two lads guarding the longhouse

314

were captured before it was burned to the ground. Having little use for three angry Norse lads, the Scots' leader sold them to a passing merchant and they lived the next ten years as slaves in Italy.

"He escaped and eventually returned to Islay where others who once were loyal to Norway secretly defied Scottish rule. MacDonald is Lord of the Isles, and has allied with King Alexander, yet turns a blind eye on those disgruntled with Scotland's rule. I cannae say he encourages the piracy, yet he does naught about it."

"Your plan to welcome Sten and Haldor into the family and give them honest work may succeed where punishment would fail. Thank ye for choosing this path."

Birk snorted. "After chasing pirates from my land these past few years, I would be justified in sending them all to Rán's net."

"Where?"

"Rán is the Norse goddess of the sea. She seeks to draw men into her net. To give someone to her net means to drown them." Birk grunted. "It tweaks my sense of justice to allow those who pick up arms against me to live."

"Yet 'tis what your da did when he brought an angry Norsewoman into his keep and made her his wife. Ye have both sown the seeds of peace. Hanna is right. Your da would be proud of the man ye've become."

Birk turned her to face him.

"It appears Colin Dubh was one of the few pirates who was not Norse, and they roamed the shores and inland more than the seas. The men who followed him were drawn to murder as well as plunder. It seems my people owe ye much, Carys."

"Are they not my people as well?"

"Ye protected MacLeans who were strangers to ye when ye killed Colin Dubh."

"Not true. I knew Fergus, Lorna and Gorrie, and had met a few others." She shrugged. "But there was never challenge of a true fight with the black-hearted *hadyn*. None of the crofters stood a chance against Colin Dubh and his men. 'Twas naught more than murderous evil. They readily killed those who were unable to protect themselves."

Birk sighed. "I wish to raise my sons in peace."

Carys tilted her head. "Ye are woefully behind on ensuring sons, my lord," she teased. "There has been no privacy or intimacy between us in almost a sennight."

He kissed her forehead. "A dire situation indeed. I will see it remedied this night."

Carys's body hummed with satisfaction—and happiness.

The ship slid gently against the dock and the children squealed with excitement. Accepting the cue, Carys leaned closer into Birk before taking her place at the rail, ever watchful over her small charges. They climbed happily into the small cart prepared for them. Carys chose to walk beside the cart, grateful for the chance to stretch her legs after the long days aboard ship. Birk strolled at her side, one hand in hers. MacLean soldiers fanned about them, providing protection on the bustling streets.

The abundance of Morvern opened before them. Scents of summer flowers, aromas of cooked meats for the noon meal, and other pungent, less pleasant smells filled Carys's nose, chasing away the sharp clean scent of the ocean. The chatter of merchants, countered with the lower banter of women and the shrill excitement of children created a happy din. Birk dropped her hand to lift Abria to his shoulders. Bodies brushed against her, and she almost missed the gentle tug on her cloak.

Carys turned, one hand partially drawing a dagger against danger, and met the nearly opaque eyes of an old woman. Carys slipped her blade back into its sheath.

"How may I help ye, *nain*?"

"The stench of death has long been on ye, my lady," the old woman replied, causing Carys's heart to lurch painfully.

"Yet I sense it fades." The wrinkled face twisted and her eyes closed as she touched Carys's cheek.

Before Carys could recover enough to speak, the woman vanished into the crowd.

"Carys! Come on!" Abria's command piped through the swell of voices. The warmth of the summer sun caressed her head and shoulders. The cackle of chickens and the grunt of a pig in a nearby pen cleared the last of Carys's surprise at the woman's words. Birk sent her a questioning look and she answered with a smile. In a few hurried steps, she caught up with the people who held her heart.

Epilogue

"I'm going to name him Alexander, after our grandda," Eislyn insisted, stubbornly planting her fists on her hips.

"Pedr was our grandda, too," Abria argued, somewhat inaccurately, but just as stubbornly.

"But the bairn isnae Welsh," Eislyn announced triumphantly, ignoring the fact the baby would be half Welsh.

"Peter, then," Abria countered, unwilling to be bested.

Birk gritted his teeth, disinclined to curb their enthusiasm for the bairn Carys struggled to deliver upstairs in the bedroom they shared. Or had shared until she'd gone into labor that morn and he'd been summarily banished.

He rose, pacing the floor as he had off and on for the past six hours. His gut was in turmoil and he'd sent the girls out to play with their nurse twice to keep from shouting for silence. It wasn't their fault Carys had been sent to bed a week ago with pains that had alarmed Hanna. And he did not wish to distress the girls with his unease. He'd never experienced this worry before, and his fear rose with each hour's passing.

"What if the bairn is a lass?" Eislyn asked, arching an eyebrow in a superior manner.

Abria frowned, giving Eislyn a dark look. "I dinnae want another sister," she replied, and Birk couldn't say he blamed her at this moment.

Gillian's bairn, left in his charge since Carys's labor had begun, toddled about the room, picking up toys Abria and Eislyn had left lying about. She threw a wooden dog across the room, the clatter as it struck the stone fireplace loud and satisfying to the wean who clapped her hands and dashed to the next toy.

"Dinnae throw them, Blaire," Eislyn scolded, plucking the doll from the lass' grasp. Indignant at being thwarted, Blaire squealed, and Eislyn promptly grabbed a bit of honeycomb from a bowl on the table and stuffed it into the child's bow-shaped mouth.

Birk didn't know if he was growing accustomed to the clamor, or if he was slowly going insane. His skin prickled and he tasted bile in the back of his throat. He nearly shouted as a hand rested on his arm.

"Dinnae fash," Gillian chided softly. "Your lady wife and bairns are doing well, but I would like ye to come up alone to see them." She tilted her head meaningfully at the squabble on the floor, but Birk ignored her gesture, lost in her words.

Bairns.

His heart stopped.

Doing well.

He released his breath, a grin spreading across his face. Gillian's gentle smile met his and she gripped his arm reassuringly. They slipped quietly from the room, his booted feet flying up the stone steps to the upper level where Carys waited.

He entered the room, light and airy with the windows uncovered. The hearth burned brightly, keeping the cold at bay, but Birk was pleased to find none of the typical dark, stuffy sickroom in evidence.

Carys, seated on the edge of the bed, turned her head at his footstep and rose shakily to her feet. He was at her side in an instant, arms about her protectively, supporting her, giving her the strength he'd been unable to offer during her labor. She took his hand. He kissed her fingers.

"Ye are beautiful, Carys. I am beyond relieved to find ye well."

Her pleased smile belied the hours of toil she'd just endured. "Come. I would introduce ye to your sons."

Startled by her move away from the bed, he sent a wild look to Hanna who merely shrugged, so he accompanied Carys without protest to the cradle at the foot of the bed, then halted, surprise rendering him speechless.

Sons.

The bairns wrinkled their faces, yawning mightily. One stuck a tiny fist in his mouth and suckled, the sound loud in the quiet room. Hanna picked him up and, once Carys was again seated on the edge of the mattress, placed him in Carys's arms. Brushing aside the lacings of her robe, Carys lifted the bairn to a swollen breast and he latched on eagerly.

"Two?" Birk's speech returned, but his mind only produced the single word.

Hanna nodded. "Aye. Her pains in the past sennight would have brought them into this world too soon, and they are still very small. But with care they should be able to hold a sword in a fortnight or two."

Birk tore his gaze from the bairn at Carys's breast and sent his ma a narrow look.

Gillian nodded. "'Tis why I asked ye here first. I dinnae wish the other children to exhaust Carys or the bairns. Ye must be firm with them."

He nodded absently, his attention already shifted to the small miracles Carys had given him. He bent and placed his hands around the second bairn, halting when he discovered his hands were larger than the babe's body.

"He is so small." Birk glanced at Carys who cuddled the first bairn as it nursed. She looked up, her form wavering as Birk blinked against the rush of pride and gratitude. He closed his hands around the tiny form and lifted him against his chest. "What will we name them?"

"Do the girls not already have names picked out?" Carys teased.

Birk caught the tiredness hiding behind Carys's light words. He gently disengaged the now-sleeping bairn from Carys's breast and handed him to Gillian.

"Come. Rest." He gently laid Carys on the bed, tucking her feet beneath the covers, pulling the edge to her shoulders. He sat beside her, still holding the second bairn.

"I want to watch them," she murmured. He settled next to her, her gaze seeking the bairns.

"Eislyn and Abria wish to name them after their granddas."

Carys chuckled. "'Tis better than last week when they thought naming their new brother or sister after the dog was appropriate."

"Alexander and Pedr."

Carys jerked her gaze to his. "Truth? They have another grandda."

"I think we should take Alex and Pedr and not wait until they decide to name the lads after something far less desirable."

This time Carys's laugh was full. Birk kissed her cheek, sensing the soft skin beneath his lips as though he'd never felt it before.

"Ask anything of me, my love, and it is yours."

Carys rolled her head against his shoulder. "I could not imagine a single thing more."

~The End~

A NOTE FROM THE AUTHORS

This book is absolutely packed with history and languages. Since the Norse, Welsh, and Gaelic words are at the front of the book, let's dive into the history behind Carys' story.

Wales, 1282 – An uneasy peace existed between Edward Longshanks of England and Prince Llywelyn of Wales. But in the spring of 1282, the prince's brother Dafydd led a rebellion against England. Though Dafydd had a rather checkered past that included siding with the English against Prince Llywelyn, the prince decided to join him, sparking the 2nd War of Welsh Independence. In December, the Welsh and English armies found themselves separated by the River Irfon. Prince Llywelyn advanced to Orewin Bridge to keep the English from crossing the river, holding the Marcher Lords at bay.

Unfortunately, someone (believed to be Welsh) disclosed the location of an area the English army could cross the river, and the Welsh were forced to retreat. Once the English heavy cavalry crossed the river and attacked, the Welsh army broke and fled.

Prince Llywelyn died during the battle, but exactly how is not known. There are different accounts that seem to contradict. We likely will never know the truth.

Dafydd took his brother's title, but failed to win the hearts of the Welsh—possibly because he'd fought against his brother in the 1st War of Welsh Independence. Sought by the English, he was eventually betrayed and captured, and his head was sent to London and displayed alongside that of his brother.

Scotland, 1283 – This was considered a Golden Age for Scotland. Though Alexander III took the crown in 1249 at only 8 years of age, he took firm hold of his kingdom in 1262, resisting his father in law, Henry of England, who wished to rule Scotland through him. Alexander (like his father before him) immediately set about securing the Western Isles from King Haakon of Norway. In 1265, after bringing a formidable force to Scotland to answer King Alexander's advances, King Haakon was defeated and died that winter in Orkney. In 1266, Alexander and Haakon's successor signed the Treaty of Perth, ceding the Western Isles and the Isle of Man to Scotland for a monetary payment.

At this point, the Isles fell ostensibly under Scottish control, though the Norse (and Gaelic) people continued to seek ways to minimize Scottish rule, and to further their control (led by Angus Mor MacDonald) over the Isles and parts of the mainland. Alexander III sought to integrate the peoples, and in 1284 (after the death of his heir) he invited trusted advisors and leaders of the Isles (including Angus MacDonald) to a conference to decide on an heir. They settled on his infant granddaughter, Margaret of Norway, who was crowned after her grandfather's death when she was three years old, and unfortunately died four years later.

More pleasant notes of interest:
The song Carys sings to the children is **Dacw 'Nghariad**, a Welsh folk song. Check it out on YouTube for the beautiful melody and lilting words.

The Corryvreckan is indeed the world's third largest whirlpool. The best site I found for information (you may find others) was here: https://whirlpool-scotland.co.uk/ The video at the bottom of the page is a fabulous compilation of actual and computer-generated footage of both the whirlpool itself and the underwater formations which cause the witch's cauldron to boil. Oh, and yes, you can take rafts and tour the corryvreckan. Let us know if you do.

Dogs. We showcased two breeds in this book. The Welsh shepherd and the Welsh Corgi. Dewr was a Welsh shepherd which is a dog bred for its working ability rather than for conformity to a physical standard. They are noted for their superior herding instincts, though the Welsh shepherd has also been used as a drover, helping drive a farmer's animals—most likely sheep, but also cattle, pigs or geese—to market. They are similar in appearance to the Border Collie, though they are typically taller, sturdier, and stronger. The Welsh Shepherd is also a good livestock (and human) protector and is a guard dog when required.

Tegan was actually named for the dam of a Pembroke Welsh Corgi Cathy owned which passed away last year. Corgis are small herding dogs developed in Wales and the two separate breeds we know today—the Cardigan Welsh Corgi and the Pembroke Welsh Corgi—were considered a single breed until 1934. 'Tis said the Pembroke was originally a gift from the faeries who rode them into battle and used them to pull their carts. A less fanciful history indicates the corgi was either descended from Valhunds, cattle dogs brought to Wales by the Vikings, or from dogs brought by Flemish weavers in the 12th century.

The Scottish Birlinn was built much like the Viking longboat—or langskip—which is very similar to the Greek galley. These shallow draft boats were extremely fast and agile, and could sail—or row—up rivers where deeper-keeled boats could not travel.

The cog ship is much larger than the birlinn and has a deeper keel. Unlike the birlinn, it also boasted an aftcastle where such weapons as a ballista could be mounted. This ship was designed to carry cargo and were sometimes used as war ships. Cogs rarely used oars, as merchants rarely wished to give cargo space to oarsmen. Typically, a rowed ship was either used for raiding, or perhaps a combination of raiding and trading.

A bit of a disclaimer:

When Carys shoots a flaming arrow into the barrel of whisky to take down the pirates, a bit of discussion arose in our critique group as to whether this would actually happen or not. Does whisky burn? Actually, the whisky and its vapors burn. Whether or not it would ignite enough to burn a pirate ship—possibly. So, in our story, Carys cracked the tun with the bodkin-tipped shaft then sent the flaming arrow into the hole (excellent marksmanship) to ignite vapors still inside the keg. At that point, the spilled whisky would ignite, even when spread upon the water.

We found an interesting video of a flaming tornado caused when whisky burning in a warehouse escaped down a creek and into a lake. Unexpectedly, a whirl of wind caught the flames and sent them soaring into the sky. You can watch a video of it here: https://www.maxim.com/maxim-man/kentucky-bourbon-fire-tornado-2015-8

Acknowledgements

We are delighted to again have our wonderful critique group, Dawn Marie Hamilton, Cate Parke, and Lane McFarland, join us in creating this story. They saw it in its infancy, helped us pull it apart and reshape it, and read the entire story yet again before it ventured out for official editing.
Liette Bougie did a marvelous job editing, and she is such a joy to work with!

Of course, the process would not be complete without the invaluable help from our beta readers: Donna, Alison, Cheryl, Barb, Ann, Sharon, and April. Thank you so much, ladies!

Many thanks to Dar Albert who helped envision the cover for The Highlander's Welsh Bride. We absolutely love this cover!

AUTHOR BIOS AND LINKS

Cathy MacRae lives on the sunny side of the Arbuckle Mountains where she and her husband read, write, and tend the garden—with the help of the dogs, of course.

You can visit with her on facebook, or read her blogs and learn about her books at www.cathymacraeauthor.com. Drop her a line—she loves to hear from readers!

To keep up with new releases and other fun things, sign up for her newsletter! (You'll find DD's news there, too!)

Other ways to connect with Cathy:
Facebook
Twitter: @CMacRaeAuthor
Instagram: cathymacrae_author
Amazon author page
Pinterest
Book bub

DD MacRae enjoys bringing history to life and considers research one of the best things about writing a story! With more than 35 years of martial arts training, DD also brings breath-taking action to the tales.

You can connect with DD through www.cathymacraeauthor.com. It's always exciting to hear from readers!

Other Books by Cathy & DD MacRae

The Hardy Heroine series

Highland Escape (book 1)
The Highlander's Viking Bride (book 2)
The Highlander's Crusader Bride (book 3)
The Highlander's Norse Bride, a Novella (book 4)
The Highlander's Welsh Bride (book 5)
The Prince's Highland Bride (book 6, available 2020)

by DD MacRae
The Italian Billionaire's Runaway Bride

By Cathy MacRae

The Highlander's Bride series
The Highlander's Accidental Bride (book 1)
The Highlander's Reluctant Bride (book 2)
The Highlander's Tempestuous Bride (book 3)
The Highlander's Outlaw Bride (book 4)
The Highlander's French Bride (book 5)

Mhàiri's Yuletide Wish (a Christmas novella)

De Wolfe Pack Connected World
The Saint
The Penitent
The Cursed

The Ghosts of Culloden Moor series
(with LL Muir, Diane Darcy, Jo Jones, and Melissa Mayhue)

__Adam__
__Malcolm__
__MacLeod__
__Patrick__

www.ingramcontent.com/pod-product-compliance
Lightning Source LLC
Chambersburg PA
CBHW030603180626
46816CB00005B/1650